A BRITISH SPORTS ROMANCE NOVEL

AMY DAWS

Published by: Stars Hollow Publishing

ISBN: 978-1-944565-25-1

Editing: Stephanie Rose
Formatting: Champagne Formatting
Cover Design: Staci Hart and Amy Daws
Cover Photography: Dan Thorson
Cover Models: Adam Spahn

To my husband:
I picked the one sport you don't watch to write a novel around.
Thanks for nothing.

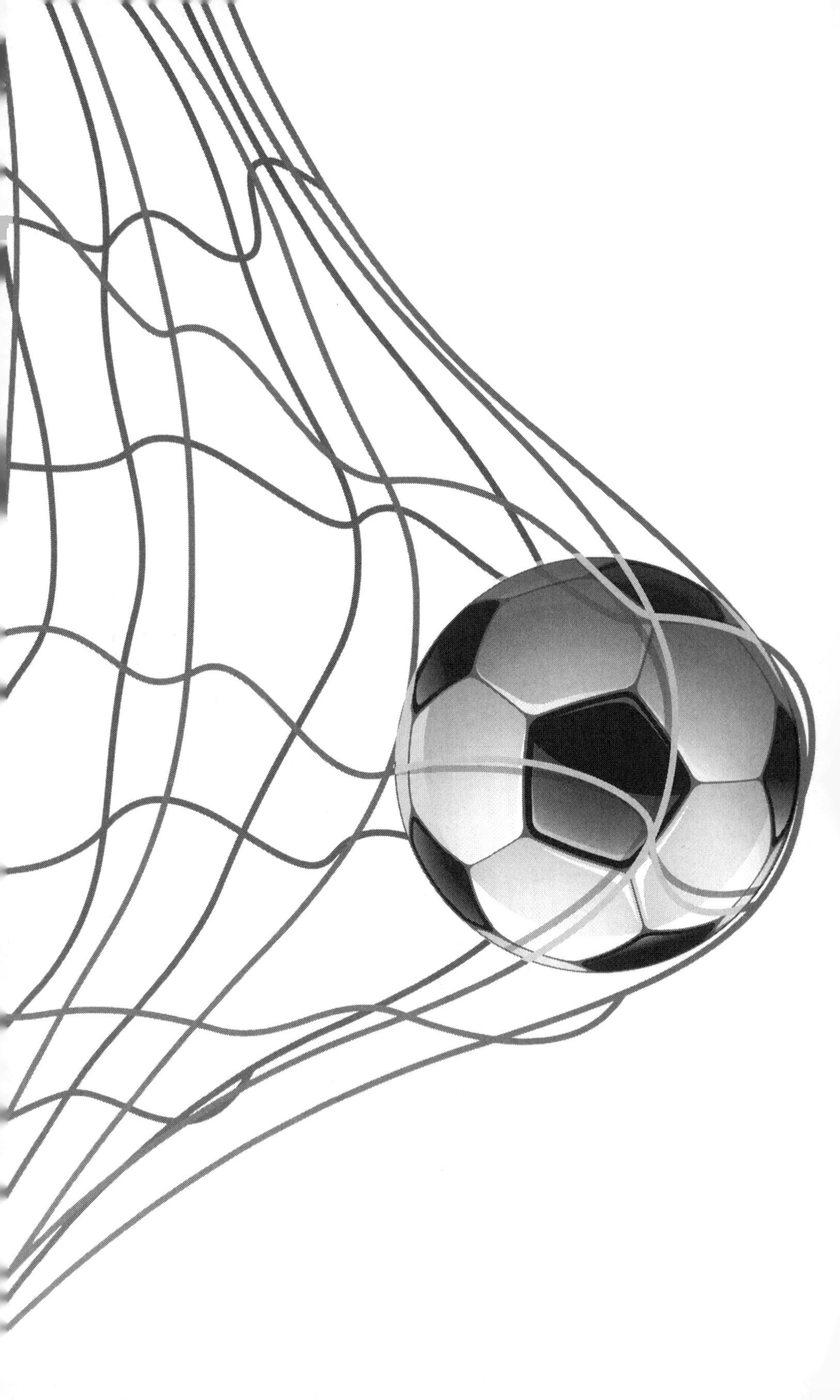

Ritual

Camden

"COME ON, CAMDEN," TANNER GROANS, STROLLING INTO THE kitchen and eyeing me at the table. He instantly deflates when he sees I'm nose deep in my book. "We've only got an hour before we need to leave. You need to get your *ritual* over with before it gets too late. Dad crawls the walls when we're late for warm-ups."

My latest James Patterson, Cross Series novel thumps closed as I gaze back at my twin brother's face. The dreary London daylight sheds little light on what emotion he's portraying beneath all those unkempt facial pubes. I shake my head. "Don't even consider judging my ritual. You're the one looking like a blonde Hagrid."

He smiles and strokes his beard. "Aww, that's the nicest thing you've ever said to me, Cam. Do you really think so? Maybe if I go for a full Dumbledore beard, our team will be promoted to Premiership."

I roll my matching blue eyes in response to the eagerness in his. Tanner and I aren't identical twins, but back when he had trimmed blonde hair instead of the shaggy mess he sports now, we even fooled each other. I once watched a taped match for forty minutes before I realised I was watching Tanner kick a football down the pitch instead of myself. Although he has a lot more ink than me nowadays.

Our other two brothers, Gareth and Booker, don't look like us at all. Gareth is the oldest and Booker is the youngest. They take after our dad with their darker hair, but since we all grew up playing football, our builds are quite similar. Years of fieldwork policed by our dad and an intense weight-lifting regime made us the largest footballers on most pitches.

To know the Harris name in regards to European football is like knowing the Mannings of American football. Football is more than our national obsession, it's the Harris way of life. So much so that Tanner hasn't cut a hair on his head since the start of our winning streak four months ago. The wanker even wears a pretentious sweatband to keep his hair out of his face during matches.

Having a twin in general is a royal pain in the arse. Having him on the same team is like a bad case of haemorrhoids. Having him playing the same position is like a jagged butt plug rammed in at the wrong angle.

However, his recent affection for hair has made my life ten times easier when it comes to the sporting game of women. Shockingly, the birds don't tend to drop to their knees for the hobo-looking players. My clean-cut appearance, on the other hand, has them quivering with need. Trust me, I'm not complaining.

"You're still not going to shave?" My eyes zero in on two scraggly pieces hanging lower than the rest. "Trim it, maybe? Wash it? I can smell it from over here. It smells worse than Booker's boots."

Tanner's eyes fly wide. "I do wash it. I even got a fancy oil for it in Shoreditch last week. But I'm *not* shaving it. *Ritual*, Camden," he adds pointedly. "Shall we talk in depth about what you do for yours?"

I lift my brows but he doesn't stop long enough for me to let loose a snappy retort. "Just get moving. Booker will be here soon to pick us up." In two steps, he has me by my shoulders and pulls me out of my seat. He all but shoves me down the hallway toward the toilet.

"I'm going, all right? There's no need to get grabby." My nose crinkles as I look over my shoulder and cringe away from his face.

"And get that thing away from me."

His hold on me tightens as he attempts to rub his beard on my face, but I manage to duck into the loo just in time to slam the door on him. He laughs in triumph, most likely because he achieved his goal of getting me to the toilet. God, my brother gets right up my nose. Living with him is trying at best, but I remind myself for the thousandth time this week that it was for a good reason.

About six months ago, our teammate Will found himself in a spot of trouble. Apparently he'd been silently losing a battle against his gambling addiction. We had no idea he even had a problem. He came to us and said he was six months behind on rent. His landlord was not only threatening to press charges, but also call our manager to get Will removed from the team. Since our dad is the manager for the team we all play for, we knew that was a highly probable outcome.

Tanner and I didn't even have to exchange words before we agreed to pay the back rent. Then, when Will wanted to move home to get more help from his parents, we offered to take over his lease.

It was a good move for us regardless. Tanner and I turned twenty-five two months ago, and living at home with our dad was getting harder and harder to explain. In our defence, Dad's house is more similar to a posh hotel than a family home—a brown-brick mansion in Chigwell, just outside of East London. Aside from the times when our sister, Vi, came around to make us all dinner, it was football headquarters for all of us. We even held team meetings there.

But now, being bunked up with a blonde Jesus in a smaller-than-I'd-like, two-bedroom flat in Bethnal Green sure doesn't seem as exciting as it did initially, even if we do live close to the pitch and above a tattoo shop and a pub.

In no time at all, I'm in the shower letting the hot, steamy water pound against the muscles on my back. Just as I do before every match, I close my eyes tightly and begin my highly-focused, visualisation technique that's become a ritual I can't seem to function without doing.

I picture the crowd chanting my name inside a packed Tower Park Stadium.

"Harris…Harris…Harris…"

Tower Park on match day is unlike any other pitch in the entire world. If I wasn't already hard, I'd be hard now.

I envision the softness of the grass beneath my feet. The spongy give of that perfect pitch. The gentle sinking of my studs. The fresh scent of newly cut grass. The nostalgic stench of hot dogs and stale lager lingering in the stands. *Christ, it's fantastic.*

Back in reality, my hand reaches low to grip myself. I slowly stroke my hardened shaft and relish in the feel of the soap over my slickened skin. I press my head against the side of the tiled wall and transform the sound of the hot water into the roar of the crowd cheering me down the pitch.

Instantly, I feel the build.

I squeeze harder and speed up my strokes. I visualise myself zigging past two midfielders who go crashing into each other in mighty disappointment. Then I juke out a defender who falls down to his knees in defeat. When I approach the goalie, he decides to come out of his box. I smile broadly.

"Never come out of your box with Camden Harris in your line of vision." My husky voice reverberates in the bathroom with a level of excitement I always get before a big score.

I pull back my booted foot and shoot.

Then…

Then…

Dead silence as the ball soars through the air. The entire stadium waits on bated breath in hopes of hearing that utterly orgasmic slap of leather hitting nylon.

Fucking.

Goal.

The crowd erupts in celebration…

...along with my cock.

I let out a groan as my hot load sprays against the wall of the shower. The release is intense. Footballing orgasm perfection. My abs bunch tightly as I shudder with aftershocks and pump a few more times, flinching at the sensitive tip firing off at every nerve ending. "Fucking goal, Camden. Well done."

When I crack my eyes open, my vision readjusts to the light as I gaze at my Cumcasso painting on the wall. Not half bad for a match-day inspiration. Smiling, I cup my hands and splash water on the mess, effectively rinsing my artful load down the drain to join all the other match-day loads I've blown on the exact same shower wall.

Ritual complete.

So yeah, I guess that means Camden Harris jerks off to images of football. And yeah, sometimes he refers to himself in the third person. There are creepier ways to spend a Saturday morning.

Truthfully, football and sex are all relative when you think about it. Loads of sweating. Loads of heavy breathing. Loads of fluids. They're both about slipping inside of a goal, finding room between two welcoming slits. It's not easy. It's a tight fit sometimes. But hell, does it feel good when that opening happily transpires, allowing your balls to hit the deepest point possible. Then the crowd—or writhing woman beneath you—goes wild.

That analogy isn't one I share with any of my brothers, who all say jerking off before a game takes the edge off and tires you out. But this season has been the best of my life. There's no way I'll tempt fate and change course now.

"Could you be any more pervy?" Tanner's muffled voice shouts through the bathroom door.

"What the bloody hell?" I cut off the water and wrench the glass door open.

"I can hear your barks of passion all the way down the hall. You sound like a chimpanzee caught in a bug zapper."

My face screws up. "You're the one standing outside the bathroom door," I snap as I snatch the towel from the warming bar and wipe my chest dry. "I'd say you're the pervert in this scenario. Piss off!"

His voice trails off as he retreats with a half-hearted protest, grumbling something about golden showers being next. I step out and wrap the towel around my waist, flinching as the fabric brushes against my sensitive tip.

Tanner can be a right bastard some days. Not only does he annoy me to no end at home, but he makes me sweat on the pitch just trying to keep up with him. Truth be told, he's always been a better footballer than me. The Arsenal scouts have been inquiring about him ever since their striker retired last year, leaving the Gunners a man down up front. Of all the London-based teams, that's the one I want watching me.

Then I went and scored nine goals by midseason. That's unprecedented. Now it's anyone's guess who they're interested in signing.

I stroll over to the foggy mirror and swipe away the mist. I shake the moisture out of my wet hair before I look at myself.

My blue eyes darken with determination. "Season's almost over, Camden. Just do what you've been doing and let the balls fall where they may. You are football. Football is you. If you want a Premier contract, now is the time to prove yourself once and for all. Show your worth."

Then, an errant thought tumbles into my head and a sly grin spreads across my face. "But when football season is over, it's the season of women. And you've always been better than Tanner at that game."

2 Tequila Sunrise

Indie

"Oh my God, I'm knackered," I say as I stroll into the on-call room and flop myself onto one of the sterile blue hospital cots, which have zero give. The hard plastic smarts against my vertebrae at the force.

My fellow resident and friend, Belle, glances up at me from her own cot. Her dark eyes are partially closed and tired, similar to my own at this time of day. "Your timing is perfect," she says, her voice perking up. "I just looked at the schedule. You're on a nine-day stretch with me. We must discuss."

I turn and prop my head on my hand and nod at the prospect of hitting the workweek finish line with my friend. "I saw that this morning, too. We've got three days down already, so I'm telling you right now that on day nine, we're hitting Club Taint."

"Hell yes," she agrees with a lascivious smirk. When she sits up, her long, inky hair falls perfectly over her shoulders. I stare at it wistfully as she adds, "Club Taint is always a wild time. I'm so excited that we're on the same rotation. Last time I missed you going out and I refuse to miss it again. Little Miss Innocent raging through the clubs of London is as good as Boxing Day in my book." She exhales heavily. "You're staring at my hair again, Indie."

My eyes snap to hers. "Sorry." Feeling a flush of heat in my cheeks, I drag myself up and stride over to the wall of lockers, knowing my fair skin does a crap job of concealing my emotions. It's not that I'm into girls. I'm just into that silky, straight, shiny—

"Your obsession with my hair is bordering on creepy, darling." Her tone is light, but her humour is dry as usual.

I crack open my locker and stare at myself in the mirror. "You have no idea how lucky you are," I sigh, silently surrendering to my fate. My messy wad of curly, red hair is in its standard messy bun on top of my head. Coming in on the ninth straight hour at work, it has grown from the size of a kumquat to the size of a melon. I attempt to smash in some of the expanse, but it's futile.

I push my cheetah-print glasses back up my nose and force a confident nod of acceptance over my appearance. These glasses are living proof of just how far I've come out of my shell since childhood—how much I've changed.

It sounds odd for a silly pair of glasses to carry so much meaning, but my upbringing was unique to say the least. I grew up in all-girls boarding schools. If that wasn't bad enough, in year three, a teacher caught me reading *The Catcher In The Rye* and made me take some fifth grade level practise tests. Next thing I knew, they advanced me three whole grades. I was thrust into a classroom of girls all wearing training bras and talking about boys.

It was like being handed a big, juicy steak without any teeth to chew. No matter how much you try to gum it, you can't seem to break it down. I wasn't able to make friends with a single girl. Instead, I lived the majority of my formative years keeping to myself and hiding behind books. I immersed myself in schoolwork because it was easier than making friends. In the end, it paid off because I received a full-ride scholarship to University and, eventually, med school.

And that is where I met the wildly bold, Belle Ryan.

Belle waltzed right up to me before our first day of class and already knew who I was, even down to where my grandmother lived in Brighton. She worked in the scholarship department on campus and had data-entered my information into the system. Med school at nineteen isn't the norm, so she set out to ensure that I wasn't a terrorist. Eventually she made some crack about a child prodigy being pretty and smart and how it's horribly unfair to the rest of the world.

In my one act of brazenness, I replied, "Well, sit tight. It's raining outside so my curls should hit Einstein heights by the end of the day."

I've always been leery of girls since some bad experiences in school, but something about Belle felt too transparent not to love. The cheeky cow stared at my hair during the entire lecture. We've been best friends ever since.

I smile at the memory as I spray myself with Evian facial spray, slather on a fresh layer of deodorant, and position myself to brush my teeth in the nearby sink. Belle calls these whore baths for doctors, but she takes it a step further and uses baby wipes in her nether regions—something that makes me feel horribly awkward.

I glance at the time and see I only have three more hours to go until I get my glorious board-required six hours of respite, even if I do plan to sleep on these horridly uncomfortable cots again.

"So talk to me about how wild you got last time. Stanley hasn't stopped leering at you since then." Belle stands up from her bed and straightens her blue scrubs, pausing as she notes a smattering of blood on her pant leg. "Damn, I didn't see that before."

"I wouldn't say I got completely wild last time." I bite my lip nervously, recalling my night with Stanley in more detail.

He's a fellow second year resident whom I know I snogged senseless on the dance floor at Club Taint last week. *But that was it, right?*

Then, as if my denial floodgates have instantly opened wide, I recall rubbing myself against him. I internally flinch when I remember that I even touched him through his jeans before ditching him like a thief in the night. Drunk, alone, and hard as a blue quartz stone.

"Gosh, I wasn't trying to be a tease." I blanch, feeling mortified because I haven't thought about that night with him until right this moment. "He just caught me in a weak moment. Wilding out is survival."

"I know, I know. Tequila Sunrise," Belle adds, voicing our own personal mantra.

Tequila Sunrise is essentially our more original version of YOLO. Actually saying YOLO makes my skin crawl. That's what immature tweens shout when they decide to purchase a full calorie soda instead of diet. Tequila Sunrise is so much more.

Our first day in Accident and Emergency—or Patch Alley as the hospital staff all call it—Belle and I were both pummeled with a crippling dose of reality when a baby was rushed in on a stretcher and pronounced dead only moments later from SIDS. The mother's screams shook us so much that Belle ended up sick in the bathroom while I stood there, frozen and shell-shocked.

The Paediatrics doctor on call that night yanked us both into her office, pulled out a sticky pad of paper, and scribbled some ingredients down on it.

Tequila Sunrise:
1 part Grenadine
3 parts Tequila
6 parts Orange Juice
Do not mix.

She told us to go home and make them when our shifts ended, and to remember that there is still sunshine above the chaos. Belle and I did exactly what she said and ended up completely wasted. We both realised in that moment that med school prepared us for the answers, but it did not prepare us for the heartache. So, rather than wallow in the sadness, we adopted the Tequila Sunrise philosophy as a part of our everyday lives.

Therefore, as a single, somewhat naïve twenty-four-year-old determined to live my life to the fullest, I thought that meant letting down my hair at clubs, drinking in excess, dancing 'til I sweat, and traveling when I can manage the time. The occasional flirting and making out is all a part of that game plan, too. It's not about being loose and easy. It's about living the one life you're given and having fun while you can. Then getting right back in the trenches when your shift arrives and doing your best to lessen the sadness in the world. Add some sunshine.

But what I did with Stanley wasn't the perfect Tequila Sunrise decision. "I'm afraid Stanley was just…there," I add regretfully. "I'd just finished a nine-day workweek, and I don't think it's unheard of for me to want to remind myself that I'm still alive and my girlie parts are all in full working order. I have you to thank for my wild side, you know," I accuse.

Belle pulls on a pair of fresh scrub pants over her black thong. "Too right," she admits proudly. "I'll take the blame because we had a blast in med school and not many people can say that. But poor, poor Stanley."

"Oh, don't feel so sorry for him," I baulk. "I hate that any time you kiss a man he just assumes it's going to end in sex. I mean, seriously. What's the rush? Foreplay is bloody exciting enough."

She shakes her head and giggles. "No. No, it is not, Indie. I'm telling you for the hundredth time, I know you went to all-girls schools and probably had to learn how to kiss on the back of your hand, but you are seriously missing out."

I roll my eyes and grumble, "I didn't learn how to kiss on the back of my hand." If I'm being honest, I didn't have my first kiss until University and it was horribly awkward. I think my teeth scraped his tongue on its way in because I didn't even know it was coming. Shouldn't there be some sort of universal signal for tongue insertion on a kiss? A little shoulder tap? Maybe a couple cheek clicks? Something that says, "Hey, lady! I'm about to ramrod your mouth with my tongue. Open sesame!" The guy probably thought I was mentally unstable because he never spoke to me again.

"Look," Belle says, striding over by me to lean against the nearby locker. "We know that you are book-smart, Indie. You're sharper than the majority of the third year residents here and probably some of the attendings. You are my little prodigy wunderkid after all."

"Oh, shut it," I snap, blocking her hand from pinching my cheek like a proud mum.

Her eyes glitter with determination. "But you have to stop saving yourself for Mr. Perfect. He's not going to come. He most likely doesn't even exist. Just give it up to someone like Stanley so you can stop obsessing over it so much. The Penis List we made is a solid plan, but not at the expense of spontaneity."

My eyes widen at her blatant dismissal of the sacred list we spent drunken hours coming up with in order to give me the boost I needed to lose my virginity. I even made a Pinterest board for it and added her as an admin.

First Tequila Sunrise judging and now this.

Okay, so I'm a twenty-four-year-old virgin who's slightly obsessed with how she's going to lose her well overdue virginity status. As I said before, though, part of the reason I'm still holding on to my V-Card is Belle. It's not her fault, per se, but when I met her, I was so focused on having fun with my first real friend that my virginity wasn't a top priority. Hell, I'd never even been to a party before Belle dragged me to one.

Then, by the end of our three years in med school, I realised that I'd focused entirely on maintaining my scholarship and barely looked at boys. Sure, I'd had plenty of interactions with blokes. I learned how to accept and give a good French kiss, plus some basic foreplay stuff. But none of them felt right enough to go all the way with. I wasn't ready. Med school had me over-flowing with firsts and the idea of getting intimate was overwhelming.

Enter the Penis List.

It was Belle's idea. She thought that if I had a game plan and a clear type to look for, it would help me look at sex as an equation and not a conquest. It started out as a half-cracked idea, but I could see the strategy behind it, even when I was sober.

The list goes as follows:

<u>The Penis List</u>

Penis #1: The virginity snatcher.

Should be a bad boy. A player. A little sleazy. Should be hot—the hottest guy I'd ever see in real life. Cocky, confident, and even arrogant. Should administer the best sex of my life. Should be well penially hung.

Penis #2: The sweetie.

Should be kind, sensitive, nurturing, and tender. The ultimate nice guy. Should dress nicely. Should tuck his shirt in. Might cry when he comes. Should put your needs before his. Above all: A penial giver.

Penis #3: The ultimate cocktail.

The perfect blend of number one and number two. Should be both a giver and a taker. Both a DOM and a SUB. Both a lover and a fighter. A blissful penial balance. Husband material.

"Look, Belle, you were there when we made the Penis List." I cup my hand and whisper the last bit, my eyes sweeping the room to double-check that we're still alone. "I'm not saving myself for Mr. Perfect. I'm saving myself for Penis Number One."

"We made that list two years ago, Indie. When are you going to find Penis Number One already?" she asks, her tone approaching shrill. "He shouldn't be the Holy Grail of cocks for God's sake. I love you, but you are in serious need of a push right now. Don't make me mama bird you out of the nest. 'Cause I'll do it. I'll shove you right out and make you fly."

I exhale heavily and drop my head back against my locker, turning my gaze up to the ceiling and begging the heavens for some act of God so I could get on with it already.

"Is it too much to ask for the universe to drop a bad boy player on my lap? I don't want to settle for a Stanley. Stanley is a number two. I don't want to lose it to a number two. I want my first to be the most epic shag ever. A night that I will never forget. A night that makes me hoarse from screaming that I love life for giving me the experience. The kind of shag I'll be able to tell my grandkiddies about someday."

"You know you're speaking out loud, right?" Belle's nose wrinkles as she asks, "Why exactly are you telling your grandchildren about how you lost your virginity?"

I roll my eyes. "It's just an expression. Although, I envisage myself as being that really cool, hip nan who shares all my wild party days with my own little faction of whippersnappers."

Giggling, she says, "Okay, couple of things wrong with what you just said. Faction? We're not post-apocalyptic, so stop being so dramatic."

I adjust my glasses and shoot her a glare, but it doesn't slow her down. "Also, nobody uses envisage in general conversation. Your prodigy-ness is showing."

"Ha, ha," I grumble.

"Okay, back on topic." Belle walks back over to her bed and slips her feet into her trainers. Her eyes are slanted deep in thought. "I think we can fix this virginity thing. What if you try just the tip?"

"The tip of what?" I ask, distracted by my own internal thoughts about finding the right kind of player to do this with.

"The tip of Stanley's cock." Her face is deathly serious. Her eyes pierce me with encouragement.

"You are such a bloke sometimes," I groan, disgusted. "That sounds exactly like what a man would say if he were trying to get in a woman's knickers."

"Indie," a proud smile spreads across her face. "A tip can be quite nice if wielded properly. You just have to have him stroke—"

"Enough!" I cover my ears. I'm over virginity talk with Belle. I am maxed out on Belle's advice on how to get this done.

She doesn't know what she's talking about. I may still be a virgin, but I'm not immature anymore. My time hasn't come and gone. I refuse to turn into a thirty-year-old virgin unicorn. That's certainly not the type of majestic creature I want to be, even if it does entitle me to a forehead horn.

A tip from Stanley won't be the way I lose this ridiculous cross I bear. I refuse. I'm not the under-developed, late bloomer I was in school. I will find the perfect Penis Number One. And I will do whatever it takes to complete this task.

Suddenly, my pager blasts from my scrub pocket. I glance down. "Yikes. It's Prichard. 999. Gotta go."

Without looking back, I turn and run out of the on-call room, bursting through the doors and skirting past a crowd of interns in the middle of rounds. Dr. Prichard is the attending ortho surgeon whom I've been working with for the past few months. His encouragement is the real reason I've developed such a focus on orthopaedics. If he pages 999, it means something big is happening.

My heart pounds as I fly into Patch Alley. Sirens blare through the automatic doors, and my face heats from the rush. This is why I love medicine. The exhilaration. The demand to think on your feet so you can save a life in the blink of an eye. The mature, capable confidence required to be a doctor.

My eyes squint at the flashing cameras outside the hospital doors, brightly popping off through the dark, pouring rain. I refocus to the foreground and see a pair of muddy boots hanging off the end of an evidently too-short stretcher. My gaze drifts up the muscular, socked legs beneath mud-soaked shin pads. Before I can clap my curious eyes on the patient, a pack of sweaty, shouting, and properly pushy men in kits comes ramrodding in behind him.

Rather than God answering my virginal prayer with a player, the devil answered it with four.

3
Go Juke Yourself

Camden

"We need the best fucking doctor here, right the hell now. I don't care if he's on holiday, get him here!" Tanner's voice booms as a man attempts to introduce himself as my doctor.

I wipe my face as small flicks of spit come raining down on me. It's shocking to see him this worked up. Granted, I've seen him get mighty upset over football before. But he's not the one being wheeled into Accident and Emergency right now. I am. Shouldn't I be the one screaming? Aren't I the one horizontal on a stretcher?

My stomach rolls as I recall what happened only minutes ago.

The slip.

One fucking slip.

And my career is probably over.

I cover my face with my hands, willing a time machine to materialise and take me back to the second when everything went horribly wrong so I can stop it from happening. Reverse the damage. Undo what has been done. Anything.

It was a wet and wild game as London's sky decided to open up and rain holy hell down onto the pitch, turning our match into a virtual mud bath. There is no such thing as rain delays in football, so the ball and every square inch of our bodies were covered in mud.

We were up two-nil—both goals scored by me. I was driving my way to a hat trick and potentially securing myself an offer from Arsenal. Suddenly, a back tackle came sliding across the mud right toward me. I attempted to cut left to dodge the harsh contact. My feet couldn't find any grip, though, and they slipped out from under me just in time for him to come crashing into me. It was that second that I felt it...The slip. That's the only way to describe it. Something in my knee slipped and I knew I was fucked.

I went down awkwardly and froze while the defender recovered with the ball and took off with my teammates down the field. I didn't care. I couldn't care. My whole career had just flashed before my eyes like it was over.

Wet.

Muddy.

Bleak.

And over.

I rolled onto my belly and punched the mud-soaked grass over and over and over with all my might. I roared in anger and glanced up, immediately connecting eyes with Tanner across the field. He dropped down to the ground, reacting to the horror that overwhelmed me. He quickly leapt up and charged toward me, sliding on his knees to my side. This was bad. Just looking at his face I could tell it was bad.

Don't get me wrong. You can't play football for most of your life and not experience the odd injury here and there. But this was different. This was a game changer.

"Fuck, Cam!" Tanner cried, his expression marred with a knowing doom beneath his dripping beard.

"I tore something, Tanner. I know it," I exclaimed. Right on cue, I felt a sharp slice of pain shoot up my quad. "Fuuuuuck!"

"Maybe it's just a cramp. Can you get up?" Tanner asked hopefully.

I shook my head but attempted to stand anyway, hoping fate was playing a mean trick on me. My stomach flipped again when it felt like both the top and bottom parts of my leg were moving in two different directions. When I stumbled, Tanner slipped under one of my arms to hold me up. My ego crumbled with that one gesture. I held my lame leg completely off the ground, unwilling to tempt fate by putting more pressure on it.

In a flash, our baby brother, Booker, was under my other arm. Panic spread across his entire face—a face that always looked so young to me, even though he was only two years below us.

"Fucking hell, Cam. Tell me you didn't!" he croaked the knowing question.

I clenched my jaw as I felt the distinct sensation of bone rubbing on bone under the skin of my kneecap.

Suddenly, the crowd erupted around us in celebration. I looked up at the board to see the opposing team had just scored a goal.

"Booker," I groaned, realising he must have left his box when he saw me go down. "You should be in your box."

"Sod football. You're my fucking brother," he growled back angrily. "That wanker was completely out of control. Utter horseshit and no card from the ref…It's bullshit."

I chomped down on my lip, seemingly fighting back pain when, in fact, I was fighting back the immense emotion that swept over me at the sight of my two brothers. The act of them choosing to leave the match mid-play to carry me off the pitch and not subject me to the scene of a stretcher was overwhelming.

These brothers of mine truly would do anything for me.

On the sidelines, we were swarmed by the team medic, a ref, the pitch emergency staff, our dad and, eventually, our raging, wildfire sister.

Vi was covered in an enormous Bethnal Green poncho and looked ready to burst. "Where was the fucking red card, Ref?" Her screams were in no way intimidating or threatening, but it wasn't for lack of trying. "That was utter shite and you know it! Get some fucking glasses, you twat!"

I winced as they settled me onto the hard stretcher on the ground and prepared to carry me away. Everyone was talking at me, including my dad. He was touching my knee and looking earnestly at my eyes with a million soundless questions. His lips were moving—everyone's were—but I couldn't hear a word of what they were saying. The blood rushed loudly in my ears as hot sweat dripped down my mud-stained face, blurring my vision. All I could do was stare down at my offensive knee.

My dream-crushing knee that just ruined any chance I had at a contract offer.

"Fuck!" I screamed loudly into my shoulder, feeling utterly betrayed. I slammed my fist down onto the hard plastic of the stretcher just as some blokes lifted it and began escorting me off the sidelines. "I blew it," I whispered on an exhale as I glanced back at Tower Park.

Tower Park.

This pitch was a place that had been my home for most of my life. From going along with my dad as a child while he attended practises with potential recruits, to now playing on it myself for the past six years. This was my career. I became a man on this grass. And now, I was being carried off of it…like a baby.

My eyes glazed as I took note of the fans all standing up…even the visiting fans. The men had their hats off and placed respectfully against their chests. The women had their hands cupped over their mouths in shock. Down below, the players had all taken a knee, even the ones on the sidelines. My chin wobbled as I admitted that for the first time in my life, I hated this fucking game.

When I finally pull my hands off my face because of the muted noise, I find myself in a small exam room surrounded by glass. I look out the closed sliding door straight in front of me and see my family gesturing wildly at the doctor who received us when we first came in.

A throat clears from beside me and I jump. "Um, sorry. Didn't mean to frighten you. My name is Dr. Porter, and I'm going to be prepping you for your MRI."

I frown and turn to eye the petite woman who barely looks old enough to drink. Her red, curly hair sits in a mess atop her head and she touches it self-consciously.

"Doctor?" I ask while wiping away the moisture on my face and trying to hide the fact that it's a mix of mud, sweat, and tears.

"I just look young. I'm not." Her insecurity fades instantly with her sharp and clipped tone like she says that phrase every day and hates it.

A loud shout snaps my attention from the doctor. I look back and see my dad running his hands angrily through his grey hair. He looks haggard and out of control. A shaken Vaughn Harris isn't a common occurrence. He has two primary emotions: protective and demanding.

The first time I ever saw the man crack any level of emotion was last year when my sister gave him a gift of our mum's poems. It was a peculiar sight and one he made us swear never to speak of again. So the sight of him flailing at the doctor makes me positively ill.

"They can't come in here," the redhead says. I turn back to catch her watching me. Her brows are knit together in sympathy beneath a pair of large cheetah-print glasses.

Disturbed by her perceptiveness and a little by those ridiculous glasses, I narrow my eyes and murmur, "I don't care."

She purses her lips, clearly unconvinced by my response. "It was kind of a mess out there, so we brought you to the ICU. Only doctors and patients are allowed in the exam rooms."

Hearing her say ICU and patients sounds ominous. A sudden

burst of panic grips my chest over what all of this could mean for me.

I'm not ready for it. I'm not ready to have a screwed up knee for the rest of my life. I'm not ready to admit this could be the end of my career. I'm not ready for change. I want to be Camden Harris, footballing star and sex god to women. That's the life I signed up for. That's the goal I want. Pun intended.

I refuse to feel differently. I refuse to let this injury take over everything I am and everything I represent.

I need a distraction. *Now.*

I turn back to take in the doctor more fully as she moves toward me. She's dressed in blue scrubs and bright neon green trainers. Inch by inch, I assess that she's a shorter frame, probably no more than five foot four. Since I can't get a good read on her body beneath those annoying scrubs, I focus more intently above her neck as she pushes buttons on the monitor near my bed.

Her face is sweet and innocent, but not necessarily naïve. Her brown eyes are too sharp and confident to be completely clueless. They definitely contradict her cherubic facial features that make me feel a bit soft and funny on the inside. I don't typically have this reaction to women's faces. Normally, I'm more interested in their body stats.

Large arse.

Large tits.

Small waist.

Down for a shag.

That's my checklist when I roll into a club. The logic behind it is that any average-looking girl can look hot with loads of makeup and dark lighting. I'm more concerned about how they look naked and spread out on a bed as I drive into them. I'm not ashamed of my taste and preference in women. Appreciating a soft, luscious bounce beneath my touch is my rite of passage as a bloke.

But this girl before me has little to no makeup on, yet I find my body instinctively reacting to the soft curves of her face. Truthfully,

I can't remember the last time I picked up a girl in broad daylight, so this all feels a bit strange to me. Then again, nothing about what's happening to me today is typical.

Suddenly, I see a rosy hue crawl up her cheeks as she catches me watching her. My brows lift in a "what'd you expect" sort of expression. Her gaze narrows in contemplation, and I swear I see a tiny spark that tells me she's not all together put off by my perusal.

The side of my mouth tilts up.

Camden Harris, you've just found the perfect distraction.

Maybe if I lie still and let this pretty, bare-faced girl invade all of my thoughts and senses, I won't turn into an emotional ninny over what's happening to my knee.

I wonder where else she's bare? I think to myself, desperate to be reminded that I am still me somewhere beneath this mess of a body.

She shuffles closer to my bed and reaches over top of me for something on the wall. The scent of lemons, toothpaste, and fresh rain fan over me in her close proximity. It's a mouth-watering combination. In the past, I've tried to steer clear of redheads because they're usually the crazy ones. But lord, between this one's scent and her pretty face, I'm quite certain that won't be necessary.

She sets a blood pressure cuff on the bed beside me. Then her cool hand touches my bicep to shove up the sleeve of my jersey. A nurse had toweled off some of the mud earlier, but I remain wet and uncomfortable in my kit.

A chill ripples over me from her delicate touch. It could be from the fact that I'm soaked head to foot in muddy rainwater. Or it could be that this bird is affecting me more than I care to admit. I choose the former.

When her eyes zero in on the half sleeve of black ink that covers the area from my elbow up to my shoulder, I wish I could crawl into her head to know what she's thinking. Is she as intrigued by me as I am by her? Does she want me? Do I make her nervous? Have I ever cared what a girl thought of me before?

I begin to notice the throbbing in my knee once again, so I willfully focus on the female before me. Her nose is small and points slightly upward, and I have a hard time not staring at her pouty lips that seem too heavy to stay closed.

Christ, she's gorgeous.

She wraps the cuff around my arm and, biting her lip, she turns away to push some buttons on the machine. I take this opportunity to check out her backside. It's difficult to tell, but I think she might be sporting a seriously sexy arse.

When the cuff begins to automatically tighten, her focus shifts and she catches my lowered gaze on her. Quirking a brow, she steps over to me and grabs my opposite wrist. "Feeling better already?" she inquires while staring at her wristwatch to register my pulse.

My brows arch. "I buggered up my knee. Not my eyes."

This conversation forces my mind back to the real issue at hand. I glare down at my knee, hot anger coursing through my veins at the seemingly normal-looking limb. On the outside, it looks perfect. On the inside, it's a stormy mess. Not dissimilar to how my entire body looks and feels.

I was born for football, bred for football, lived for football. Now the only feeling I have inside of me is utter treachery. My body betrayed me today.

A hand reaches out and touches my shoulder, causing me to jump at the touch. My gaze lifts to the redhead, and I watch her expression waver as she takes in my internal brooding. Her features are soft. Sweet. And even more beautiful.

Her brows pull together in a sympathetic way again. "I'm sorry," she says. "I didn't mean to be rude. I know you're going through a lot."

I stare back in utter confusion over how she seems to be reading me so easily. Am I that transparent? My shock over her assessment of me is halted when I catch the first clear shot of her eyes through those big glasses. Her irises are a warm toffee colour—dark and bold with flecks of honey around the edges. They are a sharp almond shape with long, soft lashes fanning out. They look softly into mine with a sense of calmness that I feel everywhere.

Everywhere.

And for the first time in my entire life with a woman, I'm at a loss for words.

Realising I'm in some weird silent trance, I clear my throat and croak out, "Most women like my eyes on them." It takes more effort than I'm used to, so I shoot her a lascivious Camden Harris knicker-dropping smirk.

Her eyes squint thoughtfully before she says, "Your vitals are good." Her tone is back to all business. "But I need to check you for internal injuries before I can take you up to radiology."

My brows lift. Could she possibly be immune to my charms? *Redheads,* I think.

She lowers the back of my bed. Suddenly, my mind yanks from the moment as the sensation in my knee of bone rubbing on bone sends shivers up my spine.

She glances down to my legs. "Are you experiencing a lot of pain?"

"Nothing I can't handle," I reply, attempting to avoid the faint feeling of nausea casting over me. She's too beautiful to be looking at me like I'm some weak patient. I want her to look at me like I'm Camden Harris, a star striker for Bethnal Green F.C.

"Well of course you can handle your pain," she says, her tone laced with annoyance. "Humans can handle a lot of pain when forced to. But since we are inside a Western medicine-practicing hospital, I need you to be more specific. On a scale of one to ten, ten being the worst, how bad is it?"

"Three." *Bugger, I'm a liar. My knee throbs! Why do we have to keep talking about it? I don't notice it when we're not talking about it and you're looking at me with those sexy, fuck-me-sideways eyes.*

She stops what she's doing and stares at me incredulously. Her hands reach up and grip the stethoscope around her neck. "You likely tore something in your knee, and you're telling me your pain is only at a three?"

"I'm a Harris. We're tougher than most." I wink at her while clenching my teeth.

She responds with a dramatic eye roll that makes me genuinely smile. Fuck, she's cute. I can tell I'm affecting her but not in the way I affect most women, which only makes me even more curious.

"Lying about your pain number doesn't make your dick any bigger," she mumbles under her breath. Her eyes fly wide when I let out a hearty bark of a laugh. It's like she didn't mean to say those words out loud. She covers her mouth and an honest-to-goodness hoot rumbles all the way into my stomach.

Even if what she said was accidental, it was challenging and funny. *An intriguing combo in a female,* I have to admit. The birds I run into usually reply to my practised lines with a giggle and a selfie. I never knew injuring myself could be this much fun.

"Believe me, I don't need any help with my cock size." I quirk a brow at her.

She barks out her own incredulous laugh this time and that colour appears on the apples of her cheeks again. The same colour that was staining her face when I was checking out her arse a minute ago.

Her smile makes me smile.

Our eyes lock, and I watch the corners of her mouth drop as her chest rises and falls with deep, labourious breaths.

Camden Harris knicker-dropping smirk.

Evidently deciding not to acknowledge my dick size comment, she says, "We'll get you some pain meds after your scan." She pauses for a beat, her hands flittering over my white jersey like she's not sure where to grab it since it's covered in mud. I help her by grabbing the hem and lifting it up past my pecs. I swear the colour of her eyes turns to lava. She can act all calm and collected, but this reaction is unmistakable.

Rolling her incredibly large pink lips into her mouth, she presses them between her teeth as she places her hands on my mud-streaked stomach. I suck in a sharp breath.

"Sorry," she croaks, her face twisting up apologetically. "My hands are always cold."

"It's okay," I groan softly against the onslaught. I'm quite certain I'd take loads more pleasure pain from her any day. "I'm always hot. Oil and water can be kind of fun to mix sometimes."

She closes her eyes for a second, forcing herself to concentrate as she moves her soft, delicate hands along the bumpy planes of my stomach. Watching her, I endeavour to think that she's a good doctor. She has a skillful touch, and the way her eyes open and inspect as she goes along makes me assume she's got eighty different facts spinning in her mind as she works.

She's obviously very focused because she's completely oblivious to my eyes trained on her, which is...problematic for me because I'm getting half hard from having her hands on me. And problematic because I'm wearing a nut cup that won't allow my erection the room it needs to stretch out.

As she works, her heavy lips slip out of her mouth and there's an audible *pop* in the room. Damn, I've never seen lips like hers on an actual human before. They look like those wax lips we used to get as kids from the old-fashioned sweet shop in Manchester. Except those lips were just something my brothers and I wanted to be perverted with. Hers...Oh, who am I kidding? I just want to be perverted with hers as well.

Fuck. Me.

Now all I can picture are those large lips wrapped tightly around my cock. So tightly I have to wrap that wild, red, curly hair around my fist and control every part of her over-eager movements. *God, I bet she'd be so eager—*

"No signs of internal bleeding," she states as she pulls my wet jersey back down.

"Good to hear," I reply, grateful for a second of reprieve to collect myself. "So now that you felt me up, do I get to know your name?" I ask.

She looks adorably confused. "I told you. It's Dr. Porter."

"I know you're a doctor with a fancy title. But you're also a woman with your hands on a man. A man named Camden. You can call me Cam if you'd like." I wink again. "Now, why don't you give me your first name. I don't mind at all."

She shakes her head. "I mind, actually. Dr. Porter is all you need to know. We'll need to get you changed into a gown for your MRI," she says, interrupting my hot-as-fuck fantasy of playing doctor with the naughty redhead. She strides over and pulls the pale green curtain around to sheath us in complete privacy from the mania I've been oblivious to outside of my room. She looks down at my shin pads nervously. "Do you need help changing?"

The side of my mouth tilts up. "Is helping me change all that you're offering?"

Her eyes slant. "Are all footballers like this?" she asks as she strides back over and unfastens the blood pressure cuff from my arm.

"Like what?" I reply innocently, enjoying the tone of her candour.

"So assuming." She adjusts her cheetah-print glasses and furrows her brow. "You just assume that I'd be willing to drop to my knees and suck you off right now, don't you? Gosh, the cheek of you!"

All air is sucked from my lungs and my brows shoot through the ceiling. She stated that phrase like she was reading a fact from a textbook, not saying a sexual comment that's turning my semi into a fully.

I let out a throaty laugh, and her fiery gaze doesn't seem nearly as amused as she continues to pierce me with a blatant challenge. She's waiting for an answer. More importantly, she's surprising the fuck out of me. I've always loved surprises.

"Hoped is more like it," I reply, noting her rigid posture. "Especially now after hearing those dirty words tumble out of those pretty lips. But it's not all about me. What about your needs, baby? I'm dying to know." I pull on my jock briefs that are about to cut off circulation.

Her eyes follow my hand and flare anxiously. "This is not the time nor the place for this kind of talk." Her voice is flustered and high-pitched, but I see a struggle in the deep depths of her eyes. "Mr. Harris, I'm your doctor."

"That sounds like an excuse, not a rejection." My adrenaline spikes with an aching need. "Name it, Dr. Porter," I add quickly, hoping to not lose momentum.

Heat flushes her cheeks again. "Name what?"

"The time and place. I'm all fucking ears, baby."

"Baby? Seriously?" She rolls her eyes and grips the stethoscope around her neck, clearly affected by the excitement vibrating in the air around us. "You can't come up with anything more original? The dictionary has lots of choices. It's even sorted alphabetically for your convenience."

"Give it time. We've just met. And you still haven't told me your first name so I'm improvising." My eyes drift up to her hair barely contained on top of her head. I'd kill to see it down around her shoulders. Or better yet, spread across my pillow as I take her from behind. I bet she has the pinkest fucking nipples—

"You do realise you have a serious injury, don't you?" She shakes her head and begins typing something into the iPad chart alongside the monitor.

I'm completely flabbergasted. Upon first glance, this Dr. Porter looks meek and unassuming, nerdy and maybe even passive. She looks like the kind of bird that when she gets the wrong meal delivered to her at a restaurant, she doesn't have the courage to tell the waiter. So she sits there and eats whatever they've dropped in front of her. Typically, my eyes would roll right past someone like her in a club. You can usually pick them out of a crowd because of how they carry themselves and how they're dressed. The types that dress for attention are generally a sure thing. But there's something about this one that makes me need to know more. She might even be a rarity. And, well, she did say "cock" after all.

She chooses that second to lean over top of me and stuff the blood pressure cuff into a metal basket above my bed. She loses her footing slightly and, well, never one to waste an opportunity, my hands reach up to grip her lower back and pull her down on top of me. Her chest hits mine, and I'm assaulted with an orgasmic scent that must be distinctly of the Dr. Porter variety.

I'm not sure what I had planned. Truth be told, I didn't completely think it through. Most likely I was just going to say something smart and see what else I could get to come out of her gorgeous mouth. But a flurry of excitement rips through me when her eyes flash to my lips and, in that instant, I know what I have to do.

I have to taste her.

Without hesitating, I sample her lips, giving her what her eyes were so quietly begging for. She lets out an audible groan, but it's not a frightened groan. It's a "you cheeky sod, I like this" sort of groan. It's the kind of groan you make when you're young and trying to fight off an orgasm that comes much too soon because you're so inexperienced. It's the kind of groan that makes all the pain in my knee completely dissipate. It's the kind of groan that gives me the slightest glimpse of how hot she would be in the sack.

I forget all about the fact that I'm kissing my doctor. Right now, she's simply an incredibly sexy woman who has managed to consume ninety percent of my thoughts since I arrived here over an hour ago. And denial is a dish best served hot and luscious, so I'm eating while I have the chance.

As soon as her soft, luscious lips part, my tongue is in, pulsing against the inside of her mouth like it's seeking refuge. Like it's seeking a way to comfort both of us from this burning, almost painful desire coursing between us. God, if I could live in this woman's mouth,

I would. It tastes like lemons, and her body has a fresh dew smell that I could lick off of her.

Furthermore, her lips deserve a medal. They deserve a plaque in the castle. They deserve to be honoured and revered and written about in pornographic novels for years to come. They are like heaven and hell combined forces and created the most intense party of all time.

She shocks the fuck out of me when one of her hands that was previously clinging to my bicep starts to skirt under my damp jersey. I release a warm groan against her lips when she drags her nails harshly down the curves of my abs. It feels like she's testing the firmness of them. *Everything is hard for you, baby.*

I break our kiss and moan out in pain when her fingers bite harshly into my flesh at the hem of my shorts. But it's not knee pain I'm moaning about. It's pleasure pain. It makes me want to rip the scrubs off her body and bite one of her nipples as payback.

My moan was evidently a bucket of ice water dumped on her head. She wrenches away from me and stares down wide-eyed.

"You just kissed me," she pants, her large lips blotchy from my assault.

"You let me," I huff back defensively, feeling so incredibly empty at the loss of her weight on me. I can't take my eyes off her mouth, nor stop silently wishing we were still kissing. If she thinks I was in that kiss alone, she's dead wrong. I probably have the nail marks on my abs to prove it.

Her eyes dance around the room nervously. "Crap. I did! Oh my God, what did I just do? I'm your doctor. That was a horrible line we just crossed. Horrible. I've gone completely mental!" She swallows hard. "Come on. We need to get you out of these clothes."

"It'll be hard to do with a buggered knee, but I'm sure I can manage if you climb on top." I quickly pull my jersey off over my head and toss it on the floor while adding, "It won't be my best performance, but I'll make it memorable. I promise."

"What?" she shrieks at my dumbfounded expression. Then her eyes feast down on my bare chest and stomach. "Your MRI, Camden. I mean! Mr. Harris! Crap. I meant that we need to get you undressed for your MRI. Oh my word. I'm sending in an intern." She rushes up to me, and just when I think I see a spark in her eyes that makes me hopeful she's coming back for more, she snatches up her stethoscope that must have slipped off during our tryst. "Crap, crap, crap," she murmurs as she scrambles away from me and leaves me with a raging fucking boner.

Just then, Dr. Prichard, the man who received me when I came in, pulls the curtain back and walks in with a wake of Harrises staring daggers through the glass behind him. The entire fishbowl imagery is as effective as a cold shower. My cock slumps back down into depressed submission.

4
Penis Number One

Indie

I drum my fingers along my lower lip as I stand at the radiology counter awaiting Camden Harris' MRI report. Prichard said he was eager for the results so he wanted to send someone over here to hurry the tech along.

Now, here I am. Alone with my thoughts. Nowhere to escape. No one to talk to. And still tasting Cam's—

"You know, staring at me isn't going to make me work any faster," the radiologist snaps.

My eyes widen because I hadn't even realised I was staring at her. I turn away from the counter and mumble a quiet apology. *Jeez, pull yourself together, Indie. It's not as if you were just mauled by one of the sexiest men you've ever laid eyes on or anything.*

Remaining calm is an impossibility at this point. I was so shaken by the kiss that I had tripped over Prichard's feet on my way out of the exam room. He caught me in front of the Harris family and did that whole awkward "are you all right" thing people do when you wish they'd just act as if the fall didn't happen. Or the least they could do is laugh with you. Both of those options are better than the "did you hurt yourself" look.

It had to be Camden's eyes. Or his abs. Or his face. But definitely his eyes are what sent me into a psychopathic frenzy. They were on me constantly and causing some seriously embarrassing things to happen in my knickers. Closing my lids, I can still see the dangerous midnight blue irises that bewitched every organ in my body. They held such danger in them. Such life. Such excitement. Even as he lay there with a career-altering injury, his dark lashes beckoned me with sinful promise. Couple that with his tousled blonde hair and abs of steel, and I was doomed.

I pop a sherbet lemon in my mouth and suck on it thoughtfully. Who knew "rock-hard abs" is a truthful synonym? I've seen countless patients and none of their stomachs have felt like that. It's positively ludicrous how they hardened beneath my touch as if they were enjoying the feel of my hands. *Good grief!*

I crunch down on the hard sweet and the juicy centre erupts in my mouth. The creamy syrupiness creates a synonym of its own for how I behaved around him: Smooth and hard on the outside, a gooey mess of molten lava on the inside.

I mean, of course I am attracted to him. That's just science. But kissing him in the ICU is about the stupidest thing I could have done. I've never, in my life, been conflicted over whether to behave like a doctor or like a woman. What possessed me to drape myself over the top of a patient and allow him to attack my lips for who knows how long?

Oh, sod off, Indie! You know exactly what was going through your head. Stop lying to yourself.

I push my glasses up my nose and swallow down the remaining bits of sweetness as I finally set the truth free inside my brain. *You wanted Camden Harris to be Penis Number One.*

It couldn't be more obvious if it was stamped on his forehead. Of all the guys in all of London. Of all the patients in all the hospitals, he had to be mine? I could lose everything if I let something that horrid happen again.

But bloody hell, when his lips touched mine, I was doomed. For the first time in my limited experience, my physical reaction to a man trumped all the mental qualifying that my brain has done with other blokes in the past.

Did I actually think I could climb aboard and let him take me in the middle of a workday? I've worked so hard for my career and am constantly having to prove myself to my colleagues because of my age. Was I going to throw it all away for abs that felt like bones, as if I'm some star-struck fan girl?

No, no. This is not me.

No man makes me act this way, no matter how hot he is. I'll chalk this up to either extremely intense pheromones or low blood sugar. Both can have some severe side effects. I pop another sweet in my mouth.

"Holy shit, you have a Harris brother as a patient!" Belle squeals from behind me. I'm taken so off guard that when her hot breath sprays moisture into my ear, I suck my sweet into the back of my throat.

My face contorts and I cough while aggressively wiping at the dewy liquid she sprayed. "Say the news, not the weather, you animal," I grumble.

Ignoring my jab, she props herself against the counter beside me and pats my back. "You have a bloody Harris brother. I heard it's one of the twins. Which one? Long hair or short?"

Her eyes are bright and hungry for more information. After I recover, my own gaze narrows with an ounce of possessiveness. Not necessarily possessiveness over Camden, but possessiveness over my thoughts. I'm still processing what I want him to be, yet Belle is going to put it all out in the open like she always does.

I swallow and begrudgingly reply, "His hair is short, but longer on the top." I'm pretty sure I copped a feel of that gorgeous golden mess during our…encounter. I inwardly recoil.

"That's Camden then. He was seen with a supermodel a few weeks ago."

A supermodel. Of course. *Way to set your sights high, Indie!*

"So is he as stunning in person as he is in the papers?" Belle's dark eyes twinkle mischievously. "God, I bet he is. Can you imagine that level of athleticism in the bedroom? Too bad it's not the oldest brother, Gareth. I'd let him stick it in any hole he wanted, even my ears if he liked that sort of thing."

"Belle!" I screech, my eyes darting over at the radiologist who seems oblivious to our conversation.

"What? I would. He's hot as hell and plays for Manchester United. They've been having an epic season."

"I don't really follow football," I croak, desperate to end this conversation so Belle goes away and leaves me alone with my thoughts.

"Don't follow football? How can you not? We're practically neighbours with Tower Park. That's who three of them play for! What, do you live in a box?" she shrieks.

"Boarding school," I shrug, using my easy out excuse for all my unsociable tendencies.

"Right. Well, let me clue you in, darling." She turns me to face her head-on and pushes my glasses up my nose so she can properly pierce me with her stare. "Camden Harris is one of four football-playing Harris brothers. Three of them are like the playboy darlings of East London. They all play for the same championship league club their dad manages. The twins are strikers and the youngest one is a goalie. The oldest makes over two hundred mil a year as a defender in the Premier League."

My eyes widen. "That's a lot of money."

"Fucking right it is. And Camden Harris has had a legendary season. Social media has all been saying that Arsenal and Man U have been fighting over who is going to offer him a contract. He could get bumped up to Premiership! His twin brother is nearly as good. This family is a big fucking deal, Indie. The hospital PR is having a field day I'm sure."

"Well, he's highly inappropriate," I add weakly.

"He's highly hot as fuck." I do a crap job of concealing my smile as a flash of his boyish smirk clouds my mind. Belle's knowing grin bursts through my bubble.

I bite down hard on my sweet. "It's weird to be attracted to someone who's at their worst, right?" I ask, leaning in closer to her.

"Why do you say that?"

"It sounds like an embarrassing creepy fetish. He's all injured and laid up. Or hell, maybe it's cool. It's probably a checkbox on Tinder."

Belle whacks me on the arm. "Screw Tinder. So you *do* think he's hot?" she asks, her eyebrows dancing.

I scoff, "I might wear glasses, but I'm not blind." Even covered in grass stains, mud, and sweat, I wanted to bend over and lick every ridge that decorated his impeccable stomach. Then, when he started adjusting himself in front of me, I had to squeeze my thighs together for fear of fluids dripping down my legs. "But he knows he's hot. I hate that," I add half-heartedly, barely convincing even myself.

"Indie…stop fighting this. You know what he is."

"No I don't," I defend, my heart leaping with anxiety and anticipation. The rush of realisation pulses through my veins.

Her eyes squint with determination. "This is Penis Number One."

"You don't know that. He might not even be into me," I lie, feeling intimidated by the idea of actually being intimate with someone as hot as Camden Harris. That kiss sure made it seem as if he is interested, but the reality of being naked with someone like him is a completely different story.

She laughs heartily. "Of course he's into you. Hell, I'm into you."

"Don't be daft."

"Stop downplaying your appeal, Indie. It's unappealing." Her gaze softens. "You're unique, smart, hilarious, and beautiful. Throw in a dash of quirky and sexy glasses and you're the fun total package. Don't ever forget that." I'm taken aback by the sincerity on Belle's face. She doesn't really do warm and fuzzy, so her coming at me like this is shocking. "And you won't find more of a bad boy player than Camden Harris, darling."

"But I'm his doctor," I nervously reply.

"Tequila Sunrise, Indie. Tequila Sunrise." Her face suddenly morphs into urgency. "But for the love of God, don't get caught. You have a lot to lose if you cross the line and people around here find out."

"I'm not stupid. I'd never do anything here," I huff as if she couldn't say anything more ridiculous.

"And don't get hurt. We've talked about this. I don't want to have to maim one of London's star footballers. You know I'm good with a scalpel."

I chuckle and bite my lip as ten tons of nerves come barreling down on top of me. A manila envelope distracts us both as it's dropped on the counter beside me. The tech walks away without a word, and I scoop up the contents, clutching them closely to my chest.

Getting hurt by a player like Camden Harris is the last fear in my mind. I'm not worried about getting too attached. Getting caught, on the other hand, is something I need to be careful about. Regardless, maybe somehow I can get this to work. Maybe when he's no longer a patient, we could get in touch. I could slip him my number, or if I'm feeling horribly brave, ask him for his. I know he's high-profile, but we can be discreet.

He's the perfect Penis Number One. I'm smart enough to find a way around this. I'm sure of it.

"I have to get these results to Prichard. The Harris family is breathing down his neck for information on this special surgery he wants to do on Cam."

Belle's mouth spreads into an ear-to-ear smile.

"What?" I ask.

"You call him Cam now, do you?" she sings.

"Piss off!" I hiss and turn to scurry down the hallway and away from my nosey bugger of a friend.

When I approach the large patient suite, I peek through the heavy double doors and spot a stunning blonde hunched over Camden. He's nestled comfortably in a large, double patient bed that's covered in expensive linens. After his MRI, he was moved to the private wing of the hospital that's reserved for A-list patients and donors. It's more like a swanky hotel than a hospital room—one of the many benefits of a privately owned clinic.

The blonde strokes his hair affectionately as if she's been doing it for years. A knife twists in my gut at their easy comfort with each other. My eyes drift down to her body, all willowy and stylishly dressed in cute jeans and a green Bethnal Green jersey with Harris imprinted on the back. When I finally see Camden's face, I feel instantly annoyed as realisation dawns on me.

Camden Harris…is a cheating wanker.

He had a lot of nerve kissing me the way he did. What if she had walked in while we were doing that? I was one heartbeat away from gripping his—

I stop that train of thought in its tracks. If I'm being honest, I should have never done anything with him before knowing a thing about him. He's a footballer for goodness sake. Of course he has some woman or *women* on call at all times. How much more green and stupid could I be?

I grip my stethoscope until it smarts inside my hand. His hair looks tamer now—more clean-cut as his blonde locks are smoothed over to one side revealing just how truly handsome he is. Even dressed in a white hospital gown, he looks like a GQ cover model. I preferred him properly mussed if I'm being frank. He wasn't as perfect looking as he is now.

Steeling myself to be unaffected by this rapid change of events, I raise my shoulders and stride confidently into the room. I avoid his eyes on me as I snatch up the iPad from the holder at the foot of his bed. Then I busy myself with typing in his results.

"Hey, Red," Camden drawls sexily.

I frown, my eyes flashing uncomfortably to the blonde and dropping back down to the iPad.

"Cam, she has a name I'm sure," the girl says, looking at me apologetically. "I'm so sorry. He can be a prat with very little effort I'm afraid." She smiles kindly and asks, "What is your name?"

Of course she seems sweet and nice. It would be asking too much for her to be a bitchy, vain bimbo with stiletto pointy nails and a vapid personality disorder. I'd do anything to see her take a selfie with Camden in the background. That would at least distinguish the two of us.

"I'm Dr. Porter," I state pragmatically. I see a flicker of surprise on her face when I give her my title. I really should have worn my black-framed glasses today. My wild eyewear makes it difficult for people to take me seriously. My first day as an intern, the chief of surgery glared at me and uttered, *"Those had better be prescription."*

"We're still at that level?" Camden states brazenly, completely disregarding the woman by his bedside. I look over at him with an incredulous glower. "I mean, after all we've shared," he adds with a waggle to his brows.

My eyes widen and glance at the blonde who's frowning in confusion. What is he trying to do? Cause a bloody cat fight right here? Whoever this woman is—girlfriend, fuck buddy, whatever—she's obviously important enough to be here for him. I'm not about to give him the satisfaction of getting a rise out of me.

I turn back to the blonde. "I'm Mr. Harris' resident doctor. I've just paged the attending ortho surgeon."

"Nice to meet you. I'm—"

"I must be going." I rudely cut her off because I don't want her to introduce herself as Camden's girlfriend. I don't want to give him the satisfaction of watching me squirm.

"You just got here." Camden winces as he attempts to sit himself up more.

"You need to stop moving," I chastise.

"You need to stop running," he retorts with a challenging spark in his eyes.

This gives me pause, but then the blonde adds, "I keep telling him to stop moving. He doesn't need to make it worse by over-exerting himself." She crosses her narrow arms over her tiny runway chest. I wish she had a flaw, but she doesn't. She's stunning all the way up to her clear blue eyes.

My boring brown eyes mistakenly flick back to Camden, who's looking at me with a puzzled expression. Before I can say another word, Prichard opens the door, distracting all of us. "Ah, Indie, I was just looking over Mr. Harris' results you entered in the system." His deep baritone voice fills the room with an air of confidence.

I sigh at his use of my first name in front of our patient. Prichard sometimes takes his friendliness with me too far and steps past the professional boundary. But he's an attending, and he's kind of too charming to get mad at. There are several nurses and interns who fawn all over him—even some of the men—but he never gives them attention. It's the ones who ignore him that he seems the most fascinated by.

He definitely has that perfect tall, dark, and handsome cliché look about him. His daily scruff is an intriguing salt and pepper, which only adds to his distinguished appeal. Compared to Camden, Prichard looks like a proper grown-up. It's like comparing crème brûlée to ice cream. They are both delicious, but for very different reasons.

"Indie is your first name?" Camden drawls smoothly, eyeing me up and down. "I like it."

I grimace and glance back at Camden's girlfriend, who doesn't appear the least bit taken aback by the way he is acting. Maybe she's used to him acting this way toward women wherever they go. Maybe this is normal behaviour for him. If so, good luck to them. My Penis List can survive without the likes of Camden Harris.

"Indie, I'd like you to double-check a couple of things," Dr. Prichard says a bit louder than necessary while he eyes Camden with a contemplative gaze.

He places his hand on the small of my back and ushers me out of the room. I hear a noise and glance back to see Camden shifting uncomfortably in bed and shooting daggers at Prichard's hand. Is he bothered? How can he be when he has a bombshell standing right next to him? Besides, I wouldn't think this looks like much. Prichard has always been affectionate in the way he communicates. It's partially what makes him a great doctor. Sometimes a slight touch on a shoulder can instantly calm an anxious patient's nerves.

When the door closes behind us, Prichard looks at me seriously through his deep brown eyes and says, "I'm going to have a meeting with the family about a new ACL procedure that cuts the recovery time by half. Due to the timing and the season being almost over, I'm afraid Mr. Harris won't be able to play the last match. But with this new surgery, he'll be up and normal in about a week. We'll have to do a follow-up surgery one month after that. Then he'll be good as new."

My brows arch excitedly. "The Wilson Repair," I state, trying to keep my voice calm and professional. "I'm very familiar. Will I get to scrub in?"

"I'm aware of how familiar you are, Indie. I read your published article." His eyes crinkle as they drop down to my mouth. "That's why I don't want anyone else to assist me."

I swallow uncomfortably at his peculiar look, but inside I'm soaring because this could be huge for me. He rubs my shoulder excitedly. "Gather the family in his room. We'll discuss the details in there."

A bit later, a pungent odour of wet, sweaty men swirls around the small amount of space in Cam's suite as three Harris brothers and Mr. Harris all file in. They are quite the family—all well over six foot tall, gorgeous, and muscled like you wouldn't believe. Two of the brothers are still in their fully soaked football gear, similar to what Camden was wearing when I saw him earlier. But now they are joined by a decidedly taller, darker, and more handsome bloke in street clothes who can be none other than Gareth Harris. Nurses keep flocking past the door, fan-girling over the man whose arrival twenty minutes earlier had to involve security. The media were already swarming for Camden, but when Gareth arrived, it became a frenzied mess.

My eyes focus once again on the blonde who is perched on the side of the bed. She's dutifully holding Cam's hand while Prichard explains the procedure that's going to get him back on the field sooner rather than later.

I know more about The Wilson Repair than most because, in med school, I wrote a paper on the materials used for the surgical grafts. I cross-analised them with a newer formula and found potential for quicker recovery times for patients. After a couple of years, my results were published in a medical journal and surgeons began adapting the new material.

Since then, The Wilson Repair has slowly been taking over traditional ACL repairs. A Spanish footballer was the first athlete to have it done last year, and he returned to the season after only five weeks. The uniqueness of this type of repair is that it avoids any bone drilling. The only drawback is that it's a two-session surgery, but the rapid recovery payoff supersedes that.

To scrub in on a procedure like this after all of my hard work is a huge opportunity. I'm hopeful this will prove to the other residents that I'm not only a skilled researcher; I'm also a skilled practicing surgeon who deserves to be here.

Since there's only one more game left in the season, Camden is done for the year. Regardless, the fact that he'll be able to start rehabilitation right away seems to please his family. I fill in all the blanks that Prichard volleys my way. The hospital's PR person and a member of the press are present so he's definitely show-boating a bit. But the Harrises are all gobbling it up as they look at us with bated breath every time we speak. Even Camden's dad, Vaughn Harris, eyes me as if I alone am going to be the one to save his son's life.

As I'm explaining to Camden that he'll be up and walking normally in less than a week, another incredibly good-looking male comes strolling in.

"Hi, guys. Sorry it took me so long to get here. There was an accident on the Tube, and it's a nightmare out front with TV crews."

The blonde girl leaps off the bed and dives into the bloke's arms. They embrace in an intimate hug. Her voice trembles against his chest, "It's fine, Hayden. I'm just so glad you're here."

He pulls back, cupping her face and dropping a soft kiss to her lips. "Man, the way you're acting, I'd swear it was you injured instead of Cam." Hayden's voice is laughing as he sweetly strokes her cheeks with his thumbs.

"Our Vi has a flair for the dramatics," Tanner grumbles in a teasing tone.

"Shut it," she says, wiping a tear from her eye. "It's the bloody pregnancy hormones." She swats Hayden's chest playfully and adds, "And it's all your fault."

It's then that Camden's cocky eyes find my shocked ones. A lopsided grin tugs on his lips as he mouths, "Sister." Then a full-blown, satisfied smile spreads across his face.

Sister.

Pregnant sister.

Not pregnant girlfriend.

And just like that, Penis Number One is back in the game.

A few minutes later, Prichard gets paged and leaves me to continue fielding any other questions they have. We schedule the first surgery for two days from now; however, to prevent any risk of further injuring himself and taking The Wilson Repair off the table, Prichard wants Camden to remain in the hospital. I'm sure the hospital also wants to capitalise on his presence here any way they can. With private ownership, this kind of press can greatly help with investor interest.

"So you'll actually be in the room when they cut into my knee?" Camden quietly asks me as his family continues filling Hayden in on the other side of the room.

I nod, walking up to his bed and standing closer to him. His voice is low with a seriousness to his tone. Looking at him now, I see that he's lost that roguish alpha air. Lying before me is a softer and more boyish version of him. Maybe even a little scared.

"I'll be right beside Dr. Prichard," I reply, fighting the urge I have to touch his arm in comfort.

Exhaling, he asks, "Will you be doing any of the cutting?" He swallows hard, and I watch his Adam's apple slide down and back up his thick neck.

I note the pensive look on his face. "It's a scope, Cam. They're tiny incisions. You probably have football scars from tackles that are bigger than these will be. Truly, you'll be up to your old tricks in no time. I promise you."

A pleased smile spreads across his face.

"What?" I ask, pushing my glasses up and frowning in confusion.

"You just called me Cam." The twinkle in his eyes leaves me no choice but to smile back.

I laugh softly and punch some pointless buttons on his monitor to distract myself from his face. "Slip of the tongue, Mr. Harris. Don't get all cocky on me now. You were doing so well."

"I was thinking I could call you Specs for a nickname instead of baby or Red, but Indie is just too sexy of a name I'm afraid. It's beaten everything I've been workshopping in my head."

I cross my arms over my chest. "You've been workshopping pet names for me?" I chuckle, secretly chastising myself for loving the nickname Specs more than I should.

He shrugs and tweaks his eyebrows while eyeing my completely scrub-covered cleavage. Honestly, the way his eyes are staring, you'd think I am wearing a wet T-shirt.

"I've had a lot of time on my hands," he says, his voice deep and husky. "And you've sort of been consuming all my thoughts since you buggered off so quickly before."

I clear my throat nervously. "I had things to do."

He growls with a speculative twinkle in his lash-framed eyes. "You thought she was my girlfriend, didn't you?"

I remain silent. The discomfort I felt in those brief moments at the loss of opportunity a girlfriend would have presented is not something I care to revisit. Him having a girlfriend should have come as a relief to me. Instead, my stupid, tortured soul was more disappointed about the loss of Penis Number One.

"My sister is more like a mum at times," he adds. "She's great. You'd like her I'm sure. Everybody does."

"She's lovely," I reply, my chest pounding with anxiety as that heated look in his gaze blossoms. "My shift is about over so I need to be going."

All cockiness drains from his face. "You're leaving?"

I shake my head. "Well, not technically. I sleep here. I only get six hours off, so I get more sleep if I stay in the on-call room." Which is mostly true. He doesn't need to know I don't go home because it's too lonely there.

"So can I have them page you in the middle of the night if I need a sponge bath?" he drawls sexily. The corner of his mouth tilts up with an impish grin.

"No," I baulk.

"Why ever not?" He actually has the nerve to look offended.

"It doesn't work like that, Cam—Mr. Harris. The resident on call is whom they'll page. Plus, sponge baths aren't resident jobs." But, come to think of it, if anyone is touching him, I want it to be me.

"I don't want just any medical person. I want you. They put me in the VIP wing. Don't I get some say?"

"This isn't appropriate," I whisper, but even I can tell my voice sounds weak. I bite my lip and look around nervously, grateful to see his family oblivious to our current exchange.

"I'm not asking for anything major. Just a simple way to get ahold of you if I have questions about the surgery. I don't do well with this…stuff." His expression morphs from cocky player to pensive patient. My instinct tells me that it's not an act, and my professional training wants to put his mind at ease. Not to mention, my heart lurches when someone looks at me the way he is, all wounded and scared, especially when I know I can make him better.

I shouldn't do this. I shouldn't do what I'm about to do. But a deep, quiet part of my mind says he needs this and this is my chance. This is where I take the plunge. This is where I stop letting my professional life trump my personal life.

I reach into my pocket for my yellow Post-it notes. With shaky hands, I scribble my mobile number down and hand it over to him. His fingertips brush against mine, but he continues to watch my face for the answer to what I'm handing him.

"Don't make me regret this, Camden Harris." I take a step back, watching the space between us shimmer with heat transference like the air above a campfire.

"Never." His tone is dark and promising as he clutches my number in his fist.

Feeling as if my legs might give out as his stormy blue eyes lock onto mine, I break the trance I'm in and turn to shuffle out, grateful that the family is still deep in their own conversation and oblivious to us.

"Oh, and Indie?" he says quietly, forcing me to pause and look over my shoulder.

"Yes?"

"When I have two good knees again, you won't be able to get away from me so easily." His eyes spark with heated warning. It's a warning that says to prepare myself for much more than a stolen kiss.

Feeling more like a woman than a doctor at this moment, I bite my lip and shrug. His gaze drops down to my pink tinted lips, which causes me to smile, spin on my heel, and haul arse out of there before my blush starts me on fire and totally gives me away.

5
Night Vision

Camden

After tossing and turning for over two hours now, I'm no closer to getting any rest than I was the second I started silently listing football stats in my head. As a child, I had the worst case of insomnia, so Vi got me hooked on listing things to help my brain quiet down. So, since ten o'clock, I've been listing every goal I've scored and I've still seen nearly every minute on the bloody clock tick by.

I should be exhausted. It's almost midnight and it was a rain match today for fuck's sake. But my mind keeps wandering back to the surgery they want to do on my knee in two days—this supposed career-saving surgery.

When everyone came in with their bright ideas, impressive statistics, and articles about other footballers who have had this brand new surgery, I didn't react the way I thought I would. I should have been jumping for joy and kissing the good doctor for saving my career.

Instead, a twisting in my gut multiplied. I began to feel weighted down like I do when I run around a muddy pitch wearing ankle weights. Did I lose my shot at a Premier contract? Am I even still a footballer if I can't play right now? Football is my identity, so what am I without it?

It's all a bit disconcerting, especially since I've been having the season of my life. This Wilson Repair is supposed to get me right back in the game, so why am I so confused about how I feel?

Oh, shut it, Camden. You probably just need to get laid, I think to myself. Instantly, Indie's angelic face invades my mind.

"Fuck it," I say while pressing the button on my bed to raise myself up. I can't keep lying here—not sleeping—and obsessing. My brain needs a break from the stress. In the past, whenever I've needed a break, women were usually the perfect release. The perfect distraction to forget and not be needed for something more than just the basic carnal act of sex.

Indie Porter would more than do for me right now. She's been invading my thoughts since I first laid eyes on her. The tremendous urge I have to know more about her is heady. I think she might be a little nuts and that makes me positively desperate to know more. Don't get me wrong. I've had encounters with beautiful women from all over the world. But kissing a doctor in an exam room ranks high on my list of spank-banking material.

Furthermore, when I get right down to the brass tacks of it, it wasn't the location that made it memorable.

It was her.

She is breathtaking. From her face to her hair, to her body, to her glasses…She gave me chills and at that point all she had done was touch my arm. I need to know what it would be like to actually be inside of her.

I turn on the dim nightlight over my bed and snatch my mobile up off the side table. Quickly, I find Indie's name that I saved in my contacts immediately after she left. She gave me her number, so whether she's my doctor or not, that act alone told me she is also open to something more than just a doctor/patient relationship. I'm just not sure she's ready to fully admit it yet.

She's probably sleeping and won't answer, but it's worth a shot.

I don't usually have to chase girls but I'll gladly make an exception for her.

Tonight is the perfect opportunity. There's something about the night that makes things look differently, too. For example, when you hear a strange noise in your flat and it's dark out, you're instantly on defence, ready for battle. But, in the daytime, if you hear a strange noise, you're certain it's just the neighbour's overweight cat tipping over his litter box again. You don't even bother closing your book.

Darkness can make you brave. That's what I want out of Indie. There's something about her that I want to break through. Maybe if I can get her up to my room now that she's not officially working, she'll drop the wall and let me in.

I press DIAL on my mobile and hear the sexiest sound in the universe. "Mmmm, this is Dr. Porter."

My groin lurches. "Are you in the middle of something?"

"Mmmm, what's that? What did you say?" Her voice is moany and scratchy, and all I can think about are the sounds she'd make with me inside of her.

My breath comes out quickly before I resume speaking. "You sound like you were either in the middle of dreaming about me, or you were in the middle of touching yourself while dreaming about me, or you were wide awake and touching yourself while dreaming about me. All of the above is an acceptable answer."

Silence.

"Don't go quiet on me now, Indie." I reach down and shamelessly cup myself, closing my eyes and imagining her all sleep-tousled and adorable in my bed with me.

"Is this Camden?" Her voice is a bit clearer now.

"Miss me?"

I hear ruffling on the other end, and I envision her sitting up in bed and putting her glasses on. Her voice is alert. "I'm just thinking about how full of yourself you are to assume that the only options of what I'm doing right now include thoughts of you."

"Who else would it be?" I ask and move my hand from my dick as frustrating thoughts of that prat, Dr. Prichard, flash in my mind. She better not be thinking of that wanker. "Did you have another someone else manhandle your lips today?"

She huffs incredulously. "What's going on? What's the matter?" she yawns.

"I can't sleep."

"Is it pain? Have they done final rounds on you already? You need to tell them your pain number and be honest, Cam. And make sure they don't forget to give you a new dose if it's been four hours."

I grin at her calling me Cam again. It sounds so perfectly casual and utterly sexy coming from her kind voice. "It's not pain."

"Then what is it?"

"I don't know exactly. I think you better get up here and check it out."

"Check what out?" Her voice rises slightly. "Are you having other symptoms? Is something happening with your knee? Are you feeling feverish?"

"I'm definitely hot."

"I'll be right there." The line cuts out and I have a fleeting sense of guilt for misleading her into thinking there is something else wrong with me. I didn't expect her to be so trusting of my complaints. But I'm not really in the position to chase her down, and she said she doesn't want me to move, right?

More excited than I feel compelled to admit, I decide to ditch my shirt to make a solid impact when she comes through the door. I fling the shirt Tanner had brought me toward my chair and lean back in my bed with my hands behind my head as I await her entrance.

In a matter of minutes, the beautiful redhead comes striding into my room. The dim yellow light above my head casts a warm hue on her blue scrubs. I didn't want to turn on any more lights for our meeting. I've found that turning the lights off when I'm in bed with a woman tends to unleash a whole other side of her that she's normally too proper to let loose. I want that to happen with Indie.

Indie's so busy tying her mass of curls up into a bun atop her head, she doesn't even look at me. Closing the double doors behind her, she eventually reaches the foot of my bed and snatches up the iPad digital chart that rests in a plastic holder by my feet. Scrolling through it for a few seconds, she says, "Your vitals were all good when they rounded on you thirty minutes ago." Her brows are furrowed. "Normal temp recorded. What's the problem?"

She looks up at me and pushes her glasses up on her nose. I'm surprised to see they are teal frames now. Gone are the cheetah ones from earlier. The colour of these make her toffee eyes stand out even more. Toffee eyes that are now taking in my black boxer briefs.

"You changed your glasses," I state, ignoring her question and smiling at her wandering gaze.

"You're not wearing your gown," she replies, frowning. "And I have tons of different glasses. I don't know what I grabbed. It was dark in the on-call room."

"I'm sorry if I woke you up," I say, surprising myself by actually caring. I don't usually do the thoughtful bloke thing, but Indie Porter is a different calibre of woman.

"It's fine. You're a VIP and Dr. Prichard told me to check in on you at some point tonight anyway."

"So do you sleep in those on-call rooms by yourself?" I ask, morbidly curious. If this hospital is anything like the medical shows on the telly, those on-call rooms are nothing short of a brothel.

"No, there were a couple other doctors in there. I'm more concerned about how you're feeling. Why did you ask me up here?" She grips the iPad against her chest and furrows her brow at me.

I cock my head. "Why do you think I asked you up here?"

Her face drops into one of unimpressed chastisement. "Are you trying to seduce me when you have a serious injury?"

Scoffing, I reply, "'Course not. That would be mental, right?"

She drops her chin. "Yes. Completely mental, Mr. Harris."

I let out a soft chuckle at her tone. "Fine then, Doctor, I think I might have insomnia or something."

Her brows lift. "That sounds like nerves, but I can give you something to help you sleep." She swipes the iPad awake again.

"I don't want drugs and it's not nerves," I lie, clenching my jaw over her perceptiveness. I decide to quickly flip the tables back on her. "So when I called, you sounded like you were doing more than just sleeping. Are those on-call rooms that comfortable?" I tweak my brows playfully.

She baulks, "I wasn't doing any of whatever your mind is wandering off to. That is my sleeping voice you heard, which is a miracle in and of itself. The cots are terrible for getting any decent rest. I'll be lucky if I am able to fall back asleep."

"So we both have a sleep problem then." She eyes me warily as my expression turns hopeful. "I think I have the perfect solution."

She lets out a haughty laugh. "Oh, do tell."

"It's simple…You can sleep with me." I give her a confident nod and prop my hands back behind my head like I just stated the most logical thing all day. "This is practically my own private apartment in here, and I'm concerned for your rest, Indie. You're not my doctor right now, but you will be tomorrow. I need you in tip-top shape. This is rather noble if you think about it."

She crosses her arms over her chest and purses her lips off to the side. "Sleeping with you would be highly inappropriate. Not to mention, I could lose out on scrubbing in on your surgery. Maybe even my job." Even though her words seem resolute, her eyes trail down my chest again.

Christ, she's worse than blokes are about checking out the opposite sex. I fucking love it.

"There's a lock on my door," I volley back.

"The nurses have keys. Besides, you may not be aware but the type of surgery you're going to have is very rare. This is a huge opportunity for me."

"No one has to know," I add.

"I would know. I'm a doctor. You're a patient. This is madness." Her stiff posture begins to shift.

"I'm not after anything except some sleep, Indie." At least for now. Sleep and a distraction is what I need, even if it isn't the naked kind. Focusing my efforts on this redhead is just what the doctor ordered. Pun intended. "My nerves are shot after today. I can't quiet my mind. We can talk each other to sleep. It'll be good for both of us."

She stops chomping on her lip long enough to say, "The best I can do is sit in here until you fall asleep."

It's a small victory, but I'll take it. "Stay as long as you'd like. The nurse said she wouldn't bother me again until eight a.m. That nurse was an interesting one, I'd say. Her bedside manner could rival Hitler. And I think her chin mole had its own beard."

She giggles and my heart races. I'm winning. I've always been good at winning.

"Don't laugh too loud. You don't want Beardie to overhear," I state. "You might want to set your alarm just in case you fall asleep," I offer, attempting to capitalise on her good humour.

She rolls her eyes but makes her way to the chair. I've had to use a lot of my charm on this girl, but something tells me she might be worth it.

"Are you sure you don't want to climb in? My bed is quite nice… VIP and all. And, unlike Beardie, I have great bedside manners."

She turns on her heel to face me. Her pointer finger is raised like a schoolteacher when she says, "There is absolutely no chance of you getting your balls wet if that's where your mind is going, Camden Harris."

My boisterous laugh is deep and genuine, and her eyes fly wide as she falls down on me and claps her hand over my mouth. "Careful. You don't want Beardie to come in."

Hearing her say Beardie is comedy at its finest, but there's nothing funny about having her close to me again. She moves her hand off my mouth and eyes my lips, probably thinking about the kiss we shared earlier, just as I am. I bite my tongue to gain control. She's even more beautiful up close as my nightlight reveals a light smattering of freckles across her nose and cheeks.

She's beautiful and funny?

I think I might be in love.

She pulls back and settles herself in the overstuffed chair beside my bed, scrolling through something on her mobile. I watch her while she wiggles to find a comfortable spot.

Being a professional footballer, I've had some majorly confident women throw themselves at me. They're usually kitted out in flossy gossamer undergarments that leave absolutely nothing to the imagination.

Indie, on the other hand, looks perfectly confident in scrubs and trainers. Maybe it's the whole doctor/patient fantasy that gets me going, but I'd like to explore everything underneath that fabric.

Tearing my eyes from her, I flick the light off. The room is cast in complete darkness aside from the faint glow of the outside light streaming in through the curtains. She moves to deposit her mobile and glasses on the end table before slouching down in the chair.

One part of my brain wants to say so much—crack a joke about what kind of knickers she wears under those scrubs, or ask her if she wants a shag after all. But the other part forces me to remain silent. This whole thing feels platonic but strangely intimate. Hearing her soft breaths, smelling her fresh scent. Her general presence is…comforting. I actually *like* having her in here. But having a woman near me and not slipping myself inside of her is foreign to me.

A heaviness creeps over me at the realisation.

She's a necessary distraction. Nothing more. I need her here because if she's not here I'll have time to think about what's really going on with me. That scares me more than anything.

No matter how simple they say the surgery will be, it's still surgery. I'm still getting knocked out. They act like this will make me good as new, but part of me fears that I'll never get back what I've lost. I was on such a lucky streak prior to this. Then, in one quick instant, everything in my career came to a crashing halt. My positive momentum, thwarted. What if I never operate the way I did before? What if this is a slow decline to a sad, pathetic end?

At least if I stay broken there's a reason for not playing well. If I'm fixed and sucking, then what?

"Are you actually scared?" Indie's voice is quiet in the darkness, but it's a question that speaks volumes to my insides. She turns her head and eyes me from the chair.

I swallow slowly before answering, "Yes." It's the first honest thing I've said in ages. I roll to my side so I'm facing her. I can barely make out the glossiness of her eyes.

"Is it for more reasons than just the surgery?"

Christ, it's like she sees right through me. "Maybe." The air is heavy with dread and fear and everything I'm too afraid to fully admit to myself.

She remains silent for a few seconds and brings her feet up to prop on the side of my bed. Her bright white ankle socks glow in the dim lighting. It's a small movement but it feels meaningful, like she's trying to get closer but not make it obvious.

"You don't have a girlfriend, right?"

My stomach shakes with a quiet laugh. It's such an innocent question dropped into such a heavy environment. "No. I'm afraid I'm not the girlfriend type."

"I didn't think so." Her tone sounds relieved and it makes me scowl.

"You don't have a boyfriend, do you?" I'm more than curious about Dr. Prichard and the way he watches her when she speaks and touches her whenever he gets the chance. Plus, how he calls her Indie in front of patients really grates on my nerves.

I can see her smirk through the darkness. "No. You're safe. It's not a part of my plan. Not yet anyway."

“Your plan? This sounds interesting.” I grin and see her chewing her lower lip while her finger wraps around a loose strand of her hair.

“Maybe I’ll tell it to you sometime.”

It’s a promising sentence. “Let’s count on it.”

Then, as if her presence soothes my insomnia, my eyelids begin to droop. I think I see hers close first, so I allow myself to drift off to sleep, enjoying the scent of lemons clinging to my bed sheets.

6 Mr. Sensitive

Indie

My alarm rouses me and I stretch, feeling blissfully rested. This is the first time in ages that I've been awakened without wanting to gouge someone's eyes out. When I come to more, I see that I'm still in Camden Harris' room. How is it possible I slept better in this chair than in the on-call room?

I glance over at the bed to see Camden's hand draped over my ankles that are propped by his side. It feels a bit peculiar—his large hands clasping my narrow ankles. Almost like cuddling, which is not something I'm at all familiar with.

Growing up, my parents weren't the snuggle in bed type. They are both archeologists who still spend all their time in the field, so I rarely see them enough to experience any type of genuine affection. My grandmother who raised me was the same. She believed sending me to year-round boarding schools was what was best, so I only went home a couple of times a year.

Additionally, since my romantic relationships are extremely limited, sleeping with someone, even as innocently as this, is something that feels odd.

I check the time and exhale when I see it's not yet eight o' clock. Reality casts over me, along with the light of day. Sickness settles in the pit of my stomach. I just slept all night in the room of a VIP, semi-famous footballer whom I'm supposed to operate on tomorrow. There is a definite blurring of lines happening here.

I stare at his sleeping face and try to remember what possessed me to say yes to him last night, other than the fact that he's a charming sod. Drunk on the cocktail that is the Camden Harris pheromones, maybe? I mean, honestly, as a twenty-four-year-old female with eyeballs, when a man like him asks you to stay, how can you resist?

My decision to stay may have had something to do with the fact that I want him to be Penis Number One, and it was nice to get to know him a bit to confirm his girlfriend status. Regardless, sleeping with him without *sleeping* with him is surely something Belle would whack me over the head for. She's always warned me that Penis Number One types are the heartbreakers.

But she doesn't realise how easy it is for me to detach from people. My upbringing conditioned me to do just that. Every summer and on holidays, girls left school to go spend time with their families while I was always left behind. Honestly, I didn't care much either way. Going home wasn't much different than staying in school. I was still alone. My parents weren't around most times. Even as an adult, I haven't seen them since my grandmother died two years ago. They do send cards with sizeable cheques on my birthday and Christmas. Other than that, they continue to live their lives with bones.

Shocked that my alarm hasn't roused Cam by now, I carefully slip my legs out from his grasp and kill the annoying chirping. I slide my glasses on and smirk as a thought hits me. *He noticed I had different glasses on last night.*

Shut up, Indie. This is not the time to swoon.

He still hasn't moved a muscle, so I lean over and press my hand to his throat. I am pleased to feel a pulse and learn that he's just a heavy sleeper. The nurses will be rounding in here soon. If I hustle, I can get a shower in before Prichard is ready for me.

I smooth down my scrubs and throw my stethoscope around my neck. Shuffling quietly over to the door, I peer out and see the coast is clear. It's quiet in this VIP wing, so escaping unnoticed shouldn't be too difficult.

I exhale with relief a moment later when I'm striding past the nurse's station and realise how easy it was to get away with something. It all felt positively thrilling and even a bit—

"Indie!" a deep voice says, startling the bejesus out of me as I'm fixing my name tag. "You're here early. Well done. I was just heading to Mr. Harris' room."

My heart hammers in my chest as I swerve to find a bright-eyed Prichard staring at me from around the corner. Camden's sister, Vi, is standing next to him looking fresh as a daisy, which is just offensive at this hour. Where's this Beardie nurse when you need a pick-me-up?

"Dr. Prichard. I didn't see you there. I erm…was just checking the vitals of Cam—Mr. Harris and all looks well." My head is nodding stupidly, but I'm powerless to stop it. "He's sleeping soundly, so…there's that." *Shut up, Indie, you sound and look like a moron. Stop moroning!*

Prichard puzzles his brow at me while I straighten my mess of hair self-consciously. "Very well then. Glad to hear it. You remember Mr. Harris' sister, Vi. We're heading his way to measure his knee for the replacement graft. Since you're here early, you can join us."

I hesitate for a split second, really not wanting to go back into Camden's room already. Part of me was hoping to avoid him until he is knocked out and draped with blue cloths in the OR tomorrow. I really don't seem to make the best decisions around him.

Plus, the way his sister seems to be staring at me is something I don't really want to stick around for. I don't know how Camden handles all his family hovering and meddling all the time. It's seven-thirty in the morning for goodness sake and he already has a visitor. I'm surprised one of them didn't sleep over with him last night. All that togetherness and rule by committee nonsense would seriously drive me mad.

But I'm also not willing to lose out on this surgery. So, despite my nerves, I follow the good doctor and Vi like the perfect little student I always was.

Time to put on your business face, Indie. No awkwardness. Just professionalism.

Prichard waltzes in and heads over to the window to open the drapes instead of flicking on the harsh overhead lighting. Vi reaches Cam's bed and begins shaking his arm in an attempt to wake him.

"Mmmm…yes," Camden's voice murmurs sleepily in a deep, throaty timbre. "Stroke lower, Indie. Don't be shy," he finishes and I swear on my life, I almost puke.

"Camden!" Vi shouts and punches him hard in the stomach. "You pig!"

He harrumphs and lets out a blast of air, wincing against her mighty blow. "Fuck, my knee! Bloody hell!" He reaches down to grasp his leg as I watch the entire scene in horror.

"Don't bloody hell me, you pervert!" Vi chastises him like a scolding mother.

"I was sleeping! I can't help it!" His eyes finally open more and immediately land on me. His lashes are dark and hooded around his sapphire blues. Damn, he even looks sexy now—horny, sleepy pig and all. "It was some dream," he adds, scowling down at the chair where I was lying moments ago. He looks at me and my cheeks feel as if they are going to melt right off my face.

Prichard's deep chortle distracts all of us. "Well, I can't say the boy doesn't have good taste." He looks over at me, not the slightest bit bemused.

I straighten my glasses and frown. What is happening right now? If these blokes think I'm the hot, nerdy librarian type, they are going to be sorely disappointed. Those are the types that pull a pencil out of their buns and their silky locks tumble down to their shoulders, right? I can't even remember the last time I brushed my hair.

Despite my intense discomfort over this entire situation, I smile politely and glance back to Camden, who's lost all good humour on his face. He's indiscreetly shooting daggers at Prichard, making me want to throw up again. If I could cover myself in an invisibility cloak and disappear, I totally would.

Prichard clears his throat and finally begins explaining to Cam and Vi where the scope incisions will be located on Cam's knee, all while taking measurements. Cam listens intently but keeps eyeing me over his shoulder with a smouldering look that's thankfully going unnoticed by everyone else.

"Indie will be on one side, running scope two," Prichard adds, "And I'll be here, running scope one. Then we'll make one more incision for the camera to show us what we're doing in there. It's a minimally invasive surgery and, because of this new 3D grafting technique, there won't be any need for bone drilling." Cam's nostrils flare in response to the last part, but Prichard doesn't seem to notice and continues, "You'll be able to go home the same day."

"So one more night here and I'm good as new?" Camden asks, his voice stiff.

"Nearly," Prichard answers. "You'll feel normal when you go home. You'll start physical therapy immediately. But to get back your full mobility on the pitch, you need to have the graft removed, which is why we'll have you come back in one month for the follow-up surgery."

"It'll take a day or two for the swelling to go down around the incisions both times," I add, feeling Camden's tension and trying to calm his nerves. "But exercise is actually good for helping your incisions to heal."

"But no football?" he asks Prichard.

"Not straight away. After the second surgery, you're welcome to train at one hundred percent. Unfortunately, your season is over for this year, but there's always next year, right mate?"

Camden looks down and nods, seemingly far away with his thoughts.

"Indie will take you for another MRI this morning. It's always good to repeat after the swelling has gone down to make sure there's nothing else we're dealing with. We don't like surprises in the OR if we can help it."

My blood turns cold as I think about being alone with Cam again after last night. After our ICU kiss, it's not a good idea. "I'll get an intern on it," I respond, pulling out my mobile to page one of them.

Prichard frowns at my lack of enthusiasm. Normally, I always do what he says, but I'm praying he lets this one time pass without a fight. I need some space.

"Well, make sure it's a good intern. This is important," Prichard orders before turning to say his goodbyes to Cam and Vi. I hurriedly follow him out of the room, anxious to get away from Camden's confusing emotions that I seem to feel instinctively. I glance over my shoulder and lock eyes with him one last time. I am overcome by my desire to know what he's thinking, but I have to disconnect. I have a full day of patients ahead of me. Additionally, if I still want him to be Penis Number One, I need to keep my distance.

Time flies through the day. By the time evening comes, I feel as if I've run a marathon. At dinner time, Belle flops down across from me in the hospital cafeteria. "Where the hell have you been all day?" she asks, picking up her apple and rolling it in her hands.

I glance down at her tray where only a Kit Kat remains. I would laugh at her odd combo, but I know she's always on a weird diet so it's best to just let her be.

I wrap my mouth around a spoonful of chicken noodle soup,

hoping to buy myself some time, so she adds, "I woke up this morning and you were gone. I didn't see you for lunch. Now it's nighttime and, if I didn't know any better, I'd say you were avoiding me. We always eat dinner together."

"I'm not avoiding you. I've just been swamped and I had a four-hour-long surgery today." Which is mostly true.

The fact is, after I left Camden's room this morning, I wasn't sure my poker face could hold up in front of Belle. I'm not ready to talk about everything so avoiding her was vital. Thankfully, it was a busy day in Patch Alley, so I really was just busy.

She hasn't been the only one I've been avoiding. I checked in on Cam's digital chart and managed everything I needed to do for him via an intern so I didn't actually have to step foot in his room. The intern said he had people swarming in and out the entire day, so I'm sure he hasn't even noticed.

"I knew Prichard would start rounds early because of the Harris brother, too, so that's why you missed me this morning," I add after downing the last bit of my soup. "I got up early to suck up to him as much as possible to ensure my position on the surgery tomorrow."

"Oh, right. The Wilson Repair. Of course you'll be on the surgery. You're Prichard's favourite and the best one for the job, you lucky cow."

Lucky isn't quite the word I'd use. I seem to be on Prichard's rotation most weeks as of late, and his demeanour around me is getting more and more uncomfortable. But I'm interested in ortho, so I'm doing my best to grin and bear it.

"The whole hospital will be talking about you even more than they already do," Belle adds, her expression full of mirth. "The third years are all moaning behind your back already."

I roll my eyes. "Nothing different there."

"But this will shut them up once and for all. This will prove that you are not only a book doctor. You're a surgeon. They know it but are too stubborn to admit it."

I gaze back at my friend, who's now focusing intently on her green apple, and I instantly feel tremendous guilt for not telling her about last night. She's such a loyal friend. Why am I keeping this from her?

"Well, hello, hello," a voice calls from behind Belle just as she takes a massive bite of her apple. I look up to see a hairier version of Camden striding toward us.

Tanner Harris flops down in the open seat beside me. He strokes his beard and Belle's mouth freezes on her apple. He flicks his head back, clearing his shaggy blonde hair away from his face and says, "Dr. Porter, am I right? Or would you rather be called Indie like that other prat of a doctor called you?"

"If she's a doctor, you should call her Dr. Porter. It's rude to call her anything else," says another voice as yet another Harris brother takes the open seat next to Belle. Her mouth is still locked on the apple, causing him to eye her quizzically.

I recognise this brother as the youngest one, Booker. I was introduced to all of them when I explained the surgery to the family yesterday. He has a slightly lower muscle tone than his twin brothers, but is still tall and broad. Trim, dark hair matches his dark, sensitive eyes. Christ, these Harrises are even more handsome in street clothes. Even the hairy one.

Tanner eyes Belle as her bite remains frozen on her apple mid-bite. "Are you just here as a table decoration? Or does that apple actually come out of your mouth?"

I smile as Belle's dark eyes turn to saucers. She completes her chomp down on the fruit, wiping away a dribble of juice that slithers down her chin.

"This is Dr. Ryan," I add. "Definitely not here for decoration."

"You can call me Belle," she adds, her voice wobbly.

"This is Booker. I'm Tanner," he says, leaning in closer, his voice dropping an octave. "Nice to meet you, Dr. Ryan. You're much too pretty to be just a table decoration."

He shoots her a wink and Belle giggles nervously. Her eyes look a bit too wide to be natural, but I don't know how to make her stop.

"Tell me, Doc," Booker says, addressing me with a thoughtful look. "What kind of meds have you prescribed our brother today? He's a moody sod and he's just kicked us all out of his room."

I cloud up. "What do you mean? Is he feeling all right?"

Booker shrugs. "Seemed okay. We were talking football like we always do and he flipped out on us out of nowhere. Told us to go bug someone else. Don't get me wrong. He is always an arse, but this arse was of a particularly bitchy variety."

"Our dad sent us to look for you," Tanner adds. "He thinks maybe Cam is in more pain than he's letting on."

The notion bothers me so I can't help myself from asking, "Maybe he's just ready for some space? It's almost eight o'clock at night. I'm sure he's exhausted. Pain meds make you drowsy, so to fight sleep this long isn't a pleasant feeling."

"Harrises don't really do space," Tanner replies, sitting back in his chair and stretching his legs out. "Something is up with him."

I nod, taking note of their concerned expressions. "I'll go check on him," I say as I stand up from the table with my tray. My shift is over, but I'm invested in this surgery that's happening tomorrow so this is my issue.

"You're leaving?" Belle hisses while not-so-subtly head nodding to the brothers still seated at the table with her.

"Yeah. A-list patient and all that." I give her a "you'll be fine" lift of the brow and scamper off, ignoring the cracks Camden's brothers make about VIP standing for Very Important Prick.

When I get to the private wing, I see Mr. Harris pacing outside Camden's room with his mobile clamped tightly against his ear. He's speaking in hushed tones, but when he sees me approaching, he cuts off whomever is talking and abruptly hangs up.

"Dr. Porter, hi," he says, eyeing me seriously.

I smile politely as I gaze into the blue eyes of an older, more weathered version of Camden. He's tall, broad-shouldered, and still extremely fit for a middle-aged man. I never knew I could be attracted to the silver fox variety. Prichard has never pinged much on my radar, even though I know he's attractive and the nurses all constantly swoon over him. But I would certainly make an exception for Vaughn Harris.

"Doc, I think my son might be in some pain. He's been quite testy all day, which isn't like him. He's usually…well, all of my boys are always very light-hearted. They don't let much trouble them, so I'm thinking he might need something to take the edge off. Can you help him with that?"

I nod sympathetically. "Of course, I was just going in to check on him."

"Cheers, cheers. That other doctor was here a minute ago, but Cam doesn't seem to like him much. I don't care for him either, to be frank, but I've done my research and I know he's skilled."

"Yes, very much so. Cam—I mean, Mr. Harris is in good hands with him. You're very lucky."

"Exactly. Cam's fine. It's probably nothing." He purses his lips and squints, causing the crow's feet around his eyes to stack on top of one another. "But if you can deal with him as much as possible, I think that'd be wise. He seems to like you."

"Absolutely. I'll take good care of him."

"Excellent. We're all heading home. He doesn't want us here anymore. I erm…won't be here for the surgery tomorrow, but here's my number. Can you text me when he's out?"

"You won't be here?" I ask quizzically. Every time I've come down this wing, I've seen Camden's dad outside his door on his mobile. I assumed he'd be here for the actual procedure.

"No. I've got an early meeting." He looks around uncomfortably, almost as if he's just now realising he's standing in a hospital. He moves to walk away but turns around and places a surprising hand on my shoulder. "Thank you, Dr. Porter. This procedure will save my son's life."

I grimace at his choice of words and, before I can stop myself, I reply, "Mr. Harris. This isn't a life-threatening injury. Some people never get their ACL tears repaired. Not athletes, I know, but I just want to make sure that you understand he's going to be okay, with or without the surgery." I say it with a smile and in a polite tone, but I feel anything but courteous. In fact, I'm feeling a bit of annoyance toward all the Harrises. I want Cam to have the surgery more than anyone. It'd be huge for my career, but it feels as if everyone is more concerned about football than they are about Camden.

Vaughn smiles in a patronising way. "Doc, you've dedicated a lot of hard work and years of education to get where you are, haven't you?"

"Yes, of course."

He leans his head down to meet my eyes. "My Camden has done the same thing. Football to us…is our life. It's more than that really. In ways I can't even begin to describe. So please, just get us through this. That's all I'm asking."

He looks as if he's saying so much more with his eyes than he can say with words, but it's not something I'm privy to understanding. Regardless, this isn't really an argument to be having with a patient's father. "I'll do my very best, Mr. Harris. I'm so sorry. I didn't mean anything by it." I smile genuinely.

He smiles back. "No need to be sorry. I'm just glad he has a doctor who cares."

Seemingly soothed enough to bid me farewell, he strides away without looking back. I turn and push open Cam's door, bracing myself for the hotness of this particular footballer, only to find an empty bed with an empty knee brace resting upon it.

Frowning, I see the light on in the attached toilet and hear water running. "Cam—Mr. Harris?" I call out, pushing the door open slightly. "Are you in here?"

When there's no reply, I take a tentative step in and eye the walk-in shower. The white curtain is drawn and steam is billowing out from the top. "Cam?" I call out again a bit louder. Still nothing. Feeling suddenly nervous by his lack of response, my emergency training takes over and I yank back the curtain. I find him sitting on the floor with his back against the tiled wall as water cascades down over him.

"Camden, what happened? Are you all right?" I ask, squatting down beside him and checking for a pulse on his wrist. His head is dropped and he's hunched over but I feel a steady beat. I pull my flashlight out of my pocket to check his pupils. His eyes are pinched shut and when I attempt to pry one open, he startles with a jump. The sudden jolt sends me flying backwards onto my rear and right under the heavy stream.

"Cam!" I screech, scrambling my way out of the water as my soaked scrubs cling to my body in a matter of seconds.

"Fuck, Indie!" he exclaims as he grabs hold of my wrist and yanks me toward him and out of the water.

It's then that I find myself unceremoniously draped over a completely naked and completely rock-hard professional footballer. "You're naked," I croak, pushing myself off his wet chest. I'm childishly grateful that his legs are bent enough to conceal his manhood so I'm not completely scandalised.

"One usually is inside the shower." His wet face has the nerve to look confused as he squints at me through the steam. Realising I'm staring, I quickly stand up and turn my back to him, but it wasn't until after I caught sight of his…well, to give it the technical term… penis.

"Are you all right?" I ask with a shaky voice.

"Yes. Of course. Why wouldn't I be?"

"You were unresponsive!" I reply in challenge.

He sighs heavily. Clearly agitated, he asks, "What are you doing in here, Indie?"

"I came in to check on you and found you passed out in the shower!" I gesticulate wildly as I find his face in the reflection of the mirror. He's scowling at me while his eyes trail down my back. Why do I have to explain myself? He's the one who shoved me into the water. "I thought you were having a seizure or something."

"I was fine. I was just sleeping." His voice drips with annoyance.

"You were sleeping in the shower?" I stare ahead in disbelief.

"Yeah, I've done it before. It's not that hard. And after having my family up my arse all day, I'm exhausted."

"Oh," I say in an exhale as reality tumbles in around me. He was sleeping. Not in the most conventional of places, but still. He's a grown man and I just swooped in and…God, I'm an arse. And now I'm also drenched.

My eyes flicker down over my shoulder to find his are still lingering on my backside. Despite his annoyed tone, his expression is one of amusement.

"If you laugh, I'm kicking you in your bad knee," I snap, grabbing a hand towel and wiping down my glasses before putting them back on my face.

He chuckles and says, "Oh God, don't. I'm not sure how I'm going to stand up from here as it is."

I roll my eyes and turn to cut the shower off without looking down at him. I toss a towel over my shoulder. "Come on now, let me help." I turn and hold my hand out to him. "And I hope you feel properly emasculated after this."

He grips the towel against his abs to conceal himself and slips his other hand in mine. Using me for balance more than strength, he stands up, putting all his weight on his good leg. His towel slips off as he steadies himself against the wall.

My eyes shoot up to the ceiling, but now that we're standing only inches apart, I can feel him watching me. "Mind grabbing that for me and finding out just how emasculated I am?"

My face screws up in disgust. "Your sister is right. You are a pig." I grab him a fresh towel from the non-penis-level towel bar before getting one for myself. I begin dabbing at my soaked clothes and hair. "This is useless. I'm soaked all the way through."

"Best just take them off." He squints at me while tightening his towel around his waist. Seriously. Washboard abs are a real thing apparently. "Are you wearing white under there?" he asks. "White and wet are almost as fun of a combination as oil and water."

I roll my eyes at his blatant come-on. "I can't leave here like this. I'm not even supposed to be working right now. My shift is over. This looks so bad."

"Just wrap yourself in this towel and I'll find you something to wear." He pierces me with a blatant challenge as he holds a towel out to me. "Or are you too shy?"

His expression is knowing, as if he's certain there's no way I'll strip down in front of him. Because of that, some dark place inside of me wakes up. I want to wipe that smirk off his face and prove I'm not some innocent, naïve little girl he can predict.

I tuck his towel under my arm, turn on my heel, and sludge my soggy feet across his room. Then I click the lock on his door. When I turn back, he's limping into the room toward his bed. He quirks a brow at the sound of the lock.

Without hesitating, I peel my scrub top off over my head. His eyes drift down to my wet, white cotton bra, and the flicker in his gaze makes my insides clench. It feels so wrong but so right at the same time. He licks his lips as I take my time wrapping the towel around my chest, enjoying the feel of his heated eyes on me. The lust crackling in the air between us is intense and—

Oh my God, it's turning me on!

Even knowing this, I still don't want to stop. I can't stop. Some dormant inner sex kitten has awakened inside of me and completely taken over my body. I'm now being commanded by my vagina and that duplicitous brain of mine is on a holiday in Yorkshire for all I know. Maybe it's this room. It doesn't even feel like the hospital. It feels like a hotel room. A hotel room where very bad things can happen.

When I conceal myself under the towel, I hear a growl of frustration come from somewhere in his throat. Satisfied, I skillfully kick out of my shoes and shimmy out of my pants, underwear, and finally, my bra.

We stand facing each other in matching towels, completely bare underneath. The only thing separating us is ten feet and a single piece of fabric. The realisation of that fact causes our breaths to come heavier than before. I can't stop appreciating the full fleshy sight of him in nothing but a towel. Good God, he really is nothing short of male, human anatomy perfection.

"Impressive," he states deadpan.

I don't know if he's referring to my body or my skilled act of getting naked under a towel. Either way, my voice is shaky when I reply, "Can you get me those clothes now, please?"

I fear if he doesn't get me clothes, I will do something even more stupid than this moment right now, which is already catastrophically senseless.

He remains frozen in place.

"Please, Camden?" I ask again and cross my arms over my chest. "Your night nurse might be coming any minute."

He glances at the clock. "Actually, we have a whole hour."

"Are you sure?" My nakedness doesn't feel as empowering as it did initially.

"Positive," he murmurs as he grabs his brace up off the bed and deftly secures it over his injured knee. He finishes and stands up straight, mirroring my pose by folding his arms over his chest. His biceps widen and flex, and my eyes take note of the veins running the length of his forearms.

"I'll get you some clothes, but I've got a bone to pick with you first and it has nothing to do with the one you're slicing into tomorrow." His familiar challenging eye twinkle is back and it's actually kind of comforting.

"We're not slicing into your bone tomorrow, Camden." I roll my eyes.

"Semantics," he grumbles. His damp chest rises with a deep breath before he continues, "You seemed awful keen on avoiding me today."

I frown, shocked by his accusation that I never saw coming. "I had somewhere to be," I retort, marching closer to him to state my case. I'm stunned to see a flicker of hurt in his eyes, but he quickly conceals it. My voice softens, "And it's a good thing I left when I did or Dr. Prichard might have caught me in here."

His blue eyes narrow further, his lashes covering the colour almost entirely. "Why didn't you want to take me for my MRI? I've heard you've been around. My family have all talked to you. That intern. But despite the fact that you are *my* doctor, not theirs, you avoided me like I had a bad case of herpes, which I know is fully cleared up right now."

"You have herpes?" I screech and slap my hand over my mouth, afraid of drawing his nurse's attention outside.

"Fuck no, Indie. It's a bloody joke."

"Why would you joke about a lifelong STD?"

He scoffs and drops his hands to his hips. "You have my damn medical chart. You'd know if I had herpes."

He's right. For a moment I forgot I am his doctor.

"Would it disappoint you if I had herpes?" he asks, his tone far too serious.

"Yes! What the hell are you going on about?"

"Why would it bother you?"

"What do you mean?"

"Why would you care if I had an STD?"

"Because it's herpes. It'd be weird if I wasn't bothered. And…" I falter.

"And what?" he volleys.

"And I'm…"

"And what?" he snaps.

"And I'm interested in you!"

His brows lift. "Are you? Because as far as I can tell, you're just a bird who fell asleep in a chair and buggered off without another word. Our bodies have barely touched."

"Oh, sod off. It was more than that." The words feel stroppy in my mouth.

"You left without a word. That was a bloke move and I didn't like it." His arms flex and my eyes fall to that perfect V-line peeking out from his towel. How is it that all footballers seem to have that V? How is it that I'm still ogling his half naked body right now?

"Camden, I'm your doctor. You are my patient." I exhale, trying to get a hold of myself. "This whole thing is an ethical disaster that I can't seem to get away from. Bloody hell, what did you expect this morning? Breakfast in bed and a goodbye snog?" I grumble.

Is this real life? Is Camden Harris seriously insecure over me? I can't even comprehend this logic. He's one of the hottest footballers in London. But looking at his face, I'd venture to say he's hurt and that my sharp tongue isn't helping matters.

"Christ, I'm sorry, all right?" I add.

His brows lift in shock, as if he's impressed that after all that I apologised.

"Are you herpes sorry?" His hard eyes hide a playful twinkle.

"I don't even know what that means," I groan.

A soft laugh shakes his shoulders. "Fine, let's get back to that goodbye kiss you mentioned." He begins moving toward me with slow, tender steps. I could laugh at how easy it is for him to change course, but even with an injury, Camden Harris moving toward me is no joking matter. Those intense eyes make me forget all about why I tried to avoid him all day.

"What about a goodbye kiss?" I ask, the pitch of my voice suddenly deeper. My treacherous gaze moves to his bare chest and curves over to his half-sleeved arm. I never knew I liked tattoos until I saw his.

"The way I see it, that kiss we had in the ICU seems like a long time ago. All day, I've been trying to determine if it was as good as I remember, or if it was just the adrenaline from my injury. Let's see if those sparks are still there. Then we'll know if these risks are worth the rewards."

I'm pretty sure I should be offended by his last remark, but I'm too busy staring at his lips as he comes within inches of my face. His warm breath is mixing with mine and it's an intoxicating combination. It invigorates a completely different part of my brain—the part that acts on raw feelings and emotion. Primitive in nature.

But the right side of my brain knows that what we're doing could get me into serious trouble and maybe even cost me my job. But his scent. His face. His body. His *being* is so overwhelming and exciting, I can't think straight. My hormones have completely taken my body hostage.

How can one person seem so very wrong but so very right all at the same time?

"I like the red specs," he murmurs before his arms snake around my waist and pull me to him. My hands land on his bare chest. The sensation of his skin against mine and the wrongness of it all are exactly what urge me on.

"I'm going to kiss you again." His lips flutter so close to mine it already feels as if we're kissing.

"Are you sure we—" My weak response is cut off by the unapologetic fervor of his mouth on mine. I squeeze out a surprised moan as he smothers me with his hard body and slides his tongue forcefully into my mouth. Reflexively, my eyes roll to the back of my head as my limbs desperately grope every square inch of his upper body, searching, pleading, grasping for some sense of sanity. Some sense of awareness of my surroundings. Some lifeline to pull me out of this danger.

But I don't find it. I only find mounds of hard, roped, and incredibly smooth muscle. God, does it feel good. And bad. And oh, so right. He's consuming me as if I'm Christmas dinner and he hasn't eaten in months. I nearly squeal with excitement when his right hand drops to my towel-covered arse and palms it decadently.

He pulls me snuggly against his crotch.

Against his erection.

It's in that one pump of his hips that I realise with a thunderous thud of my heart that the playboy flirt who kissed me when he came into Patch Alley yesterday is gone.

Instead, he is replaced by a sinfully arousing and totally mind-blowing conqueror that is Camden Harris.

And I am screwed.

7 The Last of Its Kind

Camden

SHE FEELS UNPRACTISED. UNREHEARSED. UNTAINTED. Unwrapped. Indie Porter is like a Christmas gift I've been waiting for my entire life that has finally arrived and I don't know which part I want to play with first.

I pull my tongue out from the deep wetness of her mouth and sink my teeth into her lush lower lip, sucking off the lemony sweetness. This is the same lower lip she was biting seconds earlier as she stared at me in my towel like she wanted to fuck me right then and there.

I probably would have let her. I was mad a minute ago and trying to decide if she was worth the trouble, but this woman has something on me that I can't seem to step away from. I want her. I want her more than she wants me…and that never happens to me. Ever. I woke up with a raging boner this morning thinking about this sexy redhead. Then she stood there watching me like I was some regular patient she was taking care of.

I'm putting a stop to that right now. With this kiss, I'm determined to remind her what it means to be mouth-fucked by Camden Harris. I have to even out the stakes between us.

Strangely, now that I've confirmed that kissing Indie Porter really is this bloody fantastic, I actually care what she has to say. I want to peel back the layers of this uniquely wrapped present and discover why she is the way she is, which is also a novel concept for me.

Whatever she is, it's working for me.

Last night I felt different with her beside me. Normally when I spend the night with a bird, I'm anxious for the morning so I can bugger off. I didn't feel that at all with Indie. In fact, I felt disappointed that I couldn't hold her throughout the night. I don't know if it was the pain meds or the Indie Porter Valium I had injected in me from our first kiss. All I know is that I needed to feel the warmth of her.

Now that this kiss is as hot as I had hoped, I want more. I want to feel every breath, every gasp, every shift, every contented sigh. She refused to fully let go with me last night, but tonight I see the desire in the pools of her eyes. She needs something from me and, whatever it is, I hope she lets me give it to her.

I pull my mouth away from her pillowy-soft lips and rest my forehead against hers. "Why do you always taste like lemons?" I exhale. "Tell me."

"Are you actually going to let me finish a thought this time? You cut me off before." The corner of her mouth tilts up and I cover it with mine again, kissing her sarcasm good and dead.

I break away once more, satisfied when she pulls in a big gulp of air. My morbid fascination is still demanding. "I have to know. Why lemons?" I pull back further so my eyes can feast on hers.

"Sherbet lemons." She licks her lips slowly. "I keep them in my pockets because sometimes I don't get to eat all day. It helps to keep my blood sugar up."

She smirks up at me, her toffee eyes twinkling within the frames of her glasses. I huff a soft laugh against her face. I'm grateful that she's answering my question and not ruining this moment by letting her fears seep back in.

"I like them," I say before I briefly kiss her again for one more taste.

When I pull away and open my eyes, she tilts her head. Her brown eyes flash on mine with a bewildered look. I wish I could read her mind because she seems to be making some sort of decision that I'm not privy to.

Before I can ask her about it, she wraps her arms around my neck and pulls me hard against her lips. She drives her tongue so deep into my mouth, it sends my body into overdrive.

She's definitely not afraid anymore.

"I want you, Indie," I groan, breaking our kiss and dragging my forehead down her cheek until my mouth is on her neck. It's cold and wet from her impromptu shower but feels utterly perfect. Her hand braces on my chest as she tilts back to give me more access to her towel-covered chest.

"I need you," I croak, clasping her hand and sliding it down my chest, along my abs, and over top of the towel to the firmness between my legs. She lets out an audible, throaty gasp at the proof beneath the fabric. "Now," I demand, even though I know I would get down on my knees and beg if she asked me to.

"Oh my God," she moans loudly into my mouth as her small, delicate fingers slide against the length of me.

I quickly kiss her to quiet her voice. We can't be interrupted. I need this to happen. I need to hear her voice cry out while I'm buried inside of her, even if I do have to swallow every whimper.

"I've got condoms." I pull her down onto the bed so we're sitting on the edge, angled toward each other. The relief in my knee is appreciated.

I lick and nibble my way up to her ear. She tastes like rain. Now I'm thinking that taking her in the shower sounds about perfect... and concealed. "Tell me you want me, Indie."

"I want you," she says without a second's hesitation.

Pleased, I smile against her collarbone. "Give me a second to fetch one. I'll be right back."

"Condoms." She grips my arms back toward her in some strange state of delirium. Her eyes are wide as she adds, "Condoms. No. We can't, Cam. Not here."

I cup her face, my brow furrowing with concern. "We have plenty of time. If it's my knee you're worried about, I'll let you ride on top. I'm dying to feel you, Indie." My hand trails between her towel-covered breasts, venturing lower. Her eyes flutter closed as I find a small gap between her thighs. She spreads her legs for me, shifting further toward the edge of the bed and inviting me in. She wants this just as much as I do. Buggered knee or not, we can handle this.

I push the rough fabric of the towel between her thighs. I could easily slip my hand in and palm her, skin on skin, but I want to wait. I want to be ready to slide into her before I feel all that I know she will be. She pumps her hips into my touch with shameless need, and I groan as her pink tongue darts out to lick her lips.

"What do you want me to do? Name it, Specs, and I'll do it. I know what I want."

Her drooped eyes hang on every one of my words, but she lets out a mournful groan and abruptly grabs my hand and pulls it away from her. "You don't get it." She stands up on shaky legs and awkwardly covers herself with her hands. Her eyes look wide with fear. "We seriously can't."

"Why? Is it the herpes thing?" I ask, thinking a joke might lighten her up a bit. I reach up and take her hand, stroking the soft skin of her wrist with my thumb. "I was being a sod, I told you."

"It's not you, it's me." She pulls back from me and fists her hands against her sides.

"You have herpes?" I ask, rearing back. All arousal is sucked dry.

"No!" she croaks. "That wouldn't even be possible."

"What are you saying? I'm the man-whore footballer, so I'm the only one in this scenario who could ever get the herp?" I snap defensively.

"Sensitive much? That's not what I'm saying at all. Although, if either of us were to have it, it would have to be you."

"Oh bollocks, I always use protection. I don't go bareback with anyone. Ever. And I get checked regularly. It's you innocent-looking types that are the most dangerous."

Her mouth falls open. "What does that mean?"

This is escalating quickly, but I can't stop snapping at her. She makes me crazy. "Well, the quiet ones always have the most secrets."

"I'm not quiet!"

"No, but you have the innocent bit down to a science."

"It's not a bit."

"Don't come off like you're too perfect to get an STD. You and I aren't that different."

"Typically you'd have to have some type of sex to get herpes, Cam!" she exclaims with a frustrated stomp of her foot. A deep blush crawls up her neck and hits her cheeks within seconds like she just realised what she blurted out.

I scowl, feeling completely mind-fucked. I run my hands through my hair and rise up from the bed and into her space. "Indie, spell it out for me. I have a raging boner doing all my proper thinking at the moment and he's got a one-track mind."

"Aside from the fact that I'm not going to let you rail me at my place of work…I'm a virgin, okay?" she groans and her hands move to cover the deep, crimson red consuming her face.

I swear her voice echoes in the distance like a shout from the top of a mountain.

Virgin…virgin…virgin…virgin.

My sarcasm arrives first on the scene. "Why don't you shout that one more time? We want to be sure Beardie heard it in the cheap seats."

"Shut it," she snaps, shoving me in the chest. I limp to keep the impact off my bad knee. "There is something horribly wrong with me. What am I doing? You're my patient…"

While she goes off on a rant to herself, I look down at poor Camden Junior still looking mighty strong beneath the towel. A virgin is a game changer. At least inside the walls of this hospital. Outside, on the other hand…

I look up at her, my face still the picture of stunned. "I can hardly believe it."

"What?" she barks.

"I've heard of women like you. Women that save themselves for their wedding night. But I thought you were an urban myth."

"I'm not saving myself for marriage." Her tone is admonishing.

"Then why?" I frown, wondering what other reason anyone could possibly have for staying a virgin this long, especially someone as beautiful as her.

She shrugs and murmurs, "I want it to be good."

"Your first time?" My face screws up in confusion.

"Yes, keep up!"

Her snappy outburst elicits a smirk on my face. She's cute all revved up like this. "I'm not having a go. I promise. I'm just trying to wrap my head around all this."

"There's not much to grasp. I'm a virgin. End of."

She crosses her arms and turns away from me, throwing a proper fit in a towel. It's comical really. But she's holding on to her virginity just because she wants it to be good? That can't be the only reason, can it? Most people's first time is utter crap. Then again, I suppose most people's first time is in their teens when they're poking around in the back of a vehicle to hide from their mum and dad. Their priority isn't for pleasure. It's so they can tell all their mates at school.

I'm not sure I believed in destiny until this second.

I stride up to her, mindful of my knee, and lean over her back to whisper in her ear, "Why settle for just good?"

She stiffens slightly but turns her head and answers, "Well, I want more than good I guess." She adjusts the frames of her glasses and turns to face me again. I love how small she is next to me like this. I love that when she looks up at me, her eyes have to squint a little from the lighting above my head. "I'm twenty-four, Camden. I've waited this long. Surely it isn't an impossible task to find a great shag at this age."

I chuckle at her pensive expression. "Sweetheart, you needn't even ask."

Her jaw drops as her eyes snap to mine. "Well, aren't you just a cocky sod."

I shake my head, tilting her chin up so she looks at me instead of my chest. "Specs, if you want your first time to be greatness, I'm right fucking here." I close the last twelve inches between us and twine my fingers with hers, pulling her back to my bed. "But you're right, it can't be here."

"Obviously." Her voice is wobbly as she looks away with a small flicker of disappointment and a huge splash of shame marring her pretty features.

"But it will be me." My voice is self-assured.

She pulls her large pink lower lip into her mouth and chews it nervously before looking at me and saying, "I don't think you could be any cockier."

All humour drains from my face. "I'm not cocky. I'm certain." I reach out to pull her lower lip from between her teeth and rub the pad of my thumb along it. Bits of it are raw and chapped from the overtime she's been working on it.

Her eyes flutter closed as she says, "I'm mortified."

I smile at her hunched posture. "You don't need to be embarrassed." I turn her face to look at me. "But I do think you need to stop lying to yourself about what you think we could be for each other." Her eyes flicker quickly between mine. They look sad but hopeful. "After I'm out of here and you don't have the stress of getting caught hanging over you, we're going to do this. And I'll make it better than good, Indie. I'll make it so great that when I walk away, you'll compare every bloke you ever meet to me."

She smiles, a resigned look of satisfaction on every inch of her face. "Just sex?"

"That's all I'm offering." I watch her for her reaction.

An appreciative smile takes over her face. "You couldn't be more right for this than if I hand-picked you from a catalogue."

"You're damn straight." I wink and silently beg my cock to simmer down. "Now let's get some sleep before my blue balls create a new colour in the rainbow."

8 Tearable Puns

Indie

"You think I'm sleeping in here again?" I ask, pulling out of Camden's large hands and standing up off the bed. I'm about to burst with insecurity and detaching for some space is exactly what I need.

"I don't think, I know." He looks up at me, his jaw taught with determination. "You're staying."

"Cam, last night was a fluke, and we're lucky we didn't get caught. Doing it again would be tempting fate. I could get kicked off your surgery."

There are two sides of me that I am fighting with. The old side of me that's a scared young girl being thrust into a world that's completely out her comfort zone so she follows all the rules and aces all the tests. Then there's the side of me that wants to make up for lost time and be daring and bold and take risks.

But not at the expense of my job. "My career is just as important as yours."

"I never said it wasn't."

"That's why I need to go. But me leaving doesn't change anything between us. You have my number. Call me when you're out of here. Right now I need to focus."

"So do I," he snaps in a self-deprecating tone.

"What does that mean?"

"I need you to stay, Indie." His voice is low and pleading, and his eyes are strained. "Please." He swallows hard and watches me for my answer.

"Why is this so important to you?"

"Because I'm afraid if you leave, I will, too."

His words shock me. I stare back at his gorgeous, tortured, vulnerable face. Then I walk over to him and stand between his legs, cupping his face in my hands. "You can't leave, Camden. You need this surgery. And you have nothing to be nervous about."

He closes his eyes before speaking. "You are my distraction from running out of this place, screaming." His eyes pop open as he adds, "Football is all I have and, fuck, if this doesn't work—"

"It will work," I reply, nodding my head but knowing that there are never any guarantees in life.

He looks as if he's on the brink of truly losing it this time, and I realise that what I've been sensing all along is right. From the moment he came into Patch Alley, I could see it in his face. Even in the ICU and his demeanour last night when he talked about Arsenal. He's battling something—something bigger than just nerves.

I exhale heavily because I know, deep down, there's no way I can walk away from him like this. He has to have the surgery. It's what's best for him.

"I'll stay, but only because I have it on good authority that you have nothing to be nervous about. Plus, I slept like a rock in that chair."

"If you think the chair is comfy, you should feel the bed." He tweaks his brows at me and I feel better seeing his playful side come back to the surface. Just as quickly, he closes his eyes as if he's in pain and adds, "You need to get some clothes on because I just pictured pulling that towel off and motor-boating your tits."

Camden manages to find me a pair of black compression tights that fit me like loose leggings and a white T-shirt that is so large I have to knot it around my waist. It isn't far off from what I wear when I workout at the hospital, so I'm able to duck out easily before Nurse Beardie's final checks for the night.

Back in the on-call room, I take a quick shower and brush my teeth. I change into my own workout clothes so anyone that might see me in the hallway later will assume I'm on my way to the gym. This whole set up is weird and totally horrid. But it's rather satisfying doing something wild and against the rules. It makes wearing my colourful eyeglasses look about as exciting as a bird-printed cardigan on a granny.

Running into Belle as I leave the on-call room is the only hiccup. But I convince her that I'm going home to sleep so I'm well-rested for the big career-making surgery tomorrow.

I hate lying to her. She's my one and only best friend—the person who made up this Penis List with me in the first place. I'm too terrified of what her opinion might be to come clean, though. Would she cheer me on? Judge me? Call me an idiot? It could be all of the above.

Mostly, I just don't want this bubble I'm in popped quite yet. I've managed to put this thing I'm doing with Cam in his room into a protective box that feels so far removed from the real world that I can't bring myself to allow reality in. I'll probably tell her everything after Cam's gone. But right now, I don't need the extra pressure of her opinion before I even know my own.

It's just before ten by the time I make it back upstairs to Camden's room. I find him lying in his big bed with his nose in a novel and a pen in his hand as he scribbles something inside of it. His braced leg is sticking out of the blanket and I'm pleased to see he's got a shirt and shorts on. After our heated make-out session earlier and me almost ripping his towel off, it's probably for the best.

I wince at the audible sound of me locking the door. I'd rather not take any chances tonight. "Beardie did her rounds already, right?" I whisper.

"Yes, she did. She's gone 'til seven." He's still writing inside of his book. "One second, I'm almost done."

I head over to his closet and toss his shirt and tights in with the rest of his clothes. This is all so ridiculously casual. How is it possible I feel so at ease in Cam's little suite here?

Heading back toward his bed, I get a better look at what he's writing in. "Are you an Alex Cross fan?"

He frowns thoughtfully over his note and looks up for the first time. His eyes flick down to my blue tank and black leggings. "I might be. Can I just add that I'm a fan of your aversion to traditional pyjamas?"

Ignoring the last part of his response, I do my best to school my features so they don't appear too surprised over his reading hobby. But I have to admit, a mystery-reading footballer is most definitely not a combination I would have put together on my own, especially one who writes notes in the margins.

Camden abruptly clears his throat when I move to sit in the chair. "I was thinking you should just crawl into bed beside me."

My jaw drops.

"Hear me out." He angles toward me and props himself on his elbow. "You already know we won't be having sex. Even though a secret hospital room shag sounds pretty epic, we both know that you need to be completely relaxed and that'll never happen here."

"Right," I reply, ignoring his charmingly eager eyes.

"So this is just for the sleep. You'll sleep so much better here, and it's important you're at your best when you operate on London's sexiest footballer tomorrow."

"I've met all your brothers, Cam. Are you entirely sure you hold that title?"

He watches me for a silent moment with a playful scowl and finally says, "Just get your arse in here and stop playing defence, Specs." He throws back the cover and shoots me a smouldering look. "It's not that big of a deal."

"I could get into serious trouble if I get caught. That is a very big deal."

He exhales heavily. "The door is locked. Beardie's gone. No one came in last night. We're safe. And on the Harris name, I promise you, there will be no funny business. If there is, you can blast me to the tabloids."

His eagerness is a bit shocking. For a guy who has all the qualities of a player but promises he doesn't want sex, I'm not sure why it's such a big deal for me to sleep in his bed. I bite my lip, pondering that notion.

He takes my hesitation as an opening to continue his pitch. "Haven't you ever just wanted to take a risk? Live a little?"

It's as if he's speaking directly to that meek girl in my heart of hearts—the one who only did as she was told by teachers and never experienced that wild, rebellious teenager stage.

My jaw opens to refuse again, but the words get stuck in my throat.

"Seriously, what's the last wild thing you did?" he asks.

"This would top the list." I shake my head with a self-deprecating laugh and glance back at the door. I can't believe I'm seriously wanting to do this right now.

My next question makes me wince. "Rounds at seven?"

The corner of his mouth lifts. "Yes. We'll set your alarm for six just to be safe."

The forbidden fruit is so tempting. Additionally, the deeply seeded desire I have in my body to make this a Tequila Sunrise moment and stop living my life as an inexperienced little girl is strong. Plus, the thought of lying next to Camden's large body in that comfy bed is incredibly alluring. Why can't I take a risk? Why don't I live in the moment? That's what Tequila Sunrise is all about.

With a firm nod of my head, my mind is made up.

God, why does being bad feel so bloody good?

Camden smiles triumphantly when I begin slowly sliding into his bed. I get myself situated, mirroring his position so we're both on our sides facing each other with our heads propped.

Glancing at the book on the bed between us, I ask, "What book are you on? There are like twenty in that series, aren't there?" I'm trying to come off casual when I feel anything but.

He gets the drift and picks it up. "This is Patterson's newest release. I'm a sucker for mysteries. And puns. Alex Cross is the master of puns."

Camden Harris likes puns? Who'd have thought? I begin fidgeting with the blanket and say, "Well, all I can say is 'when I get naked in the bathroom, the shower usually gets turned on.'"

I look up once I've got the blanket just how I like it and find him staring at me with his mouth hanging wide open.

He shifts his jaw to one side and narrows his eyes before saying, "'This book has some scenes about anti-gravity and it's impossible to put down.'"

I give him a mock impressed look and reply with my super casual voice, "'Yesterday a clown held the door open for me and I thought it was a very nice jester.'"

I nod my head animatedly at the end and we both burst out laughing. He quickly presses his finger over my lips to remind me about Beardie.

His touch makes me feel warm and tingly inside. When I stop giggling, I flop down onto the pillow and say, "My grandmother liked puns. It was about the only interesting thing I knew about her before she died a couple years ago."

"You weren't close?" He turns and sets his book down on the nightstand behind him and flicks the light off at the same time.

The dim exterior city lights cast a blue glow over his face as he gingerly rolls back to face me. The darkness is comforting. Makes me feel less exposed.

"She raised me, but I was always sent to boarding schools, so I only saw her a couple times a year if I was lucky."

"What about your parents?" he asks, a sombre expression on his face as if he's expecting me to tell him they're dead.

"They travel for work," I shrug my shoulders. "I hardly ever see them."

His brows lift. "I see my dad almost every day, even though I don't live with him. But he feels more like a coach than a dad." He reaches out and pulls my glasses off my face and sets them down behind him by his book.

"Thanks," I say. He smiles but he doesn't respond. It's all very… sweet. "How's your knee?" I ask, feeling a bit too intimate and needing to bring this back to my comfort zone.

"It's all right. The brace makes it feel pretty stable."

Nodding, I reply, "That's why some people never get their ACLs fixed. I was telling your dad that earlier."

Camden's good mood evaporates. "What did he say to that?"

"He wasn't pleased. I didn't mean anything by it. I know you're an athlete so it's not an option for you. But it just seemed as if…" My voice trails off.

"As if what?" Camden urges.

I shrug. "I don't know. As if his top concern was skewed a bit."

Camden sighs heavily and rolls onto his back, ruffling one of his hands through his hair. There's a sudden tension in his body that's potent in this giant hospital bed we're sharing.

Before I can stop myself, I continue, "And he won't be here for your surgery tomorrow? Is that right? After being here all day today and most of yesterday?"

"He doesn't do well in hospitals," Camden says quietly. "Never has."

Feeling like a proper jerk now, I shake my head. "I shouldn't have asked. It's none of my business." *It's totally not, Indie. Stop getting so personal with him. This is just supposed to be good fun.*

Camden's Adam's apple bobs as he wars with himself for a moment. I can't tell if he's working up the courage to argue with me or if he's thinking about something else entirely. Swallowing once, he says, "When I was little, my mum had a couple of surgeries after she was diagnosed with ovarian cancer. They said it would give her more time. It didn't."

My heart stills inside my chest at the raw and vulnerable words he's just announced to the ceiling. "How old were you?"

His lips form a hard line. "Three."

I inhale shakily and can't help but ask my next question. "Did she die in surgery?"

He closes his eyes and I almost have to look away because the stiff pain on his face is overwhelming. "No. She suffered through two horrid surgeries and didn't even get the chance to start chemo before things went from bad to worse."

Relief blankets me right before guilt crushes me. She still died. But in my mind, it would have been worse if she had died on the operating table, especially with what he has coming tomorrow. "I'm so sorry."

He shakes his head. "I was young. I barely remember her." Gruffly clearing his throat, he adds lightly, "My dad had me take a meeting with Arsenal today."

My eyes widen at his abrupt change of subject. "Here at the hospital? What did they want?"

"To see how fast I will recover. Dr. Prichard sat in on the meeting, too."

This floors me. He's lying here with an injury and they still want to talk contracts with him? He must be an incredible athlete. Regardless, talking here doesn't seem like a good idea. It's adding an immense amount of pressure right before he goes into surgery.

"You're being awfully quiet," he says ominously. "I'd like to know what you think."

His blue eyes find mine, gleaming for answers. His hand reaches out to cover my own. It feels warm and personal and so much more than a doctor/patient relationship should be. The intimacy sends shivers up my spine.

There are so many lines we've crossed in his short time here. I'm risking everything by sleeping with him like this. I went to school for so long, and now that I'm an actual doctor, I decide to shack up with a patient? This is insanity.

Pulling my hand free to tuck it under my head, I reply pragmatically instead of emotionally. "Well, as we said, with The Wilson Repair, it'll be a quick recovery and you'll be good as new in five to six weeks. Most ACL repairs take six months, which is devastating for footballers. This means you'll be able to get right back on the field for summer training. Tell them that and you're sure to get an offer."

Silence stretches out between us as Cam stares at me for a long, painful moment. He's trying to get a read on me, but I'm only giving him the business reply. Sure I'm in bed with him and it's probably too little, too late, but in my mind, I have something to prove. I can still be his surgeon. I want him to be Penis Number One, but I need to do the surgery first. I can handle both.

Without another word, he rolls over on his side, facing away from me, and the cold shoulder feels a whole lot like being slapped in the face.

Ten o'clock turns to eleven. Eleven turns to midnight, and midnight turns to one in the morning, and I'm still staring at the window, begging sleep to take me. Cam's soft sounds of sleep taunt me, making me feel like a boat with no water.

Lying next to him in his hospital bed when I know, without a shadow of a doubt, it could be a matter of days before I have sex with him is weird. Weirder than weird. It's like intimate or something. It feels gentlemanly that he's not trying to have sex with me anymore, which is all wrong because he's not supposed to be a gentleman. He's supposed to be Penis Number One. I'm supposed to be his surgeon.

What a mess.

Unable to lie here alone with my thoughts any longer, I grab my mobile from under the pillow and pull up Belle's name.

Me: Hey, can you talk to me for a minute?

I wait for a moment, knowing Belle's ring will wake her. Being a doctor trains your brain to be a light sleeper.

Belle: Sure. Let me go into the bathroom so I don't wake Stanley, who's probably approaching a wet dream about you right now.

I roll my eyes and slide off the bed, glancing down at Cam for a moment. He's clearly in his REM sleep cycle. Since I know he's a deep sleeper, I creep into the loo, leaving the lights off so there's absolutely no chance of waking him.

I slide down the shower wall just as my mobile lights up with Belle's call.

"Hey," I croak as I tuck my feet under my legs on the shower floor.

"Hey, why are you whispering?" she asks. "Aren't you at home right now?"

I purse my lips. "Promise not to get mad and promise not to judge. And promise not to do that thing where you sound as if you want to pet me on the head."

"Indie."

"You do it sometimes. I know you're not trying to be patronising, but I just need you to promise."

"Okay, I promise."

I drop the bomb. "I'm up in Camden Harris' VIP suite."

"Why? Did something happen to him?" Her voices raises with alarm.

"No."

"Then why are you there?"

I drop the second bomb. "I'm sleeping with him."

"You had sex with him?" she squeals, her voice louder than before.

"Stop shouting! Oh my God, you're going to wake up Stanley," I groan. "And no. I didn't have sex with him. I stayed in his room with him last night and slept in the chair, but tonight he convinced me to sleep in his bed. I was trying to just sleep with him, but I can't sleep because that's all we're doing."

"I'm so confused."

"I don't know how it happened, but it did. He knows I'm a virgin. He knows I want to have sex with him, but we're waiting."

"For what? The operating room?"

"Belle!" I growl. "Be serious. I know this sounds crazy. But he's so hot and he's actually kind of fun, and he's really persuasive and charming. Somehow he got me to stay in his room last night. Then he was nervous about the surgery, so I said I'd sleep with him again tonight. But I can't sleep because all I keep thinking about is the fact that everything we've been doing for the last forty-eight hours is very Un-penis Number One. I'm breaking the rules, Belle, and I'm terrified that this is going to mess up more than just my Penis List!" I drop the final bomb and it feels like a stinker.

"Got it. Okay, hang on a tick. It's like I just found out Mary Poppins was a pedophile."

"What?"

"I'm processing. My sweet, perfect student, Indie Porter, has gone rogue on me. You skipped like eighteen steps, darling. I thought we made this list and these rules so you would know exactly what to do."

"Well! He's really charming." I sigh heavily and listen to her breathe in and out for what feels like forever.

"Okay. It's going to be okay." Her voice is confident and resolute.

"It is?"

"Yes. I decreed it and so shall it be. You're worried he's being too nice? Like he's not Penis Number One material? Don't. I've been Googling him since he came in. There's this entire hate mail blog post from that model he was dating last month about how he fucked her over. She doesn't actually state his name, but you don't have to be a genius to know who Hamden Carris is."

"What did the article say?" The inner voice in my head wants to know what he could have possibly done for her to publicly smear him like that.

"Indie! It doesn't matter. You need him to be a dog. I'm telling you, he's a player. Don't get attached. Caring about what happened to some leggy, jilted blonde is irrelevant.

"Furthermore, if you can't sleep, get the hell out of there now. Nothing needs to mess up your ability to operate tomorrow. He's asleep. You've coddled him. Your customer service job is done. Leave so you can get your head straight and be ready for this surgery. He won't care. You're an innocent virgin unicorn…He'd be a fool to walk away from you."

"Okay." I swallow hard. "Bloody hell, you give good advice at one in the morning."

"Well, I hadn't gone to sleep quite yet."

"Do I want to know?" I ask nervously.

"No."

"Okay," I reply with relief. My shit sandwich is large enough without adding her drama to it. "I'm sorry I didn't tell you."

She huffs a laugh into the line. "I couldn't be more proud of you.

Now get out of there."

I creep out of the bathroom and throw on my trainers. Cam's still out cold, but before walking out the door, I decide to leave him a note—something he'll see in hopes he doesn't think I've changed my mind about the Penis Number One thing.

My eyes scroll through the notes in the margins of his book until I get to the place he left off. Biting my lip, I grab his pen and scrawl out something of my own just below his last note. It's something that I hope he'll be able to appreciate.

Then I creep out like a thief in the night, clutching tightly to my nerves the entire way.

9 Bye, Felicia

Camden

"YOU'RE GOING TO BE GREAT. DON'T BE NERVOUS," VI COOS AS she strokes my hair over and over. I know she does it to calm herself more than me, so I bite my tongue to stop from telling her to piss off.

Two nurses just left my room after prepping me for surgery. One shaved my leg, the other started an IV drip. I already feel the effects of whatever meds they put in there to relax me, but they're making me feel more emotional than calm.

I shift uncomfortably as I'm sprawled out on a hard, mobile bed that's to take me to surgery any second. It's different from the large VIP bed that smells like lemons and rain. *Thank goodness for small favours*, I think sullenly.

"You have to stop," I growl, unable to bite my tongue any longer and shooing my sister's hands off of me. My mood is dark, and the fact that I woke up to Beardie's face instead of Indie's didn't help matters. "Where are Tan and Booker? Gareth?" I ask, feeling like I'm overwhelmed with the maternal hovering of my sister. Some annoying brotherly distractions could serve me well.

"They're in the waiting room. I didn't think you'd want everyone swarming you before the surgery. I can call them in here if you want," she adds, her eyes bright and helpful.

I shake my head. She's right. I'll just get prickly and bark at them like I did yesterday. Best to just get this over with. "Dad?" I ask knowingly.

Her eyes turn soft. "Sorry, Cam. You know this is hard for him."

Hard for *him*? I want to laugh. Imagine how it is for me since I'm the one going under. Surgery and my family do not have a good history, but nobody seems to be talking about that.

"Well, are we all ready for action?" Dr. Prichard's deep voice bellows as he comes striding into the room, adjusting his blue scrub cap.

I look behind him, hoping to see Indie on his tail, but am disappointed when no one follows.

I'm angry. I'm angry that I'm angry. I'm angry that I care. She did exactly what she did yesterday and just left. I can't get a read on her and it's infuriating. I don't like feeling powerless.

"Ready as I'll ever be," I murmur, trying not to roll my eyes.

"As I mentioned to you in our meeting yesterday, we'll be video streaming the procedure to other clinics since it's only the second time The Wilson Repair has been done in the UK. There are a lot of interested sports medicine surgeons eager to watch this all unfold. It's exciting times in medical history."

"You hear that, Cam?" Vi says, nudging me. "You're helping other doctors by doing all of this. Isn't that great?"

"Great," I grind out. "Where's...Dr. Porter?"

Dr. Prichard's brows furrow. "Scrubbing in I'm sure. She had patients of mine she had to do rounds on before the surgery so..." His voice trails off and I look over to see what his eyes have zeroed in on. A pair of feminine red-framed glasses rest on my bedside table beside my Cross novel. I didn't even realise she left those there. She must have run out in quite a hurry to leave those behind.

I glance back at Dr. Prichard's narrowed eyes. "James Patterson fan, are you?" There's a definite edge to his voice.

"For some time now," I bite back, feeling certain we're not talking about mystery authors. "It's right up my alley."

"I'm sure." He forces out a laugh. It reminds me of Dr. Evil. All he's missing is a facial scar and a hairless cat. "Well then, I best go join Indie and scrub in. This is a very big day for her. She had an article published in a medical journal on The Wilson Repair. Did you know that?"

"Why would I?" I feign ambivalence.

"She was an intern at the time and it's how she got her job here. So she'd do about anything to scrub in on this procedure."

I nod but remain silent. What is this spunk bubble trying to do? Create a divide? Well, I felt it before he even came in here, so he can pack away his cock feathers.

"We'll see you in there, Mr. Harris." He turns and walks out the door, and it takes all the control in my body not to throw my book at the back of his smartarse head.

"What was that all about?" Vi asks from beside me.

"Nothing," I reply flatly. "Absolutely nothing."

The amount of time it takes for an intern and a nurse to begin wheeling me through the hospital toward the OR is the same amount of time it takes for everything inside of me to crack. I feel like a bull in a china shop, ready to snap at any second.

First, a sleep and ditch from Indie. Then that prat of a doctor making it clear what I truly am to Indie: a step up in her career.

She never told me about the published article. When I think about how I told her I was scared, that I didn't want to have the surgery, it's no wonder she did anything she could to get me to stick around. She has everything to gain from this surgery. Hell, for all I know she's laughing to her doctor friends about the footballer who actually believed she was a virgin.

As if I needed any more to Hulk out over, a text from my dad sends me toppling over the edge.

Dad: Cam, you may be a Gunner sooner rather than later. I'm so proud of you, Son. Call me after.

He can't even bring himself to text the word "surgery." His priority is all football and contracts instead of the fact that his son is going under the knife in less than thirty minutes. Defence mechanism or not, I've never felt more alone in my life.

My sister tries to hug me goodbye at the door, but I can't even bring myself to embrace her back. I hand her my mobile and watch her retreat, envious that she's out of the spotlight. She's with Hayden and they're going to have a baby. She's always been the matriarch of our family. Our voice of reason. Our problem solver and our referee. When I think about all the times that Tanner and I have barged into her flat so she could settle a fight between us, it makes me wince. Now she's going to be a proper mum to her own child. She's not going to have time for our trivial shit anymore.

Everything is fucking changing. If I lose football after all this, I'll truly have nothing. In a matter of two days, I went from having the world by the balls and being a sure-footed, footballer to an insecure, injured, emotionally-stunted pussy.

The nurse leans over me as she prepares to push me in. "Mr. Harris, are you all right? You're looking pale."

"Let's just get this over with," I brood.

A haze of neon lights cast over my head, and I look around to get my bearings. The OR is full of at least fifteen people all busying themselves with medical instruments. There's a crew adjusting a huge telescope-looking camera above the operating table and a couple talking into headsets as they stand in front of some TV monitors.

They transfer me to the operating table and, before I lie back, my eyes land on a large glass window on the far wall. Behind the glass is Indie and Dr. Prichard. They are standing face-to-face, oblivious to our entry. I see his hand reach up and touch her cheek in a tender, intimate, and definitely familiar gesture.

Fury courses in my veins as I lie back on the table and, in a flash, my mind is made up. Whatever Indie Porter and I could have been will never happen. Camden Harris competes with no one, especially not wankers like Dr. Prichard. She's not worth this much effort.

The anaesthetist is talking to me as he places sticky, round pads all over my chest and shoulders, but I can't hear a word over the frustration roaring in my ears. He places a mask over my face, and the last thing I see before black is familiar, feminine, toffee-brown eyes behind a blue mask.

Bye, Felicia, I think ironically and do my best to ignore her tender touch on my shoulder as my vision fades to black.

Red Card

Indie

I MAINTAIN MY PROFESSIONALISM AND CONCENTRATION DURING the surgery, but I feel everyone's eyes on me the entire time. Watching, judging, and wondering exactly how I got to where I am, holding a camera scope during a nationally-televised rare surgery.

I'm a twenty-four-year-old second year resident. I already have a target on my back for being the youngest doctor here. People already expect me to fail. I don't need to give anyone any indication that I don't deserve everything I've gotten.

So when Prichard stroked my cheek in the scrub room in front of the entire surgical staff, it took everything I had not to knee him in the balls. He said I had an eyelash on my cheek, but then a gentle swipe turned into a caress and a caress turned into a cupping. When he leaned in, I couldn't believe what was happening. I yanked myself out of his grasp, pulled my mask up over my face, and gave him clipped, one-word responses the rest of our time together.

Thankfully, he didn't seem angry with me during the surgery and even allowed me to present some of the particulars during the procedure. Camden's knee accepted the graft perfectly and, technically, it couldn't have gone better.

But the look in his eyes before he went under still chilled the blood in my veins. His blue pools were swimming with anxiety and…loneliness. I almost regretted my decision to not see him prior to operating, just to help put his nerves at ease. But I'm so attracted to him and in tune with his desires. I was scared he would rattle me. Letting my relationship with him cloud my focus was not an option. I needed a clear head and I needed to trust myself to do his surgery properly.

I hurry and scrub out, anxious to see Camden after he wakes up from his anaesthesia. I nod and smile politely at Prichard, even though I want to be a cold bitch to him. I can't lose my spot on the follow-up surgery in a month, so I plan to avoid any personal interaction with him until then. It shouldn't be too difficult because I'm coming up on some time off here soon.

Striding into the post-op room, my eyes find Camden right away. He's the only patient whose feet are hanging off the end of the bed. His eyes are closed and his face is moving side to side as he stirs. A nurse has just finished replacing his IV fluids.

"Has he woken up yet?" I ask, approaching the other side of the bed.

"Yes, he was awake for a bit but has been in and out since then."

"How's his pain?" I ask.

"Good. He said he had none."

My brows arch. "You can't always trust his answer on that. He looks restless, so let's give him eight hundred milligrams of Ibuprofen."

"You're talking like you know me," Cam's voice croaks. His blue eyes crack open and he swallows as if his throat hurts. I grab the lidded cup with a straw and try to offer it to him, but he shakes it off. His blonde hair is disheveled and his normally tan skin looks pale beneath the fluorescent lights. Regardless, he's still painfully handsome.

"I just know from experience that you like to minimise your pain," I smile sweetly.

"I don't need you to speak for me." He grimaces and closes his eyes tightly, as if he's trying to fight off a sharp jab of pain somewhere. "So how did the surgery go, Doc?"

My brow furrows at how he addresses me, but since the nurse is standing only a few feet away, I decide to ignore it. "It went really well. Your ACL accepted the graft. Your knee should feel great in a day or two, just like we said. You can start working out with the PT tomorrow. It should feel pretty normal. Just avoid football until we pull the graft out in a month. By then your ACL should be fused back together and you'll be good as new. Really, it all went perfectly. From the procedure to the broadcast, everyone is buzzing about how this will be changing recovery time for ACL tears in sports medicine. It's exciting. Dr. Prichard is talking to your family in the waiting room now."

"Great." He slow blinks a couple times and stares at me with a hard look in his eyes. "Glad I could help you get ahead."

I frown as he looks away and can feel the nurse's curious eyes on us. I shrug as if I don't have a clue what he means by his remark, but deep down I can tell something's wrong. "Well," I begin awkwardly, "you helped a lot of people get ahead, I'd say. We're very grateful. I'll let you get some more rest. I will check on you again soon, Cam."

I reach out and touch his shoulder, mindful to not appear too personal, and he doesn't even look at me. I turn to leave and hear him quietly say, "Bye, Dr. Porter."

I look back and he closes his eyes as if he's closing the door on something so much bigger than this moment. I have no clue what's going through his head, but my only hope is that I can get a better handle on him later. Or better yet, when he's out of the hospital.

A while later, Belle finds me in the cafeteria throwing away the remnants of my lunch. "Hey! I heard surgery went well. How was your goodbye?" she asks, adjusting her tray on her hip.

"My goodbye?" I ask, setting my tray on the conveyor belt.

"With lover boy. I saw a nurse pushing him out the back exit door a little bit ago. I suppose to avoid all the paparazzi and media crews. I assumed you already spoke to him? Arranged your first date." Her eyes flash with a dirty look in them.

My face crumples. "Prichard said he wasn't getting discharged until after three o'clock."

"Well, he must have changed his mind because Camden was definitely leaving just now. He was in street clothes—"

I don't even let her finish before I take off, moving through the hospital as fast as I can, not caring if I look like a lunatic. This probably reeks of desperation, but after his chilly demeanour in post-op this morning, there's no way I'm letting him leave on that note.

I head to the back area of the hospital where they deliver the hospital beds because I know that's where they've released VIPs before. I burst through the large metal door and squint as my eyes adjust to the London daylight.

"Looking for someone?" a voice asks. I swerve around to find Camden sitting all alone in a wheelchair alongside the building. He's hiding back in the shadows, dressed in a zip up hoodie that is pulled up over his head. His legs are bare in a pair of athletic shorts with a cloth fabric bandage wrapped around his right knee.

"I was looking for you," I reply breathlessly. "I didn't know you were getting discharged so early." I walk over so I can see his face better, and he looks off to the side as if he doesn't want to make eye contact.

"Same-day surgery. All a part of that magical procedure you performed on me today." He turns back and his blue eyes are icy cold. I think I preferred the no eye contact thing.

"Are you waiting for a car?"

"Vi had to drive around because some paparazzi was following her."

"And the nurse left you out here alone?" That's against hospital policy and I immediately want to ask what her name is.

"I wanted to be alone." He pierces me with a look in his eyes as if he's trying to convey more than what we're talking about. "Don't worry about me."

"So...that's it then?" I ask, the words feeling odd and sticky in my mouth. We're finally outside the hospital, breathing fresh air with no one around to overhear us. This is what I wanted, so why does it feel so awkward?

He looks at me, his face hard as stone. "Did you expect more?"

"I mean...I guess. I thought..." my voice trails off. How do I put into words that I had hoped we could have sex sometime soon.

"Let's not drag this out." His words are sharp and clipped and final. I can't, for the life of me, figure out when things shifted between us.

Steeling myself, I say, "I'm just surprised. I thought we had an arrangement."

"Things change," he adds with a careless roll of his eyes. "It's not really that shocking."

My jaw drops as he continues looking at me as if I'm nothing more than his doctor. As if I didn't risk everything by kissing him and sleeping in his bed with him.

Gosh, I'm such a fool for believing that he even liked me. A brief flicker of irrational anger toward Belle crashes over me. *"Stop downplaying your appeal, Indie. It's unappealing."* The only thing unappealing is me continuing to let this tosser look at me as if I'm nothing.

I adjust my glasses and retort back, "You know what...it's fine. I don't know why I thought this was a good idea. There's a chance this could have ruined my career, and for what? A footballer? You've probably had more rides than the London Eye."

"Oh, real original," he sneers.

My voice trembles with anger. "Better than a pun." Then a

moment of silence stretches out between us, both of us leaning in, eye-fucking each other with quiet rage. This entire exchange is childish and juvenile, but bloody hell, does it feel good on some deep, dark level.

"It was nice to meet you, Dr. Porter." He turns his wheelchair to look away from me, and my anger flatlines at his formal address.

Our little affair is truly over before it even started. I'm left blanketed in the shame of everything I risked for someone like him.

When I first met Camden, he was warm and playful. Charming even. I escaped into a secret world where I was wild and carefree and broke all the rules. I laughed a lot.

Now, he's cold and indifferent—exactly everything I thought a player might be.

"I'd say it was nice to meet you, too, Mr. Harris, but I'm not sure it was. I'll see you in a month."

And just like that, I red card myself back to the real world.

11

The Cymbal in the Pun Was Rather Loud

Camden

"ALL RIGHT, THAT'S IT. IT'S BEEN FOUR DAYS. YOU HAVE TO DO something." My brother Tanner doesn't bother to knock before his heavy steps bound into my room. He stops quickly and wrenches open the blinds.

"It smells in here," Booker says quietly, his nose scrunching up as he props himself on the doorframe. "It smells like stale tears and crushed dreams."

I roll my eyes and squint at the onslaught of light. The bright London daylight pours in behind Tanner, giving him an eerily similar silhouette of Big Foot.

I roll over, shove my hands beneath my pillow, and bury my face in darkness again. "Go back to the casting set of *Planet of the Apes* and leave me be," I groan. Despite my desire to be alone, Booker's amused laugh pleases me.

"Ha ha…Great hairy joke. At least your brain hasn't reverted back to ape status quite yet." He pulls the duvet off me in a dramatic fashion. "Cam, all you've done since you got home is sleep and physical therapy."

"That's called healing. What more do you want?" I ask, glowering at him over my shoulder. My knee isn't bothering me at all. Truthfully, I've been working out in our gym after the therapist leaves and it feels completely recovered. It's almost like it was never injured, which I wish was the case.

I've been in a funk ever since I left the hospital. Not because of what happened or didn't happen with Indie, even though I'm almost embarrassed of myself for caring about that situation as much as I did. No girl gets under my skin like that. Not even a doctor.

Instead, I'm going stir-crazy without football in my life.

"The doctor said, aside from football, you can go back to things as usual. You skipped dinner at Dad's today. No one skips dinner at Dad's."

Booker chimes in, "Vi made Swedish pancakes."

"With lingonberry jam," Tanner finishes, his tone obvious.

Damn, I love Vi's Swedish pancakes. Then I remember that if I had gone to dinner, I would have had to talk, and I'm avoiding the whole talking thing in general. My first conversation with my dad did not go well since he failed to ask me how the surgery went. He just wanted to know how soon I thought I would be able to play after the second surgery. I can't predict the fucking future so I'm not sure what he wanted from me exactly.

"You need fresh air. You need some food that's not chicken and rice. You need to get laid. Booker and I are leaving right now for our last match, but I swear I'll skip it if this is how you're going to be while we're gone."

"Oh for fuck's sake," I grumble, rolling over and sitting up to hit Tanner with a death stare. "Why don't you just leave me a honey-do list before you go like a proper footballer's wife."

"Great. We haven't Hoovered in weeks, so go ahead and start there. Then…I don't know…maybe read a book or something. I haven't seen you touch this one since the hospital." He pulls the novel out of my duffel bag that's remained packed since I got home.

"You want me to read?" I ask. "What does that have to do with football?"

"Nothing. I don't give a toss about football right now. I care about you. You're acting weird and depressed or something. I actually considered buying you a puppy today for Christ's sake."

I look at Booker and he nods in confirmation. "What the hell would I do with a puppy?"

"Walk it. I don't know. Ask Vi. She's the one with a dog. I just want you to stop being weird and mopey. It's making me feel awkward."

"Give it here," I groan, taking the book from his outstretched hands. "If I read this, will it make you go away?"

"Yes. It will." He smiles like a dope and bats his eyes happily. In a high-pitched falsetto voice, he adds with a shake of his pointer finger, "And I want a full book report once you've finished."

I roll my eyes as both Tanner and Booker continue watching me, evidently expecting me to start reading right in front of them. I crack the book open. "There. I'm reading, now get out. Go kick some arse, but don't score any goals and show me up, all right?"

"No promises," Tanner says, smiling broadly. "Someone has to keep the Harris name in good standing while you're on holiday."

"Suck my balls," I grumble.

"On that cheery note, I'll see you when we get back in a few days. Call if you need anything, but I think Vi is bringing you lunch tomorrow, so consider yourself warned." He walks over and kisses me on top of my head, his nappy beard tickling my face.

"Get away from me, you freak."

"Later, Broseph," he beams as he hustles out, shoving a quiet Booker ahead of him.

It bothers me to not be going to the match, but not as much as it would bother me to sit on the sidelines and not play. Plus, if I go to the match, I'll be expected to talk to the press. I'm not ready for any of that until I have my follow-up surgery and can start training at full throttle again. I need to lie low for the next month or two. Then we'll see how things turn out.

As I thumb through the pages, the familiar scent of paper and ink wakes a part of my brain that's been dormant the last few days.

I've loved reading for as long as I can remember, and writing in the margins makes me feel like an active part of the story. I highlight plot points and underline areas that might be symbolic to what's coming. I think I love puns so much because of the double entendres they can represent. Plus, I've always thought it might be something my mother would have appreciated about me.

Last year, Vi gave our brothers and me a bunch of poetry our mum had written. She was a full-blooded Swede so some of it had to be translated. She and our dad met while she attended University in London. Gareth told me once that he remembers Mum yelling at Dad in Swedish when they fought. I would have liked to have heard more, but pulling memories about Mum out of Gareth is more difficult than pulling teeth. Reading her poetry made me feel connected to her, though. Her poems were chock-full of symbolism and clever rhymes, not terribly unlike puns.

I start rereading my margin notes to familiarise myself with where the plot was headed last I left off. An unfamiliar script stops me in my tracks.

"What the hell?" I whisper and turn the book sideways to get a closer look.

It's not that the woman did not know how to juggle, she just didn't have the balls to try.

I touch my fingertips to the inked pun inside my treasured book and know instantly it had to be Indie who wrote it. After our bit about puns, there's no one else it could have been. Did she do it when she left my room that night?

I recycle the words over and over in my mind, attempting to look for the hidden message within the phrase. That's what I love most about puns. They aren't just funny one-liners; most are full of symbolism. I know she's trying to say something more than what's written here.

I check the time and note that Indie should still be at work right now. After my harsh brush-off, I'm not sure she will be receptive to a phone call or a text, though.

Plus, mysteries are easier solved in person.

My well-rested brain kicks into overdrive. Before I realise it, I'm sliding my legs into a pair of jeans and throwing on a T-shirt.

Maybe my redheaded distraction still has some potential after all?

12

Tequila Sunset

Indie

"It's Tequila Sunrise time, baby!" Belle hoots, chasing me out the door of the hospital and into the unseasonably warm spring evening. She throws her arm around my shoulder and pulls me to her. "Stop moping now, Indie, darling. We have finished our nine-day stretch and we're going to Club Taint as planned. We're going to have a wild time."

My lip curls. "My own bed sounds better right now."

"No!" She halts me in my tracks and turns me to face her. "I let you mope these last few days at work, but now you're done. You've earned the respect of the resident staff and most of the attendings. You should be feeling on top of the world after the week you've had. We need to celebrate!"

"I know," I reply with a sigh, even though Prichard has been acting cold toward me ever since we finished Camden's surgery. I keep trying to convince myself that maybe he wasn't trying to kiss me in the OR, but his mood shift begs to differ.

"Who cares about that wanker, footballer Camden Harris? He's probably gay. That's the only logical conclusion."

"He's not gay," I reply, horrified as the memory of his firmness creeps to the forefront of my mind. I can't believe I groped him like that.

"Bisexual then. Who cares? He probably wanks off to images of football for God's sake." She turns, linking arms with me, and continues walking down the side of the hospital where we have to split off in different directions. "The Penis List is still a solid plan. You won't convince me otherwise. We're going to find an even better player tonight. One who's much less needy. Footballers are dramatic pansies anyway. Let's go for a rugby player. Or maybe one of those underground fighters. You need a bloke you won't be inspired to break the rules for and then *get to know him*." She pierces me with her dark eyes. "This is happening, Indie. We have five days off. Now is our time."

I exhale at the knowledge that fighting a determined Belle is useless. Deep down, I know she's right. The whole scene with Camden was horrid. It reminded me of a time in primary school when I explained that the poem *Autumn* by Emily Dickinson wasn't about the changing of the seasons, but about death and the decline of Christianity. Everyone laughed, even the teacher.

I've just always seen things differently and still do. The way he was so aloof and brushing me off outside the hospital after everything we talked in depth about is ridiculous. I can't let him or anyone revert me back to that guileless, insecure girl ever again. That's not who I am anymore.

I force a smile and push my black-framed glasses up my nose a bit. "You're right," I agree. It's time to move on from Camden, and I'm ready for a night out with my best mate. "I'm sorry and I promise I won't let one stupid arsehole spoil our Tequila Sunrise time."

"Too right!" she sings, breaking away from me to head toward her flat in the opposite direction. Walking backwards she shouts, "Go home. Shower. Shave your wobbly bits...Do whatever you need to do to get tarted up and ready for our night."

I turn the corner, still watching her retreat and frown when her face falls. "Indie...look out!"

Smack. I run right into a large hard object. I let out an embarrassingly girlie yelp and hunch over to grab my aching knee. I wince at the searing pain and glare at the metal pedestrian sign. The bastard has a lot of nerve being stuck in the concrete so firmly. As I release a slur of expletives, a pair of helpful warm hands wrap around me from behind.

"Holy fuck," Belle says. Her voice sounds far away, though. *If they aren't Belle's hands on me, then whose are they?*

I turn around and find myself in the hands of The Penis Prodigy himself: Camden Harris. The setting London sun is bathing him in golden light, turning him into a beautiful bronze, god-like wonder.

"Are you kidding me?" I groan, looking down to rub my knee.

"Are you all right?" he asks. His deep voice is soft and low, vibrating through my body with concern as he hovers over me with his hands on my back.

I shuffle away from him as he tries to inspect my knee. "I'm fine," I snipe. "I don't think I'll need The Wilson Repair."

He huffs out a laugh. "If you did, I know a good doctor."

I hobble over to a nearby bench and silently curse the universe for making me look like such an arse at this particular moment. Camden tries to help me sit, but I reject his assistance. "What are you doing here? Something wrong with your knee?"

"I came to see you." He looks down at me, shoving a shaky hand through his hair and scratching the back of his neck. "Can we talk?"

I look over and see Belle walking backwards away from us. "I'll pick you up for the club in two hours!" she sings merrily as if it's completely normal for a hunky, famous footballer, whom I've just operated on, to pry me off a street sign. She gives me a "toodles" sort of wave and I squeeze my knee to stop myself from giving her a wave of my finger.

A rueful smile tugs at Camden's mouth. "Are you off work tonight?"

I lick my lips slowly. "Yes. Belle and I are off for five days, and it's sort of a tradition after we work long weeks to go out on our first night."

"I can understand that." He sits down beside me, propping the side of his leg on the bench and draping an arm over the back. He smells better than ever.

"Are you doing your therapy I hope?" I ask, eyeing his denim-covered knee and noting how annoyingly hot he looks in dark jeans and a fitted, black T-shirt.

He nods thoughtfully. "Yes. The physical therapist is about as exciting as dry toast, but I feel great during our workouts. Normal even."

I purse my lips and let go of my knee to sit up straight, mindful not to sit back and brush against his arm. "That's sort of the point."

A fleeting look of nerves shadow his eyes before he blurts, "I just started reading my book again."

I frown. "What book?"

"My Cross novel."

My face falls. *Fudge.* In my anger, I'd all but forgotten about the note I wrote inside of it.

"I'm guessing by your reaction that note was from you?"

I look away. "That was before."

"Before what?"

"Before you turned into a prickish footballer who gave me the cold shoulder."

He deflates and shifts closer to me. "Indie—"

"Don't," I cut him off and slide down the bench away from him. "I'm not some baby who needs coddling."

"I know it. I was the baby," he replies while running a hand down his thigh. "I saw Dr. Prichard with his hands on you in the OR and I didn't like it. And I didn't like that I didn't like it."

I actually have to shake the stupor from my brain before I can reply. "The Prichard thing was nothing."

"Well, I'm not a sharer," he adds, piercing me with his stunning blue eyes. "Then you left the night before and it all just got to me. A bloke's ego can only take so much."

"You're a professional footballer. Your ego should be bigger than London."

His lips form a line. "It usually is…but not around you."

I shoot him an "are you kidding me" expression. Does he really expect me to believe that I have the ability to make him insecure?

"Look, this is my fault. I'm taking full blame here. I just let what Dr. Fuckwad said get to me." His jawbone ticks with obvious anger.

"Who?"

His eyes narrow. "Dr. Prichard. He made it a point to tell me about your published research on The Wilson Repair and it made me feel like I was being manipulated."

"Manipulated? How?"

"Well, I started questioning everything after that. Why didn't you mention it to me before? I'm usually the player, not the playee. It's not like we didn't have the chance to discuss it. You slept in my room two nights."

My jaw drops. "I didn't think you'd care."

"What the hell does that mean?" He looks offended as his jaw muscle ticks violently.

"Nothing! I didn't mention it because it didn't occur to me. I don't seem to make the best choices when I'm around you, Camden. I have a bit of a one-track mind when you do that glittery eye thing to me. But fine, let's air it all out," I bark, feeling as if I'm on a roll now. "Yes, I have a heavy interest in your surgery. I have a heavy interest in ortho. It's what I've chosen to focus on. I don't have any reason to hide that. I probably didn't tell you because—" I pause and he urges me on. "Because I was embarrassed by my behaviour. What happened to you was the surgical opportunity of a lifetime. It was great for my career, yet I was risking it all by getting involved with you. I didn't want you to look at me as if I was a silly little girl with half a brain. I don't like feeling as if I'm being run by my hormones."

He jeers, "I wouldn't have thought that."

"Well, what I did was unethical and I still don't know exactly why I did it."

"Could it be because you want to fuck me?" He slides closer to me. His vulgar word mixed with his scent of soap makes my mouth water.

I scoff at how he's managed to simplify a whole slew of personal and ethical issues into one stupid sentence. "No, definitely not."

"Maybe it's my glittery eye thing you mentioned?" He's doing an absolute horrid job of hiding his smirk.

"God, you're an arse." My shield drops like the adulterous Brutus it is. How does he make me lose myself so quickly?

"Indie," he whispers, leaning in. His close proximity confounds my mind so much that I want to fall into his warm, manly embrace. Somehow, I manage to resist...but just barely. "I was a wounded, egotistical jerk. But that was temporary. Your note cured me. I'm sorry for being jealous and brushing you off." The feel of his breath tickles as he inhales over the skin exposed along my neck. "It's okay to want me."

"No, it's not. You suck." My voice is raspy, which makes me roll my eyes. "Did you even get what my pun meant?"

"Yeah, you're considering becoming a juggler of testicles after you finish this whole doctor phase." His face is expressionless and, like a silly girl, I smile.

I turn to shove him away. "You don't deserve my pun." He catches my hand and holds it against his chest. I nervously look around to confirm that no one is watching us. I shouldn't be touching him. I should be pulling my hand away from him and act halfway professional. But then I feel the ridges of muscle beneath the soft cotton of his T-shirt and the pounding of his heart as he clutches my hand. I take a quick guess that it's beating around 80 bpm, which is fast for a resting state athlete. His eyes sparkle with so much desire, and the danger of the whole scene makes it impossible for me to look away.

"You're scared," he says. "But why?"

Embarrassment forces me to look down. "I've never made men a priority in my life. I'm not like this. I don't sleep with patients and jeopardise all that I've worked for."

"It looked to me like you were just living a little." He releases my hand. "And I'm sorry if I was pressuring you too much."

The remorseful look on his face gives me pause. "You didn't force me to do anything I didn't want to do. Just…this place," I say, gesturing to the hospital behind me. "I'm normally a different person in that building. I don't *live* my life in there. I *save* lives in there."

"I completely understand." He stands up and shoves his hands in his pockets as if he's getting ready to leave.

"Okaaay?" I ask as he looks at me expectantly.

"How about I escort you home and we get to know each other away from the hospital." He winks and gestures for me to follow him. "Let's have a do-over, Specs."

I couldn't say no. I didn't want to say no. It wasn't because he's hot or charming, or because he apologised profusely, or because I still want him to be Penis Number One. It's because I'm genuinely curious about him. I get a sense that there's a lot more to Camden than what he shows on the surface. He feels like a brand new textbook just waiting to be read, and God I love textbooks.

"I don't live far," I say as we make our way down the sidewalk and away from the glow of the hospital. A weight lifts off my shoulders when I can no longer see it behind me.

Camden squints as a thought strikes him. "You sleep at the hospital, though." He looks at me curiously. "Even though you live so close?"

A twinge of anxiety fleets through me at his perceptiveness.

"It's...complicated."

"Try me," he states.

"I'm impressed by how you're getting around," I deflect, eyeing his movement appreciatively. This is the first time I've seen Camden Harris at one hundred percent. No limp, no favouring. Just long, powerful strides, eating up the pavement of East London. I can only imagine how incredible he looks on the pitch.

"Yeah, it's been good. The therapist has been working with me all week."

He shows me some of the movements he does with the therapist and how when he twists it a certain way, he can feel the graft. I tell him that's normal, relishing in the fact that we're talking in my comfort zone right now and not about the fact that he's coming back to my flat.

"Stitches still there?" I ask.

"Yes. They haven't dissolved yet, but I hardly notice them. The incisions are small. You and Dr. Prichard are true to your words."

"Don't you mean Dr. Fuckwad?" I laugh and he smirks knowingly in response.

"You have to admit he's got a creep factor to him."

"But you luring a naïve doctor into your patient room at night is so innocent?"

"'Naïve doctor sounds like an oxymoron, doesn't it?" He stuffs his hands in his pockets and narrows a playful gaze at me.

I bob my head from side to side. "Experienced in books, but not in life I'm afraid."

He winks and responds, "That's all right. Life happens to be my specialty."

We arrive at my basement flat, and he follows me down the exterior concrete steps. I've lived here since I was an intern because it was the only place close to the hospital that I could afford. Belle and I talked about living together after med school, but she comes from a lot of money and I knew she wouldn't let me pay my way.

Being a doctor in England isn't as lucrative as it is in the States. Since Royal Hospital is partially private owned, I make more than a lot of residents working for the NHS. But as a second year, it's still pittance considering what we do for people every day. Thanks to my scholarships, I don't have the outrageous student loans that so many others have to pay back. That, along with my parent's guilt money, helps keep me comfortable.

I feel Cam's warmth behind me as I unlock the door and it all feels strangely ordinary. He's a famous London footballer. He plays in a stadium that's a mile from my flat. People chant his name in the crowd, and girls throw their bras at him in hopes he'll just look at them. What on earth is he doing here, and how is this my life?

"No roommate?" he asks, walking around my studio flat and taking in the tight quarters. He looks so large in here, his head only six inches from the ceiling. Everything looks tiny with him in here, right down to my gold, floral loveseat.

"No roommate. I erm…grew up in all-girls boarding schools with roommates all the time. So…" my voice trails off as I drop my keys in a bowl and desperately wish I had something to do with my hands. I also wish I wasn't in my scrubs at the moment. I also wish he wasn't peering into my closet.

"That's right. You mentioned boarding school before." He turns back to face me, crossing his arms over his chest and leaning against my closet door. A dirty smile teases his mouth. "Have any pillow fight stories you want to share with me? Girl on girl experimenting perhaps?"

My cheeks heat as I laugh through my nose. "I'm afraid you'll find my boarding school stories quite dull." *If he only knew what the other girls did there.*

He steps back for me to place my trainers in the closet and makes his way over to the adjacent wall. He grabs hold of what looks like a shelf and pulls out my Murphy bed as if he's done it a thousand times before.

"I share a flat with Tanner. I envy your solitude." He flops down on my multi-coloured quilt, and the view of him on my bed is... disarming.

"Do you want something to drink? I'm going to have something to drink." I walk over to my refrigerator and rummage for something alcoholic. I could sing when I find a bottle of Prosecco that Belle left here last time she was over. I grab two tumblers and pour generous portions into each, turning around to find him watching me.

His brows arch. "Nervous?"

"No," I baulk. I reassess. "Yes."

"Indie..." He says my name in that way again. That way that makes my knickers feel warm and my heart feel fast. "I'm not expecting us to fuck right now."

"You're not?" I ask, deflating a bit but still affected by his cavalier use of that word. I don't know why I assumed he was coming here for sex. I don't know why I thought that I'd even be ready for it right now. In a way, I wish we would do it right now so there's no time for me to overthink it. This is what I've been waiting for. Why doesn't he want it?

"Well, not entirely." He stands up and walks up to me, placing his hands on either side of the counter, caging me with his hard body. I clutch my sparkling wine to my chest as my back presses against the worktop. He's so close he has to bow his head to pierce me with his eyes. "Not tonight away."

A playful twinkle in his gaze relaxes my nerves. "Then what are we doing?" I ask, pulling my lips into my mouth and rubbing them together.

"We're reacquainting." He leans down, and just when I think he's going to brush his lips against mine, his hand comes up between us and he grabs his glass from me. A smirk plays on his lips as he takes a drink. "It'll make it that much sweeter."

A soft smile creeps across my face as I muse over his playful demeanour. Suddenly, I'm taken completely off guard when his lips land firmly against mine. The sweet, fizzy bubbles of the Prosecco are still fresh on his lips as he works himself into my mouth. I nearly drop my glass when his hand blindly takes it from me and places it on the counter somewhere beside us. He bends and grips behind my thighs, hoisting me up onto the counter to give himself better access to my face.

When he presses himself snuggly against my centre, I want to moan. Or sing. Or whimper. But definitely moan. His tongue enters my mouth, but it's not greedy and demanding. It's passionate and warm, sensual and hot. It's delicious and even better than I remember it being at the hospital.

His hand slices into my tied up hair, snagging in the messy bun. As a result, he grips my top-knot with need and a command that has me arching into him and sliding myself closer. When his other hand slides up under my shirt, tickling my ribs, I stupidly realise that my hands have been frozen in fists on the countertop this entire time.

I quickly reach up and grip his biceps, shoving my hands under his short sleeves to stroke the tensed muscles. They're smooth and hard, promising and powerful. They're exactly what I want.

"We should stop," he groans against my lips while need courses between us like bolts of electricity with every exhale.

"I'm not the one who started," I murmur.

He swallows and presses his forehead against mine, further separating our mouths. "You're always the one to kick it up a notch, though."

My eyes widen. "That seems unlikely. Who's the virgin here?" I ask, laying it all out there in my lust-induced state.

He laughs and pulls his head away from mine, glaring at me through his lash-framed eyes. "It's the innocent ones that are the most dangerous." His jaw muscle ticks as he appears to be pondering something while tucking a piece of hair behind my ear. "Maybe you should blow off your friend tonight after all."

His caress on my face is so sweet that I almost forget he's a slutty footballer. Pursing my lips, I shake my head. "I really can't. Belle is my best mate. We have to go dancing at Club Taint for our Tequila Sunrise tradition."

He moves out from between my legs and crosses his arms over his chest. "This sounds interesting."

"Oh, it's nothing. I just can't bail on her. It's her night, too."

"Which is…?" He waits for me to fill in the blank, and I can tell by his expression that he's not going to let this go.

Exhaling, I try to come up with a way to funnel this philosophy down as much as possible. "It's our thing. Our jobs at the hospital are anything but typical. My drama at work isn't someone eating my labeled yogurt out of the company refrigerator. It's the fact that I've had to call the time of death on three patients and I'm only twenty-four-years-old."

His face falls at the sharp turn this conversation has taken.

"I don't mean to be a downer, but we see death or immense sadness every single week. A terminal diagnosis, telling a wife she lost her husband, a kid in a horrible car accident. The entire gamut of emotions all happen inside that hospital. So outside, we make it count. We have fun. We act our ages."

"Tequila Sunrise," he finishes.

I shrug. "Tequila Sunrise."

A look of respect is evident on his face. "So…tomorrow then?"

I nod my approval, a flurry of excitement and possibility overcoming my insides. He'll be my most exciting adventure so far.

His smile suddenly falls. "But you're sure you don't want something more, right? I don't want to mislead you into thinking I'm someone I'm not, because I don't do girlfriends. I do casual and safe. But never girlfriends…Except for a girl in fourth grade who kicked me in the balls and told me she'd do it again if I didn't agree to be her boyfriend."

"Oh my God, is that true?" I ask, poorly concealing a laugh, which makes him laugh, too.

"Yes. I cried real tears and was so afraid of her that we stayed together for a whole year. Eventually I convinced myself that the pain couldn't have been that bad, so I broke it off with her. But I did it in the car with her mum there just to be safe."

I laugh so hard my side hurts. I'm not sure if it's the story that's so funny or the tiny bit of horror I can still see in his eyes as he retells it. "That's awful."

"It was. Ruined me forever I'm afraid."

"Well, you're safe with me," I add after my fit has subsided and I can breathe again. I slide off the counter, using his shoulder for balance. Patting him in a matey way, I assure him, "I have a plan all worked out and latching myself on to you isn't a part of that. This is a one-night thing. I promise. My adventures in life have only just begun, Cam."

He loses a little brightness in his eyes and looks down.

"What is it?" I ask.

"Nothing." He looks toward the door. "Right." He purses his lips and leans in, dropping a kiss on my cheek. "I'll call you tomorrow." Then he leaves without a look back.

My Penis List is finally going to start.

Tequila Sunrise, baby.

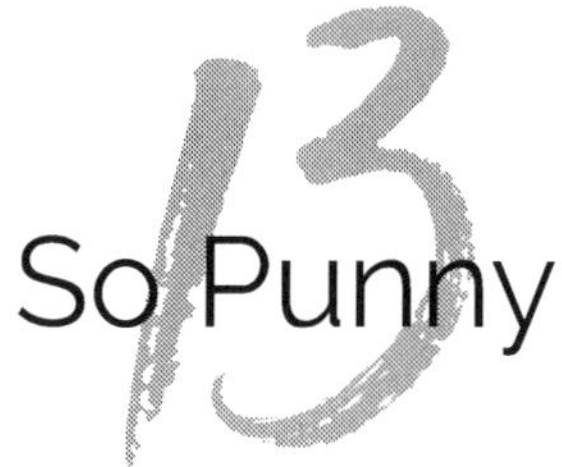

13 So Punny

Indie

"SO YOU'RE SURE YOU WANT IT TO BE THAT HARRIS FOOTBALLER? Not one of those blokes over there?" Belle asks, gesturing across the sea of people grinding against each other and waving flirtatiously toward the guys we just left.

"Yes I'm sure," I almost growl, but hold back. We've been dancing with the same two guys since we arrived at Club Taint. They are cute and nice, and I'm trying to be fun because this is Belle's night off, too, but all I have is Camden Harris on my mind. The more I moved my body, the more I thought about his pressed up against mine back at my flat. *God, I bet he would be an incredible dancer.* Before I knew it, I was feeling flush everywhere and didn't want the guy I was with to get the wrong idea, so I told Belle I needed to cool off.

More like hose off.

"You look hot enough, you could get pretty much any guy here," Belle adds. "Even the gay ones."

I roll my eyes and look down at the mustard yellow dress she insisted I wear. It's sleeveless, tight, and has a short asymmetrical hemline with a slit up one side. Paired with black, peep toe ankle boots, my red hair tamed into some halfway-decent curls, and Bad Blood lipstick, I can't help but feel pretty good. It's just too bad I can't apply this effort to my *chosen one.*

I giggle to myself at that label for Cam and press my lips together, recalling the feel of his firm, sculpted arms and soft, needy lips. God, if he can fuck as good as he kisses, I'm more than ready for tomorrow.

I take large gulps of my cold beer and slightly sway, annoyed that the alcohol is doing nothing to stave off my desire. Belle downs the last of hers and waves the bottle. "You've got the next round."

I polish off mine, too. "Hold our spot. We'll have one more and then I'm done. I don't want to be hung over tomorrow."

"Oh yes. This I know." Belle shoots me a lewd smirk, her tongue darting out to lick her lips. "It's why you took so long getting ready tonight. Had to pamper all your wobbly bits to ensure they are ready for tomorrow night's performance!"

"Shut it, you cow." I shake my head at her. We're so different, but her need to constantly shock me is my favourite part about her.

I make my way through the horde of people and up to the bar. I'm hopeful that redheaded bartender, Frank, is still here. He took one look at my hair earlier, ignored everyone else and insisted on taking a shot of Fireball with me. He is certainly gay and wonderfully hilarious. A few more drinks and I'll probably end up asking him to be Penis Number Two.

I find a random spot open at the packed bar and see Frank elbows deep in a round of shots for a bachelorette party. It's going to be a while before he's free so I prop myself on the barstool. While I wait, inspiration strikes. I pull my mobile out of my clutch and find Camden's number.

Me: Remind me why we're waiting until tomorrow again?

Nerves erupt in my belly over my brazen text message. I shoot him an awkward grin emoji and check the time to see it's half past eleven. What if he's asleep? God, this was a bad idea. Belle always says to never drink and text.

Camden: Hiya to you, too. Are you home?

can be.

A lightbulb goes off in my head when I realise all of that can't be taught in one night.

No matter how skilled I consider myself to be in the bedroom, her first time won't be as good as her third or her fourth. I hate that some other bloke will be the one to show that to her. Like one of those blokes she's probably dancing with at that fucking club right now.

All right, Camden Harris, once your balls drop, you need to get control of this situation.

One night doesn't work for me anymore. With other girls, yes. But Indie is different. I need more. I need an addendum to our arrangement, and I need to make it tonight before those other tossers get any bright ideas.

I grab my mobile and pull up my brother's number. Without another thought, I hit DIAL.

"Cam?" A deep timbre vibrates into the line. "Everything all right?"

"Yeah, Gareth, I'm fine. Are you back in Manchester? Or are you still at Dad's?"

"I'm still at Dad's. How's the knee? You missed dinner, you know. Vi's pissed." Gareth's accent is sounding more and more Mancunian every time I talk to him.

"I'm not scared of my big sister."

"Yeah right," he objects. "Wait 'til you see her next time, and tell me that when she's detached your balls and buried them with Bruce's dinosaur-sized shits."

My face contorts at the image of Vi's huge Saint Bernard's massive craps. Her dog is a slobbering beast but, for some reason, she loves him.

Ignoring his comment, I say, "The knee's fine. Feels great, actually. It feels weird if I twist it a certain way, but Indie says that'll be gone after the graft is removed."

"Indie?" Gareth asks. "Do you mean that Dr. Porter girl? You're on a first-name basis with your surgeon, Cam?"

"That's why I'm calling, actually."

"Oh, here we go."

I tell him everything that happened between Indie and me at the hospital, leaving out the bit about her being a virgin. No one but me needs to know that. Ever. Not that my brother would give a shit. He'd probably call me a scumbag if he knew I was planning to take her virginity and then leave her, but that's partially why I need to tweak our arrangement.

"I need you to come with me to a club tonight. Dad, Booker, and Tanner are all away at the match, so I know you have nothing better to do. Come on, Brother. Be my wingman."

He sighs heavily. "It's almost midnight and it's always a shit show when I go to clubs, Cam."

"Get over yourself. You're in London now, mate, not Manchester. If I can go into a club and not be mauled, so can you. Besides, I know the club she's at. It's basically a gay bar. We'll be safe."

Saying that is probably the deciding factor for why he agrees to help me. I know Gareth's not gay because I've seen his porno collection. But he's almost thirty and, truth be told, I've never seen him with a girl. Tanner and I have tried to drag him to the clubs with us when he's in town, but he always avoids that kind of scene. Booker thinks he's celibate for football. I think he's got a secret girl in Manchester. Regardless, he doesn't date publicly. Ever.

"I guess I should be glad you're getting out of the flat."

"Exactly," I reply. "Let's go."

It's just after midnight when we get to Club Taint. This place is a bit of a wonder. It has a gay bar vibe to it with the pedestal go-go dancers and the dubstep music, but it's still diverse enough of a crowd to be able to kick back and feel welcome. I've been here once before with the team when we were trying to get our midfielder, Clive, to come out of the closet. Truthfully, we all know he's gay and couldn't give a shit. We just want to know. It's like having a friend who's allergic to peanuts—it's nice to know so you don't embarrass yourself by handing him a Walnut Whip.

Gareth leads the way, pulling down his baseball cap, keen on not being recognised. I didn't bother wearing a hat. You don't see many baseball caps in London, so my theory is that you draw more attention to yourself by wearing one.

While my brother orders us drinks at the bar, my gaze scans the dance floor for a red, messy bun, preferably surrounded by happy gay men and not straight, trolling blokes. I know it's a bit intense to show up here without a warning, but there's a part of me that's excited to see her in public. Not in the hospital behind closed doors, or in her flat where her curtains are drawn. I want to see her in a dress, dancing and maybe a little bit intoxicated so that when I throw my ideas at her, she's open to them. Plus, I'm much more persuasive in person.

"Relax and have a drink. You look like a fucking stalker," Gareth says, passing me a bottle of lager. "Are you sure you know what you're in for with this bird?"

I suck back a cool drink and frown. "I'm not a stalker, and I'm not *in* for anything other than adjusting our arrangement."

"And what arrangement is that exactly?" His hazel eyes are judgmental under the shadows of his cap.

I lean in so he can hear me. "She's not wanting a boyfriend, and I already made it very clear how I am. I just want a bit more than the one night she originally proposed."

"Are you telling me a surgeon at a private hospital wants a one-night stand with you? What is it…some bucket list thing? Are you fulfilling her make-a-wish dying request?"

I scowl. "Don't be a prat."

"Well, good luck to you. Just find this girl so we can get out of here." He turns around as a group of girls looks in our direction.

I put the bottle to my lips and nearly choke when my gaze lands on the most stunning woman I've ever seen. I thought Indie Porter was hot in scrubs and messy hair. The woman standing before me now is completely out of my league.

A long game plan with a bird never looked so good to Camden Harris.

15 Penis Addendum

Indie

When I get a glimpse of Belle's tongue ramming down her dance partner's throat, I decide it's time for another drink. I break away from the guy I'm with and interrupt Belle just long enough to tell her I'm going to the bar. When I turn around, my guy has already grabbed another girl, so I don't feel much love loss there.

I finally get myself out of the throng of people, feeling as if I just got mauled, and my gaze collides with a pair of eyes that I've been picturing in my head all night.

The Chosen One.

"Camden?" My voice sounds weak and unsure as I approach him, drinking in his entire body. He's dressed in a pair of faded blue jeans and a thin, holey grey T-shirt. It's the kind of shirt you pay a lot of money to have artfully distressed because if you tried to do it yourself, it would look as if you took a paper puncher to it. His hard muscles are on full display beneath the soft fabric and the touch of ink snaking out on one arm adds edge to a drool-worthy boy next door look.

"Indie." He utters my name so quietly I have to step closer to hear him. Even his blonde hair looks perfect, smoothed over to one side. "This is what you look like outside of work?"

I glance down shrugging. "No, not always."

"Good," he replies with a scowl. "Were you dancing with someone out there?"

"Hello, Dr. Porter," a deep voice interrupts from beside him. I hadn't realised Camden's brother, Gareth, was standing right next to him. "Nice to see you."

"Please, call me Indie." I look over and smile at him politely, immediately wondering what Camden has told him about me. "What are you guys doing here?"

Camden's face softens and he replies, "I need to talk to you."

A pit forms in my stomach from the look on his face. Were my texts too much? Is he wanting out? Without another word, he grips my arm and ushers me away from the bar. His hand is hot on my back as he gestures toward a quiet corner of the club with tall, empty cocktail tables and no chairs. Most of the clubbers are pressing in on the dance floor, so this area feels like a place you could go to murder someone and no one would hear their screams.

"What's going on? Is everything okay?" I ask, as the music thumps along with my heart. "What does your brother know about us?"

"Everything's fine." He gestures for me to stand on one side of the table and positions himself across from me. "Don't worry about Gareth. I wouldn't tell him more than he needs to know."

"So he knows we're—"

"Forget him. He doesn't care. But you may as well know there's not much you can do with a Harris that the others don't eventually suss out. We're like fucking psychics when it comes to each other's business. It's annoying as fuck."

"Oh great," I moan.

"But we don't judge. Ever." Camden pins me with a serious look that somehow calms my nerves.

I nod my assent. "So what are you doing here then?'

"I need to make some changes to our arrangement." Camden is so tall that when he goes to rest his elbows on the table he has to hunch over, bringing our faces only a foot apart now.

Frowning, I ask, "What kind of changes?"

"I need more than one night." His blue eyes flash back and forth between mine, revealing a touch of uncertainty.

"What do you mean?"

"I can't just take your virginity and leave. It'll be awful." My face falls but he catches himself quickly. "What I mean is, I'm going to make it good, don't worry. But your first time won't be as great as your third time. I want a third time. At least."

My gaze drops. "Camden."

"I'm not asking for a relationship or dating, or even friends with benefits. I'm just asking for more…sex." He has the cheek to look sheepish.

"More sex," I huff. He has an uncanny way of simplifying meaningful conversations into two words.

"And other stuff," he adds. "I don't know how much you've done and I want to be thorough. You have five days off, right?"

"Yes," I reply.

"That's just enough time. We'll have some time to cool off before my final surgery and bam. I'm out of your life for good, satisfied that I've given you a lifetime of memories to make even your future husband look inadequate. It'll be perfect."

I can't help but smile at his arrogance. "You came all the way here, to Club Taint, to tell me you want more sex?"

His eyes narrow. "I thought maybe if you were boozed up a bit, you'd be more amenable. You have a history of being a bit…tense."

My jaw drops. "That's only at work. You haven't seen anything yet."

He straightens, a broad smile taking over his entire face as he walks slowly around the table. I look down nervously as he grips my waist in his hands, squeezing my sides with delicious promise. Hovering over me, he walks me backwards until I'm pressed up against a nearby wall.

"*You* haven't seen anything yet, Indie." His voice is deep and husky, and the intense look in his eyes drains all good humour from my face. "I might have had one other reason to come here."

He leans the rest of the way in and kisses me…like a savage.

Everything I remembered about our first kiss, and the second kiss, and the third kiss…is gone. Erased. The bar has been risen so high, all the other bars have disappeared.

My inner voice cheers in triumph at the fact that I'm actually doing this. I'm not just a doctor completely focused on my career. I'm going to be wild and have sex with Camden Harris and shift my one-dimensional life into glorious 3D.

He is the perfect Penis Number One.

Pulling back, he breaks our kiss, leaving my lips feeling raw and swollen. "What are the odds of you coming home with me right the fuck now?"

I swallow once. "I'd say pretty bloody good."

16 Oral Fixation

Camden

TONIGHT IS THE FIRST TIME I'VE EVER SEEN INDIE WITH MAKEUP on. Even behind yet another new pair of glasses, she's striking. The ones she's wearing tonight are vintage with a black browline and an invisible bottom frame. Combined with the dress and the hair, it all works really well.

And I'm not sure I like it.

Women are a different kind of beautiful when they have makeup on. It puts them on display for all to see, and they want to be seen because they put in the extra effort. So their confidence is higher and their shoulders are straighter. They're different.

But when Indie's face is bare, she's a secret kind of beautiful only noticeable to those who care enough to look.

I liked that I was the only one looking then.

Now, with her lips fire engine red and pouty, every bloke in this club had to be checking her out, gauging their odds and how much work it would take to shag her.

So I had to kiss her. I couldn't stop myself. It was erratic and messy and wet, but my dick cheered when I pulled back and her lips were swollen and her eyes were filled with lust. It was either kissing her or peeing on her so every guy knew to back the fuck off. Indie

Porter belongs to Camden Harris.

For the next five days that is.

Indie goes to talk to Belle while I go to find Gareth, who's none too surprised when I tell him I'm getting a cab home.

"That didn't take long."

I smile. "I'm a Harris."

He laughs and sets his beer down. "Can I go now?"

"Yes, my brother, you can. Thanks for the support."

"Not that you needed it," he states as he pulls his hat down and makes his way out of the club.

A few minutes later, Indie finds me at the bar and I usher her outside to the bank of cabs. "Your friend doesn't need a ride?" I ask as a black cab pulls up in front of us.

"No, she's going home with a guy she met." Indie shrugs like this is perfectly normal behaviour.

She slips inside first. As soon as I fold myself in behind her, I stare hard at her. "How are you feeling?"

She bites her lip. "Fine."

My gaze narrows as I put my arm on the back of the seat and eye her carefully. "How much did you have to drink?"

She looks away and I sigh. She's not falling over drunk, but there's no way I'm having sex with her if there's even a chance of her not being sober.

She scoffs and turns to face me. "Well, I had this really cheeky footballer, who thinks he's God's gift to women, manhandle my lips right before I went out tonight. I had to cool off somehow."

I'm across the bench in a blink, pressing my lips firmly to hers again. *God, she tastes good.*

"Where are we going?" the driver barks, interrupting our kiss.

I give him my address and pause when I realise what I've just done. Tanner and I have an unspoken rule to never bring women home. I suppose we never did it when we lived at our dad's so it's just something we continued when we moved out.

As athletes, our home is our sanctuary away from the pitch. It's where we prepare and recover ourselves from the grueling parts of our jobs. It gets pretty nasty after we get back from matches. We're athletes. We stink. But it's who we are, and we don't need a woman coming in and judging our system.

Plus, if we don't bring women home, there's never the whole awkward "do I have to offer her coffee" sort of vibe. Making coffee for a girl is basically like getting down on one knee—something I can't even fathom doing.

I actually want to bring Indie back to my flat, though, which is a notion that strikes me as odd. Maybe it's the virginity thing that makes her different because I've never wanted it with any other girl.

I can't explain it and I'm not going to obsess over it. Or make her coffee. Tanner is gone and, right now, I want to see how Indie Porter looks on my bed.

We arrive at my building and take the lift up to my fourth floor flat. As I'm unlocking the front door, she asks, "Are you a good dancer, Camden?"

This question is odd, even for her. "Why do you ask?"

She sighs and leans against the wall just as I open the door. "I envisioned you were tonight when I was dancing with some bloke."

My jaw clenches. "I don't need to hear about you dancing with other guys."

She smirks. "But I was thinking about you so it shouldn't count."

"It counts."

"I think I like this jealous side of you. I might have to use it to my—"

Her snarky comment is cut off by a satisfying yelp as I wrap my arms around her waist and throw her over my shoulder.

"What are you doing?" she squeals as I savour the feel of her bare legs in my hands.

I turn and walk her inside, kicking the door closed with my foot. "Do you think you're smart, talking to me like that?" I ask, completely unable to hide the smile on my face.

Her hair tickles my back as she giggles. "I am quite smart, actually. I skipped three whole grades in primary school. Did you know that?"

"I didn't know that. Tell me then, what did they do to punish clever girls with smart mouths in boarding school?"

"Oh, naughty, naughty things." She giggles again and I have a momentary desire to put her down just so I can see her face when she does it.

"I might need a demonstration." I walk down the hallway and straight to my room, forgoing the polite flat tour, the offering of drinks, and the inane small talk. Our arrangement is for sex and sex alone.

"I might be inclined to oblige." Her voice is breathy when we reach the quiet darkness of my room.

I don't turn the light on. The streetlights streaming in through the white, wooden blinds are plenty bright enough for me to see all I need to see. I want her to feel confident. I want her to feel safe. Her breath is heavy and I can feel her body tense with anticipation.

Instead of tossing her onto my bed like she probably deserves, I slowly slide her down off of my shoulder to the floor beside my bed. I savour every soft curve, peak, and warmth of her body against mine. In her heels, she's eye-level with my chest, which is where her shaky hands and gaze are both glued to.

I tilt her chin to look up at me. "Don't be nervous. We're not going to do this now. Not with you being pissed."

Her thick, mascara-lashed lids bat up at me. I note that her hair looks more wild now, long and loose down her back. "I'm hardly pissed," she defends quietly.

"Still. If you want it to be memorable, you need to be sober, Specs."

"So what are we going to do?" she asks, adjusting her glasses and slumping her shoulders.

My brows arch as I lean down and kiss her. Her lipstick is much lighter than it was when I saw her earlier this evening. She looks more like the Dr. Porter I remember from the hospital.

I pull back from her and murmur, "I want to explore your body." I move over to the side of her neck. "I want to get to know your curves." I crouch down and kiss the swell of her chest. "After all of that…there's nothing holding us back."

"Okay," her voice wavers.

"Does that sound all right?" I ask, gazing down into her eyes and needing to make sure she's up for this. Everything we've done up until now has been very tame. I want to make sure this is still what she wants.

She nods, biting her lip and giving me her glorious consent. My hands immediately reach around her sides and find the zipper on her dress. The noise of its descent is the perfect soundtrack to the raging desire simmering between us.

"So tell me, Indie. How far have you gone before? With…others?" I can't even bring myself to say guys. What is it about this girl that makes me so territorial?

She swallows slowly as I slide the straps of her dress down to her shoulders. I pause my momentum, awaiting her answer.

"I've hit a couple of the highlights."

This makes me smile. "Like what?" The dress drops to the floor.

"Oral?" She says it like a question. I glance down to appreciate her black bra and underwear, my jawbone ticking with desire.

"Giving or receiving?" I whisper against her mouth as my fingers rub along the hem of her panties.

"I've received. But I've never given."

This disappointments me. I would've liked to have been the first to taste her, but my displeasure isn't enough to deter me. "Well, I'm not convinced whoever it was knew what they were doing. And in the interest of research, I'd like to be thorough."

"Okay."

I reach behind me and pull my shirt off over my head, then drop it to the floor. She sucks in a sharp breath when I grab hold of her knickers and slide them down her legs. I continue watching her eyes, bright with arousal as my hands trail up her soft, smooth inner thigh. I can smell her scent already and it's beckoning to me.

I turn to sit her down on the side of my bed and take the opportunity to stroke her hair before laying her backwards. I envisioned her hair splayed across my pillow the first time we met. Now I have her, right here in my room, seconds away from having my lips on her body. While I'm stroking her hair and relishing in the feel of it on my hands, something happens. I didn't notice her eyeing my arousal. I didn't notice her touching my hips. But I definitely notice when she undoes my jeans and pulls me out of my boxers.

She grips my shaft with her small hand and I croak out her name. "Indie?" I close my eyes, trying to remain on my feet, even though my legs want to give out. "What are you doing?"

I look down and she opens her mouth, but not to speak. Her large, thick lips wrap around me, drenching as much as she can fit of me in her mouth. Once she's soaked every inch, she bobs her head along the tip. She's applies the perfect amount of pressure with her lips while her free hand cups my balls, massaging the orgasm building from deep within. It's perfection. There's no way she hasn't done this before. Or maybe I heard it wrong and she has. I don't know. I can't think straight.

"Indie." I cry her name out more forcefully as she tightens her lips around me and quickens her pace. I reach out and wrap her hair around my hand. I follow her thrusts, allowing her to set the pace, and twitch when I hit the back of her throat. I'm a torn man. I want to live in this moment and enjoy what she's doing to me, but I also want to toss her back and slam myself inside of her.

My voice is gravelly when I say, "You need to stop soon. I'm going to come." I force myself to open my eyes and watch what she's doing to me. It doesn't help. It makes it worse. So much worse. "Indie!" I exclaim, cursing the world for how fucking hot she looks with me in her mouth.

Pulling her mouth off of me, she says, "It's okay. I've always wanted to try this."

Wait, what? No fucking way. "I'm going to come," I warn one last time. Right before I tell her I'm going to let go, she drags her teeth along my dick and sucks hard right at the crown.

I erupt. And I think I die a little.

I've had tons of women suck me off before. I've had a handful of them swallow. But what Indie did…is the best blowjob I've ever had.

I'm barely through the aftershocks of my orgasm when I drop down onto my uninjured knee and shove her onto her back. I gaze up at her, spread out on my grey duvet in nothing but a black bra. I want to pay homage to her breasts, but the scent of her is needful to me.

Throwing her legs on top of my shoulders, I waste no time devouring her. Tasting her. Sucking her. Relishing in the hoarse cries she lets out every time I pay special attention to her clit. I find the rhythm she likes, but torment her by bringing her to the edge and backing away, over and over.

I want her to remember this the same way I'll remember what she did to me.

I sink one long finger inside of her, closing my eyes to stop from blowing another load when I imagine how tight she'll feel around me tomorrow. I pump into her a few times, watching her hands flit from her face to the sheets, to her breasts as she climbs higher and higher.

My dick is rock-hard again. She is such a vision. And she has no idea.

I slide a second finger inside of her and press my lips to her, flicking my tongue rapidly. That's all it takes. She explodes, pulsing around my fingers as she comes. Her chest rises and falls in rapid succession as she blinks up at the ceiling a few times.

"Oh my God," are the first understandable words she's uttered since I put my mouth on her. "Are you for real?"

Her words make me smile. *Camden Harris is always fucking real, Specs.*

I slide up on top of her and kiss her ruthlessly, hoping that whatever experimenting she's done with oral in the past is good and forgotten now.

"How was that for a highlight?"

17

Penis Number One, So Not Done

Indie

MY SKIN IS WARM AND TINGLY AS WE LIE TOGETHER IN HIS BED, naked and staring at the ceiling.

"I'm impressed." Cam's voice is low and awestruck as he props his hands behind his head. "For someone who's never given head before, that was like…choreographed excellence."

My cheeks flush at his compliment. "Thank you."

"You really haven't done that before?"

I shake my head and duck beneath the blanket.

"What?" he asks, chuckling and pulling the blanket back. "Tell me."

I sigh. "Belle gave me detailed instructions once and I retain facts forever." I tap my temple. "Once I hear something, it's in the vault. Although, she told me I didn't have to swallow. She said that if a man's cock is in a woman's mouth they've already won the lottery."

He roars with laughter and murmurings of the fact that she has a good point. But I still don't regret swallowing. I had to try it just once. I was also so turned on, I couldn't stop myself.

I roll over to face him, tucking my hands beneath my head.

"That felt kind of awesome."

He glances at me out of the corner of his eye. "Which part?"

"Well, both. Obviously. But I always thought giving it would be something I hated. When women talk about it, they sort of make it seem like a chore. But I loved doing it. It made me feel powerful."

His brows lift with a satisfied smirk. "You literally had my balls in your hand."

"Shut up." I swat him, smiling the entire time. "It felt good to make someone feel that good. You really did like it, right?" My smile fades as I wonder how many other women have done that exact same thing to him, only better. Maybe I was crap at it after all.

"I liked it too much. It felt like you were topping from the bottom there for a second, but we got things evened out in the end I think."

He winks.

I smile.

"This experience was certainly better than my last," I say.

He groans. "I thought I was clear that I don't want to hear about you and other guys."

"Okay, okay, sorry," I wince, recalling the last time in my mind.

It was someone I knew in med school. It happened when we were studying late one night. I didn't even orgasm before he stopped to grab a condom out of his wallet. Then he threw a big fit when I told him I didn't want to have sex.

What Camden did obliterates everything that guy even attempted.

"I'm exhausted," he says, glancing at the clock to see it's after two. "Let's get some sleep. We have a big day tomorrow." He tweaks his brows at me with sexual promise.

Camden rolls toward me to pull my glasses off my face and deposits them behind him on the nightstand. Then he snakes his hand around my waist and pulls me against him so we're front to front. I'm breathing in his chest and have no clue what to do with my hands.

They're all awkward and bent under my chin. He arranges his head on top of mine and lets out a contented sigh as if he's perfectly comfortable, yet I still don't know what the hell to do with my hands.

"Can we...maybe not...cuddle?" My voice is weak, my body frigid.

Camden pulls back and frowns down at me. "Okay. That's a first."

"I don't mean to make it weird, but I like my space when I sleep. It's peculiar because I like the companionship of sleeping next to someone, but I can't seem to get comfortable with the cuddling part." I'm rambling. "It's probably something I should address with a therapist at a later date."

He huffs out a polite laugh. "We don't have to touch, Indie. It's fine."

His voice is flat, revealing no emotion, good or bad, as he rolls over to face away from me. His large shoulders look strong and comforting, but no matter how hard I try, I can't bring myself to want to spoon him. I've never had to deal with this before. The limited encounters with men in my life were brief and I always left afterwards. Experiences with Camden are new on so many levels.

I sit up on my elbow, watching him. His eyes are closed. "Are you mad? You seem mad."

"I'm not mad." He doesn't open his eyes but a smirk tugs at his lips. "You just never cease to surprise me."

I wince. "Is that a good thing? I can't tell."

His low chuckle is genuine. "It's a good thing. I just hope you like surprises, too."

My brows rise. His words sound ominous. And promising. And his tone is decidedly sexual. After all this spontaneity, I'm not sure how this night can be topped. I roll over and exhale with relief.

I don't think he's mad. He gets my weirdness. I feel better. And sated. And venturing on happy.

I think I picked a great Penis Number One.

Drowning

Camden

I AWAKE ON MY SIDE WITH A PAIR OF PALE, NARROW ARMS SNAKED around me, spooning me from behind. One arm is resting on my waist, the other tucked between me and the mattress. A smooth, sculpted leg is draped over my hip, but the grey sheet is hiding all the parts that I acquainted myself with so well last night. For someone who likes space, her subconscious evidently hasn't received the memo.

The morning bathes us in a golden light. Dust motes float in the sunlight slicing through the blinds. A smile stretches across my face as I peek under the sheet to find myself charged and ready for round two. I glance at the clock and see it's not even eight o'clock yet.

But I have a virgin…in my bed.

Last night with Indie was hot, hard, fast, and the perfect stepping-stone. Then, when she didn't want to be too close in bed, a part of me was grateful. I'd somehow slipped into a different place with her and I needed a swift kick in the balls to be reminded this isn't anything more than physical. This is sex. Virgin sex. With an expiration date.

I'm breaking all sorts of rules with Indie. In my entire life, I've never slept with a woman and not had sex. I've never done the pillow talk thing. Now I've done it three times with the same person. I guess I can blame it on the injury, but I'm doing all I can to *not* think of any of that.

Those four days after surgery, my mind was obsessed with football and what my future could look like. How everything for me could be changing soon. Tanner thought I was depressed, but I wasn't. I was consumed. If I'm being completely truthful, there was a part of me that was consumed by Indie, too. I've never let anyone get inside my head so much. When I thought she was manipulating me, I flipped.

But having her here now, like this, naked and having no anxiety over getting caught, no request for space…it's nice. She feels like the first real breath of life I've inhaled since I started playing football so many years ago.

My perfect, redheaded, innocent distraction who feels pretty fucking great pressed up against my backside.

I roll over so we're facing each other, trying to be smooth and not ruffle the bed too much. She sighs with a little hitch in her voice and nuzzles into my chest, still completely out of it. It's way too adorable, so I decide to sex up the moment.

I shift out of her grasp, propping myself on my hand to gaze down at her. Her face is relaxed as she moves into the fetal position, exhaling peacefully and tucking her hands under her chin. She's completely on my side of the bed, and I didn't have much room to begin with.

Biting my lip, I peel back the sheet and feast my eyes on her gloriously naked body. She's curled into a ball so it's mostly just creamy skin and curves; however, her sculpted legs tucked up into her evoke a flashback of them wrapped around my face last night. Plus, that arse…good God. I immediately fantasise about cupping it in the shower, in my kitchen, in the streets. Hell, anywhere she'd let me.

It's all more than enough to get me excited.

I lower my head and blow a cool stream of air along her ribs. She squirms just as I place a soft kiss on her shoulder.

"Cam?" she whispers, her eyes fluttering open. She rolls onto her back, and her face brightens when she sees mine. Her makeup is smudged around her eyes and there are still hints of her red lipstick on her lips. She looks back over her shoulder and frowns at the rest of the empty bed. "I moved in my sleep, didn't I?"

A laugh escapes me. "You could say that."

"Did I wake you?" She looks insecure.

I want to wipe that emotion off her face, so I lean down and nuzzle her breasts. She cradles my head in her hands, and everything about her feels so good.

I turn and place a kiss to her palm. "Wake me any time you want."

I shift myself over top of her, and she opens her legs to allow me room to tuck in. Her lip slips between her teeth as she watches me tilt my head and pull her soft nipple into my mouth. It hardens against my tongue. I look over to see the other one has also perked up and reach out to roll it between my fingers.

"Oh my God," she groans when I roll my hips and press myself into her centre. Her body waves beneath me as her fingers slice through my hair, ruffling the length on top.

"Does that feel good?" I ask.

She nods eagerly.

I shift to the side of her and trail my fingertips around her nipple before cupping the heaviness of her breast in my hand. Her nipples are paler than any I've ever seen before, but perfect in that angelic way she has about her. "Does that feel good?"

She nods again, so I continue moving my fingers down inches of creamy white skin and stop right at the top of her thighs. I teasingly skirt my touch along the top of her slit. "Does that feel good?"

Her hips pump into me and she sighs heavily while nodding her silent answer. I begin to palm her, massaging her smooth swell without slipping inside her folds. She inhales sharply as her feet squirm against the sheets.

She wants more. No more questions necessary.

I slide two fingers inside of her and connect our lips just as she lets out a throaty moan. She grips my head, firmly kissing me back, making no mistake of her gratitude.

My dick throbs against her thigh, and the ache is almost unbearable as she reaches down and grips me in her hand. I need to take my time with her, prep her, prime her, tease her. But then she does that thing with my balls that makes every drop of willpower I have evaporate.

"You need to stop touching me, Indie," I groan.

"Why?" she gasps.

"Because there are things I need to do to make sure you're ready."

She stills instantly now that she knows my full intentions. Swallowing and nodding, she moves her hands away from me to grip the sheets. I make my way down the bed and position my face between her thighs. I am more than pleased to find she's already damp; however, I need to make absolutely certain she's prepped. I press my tongue to her opening and she begins groaning with needy desire.

As my tongue begins moving, her hands find my hair and comb through it in perfect sync with my rhythm. After last night, I already know the places that get her there the fastest, so there will be a lot less teasing this morning.

I slide two fingers back in, massaging her from the inside, relishing in the feel of her on me. She responds loudly and that encourages me to push a third finger in. I pause my tongue assault to focus on widening my touch inside of her. Watching her face, I crook my three digits to hit that special spot that sends most women over the edge.

"Camden," Indie gasps loudly. Her hands fly into her hair in uncontrolled raptures. "I'm going to—"

I bring my thumb up and press hard against the area I know will set her off.

She screams my name again as she reaches down and holds my

hand in place like she's terrified if I move it, it'll all stop. My face breaks into a proud smile at her desperate reaction to my touch. *It's fucking hot.*

When she stops gasping for breath, I move back up her body and whisper into her ear, "Do you want me to fuck you, Indie?"

She looks back at me, eyes wide, lips swollen, hair a mess. "Yes."

My body goes into autopilot. I move off of her and grab a condom out of my nightstand. She sits up on her elbows and watches me roll the slick rubber on. Her body is squirming and needy with the aftershocks of her orgasm. When I finish, I look at her face and expect to see fear, anxiety, or nervousness.

But I don't see any of those things.

She looks ready.

I move back between her legs, resting on my knees and stroking her thighs in comfort. I notice a small twinge in my knee when I bend it that much, so I shift into a better position. I'm not sure this is the kind of rehab my physical therapist had in mind for me, but I did ask about intercourse and he indicated it was a grey area.

I took that as a resounding go ahead.

Indie's eyes are on me as I slide my fingers into her one more time to check and see that she's ready. I position myself between her, rubbing my crown along her to wet the tip and make my entry as smooth as possible.

"Indie," I say and her eyes tear away from the action and land on my face. She puzzles at the serious look I'm giving her. "There's a fine, fine line between the moment it hurts and the moment it feels fucking brilliant."

"Okay," she says breathlessly.

"Are you sure you want to do this?" I ask, giving her one more chance to stop.

"Yes, Camden."

I cup her face in my hand. "Stay with me, Specs, and I'll get you there."

I nudge in a couple of inches and her eyes fly wide. So wide that I slam my lips to hers and kiss her as hard as I can—anything to distract her from the ache she has to be feeling because, if it's this tight around me, it has to be even tighter for her.

Her thighs squeeze around my ribs like a vise. Her hands flit nervously around my face, arms, and shoulders like she doesn't know what to do. I thread our fingers and press them into the mattress by her head. When I pull back to look into her eyes, she gives me a small nod, silently telling me she's okay. My gaze remains on her face as I push the rest of the way into her. Her wide eyes water and it makes me want to stop. It makes me want to pull out and apologise and kiss away the pain, but she keeps nodding and chewing her lip.

I still inside of her as she breathes heavily. "Are you all right?"

"I think so," she replies, squeezing my hands so tightly that I have no choice but to close my eyes from the onslaught of her grip.

"This is that moment, that fine line. It'll start to get better," I promise.

"Okay." Her voice is gravelly, so I kiss her again, comforting her with my lips, moving down her jaw and neck and on to the swells of her breasts. I suck each nipple and give her a little more time to adjust to me being inside of her.

When I move back up to her mouth, I thrust my tongue between her lips and match the movement inside of her. She's so snug, it's overwhelming. And painful. But it's also so great.

It's like the reason you groan after taking a bite of a delicious dessert. Your taste buds can't handle so much goodness without some outward reaction.

Her hands finally relax in mine so I let them go. They instantly begin roaming over my body more purposefully than before. She drags her nails down my back. I thrust myself in and out, her body swaying with mine as she welcomes me more with every thrust.

I need this experience to be better than great for her. It has to be perfect.

I continue to pump into her, more deliberately this time, watching every inch of me disappear inside of her over and over again. Every time I hit the deepest point, her cries grow louder and louder. She grabs my arse, cupping me against her, so I pull her hips up to meet my thrusts more deeply.

When I decide to reach down between our bodies and touch her clit with my fingers, she begins moaning.

Like, really moaning.

I sync my hand to slide on her nub with each plunge. Within seconds, I can feel her tighten around me.

"Camden!" She screams my name, her orgasm surprising us both. Her eyes find mine and they're wide and wild, terrified and grateful. It's an intense look—one that pierces right through me and breaks something deep inside of me.

Unable to withstand another minute of her expression, I crash my lips to hers, swirling a silent reassurance that she's not alone. I'm right here with her and, even though this isn't my first time, it's still important. I still feel what's happening.

And then…and then…when she clutches me to her…trembling and thanking me for giving this to her…

I'm drowning.

I'm drowning in deep, dark, delirious destiny. I'm in a place I never want to leave. A place I never want to say goodbye to. A place I never want to let go. Just sinking further and further into a world I've never known.

19

It's Just Coffee, Bucko

Indie

HEAVY BREATHS, SLICKENED BODIES, AND PUMPING HEARTS ARE the three most outwardly obvious things in the room right now. The less obvious is the ache between my legs.

The pain.

It's a raw throb that's positively tortuous. How do teenage girls get through this with guys who don't know what they are doing?

After the sharp, initial part was over, the build of my orgasm helped mask the pain. Now that it's all over and I've come back to the land of the living, I feel it everywhere.

Regardless, the soreness doesn't discredit the part when it got good. Really good. Deep, penetrative, mind-blowingly good. The entire experience was nothing like I had imagined.

From the look in Camden's eyes to his tender touches and words of affirmation, it was all surprising. Very unlike what I had expected from a Penis Number One.

At one point, I swear he looked at me as if he could see my soul. It was unnerving. But I suppose it's normal to feel some natural connection when your bodies are literally joined in the most carnal way possible. He was inside of me after all.

Plus, I know virgin sex is huge on a bloke's bucket list, so that had to be all his expression was about at the end. And that is precisely why I wanted my first time to be with someone experienced. Because, regardless of all those strange feelings, it was still *incredible*. The whole area between my thighs is raw and needy as if I want more but can't possibly take it. I can now say that "hurt so good" is an expression I fully endorse.

Camden remains collapsed on top my body with his face buried in the pillow beside my head. His muscled back rises and falls with each lung intake.

"Are you okay?" he mumbles into the pillow, finally showing signs of life.

"Yeah," I reply, noting him softening inside me.

He rolls over and stands up, naked and completely unashamed of his softening erection. I feel awkward and unsure what to do until he bends over and scoops me up in his arms.

I wrap my hands around his neck and ask, "What are we doing?" But he doesn't answer.

He carries me down the hallway and into the loo, where he sets me down on the counter and turns the water on. He grabs two towels out of the cabinet, places them on the warming bar, and opens the glass shower door. He avoids eye contact with me as his head motions for me to get in.

So I do.

Once encased in the small glass space with him, I feel a bit awkward. He hands me the shampoo and finally looks at me with a meek, sort of small half smile.

Okay, so we're showering together as if this is a normal thing we do. He holds my shoulders and positions me so I'm beneath the stream. Then he tips my head back, using his hands to help soak all of my hair.

And now he's washing my hair.

When I close my eyes to rinse out the shampoo, I feel his lips on my collarbone but can't open them to see him yet. He moves up my neck, dragging his chin along my neckline with every kiss.

We switch places and I attempt to help him wash his hair. With our height difference, it's not as easy for me, though.

He loads up a sponge and rubs soap all over my body. I flinch when he gently swipes it between my legs.

"Sensitive?" he asks quietly. "Or does it hurt?"

I swallow and drop my chin, embarrassed by how badly I want more when I'm so clearly hurting down there. "Both. Sensitive on the outside." He nods and pulls his lips between his teeth.

After we finish rinsing, he cuts the water and we step out to towel off. He casually wraps one around his waist, leaving his chest damp with water.

Camden Harris in a towel is still a sight to behold.

He begins brushing his teeth and offers me a toothbrush with paste on it, too.

"This isn't Tanner's, is it?" I ask, joining him at the counter.

He shakes his head and passes it over. We brush our teeth next to each other like two normal folks. I mean, never mind he just took my virginity and gave me an earth-shattering orgasm to boot.

The aching pain he's left behind just makes me want more. So much more. I'm glad I agreed to adjust our arrangement. These next few days are sure to be the best Tequila Sunrise moments yet.

After we rinse off our toothbrushes, he finally speaks again. "I want to try something."

He moves toward me, my butt hitting the countertop as I turn to watch him. "What?"

"Just trust me." His gaze drops down to my body as he turns me so my back is pressed against his front and we can see our towel covered bodies reflecting in the mirror.

He slowly unravels mine and then his own. Staring at our naked reflections in the mirror, my first instinct is to cover myself; however, the heated look of his eyes on me is so intense, I automatically arch into him.

His hands reach around and cup both of my breasts. "Do you know how hot you are, Specs?" he whispers in my ear while kneading my breasts in his hands.

Unable to find my voice, I swallow hard and my breaths come out shaky.

"Your body is like a sweet, juicy morsel that begs me to fuck it." I moan softly when he rolls each nipple between his fingers.

He stops his assault on my nipples and trails his fingers slowly downward over my abdomen, finally stopping at the area between my legs.

"I'm going to touch you here. Right on your sweet little pussy." His hands spread my thighs apart. "But don't worry. This won't hurt."

"Okay," I all but moan, the combination of his naughty words and the growth of him pressing into my back nearly sending me over the edge all on their own.

Then he's touching me again, just on the clit this time. His skilled motions take an embarrassingly small amount of time to get me off. I was still so keyed up and raring to go, it isn't more than thirty seconds before I am coming apart all over.

When I'm done crying out for the man upstairs, Cam smiles, kisses the side of my neck, and murmurs, "I think I found your button." Then he strides out of the bathroom without a look back.

After a moment of confusion, I grip my towel around me and make my way back to his room to find him putting fresh sheets on his bed.

He watches me carefully as I move to the other side of the bed to help. He's found a pair of shorts now, thank God. Maybe now I can think straight for once.

As I pull down the corner of the fitted sheet, I can't help but ponder over what the next couple of days will be. This feels more intimate than I thought it would. More personal. Not like sleeping with a player. Unless this is all a part of his well-practised game?

"Are you going to tell me what has you chewing your lip like it's a piece of bubblegum?" he asks, tossing the pillows back on the bed and launching the last one at me.

I catch it and concurrently release my lip. "Probably not."

He huffs once. "Am I going to have to force it out of you?"

He seems less introspective after our bathroom antics. "I don't have to spill all my thoughts to you just because you say so."

"After I fuck you for the first time you do." His face looks cocky but his eyes look tense. "Don't tell me it wasn't good. I'm not stupid."

"It was better than good," I offer and definitely mean it.

"Then why the sour face?"

I know I won't be able to get away from his question. Honestly, he deserves an answer. I don't want him to think that I didn't like it. "It just felt…different than what I imagined."

"Different how?" he asks.

"Nothing. This is daft." I quirk a brow at him. "That was the best sex of my life, Camden Harris. Is that what you need to hear?"

"That was the only sex of your life, Indie Porter."

The sound of a buzzer interrupts the tension brewing between us. Camden looks at the time. "Fuck."

"What?"

"I completely forgot."

"Forgot what?"

"My sister was coming over."

"Vi? Oh God. Should I hide?" My eyes are wide with worry. I don't want his sister to know what's going on, no matter how psychic his family is. His brother last night was one thing. We were in a public setting. But his sister seeing me here is a whole different thing. I'm still his doctor for the next three weeks. I'm going to be operating on him. This is bad. This is very, very bad.

"No. You're not going to hide," he says as he rustles in his dresser for some clothes.

"Cam, I wouldn't feel right operating on you if your sister knows we've—"

"Had the best sex of your life?" he finishes.

"Yes!"

"She's not going to care. What she would care about is me hiding a girl in my closet. My sister would castrate me. And she'll know. There's no use hiding it."

"This is awful," I groan. His family is everywhere. How do people live like this? "What should I do?"

"Put some clothes on to start."

He tosses me a pair of compression tights and a T-shirt, reminding me of our tryst in the hospital bathroom. Gosh, that feels like ages ago now.

"Hey," Vi's voice calls from the entry.

I yank the shirt down over my head and bounce on one foot as I shove my legs through the leggings. "She has her own key?"

He shrugs as if it's totally normal for his family to waltz in and out of his flat.

"Where are you—Oh!" Vi comes face-to-face with Camden as he tries to exit his room to stop her before she walks in. He puts his hand on the doorframe, blocking her view of me, but she drops her head and catches me adjusting the band on the leggings. "Well, hello to the both of you. I didn't realise you had company, Cam."

"Hello, Vi." I give a self-conscious wave, wishing like hell my hair wasn't still wet from our shower. I wince when I see Cam's is still wet as well.

"Hiya, Dr. Porter." She grins lasciviously. "Nice to see you again."

"I was just—"

"Dr. Porter was just making a house call." Camden turns away from the door and strides over to stand beside me. "My knee needed tending to."

Vi looks at the both of us skeptically as he throws a casual arm around me. "I'm sure that's not the only thing." She cuts Cam a glare. Her tone isn't chastising, it's laughing. It's laughing a lot. She's taking the piss as if this is something she sees from her brother on a regular basis.

This is far too embarrassing. I don't want her to look at me as if I'm one of those girls, even though I am. I know this isn't going anywhere…and I'm okay with that. But I'm not okay with nice people like Vi getting the wrong impression of me, as if I'm a slut who bangs her patients on a regular basis. I need to leave before I do something stupid like mentally justify my Penis List…out loud.

"I'll be going now so you two can have your…erm…family time." I shimmy out from under Camden's arm and wince at the fact that I'm going to have to put my heels on with these tights.

"Do you like pancakes?" Vi asks as I grab my shoes up off the floor and move past her. "They are Swedish so they're better than regular pancakes. They're like a French Crepe and a pancake had a Swedish baby."

I pause in the doorway, staring back at Vi with Camden standing behind her. He looks as if he's trying to hide a smirk and failing miserably. I think I die a little. "I'd really rather not."

"Hush. You must be hungry."

Camden surprises the both of us by barking out a laugh. "Oh yes, she worked up an appetite all right."

My eyes turn to saucers just as Vi twirls on her heel and punches Camden right in the abs, catching him completely off guard. He topples over, squatting on the floor and gasping for air. "Fuck, Vi. What happened to your fists of ineffectual fury?"

She crosses her arms and smiles proudly. "This baby gives me super powers. One of which includes smelling an arsehole when I see one." She looks back to me. "Come on, Dr. Porter. It's lunch time and you're getting pancakes."

After insisting she call me Indie, we make our way down the hall and into the kitchen. It's the first time I realised that I've only seen Cam's bedroom, the hallway, and the bathroom since I arrived here last night. It's a standard bachelor pad. Not much for décor, but the furniture all looks really comfortable.

Camden says he has a call to make, so I sit at the kitchen island and watch Vi busy herself by making coffee and food.

"Is there anything I can do?" I ask, feeling like a prat just sitting here.

"Nope. I made these yesterday, so I'm just popping them in the oven to reheat." She moves confidently around the kitchen as if she's cooked here before. When she's done, she sidles up beside me. "Our mum was from Sweden, so this recipe is truly authentic. They are impossible not to like. I make them all the time for the boys."

I smile softly. "That's a lovely way to remember her."

A fleeting look of surprise mars her face, but she's quick to conceal it. "So…you know about our mum?"

I open my mouth to defend my remark, realising how what I just said was so incredibly personal and horribly inappropriate. "No… erm…not much. Just that you were all young when she passed. I'm so sorry. I shouldn't have said anything."

"Don't be sorry." She looks off into the distance. "We probably don't really talk about her enough. I've been thinking about her a lot more now that I'm starting my own family."

"How far along are you?" I eye her abdomen as if it would have grown since I last saw her.

"Just hit fourteen weeks yesterday." She touches the nonexistent bulge. "I never even knew what the weeks meant before. I'd hear someone say how many weeks they were and ask, 'How many months is that?'" She laughs and I laugh with her. "I'm excited to see how my brothers do as uncles. It should be a riot."

"You and your family all seem so close." I vaguely wonder what that would feel like.

My grandmother was so distant even when I was home. My parents were even worse. The Harris family all seem to be on top of each other constantly. Ruling as a committee on the surgery; hanging out in Cam's patient room so long they got into a fight; Vi having a key to Cam's flat. It's crazy.

Her brows lift. "We are…Sometimes annoyingly so." Her blue eyes are bright on me now. "So are you off for the rest of the weekend then?"

"Yeah, as second year residents, we work really long stretches. Then we get four or five days off. I go back to work on Thursday."

"Oh good, you'll be back in plenty of time for Cam's surgery. We're all ready to get this over with and see him back on the pitch. Although, who knows? It could be a different stadium by then. He's so talented. I'm really excited to see what the next few days bring for him."

"Different stadium?"

She lifts her brows. "Arsenal is a great step up. If he got an offer from them? It would be a long time coming for him. I'll miss watching him at Tower Park, but at least he'd still be based in London. It's just hard because we all grew up in Tower Park"

She continues on about the magic of Tower Park Stadium and watching her brothers play together. While I appreciate her vigour for the sport their family has built their lives around, the voice in the back of my head wants to speak up. Healing, refocusing, and rehabbing should be Cam's focus, not his contract.

I bite my tongue, though. Partly because I genuinely like Vi, but mostly because, right now, I'm not his doctor. I'm certainly not his girlfriend. I'm just someone he's having sex with, no strings attached.

Disappointment creeps into my soul over the powerless feeling mixing my professional career and my social life affords me.

"…What are yours and Camden's plans for the weekend?" Vi's question snaps me out of my internal musings.

"I um…er—"

"I can think of aerobic exercises we could try," Camden says, his voice surprising us both from the kitchen doorway behind us.

"Cam," Vi starts, pinching the bridge of her nose. "Can you maybe, just once, not be the gravy-sucking sex pig you'd like us all to think you are?"

His lips squish off to the side as he contemplates her question. "No can do, Vi. I like seeing that lightning bolt vein pop on your forehead every time I say something that sets you off."

She rolls her eyes and stands up to check the food. Camden flops down on the stool beside me, spreading his legs wide so our thighs brush together. He waggles his brows at me, and I hate myself a little bit for smirking.

"You know what would be brilliant?" Vi asks, snapping our attention away from each other. "Camden, you should give Indie a tour of Tower Park. The guys are all away this weekend so it'll be dormant. Tower Park completely empty is even better than packed to the roof with roaring fans…It's…It's magic." She shakes as if she's just given herself the chills.

"It is magic," Camden agrees, his brow rising with a naughty gleam to it.

I frown at his weird expression. "Sounds nice?" I have no idea what to say in response. A tour of Tower Park sounds rather date-like and that is definitely not a part of our arrangement. I'm feeling twitchy with all this familial meddling.

"It's better than nice. You'll see," Vi says, placing a mug of coffee in front of me.

Camden's eyes lose all good humour as he stares at the cup in my hands as if Vi's just given away his favourite toy. I silently offer it to him. He scowls and shakes me away as if he wouldn't touch this cup with a ten-foot pole. It's all very peculiar, which is nothing new for Cam.

After we finish eating, I head down the hall to Camden's room to switch back into my dress from last night. With Vi projecting all this girlfriend type warmth at me, I had to get away. Add in Cam's weirdness over coffee and I'm bursting for some space.

When I come out, he's propped up on the counter by himself as if he was waiting for me.

"Your sister leave?" I ask, looking around the room.

"Yep. Her and Hayden are going baby gear shopping or something."

I nod and stare down at my feet. "I think I need to go home and get some clothes and, I don't know…just relax a bit."

Camden frowns. "We don't have a lot of time to waste here, Specs."

"I know but…erm…"

"What?" he prods.

"Well, I'm sore for one." I feel a flush of embarrassment move over me. There's an ache between my legs that is not all together pleasant. I'm afraid that if I stay we'll only make it worse.

The corner of his mouth tilts. "Where exactly are you sore?"

"Shut up, you know where." I adjust my glasses. "And I'm not sure we should do this Tower Park thing your sister suggested."

He shoves himself off the counter and folds his arms over his chest. "Why not?"

"Because it sounds like a date and that's not what we're supposed to be doing here." My lips form a thin line as I try to gain some semblance of control back over this plan of mine.

"I'm aware of what we're doing."

"Oh…well—"

"I have plans for you, Specs." He moves toward me and pushes me up against the frame of the doorway. Back in my heels, I reach just below his chin now. One of his hands cups my waist and the other snakes around and palms my arse, bringing me into him. "You see, football and sex are interchangeable for me, and fucking you at Tower Park is going to be fun…for both of us." He waggles his eyebrows, barely lightening the mood of his hot hold on me.

My groin actually pulses with need and it hurts. The wickedness of his mouth, the promise of his firm grip, and the challenging twinkle in his eyes excites every part of me.

I smile. "Well, when you put it like that."

26 Dirty Hot

Indie

After making firm plans for tomorrow and leaving Camden's flat, I couldn't wait to postmortem things with Belle. Growing up, I never had friends to confide in so she has certainly become my sounding board. Plus, since she created the Penis List with me, it's only natural that she earns some dirty details.

"Oh my God, you look different," Belle says as she slides into the velvet green booth of our favourite pub in Bethnal Green, Old George. It's a renovated 18th century pub with exposed brick, mismatched furniture, and a cool, dark atmosphere. The hipster bartenders with swirlie mustaches fit right in with the vintage décor.

"I do not look different, do I?" I hold my cheeks because I can feel the heat of my blush.

Her dark eyes widen. "I bet if you stood up and walked, you'd look like one of those cowboys from *Brokeback Mountain*."

I frown. "Why would you say *Brokeback Mountain*?"

Her shoulders lift. "I dunno. It's the only cowboy movie I can think of that has a lot of *riding*." She waggles her eyebrows suggestively.

I shake my head at my severely strange friend and hand her my glass of red that I ordered while waiting for her.

"So how was it? How did you leave it? How big is he? Did you spend the night? Or did you go home right after?" She takes a big gulp and hands my glass back to me while gesturing to the sever to bring another.

"Down, Sheba," I jest. "Let's start with what's most important." I lean in and whisper over my wine glass, punctuating every word, "The sex was intense. Intensely good. Intensely fun. Intensely hot. Intensely overwhelming. Just…very intense."

Her eyes are on fire with barely contained excitement. "Sounds intense."

"But it was also sweeter than I expected." I take a sip, contemplating everything in my head. As mind-blowing as everything was, he did confuse my Penis List a bit.

"What do you mean?" Belle asks.

"He was gentler than what I expected. I'm not complaining, but in the hospital, he was all cocky, arrogant, demanding playboy. This morning when we did it, he was patient, calm, and attentive. There was no spanking or throwing me up against a wall…or anything horribly naughty like I thought a typical Penis Number One would be like."

Belle rolls her eyes as a bartender hands her a glass of red. She doesn't even look up. "I wouldn't have wanted that to happen during your first time anyway, Indie! That would have been terrible. You have to build up to that stuff."

"I know. But I just…I don't know…There were moments he looked at me as if…"

"As if what?"

"As if he was deeply connected to me. It was…unnerving."

Her brows lift. "The guy is good."

"What do you mean?"

"I mean, he's a master. Only the best players know that if you can make a woman feel more than just the physical during sex, it makes everything better. He's obviously very experienced."

"Well, that's what we wanted, right?" I ask, feeling a strange pull in my belly at the fact that I'm reading into him so much. Even if the way he's doing it with me isn't unique, I'm not complaining. I checked a very important box today. And by box, I mean my vagina.

"Right! This is all good. This sounds perfect. So how did you leave it?"

"Well, we sort of fooled around afterwards in the bathroom."

"You slut! Continue."

I laugh. "The bathroom stuff was hot. Like, crazy masculine hot. He talked dirty and only used his hands on my clit, nothing more. I thought I was going to pass out."

"I'm hating you a little bit right now."

Ignoring her remark, I add, "After all of that, I was sore, so we both agreed a night apart would be good. But we made a date to see Tower Park tomorrow and continue our *arrangement* there."

"Like screwing at Tower Park?" She starts to giggle when I smile and nod. "This all sounds perfect."

"It kind of is. But God, it's so hard. My vagina is like…awakened or oversexed or something. It's tender and I'm hyperaware of it, which only makes me want to have more sex."

Belle shoots me a knowing smile. "You're like how a person is when they first get Netflix. They can't stop binge-watching all the shows. It's quite cute." She giggles again affectionately.

"He got weird at lunch, though. His sister stopped by unexpectedly with food. I thought it would be awkward, but she was great. He was fine at first, but then he got cagey. He kept eyeing my coffee. At first I thought maybe he was against caffeine because he's so dedicated to his health, but he had a cup, too. He kept staring at me over the rim of his mug the entire time. I can't wrap my head around it."

Her nose scrunches. "Was it a sentimental mug?"

"I don't think so."

"That's odd. But he still wants to screw you at Tower Park?"

"Yeah."

"Then that's all that matters. Forget the rest. You're in it for the sex. Not the coffee." She winks naughtily at me.

When I get back to my flat, a strange sensation overcomes me.

I kind of miss Camden.

It's so stupid because analytically I know I don't want anything more from him. We're just screwing. But he's so much fun that I can't help but wish he were here.

I grab my mobile to send him a text.

Me: So teach me about this sexting that all the kids rave about.

Camden: Who is this?

Me: Shut up.

Camden: Gran, I told you to stop making me explain the millennials to you.

I burst out laughing so loud that I cover my mouth in embarrassment, even though I'm lying here by myself.

Me: Your gran sounds more fun than mine.

Camden: Actually, I never knew her. She passed away before I was born.

Me: That's too bad. But if all grans are like mine, you're not missing out. Mine was glacial cold.

Camden: Luckily you turned out pretty hot regardless.

I smile.

Me: So back to this sexting…

Camden: I think I can teach you better in person. Maybe I should come over.

Me: No way. My vagina can't take it.

Camden: No funny business. I promise. I'm saving up for Tower Park.

I hesitate to respond. I want him to come over. I want him to come immediately. But this is all supposed to be about sex, and if we're not having sex, there's absolutely no reason we should hang out. I can't get wrapped up in Penis Number One. I have goals and a list and more penises to try in the near future.

Cam: Get out of your head, Specs. We have five days. We should be able to do with those days as we'd like.

I bite my lip.

Me: Okay.

Thirty minutes later, a rather cosy looking Camden Harris stands on my doorstep in sweats and a soft white T-shirt. His blonde hair is smooth and floppy on his head. His eyes are blue and warm as they drink in my own cosy pyjamas that consist of leggings and a pink camisole. Just looking at him, I already regret the pain between my legs and the fact that we can't have sex again yet.

He grins lasciviously and props himself on the doorframe. "I knew you couldn't say no to me. I'm too irresistible."

"Oh, shut up," I growl and close the door behind him.

He hands me a bottle of Prosecco and I get us situated on my Murphy bed with some crisps, drinks, and a DiCaprio film on the telly.

I set pillows up behind us on the wall so we're sitting up, and I adjust my glasses before taking a drink.

Camden watches me carefully. "How many pairs of eyeglasses do you own?"

My brows lift and touch my basic wire frames I currently have on. These are my nighttime eyewear—the ones I leave on my bedside table every night. "I think twenty now. I had twenty-one, but a patient broke a pair last month when I was setting a bone."

"Ouch." He winces. "Good thing you had a spare."

"Yep," I grin and nibble on a crisp.

"Is there a reason you have so many?" He takes a sip of his drink.

I roll my eyes. "Yes, but it's daft."

He frowns and a low rumble comes from his chest. "You say a lot of things about yourself are daft, do you know that?" His eyes pin me with a serious glower.

"No." I frown back.

"Well, you do, and you should stop because I never agree." He angles toward me and bends his large leg up, watching me expectantly. "Now tell me why you have so many eyeglasses. I'm sure there's a reason."

"All right." I pull my glasses off and stare at them while I speak, a bit disarmed by his adamant interest. "So in school, there was this girl named Sinique Simon. Everyone always wanted to be her. She could sing like Beyoncé and spoke like four languages. She could even do the splits so far that she touched the bottom of her foot to the back of her head."

"Impressive." His eyes widen as I slide my glasses back on. "You should give it a go."

I whack him on the arm and an involuntary smile spreads across my face. "I can see why your sister hits you so much."

He chuckles. "It's all a part of my charm."

"Anyway," I continue, "Sinique always wore the coolest sunglasses, even in class. And I guess it was sometime after med school when things started to change for me. I felt different on the inside, so I wanted to represent that on the outside." I adjust my frames again with a sheepish smile. "It's silly, but I didn't want to blend in anymore. I wanted to have oodles of glasses so that every day I could select a pair that suited my mood." I shrug.

He reaches out and tucks a piece of wayward hair behind my ear, and I feel warmth radiate between us. His face is serious when he asks, "What made you feel different on the inside?"

I swallow, my cheeks heating a bit with embarrassment. "I suppose Belle, maybe? My friend from the club. She's a doctor, too. I met her in med school and she was always urging me to try new things. I didn't have anyone like her in my life before."

He glowers at my last word but doesn't push it. "Well, they all suit you." He leans in to drop a soft kiss on my neck and murmurs, "You're very colourful, Indie Porter." He lingers for a moment, running his nose along the length of my collarbone. When he finally pulls back, he sighs as if he's just feasted on the most delicious bouquet of flowers.

The look in his eyes makes me squirm. It's completely open and unprotected, devoid of any Penis Number One characteristics. We need to get back to our arrangement.

"So when are you going to teach me about this sexting?" I ask, turning on my side to face him. "This isn't a movie and cuddle date here. I have goals with you, you know."

His brows lift. "I'm great at scoring goals, Specs. Don't you worry."

I giggle.

He looks forward and adds, "And sometimes being spontaneous in life can be a great adventure. You don't always have to stick to a plan." He turns to watch me for my reaction but apparently isn't happy with what he sees. Rolling his eyes, he sets his tumbler down. "Get out your mobile."

I could almost giggle with excitement over how this could go. He slides down the bed on his back, his mobile clasped in his hands. I mirror him so we're lying beside each other but both focusing on our mobiles.

I get the first text.

Camden: What are you wearing?

I giggle. "Well, have a look, why don't you?"

He smirks and shakes his head as he waggles his mobile as if that's the only way we can communicate right now.

Camden: I'm in my boxers.

I read the text and, out of the corner of my eye, see him slide his sweats off and yank his shirt off over his head. He's now laid out, chiseled and gleaming in my dim lamp lighting.

Me: I'm in my knickers.

I too slip off my leggings. Then I sit up and pull off my cami. I reach behind myself and glance over my shoulder to see if he's watching. I'm pleased when he is as I unclasp my bra and fling it to the floor.

He inhales sharply when I lie back down and squeeze my breasts together while gripping my mobile.

Camden: How do your breasts feel?

I huff a soft laugh and then bite my lip. Closing my eyes with embarrassment, I steel myself to reach down and cup one breast in my hand. I roll my nipple between my fingers and hear him tsk between his teeth.

Camden: Are you wet?

Oh my God.

Not wanting to be too chicken, I grip my mobile against my chest and slide my free hand down inside my knickers. I swipe a few times and feel my arse rise off the bed with excitement.

"Yes," I groan, closing my eyes and picturing him.

"Mobile, Specs." His voice is coarse and laboured as he watches me.

I nod and pull my hand out and bring it back to my keypad.

Me: I'm soaked. Are you hard?

I watch in gleeful delight as his hand reaches down into his boxers and pulls himself free. He is long and proud as he strokes himself, the tip glistening with promise. I immediately want to wrap my mouth around it, but I have a feeling if I do, I'll lose the game.

Camden: You make me harder than any woman I've ever met.

Me: Bet you say that to all the girls.

Camden: Touch yourself again.

I slip my fingers inside of myself again, and it becomes a huge battle between closing my eyes in ecstasy or watching Camden's ripped arm pump himself faster and faster.

Me: I want to taste you.

Camden: I can still taste you from last night.

Me: I want to fuck you again.

Camden: Soon, Specs. Very soon.

I grind into my hand and flick my clit the way I remember Camden doing to me this morning. The sensation causes me to cry out as I feel the build coming.

Camden: I'm going to come on you.

His text is the dirtiest thing he's sent me so far, but the hope of him ending this texting and actually touching me excites me so much that I respond immediately.

Me: Yes, please.

The bed dips as Camden moves to straddle me. I slide up the wall so I'm no longer lying flat, allowing him to rub his crown between my breasts. I squeeze them together with my biceps to form some pressure around him while his other hand drops his mobile and reaches to find my aching centre.

Two fingers disappear inside of me and I moan, grabbing hold of him in my hands and taking over the movement in front of me. He gasps at my touch and uses his thumb on my clit, doing that firm sideways motion again.

"Oh my God, Cam," I exclaim, pumping myself against his hand. His fingers on me are so much more effective than my own. I cry out another time when my release catches me completely off guard. "Yes!"

I grip him so hard in my hands when I orgasm that he yells, "Fuck!" Then his warm release spasms all over my chest.

I open my eyes and look up to find Camden with a sexy smirk on his face as he gazes down at the display he's made. His fingers slip out of my centre and he sits back on his haunches.

"Another shower?" he asks, waggling his brows.

I giggle and shake my head. "Ye think?"

21 Challenge, Accepted

Camden

It's nearing five o'clock by the time I get to Indie's flat to take her to Tower Park the next day. Last night with her is what I call dirty hot. It was exactly what I needed after the overwhelming feelings I had during our first time together.

I took a girl's virginity once when I was seventeen. She was sixteen and we did it when her parents weren't home. But I don't remember it feeling so…emotional. Maybe Indie is just as expressive as she is responsive, and that's what I was reacting to? I don't know, but bloody hell, that felt different than what I'm used to.

When my traitorous sister gave her coffee, I knew I needed to get control of the situation. Having coffee in the Harris house with a girl who's not blood-related is like picking out china patterns together. Way too far, Vi. Way too far.

But when Indie messaged me about sexting last night, I thought a down and dirty tryst that involved me leaving when we were done would get us right back on track. And it did. She didn't seem bothered when I left after our shower. She seemed relieved.

Which is how it should be.

I don't do relationships. I just like sex. I don't see it as using women. I see it as appreciating them. At worst, I'll be remembered as that footballer who shagged them once and taught them what great sex feels like. Some women accept that notion better than others.

This arrangement just feels different because it's happening more than once. That's all.

Indie opens the door and my eyes drink her in. It's been great fun seeing what she looks like outside of the hospital. Tonight, she's wearing a pair of tiny denim shorts and a thin white tank top with buttons down the chest. Her top is covered with a red plaid, long sleeve shirt that she's left unbuttoned with the sleeves rolled up. The outfit is topped off with her red-framed glasses.

The glasses are the same ones she left in my hospital room after the second night she slept with me. I returned them to her before she left my flat yesterday. I chose not to mention the fact that I am pretty sure Dr. Prichard noticed them that day at the hospital. Indie is already so paranoid about people finding out about us that I didn't want to add fuel to the fire.

Plus, I don't think Dr. Fuckwad is the type to blow the whistle on Indie—mostly because he wants to fuck her. There's not a doubt in my mind about that fact. But he knows that if he wants a shot, he has to stay on the right side of this. No one wants to fuck a snitch.

"You look good enough to eat…out." I bend over to drop a kiss on her lips as my hands find their way to her backside, taking a cheeky squeeze.

She blushes and tucks her long red hair behind her ears. I'm pleased to see she left it down again. "Another pig moment…How novel." She smiles at me in a way that tells me she likes my shocking comments. She gets me. "You look good, too."

I'm wearing dark jeans and a navy T-shirt. It's pretty much my standard everyday clothing that's not a football kit. I'm not into fashion. Never have been. Gareth has a stylist now, who purchases everything he wears. He brushes it off like they're nothing more than an errand runner, but I know the prat prides himself on how he's dressed when the tabloids get shots of him.

"Are you ready?" I ask, eyeing her creamy, muscular legs and wondering if it would be a better idea to push her inside right now and mess up our plans for the night.

"Yeah. I'm intrigued, actually. I've never been to a stadium."

"Good," I say and follow her up the stairs to the street where I hail down a cab.

Tower Park is only a mile away but her brown-heeled ankle boots don't look up for the walk. Plus, the less time we spend doing this tour, the more time we get to tour each other.

When Vi proposed the idea, my first thought was sex. It didn't even occur to me that it would be considered a date. I just pictured Indie spread out on the pitch and me slamming myself into her. I've been sucked off at Tower Park by a couple different fans in the past, but shagging someone there will be a first for me as well.

I instruct the cab driver to drop us at the private entrance of the stadium where I have keys to get in through a small door. I suggested grabbing dinner first, but Indie is paranoid about someone from the hospital seeing us. She only agreed to Tower Park after I assured her that no one would be around and we'd have the place to ourselves.

Indie's eyes are wide and eager as she takes in the expansive structure all around us. It is rather grand, but this entrance is less so. Unfortunately, there's no other way for me to get her in when it's not fully staffed.

Grabbing her hand, I pull her through the dimly lit concrete hallway. The ceiling is low and I have to duck from some of the light fixtures.

"Is this where I go to die?" Indie mock whispers.

"Yes, Indie," I reply. "I get murdery with all my best girls."

She giggles and it makes me smile. The comfort between us in such a short amount of time is nice. It's easy. This whole arrangement is so easy. No drama. Most girls are crazy with the drama. Indie is unlike any of them.

I stop right before turning the corner and look at her. "Okay. So around the corner is the home-team entrance tunnel." Her eyes fly wide. "You can't miss it when we walk by so I'm going to show it to you before everything else. I'm kind of fucking you with no foreplay here, so just promise me you'll appreciate it."

"Okay." She smiles brightly, but then her face crumples with worry. "But not like...actual fucking, right?"

Her innocence is hot. I cup her face in my hands and kiss her, softly flicking my tongue in her mouth just because I like to shock her. Also, I actually ache to taste her again. I'm pleased when I discover that she still tastes like lemons, even outside the hospital. I pull away and murmur, "Is that a request?"

She chews on her lip.

Laughing, I say, "We'll save the exhibitionist stuff for day five, Specs." I throw my arm around her. "But I won't judge if you come a little."

Pulling her around the corner toward the solid concrete tunnel that's painted in bright white, I can't help but squint at the light pouring in from the end. I hear her inhale and hold her breath as I walk her down the long stretch. I don't say anything. I never say anything inside this tunnel.

Whenever I get angry at the sport of football, I remind myself of this feeling—this simple walk through a tunnel. Every time I feel defeated, frustrated, overwhelmed, or over-worked, none of it seems as bad when I remember how *this* feels.

We break through the opening and the London sun is low, casting a warm glow on the entire stadium. Across the pitch, one whole side of the stadium spells out TOWER PARK on white painted chairs. The grass is a lush green, and the seats are old and wooden. This entire stadium is over one hundred years old. It reeks of history.

We walk to the corner of the pitch and Indie stops suddenly, bends over, and takes off her heels. I stare at her for a minute, the image of her bare toes wriggling in the grass overwhelming me. It's completely unnecessary to take off her shoes. It's just grass. We wear studs on the pitch every day. But something tells me she's not doing it for fear of hurting the grass. She's simply showing respect.

How? How does someone like her think to do something like that? She's not even a proper football fan. She's just a doctor. She's just a girl I want to fuck, but she keeps doing things that make her so…*different*.

I'm still gobsmacked when she reaches for my hand, silently asking me to take her out to the centre of the pitch.

I finally snap out of my trance when we reach the middle circle. Pride radiates from me as I spin Indie around to take in the magnificence of it all.

"Nothing in life has ever made me feel so small…and yet, so big," I say and her brown eyes look up at mine.

"This place is pretty impressive."

The corner of my mouth perks up. "I grew up here." I drop down on the grass and stretch my legs out in front of myself. "I don't have a clue who I'd be without this place."

Indie sits criss-cross beside me. "How did you and your brothers all come to play for the same team?"

"That's a bit of a loaded answer," I reply, tilting my head thoughtfully. "Essentially, it was our dad. He was a star striker for Man U when they won The Cup in the 80s."

"Oh wow, I didn't know that."

"Yeah, so we lived half the year in Manchester during his season, and the other half at our house in Chigwell. But when Mum died, he quit the team without a second thought. He was making loads of money but just up and left. I was only three when all that happened so I only know about it from retellings."

"He must have been devastated." Indie watches me carefully, sympathy knitting her brows together.

I shrug. "I suppose so, but he doesn't ever talk about her. Most of my memories of him from when I was younger aren't good. He refused to hire a nanny, even though he could more than afford one.

I think he didn't want anyone to see his grief."

"That's heart breaking," Indie says, looking down at my hand in the grass.

"I remember one night he threw all of our mum's clothes into the fireplace. Vi was sobbing and trying to grab a sweater of hers, but Dad refused to let her get it. I was comforting Vi but didn't understand why she cared about some silly sweater that was too big for her."

Indie's hand reaches out and covers her mouth, but I'm too busy haemorrhaging feelings like a broken blood vessel to stop.

"Then Bethnal Green F.C. came along, which is Championship League, so it's one division down from Man U and Arsenal. I was ten and had never touched a football when one of Dad's old teammates came barging in every day for a month straight. He was the Bethnal's coach and he wanted my dad to be the manager. He wouldn't take no for an answer."

"Is that guy your current coach?" Indie's soft voice reminds me I'm not alone, and I look up and see her listening intently.

"Yes. He's a screaming arse most days, but he taught us everything we know. In many ways, he turned our life around. After Dad accepted the offer, everything changed. He got happier, and we went to work with him just because we were star-struck. Then Coach gave us jobs with the team doing basic stuff like picking up loose balls. Eventually we started helping with dribbling drills and, hell, before we knew it, Gareth was scrimmaging with them as a teenager.

"Arsenal wanted to offer my brothers and me a place in their youth academy, but Dad wouldn't let us be promised to any league. He was angry at league football. Maybe because of everything that happened after Mum died. I don't know. It was a pretty epic battle when Gareth signed on with Man U."

"But now your dad wants you to sign with Arsenal?" Indie asks.

I nod. "I think my dad is still trying to get back at Man U. A twenty-year grudge maybe. I can't be sure, but I think he's been trying to work a contract with Arsenal for me, Tanner, and Booker. He's been tight-lipped about it all, so who knows?"

"How do you feel about that?"

I look into her wide, probing eyes. "You know…I don't fucking know. When I was young, Premier was my dream. But Championship League is still incredible. The money is great and I get to play with my brothers every day. That's huge. Hearing our name chanted is like the most immense amount of family pride I can fathom. And my brothers are right beside me. They are my family. My teammates. My best friends." I shrug, feeling myself lose control. "My family drives me crazy and we fight constantly, but they are mine and I can't imagine a better life without them."

"Then don't sign with Arsenal." Indie says it so simply, like it's an easy choice.

I shrug, annoyed by even myself at this point. "I don't think that's the solution. It's just that I can't figure out what I want out of football. I don't know what it's given me."

"How do you mean? I thought you said it saved your life?"

"We had no life before. Football gave us a life. But what else?" I reach down and touch the grass, instantly transported back to the feelings that overcame me when I went down over a week ago. "It wasn't just my ACL that tore in me. It was my home. I am football. Nothing more. If I can't play, what the fuck am I?"

"You're a lot of things, Camden," Indie exclaims, leaning forward and squeezing my arm urgently. I look up and her eyes don't hold pity for me like I expected. They look exasperated, like nothing I've said makes any sense to her.

"Off the top of my head, Cam, you're witty. Like the kind of wit you're embarrassed to laugh at but even a grandmother would laugh…because, bloody hell, it's funny."

I smile and she continues, "You like to act like a cocky bugger, but you're really smart and insightful. Those notes in the margins of your book are a whole other side of you."

"I liked your note." I pull her toward me so she has to climb on my lap. With her straddling me now, I grip the edges of her open shirt and I drop my head to her chest.

This is the first time I've said most of this out loud and I'm exhausted from it.

Fuck feelings. Feelings suck.

"We've been pretty good at juggling so far," I add, referring to her pun in my book. Her words about me are too nice. I need to change the focus off of me.

She doesn't take my bait. "You need to know that you are so much more than football. It's not even the product of a reasoned list of items. It's just something you innately are, Camden. You are beyond what words can articulate."

My eyes are seeing her. My ears are hearing her. But my soul still can't open itself up to the possibility of being more than football. As if sensing my anxiety, she adds with a laugh, "And you're a great lay."

I squeeze her sides and she falls down on my chest, laughing. She sits up and kisses my cheek once before whispering, "Can we go see your changing room now?"

Yes, Indie Porter. Yes, we fucking can.

I lead her into the home-team changing room, pointing out the differences between this one and the visitor's. Visitors get hooks on a wall for their kits. We have cubbies with backlighting, bronzed nameplates, and a whiteboard for words of inspiration. It's posh. The visitor's resembles a prison cell.

"What's that?" Indie asks, pointing to some text that's woodburned into the wall above the changing room exit door.

"It's a saying that the original owners put up. It's been there forever."

"'I am thine, thou art mine.'" She reads the words and admires the glimpse back in time this area of the room represents. The rest of the room was sheet-rocked and refinished a few years ago—all updated to a more modern, state-of-the-art feel. But this one old, weathered slab remains original.

"We all touch it as we walk out before every game."

"Interesting. What's the story behind it?"

I exhale. "Coach says it's to represent the player's relationship with the sport. You give yourself to football and it will give itself back to you. But there are other stories out there."

"Like what?"

"Marty is a janitor who works here. I talk to him sometimes 'cause he's old and knows stuff."

Her brows lift as she turns away from the sign to eye me. "Old and knows stuff?"

I shrug my shoulders because I'm not about to sound like a complete wanker by admitting Marty is like the grandfather I never had. "He's worked here for forty years, and he said it was a vow the old owner made to his wife on their wedding day. Since they got married on the pitch, it must've seemed fitting to burn it into the wall here. I don't know. Marty's a romantic I think."

"What a cool mystery," she states with a smile. "But I agree. A bit overly romantic."

"You're not?" I ask, watching her carefully.

She shakes her head with a light laugh. "No, I look at things too critically. I see the seams of a relationship and it just looks like something that could pull apart."

"I tend to agree with that," I reply, mulling over what she's said when something else catches my eye. "Come in here. You'll find this interesting, too…'cause you're a nerdling and stuff."

I grab her hand and drag her behind me. I swear I can hear her eyes rolling. "This is called the Cry Room," I grin. "It's where injured players are brought in to be examined."

Her eyes are wide. "Wow, you guys have an X-ray machine in here?" I try not to take it personal that this room impresses her more than the pitch.

"Yeah. They X-rayed me before I left the field last week."

"Interesting." She walks around the room, touching anything of interest, which is pretty much everything. I stand in the doorway and drink her in like a creep, eyeing every square inch of her legs the entire time. "You have a staff doctor at every game, too? Does he travel with you?"

As I'm answering her, she slides her plaid shirt off her shoulders and ties the offensive material around her waist. Now she's in nothing but a skimpy white tank top with tiny metal buttons begging to be unsnapped.

"Let's revisit that part of our conversation where you said I was a great lay."

"After all you shared out there, that's what's on your mind?" She stops in front of the large padded exam table and hoists herself up, kicking her feet nonchalantly.

I smile and walk slowly toward her. "You know, I was inside of you over twenty-four hours ago."

She smiles and her cheeks flush. "I remember."

"Think you're feeling better down there?"

She looks down, revealing her innocence again. "You want to do it in here?"

I nod. "There are security cameras on the pitch. And since this is a medical room I thought it would be kind of poetic. I've been dying to play doctor/patient with you since the first time you kissed me in the ICU."

"I didn't kiss you! You kissed—"

I kiss the word kissed right off her mouth. With one flick of my tongue, she grabs me by the shirt and yanks me between her legs.

My hands stroke up her sides as she wraps her legs around my waist. "Is that a yes?" I murmur with a smile.

"Yes," she gasps, and I finally get to rip those stupid fucking snaps open on her chest.

It was mostly just for dramatic effect because, five seconds later, I pull the whole bloody thing off of her, along with everything else she's wearing. She immediately returns the favour, all but ripping my clothes off. Now, with her on the footstool, we're standing skin-to-skin and eye-to-eye. She's completely pressed flush against me as I ravish her mouth with my tongue.

After palming her arse and groping every delicious curve of her, I'm desperate to be inside of her. Without hesitating, I turn her around and bend her over the exam table. Her gorgeous hair splays out wildly, and she lets out an excited groan when I press myself against her backside. Propped on the footstool, she's at the perfect height. I waste no time sinking my fingers into her wet, tight channel. I throb with appreciation, but I continue spreading her, prepping her for my entry. I need her ready for what I want to do to her next.

When my thumb grazes her back hole between her lush cheeks, she lets out the sexiest fucking groan. It's a sound that makes no mistake that she likes what I'm doing to her. And that pleases me greatly.

When she begins bucking against my hand and begging for more, I pause my actions and dig a condom out of my jeans. I watch her back rise and fall with laboured breaths as I slide the rubber on.

Smiling, I bend over top of her, brush her hair off to the side, and breathe, "Now, Specs, this isn't going to be slow and careful like last time. It's going to be hard and fast."

"Yes," she exhales, moaning out loudly when I press my fingers down firmly on her clit, teasing the flesh in slow, rhythmic strokes.

"I'm going to really fuck you this time."

"Yes." She sounds like she's going to come already.

"Have I mentioned I love your noises?"

"Camden, just do it already!"

A mighty cry erupts from her when I slam myself inside. I have to close my eyes because she's still so tight and it feels even better than the first time. I pause, allowing her body to adjust. Her laboured breaths come hard and fast.

"Are you good?" I pant.

"God, yes," she cries.

I position one hand on her cheek, massaging and gripping while the other skirts around to her front and swipes at her slickened nub.

"Oh my God," she cries out as I start to move inside of her.

My head drops back as I thank the world of football for giving me this after taking so much away. "This is why I needed more time."

I pump into her faster, feeling every inch of me slip in and out with wet, firm strokes. Her body squeezes me like she doesn't ever want me to leave and, God, I could imagine living here just like this.

My continued assault on her clit it fruitful. "Oh my God!" Her voice is high and alarmed.

"Not yet, we're doing this one together," I say, letting go of her front and gripping her hips in both of my hands. I pull her back into me with every hard thrust I push forward. I bounce her supple arse on me and hit even deeper than before.

"Camden," she cries again, and I feel everything inside of her tighten around me. It's so incredible that I can't hold back.

I slam into her one final time. The cries of her release are what push me over the edge, too. Quaking, shaking, and trembling as I pulsate everything I have inside of her. Or inside the condom, I should say.

When I finish, I hunch over her back, both of our breaths heavy and sated. *Christ, I don't remember anyone ever feeling this good.*

That's a disturbing thought, so I quickly pull out and walk to the loo to clean up. While I toss the condom, I recall the last time I had sex with a girl twice in this short amount of time. It was probably that model a few months ago. I knew the second time with her was a mistake because, as soon as we finished, she tried to make plans with me for the next night. When I refused, it turned into a social media smear campaign that had my dad breathing fire at me for weeks.

Thank fuck this has a clear kill date on it because things are already getting confusing.

Indie's already dressed when I come back. As she watches me put my clothes back on, I do my best to forget about the odd thoughts racing through my mind.

When I look up, she's shaking her head in wonder. "There's no way the next one is going to be that good."

"What are you talking about?" I pull my shirt down over my head and button up my jeans.

"You don't want to know. You'll think I'm a head case."

"I already kind of do and I still want to fuck you." I force a congenial smile. "Tell me."

"I can't. I refuse." She crosses her arms over her chest.

"I could force it out of you." My brows lift playfully, but deep down I'm frustrated by how badly I need to know what's inside her mind.

She makes a move like her lips are sealed. Without hesitation, I shoot toward her, clutching her sides in my hands and fiercely tickling her against the exam table. Her noises are infectious. Before long, my crabby mood is all but gone as I laugh at her squirming reaction.

She begs for mercy with tears in her eyes and exclaims, "Okay, I'll tell you!" I pull back with a triumphant grin. "I have this Penis List I made-up with Belle."

"A penis what?" I release my hands from her waist and stand back. "Is that like a Christmas list of dicks?"

"No, it's just a Penis List," she says with a huff, leaning on the table. "It's that plan I've mentioned. About why I'm not worried about falling for you. Because of the list. The plan. You are Penis Number One, which is a very distinct type. Number one is supposed to be a playboy. Someone…experienced."

"Okay…and?" I cross my arms.

"And, I'm just saying…Penis Number Two is going to have big shoes to fill because you and I have been doing quite well, I'd say."

Her talking about other men again is not amusing. "What the fuck is Penis Number Two?"

She counts the descriptive traits on her fingers like she's listing off items on her grocery list. "Total opposite of you. He's got to be sensitive, a giver...takes nothing, gives everything. Emotional..." Her voice trails off when she notices the look on my face. "Why are you looking at me like that?"

"Are you saying I could never be Penis Number Two?" I can't help but think I've given up a lot these last couple of days with her. I've screwed her in ways I've never screwed anybody else. So how different could a Penis Number Two be?

She eyes me skeptically.

I move toward her and trap her against the table with a hand on either side of her. "Indie. I've fucked a lot of women. You don't keep women coming without being a giver. Has there ever been a time you haven't gotten off?"

"Well, no." Her face looks uncomfortable.

"See? That's my primary goal every time. When you come...the face you make...the sounds you utter...that is what makes me come."

She opens her mouth but no words come out.

"So your Penis List has some holes in it I'm afraid."

"Well, thankfully...it won't concern you once our arrangement is done." She crosses her arms with a determined scowl.

I push myself away from her. "I think I could show you whatever else you're trying to get from that list. Easily."

"I highly doubt it." She puts her hands on her hips. "And besides, this isn't a contest, Camden. There's no winner."

"No, but it sounds like you have goals. Pun intended. So you need a sensitive lover? Challenge accepted."

"Challenge not accepted. This isn't how it's supposed to go. The point is to have multiple penises, not one. And you're Penis Number One. Not Two! End of."

I scoff, "Relax, Specs. You'll have plenty of time to shag other blokes when I'm gone."

For some bizarre reason, the notion feels like razors in my stomach as it tumbles out of my mouth.

22 Under Pressure

Camden

The next morning, I wake up alone in my bed. Tanner came home late last night, so that was a big reason I didn't invite Indie back to my flat. Or stay at hers. I don't need questions about where I am or what I'm doing right now.

Because I'm not even sure I know what the fuck I'm doing.

This Penis List of Indie's has my stomach in knots. I'm not sure if it's just the jealousy factor, or if it's the fact that I've always loved a good challenge.

I don't even know what this is between Indie and me, but I know I have a strong intensity with her that I'm not sure I'm done exploring yet.

I ruffle my hair and stride out of my room to find my father and Booker sitting at our kitchen table as I thought they would be.

Ever since Tanner and I moved out here, Dad and Booker have come to our flat following every match to go through the footage. As a manager, our dad's job is to recruit. As our dad, his job is to sideline coach.

"Camden," my dad says, setting down his cup of coffee and standing up to get a look at me. "Your mobility looks improved. How do you feel?"

I toss a quick nod toward Booker and smile tightly at my dad's words. "I feel perfectly fine."

Dad's brows rise. "Your physical therapist says you're doing better than fine. He says he's never seen such a quick recovery after an ACL tear."

"You spoke to my therapist?" I frown and zip up my hooded sweatshirt over my bare chest, subconsciously suiting up my armour.

"He called me while we were on the road. We won the match, you know. Tanner scored one goal. Booker blocked three attempts."

"Aces, Book."

Booker smiles softly as Dad adds, "It was a great match. You were missed."

"I got it all recorded and watched some of it," I mumble, striding over to the coffee pot and pouring myself a cup.

"Great. I think it's a good idea for you to go through the match footage with us. We need to keep your head in the game." His voice sounds so much like Coach, it makes my skin crawl.

I sit down on the chair beside him and listen as he spouts off some of the highlights. He's aged so much in the last few years. Did I even notice? His dark hair looks greyer every time I see him. Is football causing that? Did losing Mum cause that? Or is it something more? The only time I see him behave even remotely human is toward Vi. Why haven't I noticed any of this before?

"So are you going to tell me what's going on then?" I ask, cutting my dad off midsentence. Booker shoots me a quizzical look.

"What do you mean?" Dad asks.

"The meeting with Arsenal. The text message about becoming a Gunner. Your hints haven't been subtle, Dad."

His face lengthens as he pulls his brows back. "I'm just trying to motivate you, Cam. Nothing is set in stone yet."

"Motivate me?" I ask with a huff. Booker leans toward me over the table, attempting to silently calm me with his thoughts. "So nothing is coming of all this?"

"I signed a non-disclosure agreement, Cam. I can't really say anything until—"

"Until what?"

"Until after your second...*visit*." He bites the last word out awkwardly and looks down at my knee. Once again, he can't actually voice the word "surgery" and it makes my temper rise. "I'll be able to tell you everything after we see how things turn out."

The pressure of those words pushes me down with the weight of a thousand pounds. My head feels heavy. My hands feel caked in sludge. My stomach sinks to the floor. But my temper is pushing back against all of it. "And if things turn out badly?" My voice is quiet, restrained.

"Don't think like that, Cam. You're a Harris. You'll bounce back and be better than ever. I'm sure of it."

"And what if I don't?" My jaw muscle ticks. My hand grips my mug, turning my knuckles white.

"What do you mean?"

"What if I don't bounce back from this? What if I can't play football again?"

"That's the kind of thinking that will make your recovery harder. Just focus on the prize. Focus on being the best. You're a Harris. You boys were made for this."

I huff out a laugh. "This is such crap."

"Cam." Booker's tone is a calm warning that Dad ignores.

"What's crap?" Dad asks, his hazel eyes piercing me.

"How you are. All this secrecy. All this tip-toeing around shit. The added pressure. You pile it on with your empty words, and I still don't know anything."

"It's for your own good. You don't need this on your shoulders."

"It's there with every word you say!" I rake my hands through my hair and grip the back of my neck. "Why didn't you come to my surgery, Dad?" I throw the question at him, catching him completely off guard. If he's going to poke me, I'm going to poke him back even harder.

He scoffs, "I'm a busy man, Camden. It's the end of the season. The scouts need to know what final matches to go to for recruits."

"Bullshit," I say, pushing up out of my chair. It scrapes along the floor and hits the wall behind me. "You didn't come because you can't handle anything that reminds you of Mum."

"Camden," Tanner's voice bellows from the archway of the hall, jolting me out of my rage. His hair is a mess and his beard is mis-shapen, but his eyes have that look that tells me he's not in a joking mood. "What's going on with you?"

"Nothing. I'm just sick of talking about fucking football. It's all we ever do!" I turn on my heel, determined to get the hell out of here before I completely break down like the emotional sap I am.

Tanner steps in front of my path to the hallway and places both hands on my shoulders, gripping them firmly. But it's not to stop me. It's not to scold me. It's to show me that he hears me. Our eyes lock for only a couple of seconds before he nods and lets me go.

Go where, I don't know.

23
Thou Art Mine

Indie

THE NEXT DAY, I BURST OUT LAUGHING WHEN I OPEN THE DOOR and find Camden dressed in a pair of tan trousers and a pale blue button-down tucked all the way in. I think he's going for conservative church boy, but his slacks are tailored perfectly to his muscular quads, and his metal plaque brown belt and expensive leather shoes make him seem way too fashionable to fool me. Even his blonde hair is perfectly styled off to the side, revealing the horizontal line of his undercut.

My clothes are more casual than his because I didn't realise he was playing dress up. I'm barefoot and wearing denim leggings and a loose purple tank. At least the leggings are my hottest pair.

I glance down at the bags in his hands. "What are those?"

"Hello, Ms. Porter. I was wondering if I might call on you?"

I puzzle over his formal voice. "Don't you need a mobile for that?"

"I mean, *call on you* in the old-world sense. Like…a courtship. But with all the conveniences of modern-day sex." He flashes a smile at me.

I laugh again. "Is this how it's going to be all night?" I cross my arms and prop myself against the door. "Because I definitely prefer

Penis Number One Camden."

"Oh hush," he growls, pushing me aside to enter my tiny flat. "Think of this as role-playing. I'm making you dinner and you're going to like it."

I watch him as he sets the food on the counter and busies himself with unpacking and prepping. He looks rather good with his sleeves rolled up and behaving all domestic. A girl could get used to a Penis Number Two type maybe. But he can't fool me. A zebra can't lose its stripes.

He informs me he's going to make us a steak salad; however, by make, he means arrange takeout on plates. It sounds fine by me because my cooking skills have never been my strong suit.

He pauses for a moment, and I watch his shoulders rise and fall a few times. When I'm about to ask him what he needs, he turns and rushes toward me. His lips find mine as he backs me up against the closed door. Once our movement stops, he pulls back—mouth open, nostrils flared, eyes locked on my lips— as if he had to look at me to make sure I was real. Then he attacks my mouth again. The kiss is firmer this time, fierce and spinning hot jolts through my entire body. When I'm about ready to beg him to rip my clothes off and take me right here against the door, he pulls back and murmurs, "That was too much. I'm sorry."

"Don't be sorry." My voice is husky as my eyes find his.

His brow line creases with apprehension. "I just needed to get lost for a minute."

I want to ask why but my mind won't let me. This stuff with Camden is supposed to be casual. Sexual. Fun. Asking the deep questions will open up too many feelings. Feelings that I started to experience at Tower Park yesterday. Feelings that I need to detach from straight away.

"I can think of another place you could get lost." I pull him into me and slide my hands up his firm back.

"No, Indie. I'm determined to be your Cock Number Two." His

face is boyish and innocent again, like a child who wants to win the big game.

I huff an exasperated laugh. "You just like a challenge."

His brows waggle, lifting his pensive expression from before. "That I do. Shall we begin?"

He grabs my hand and leads me to my small table where he pours me a glass of red wine from the bottle he brought over and pops the tab on his Guinness. When he hands me the glass, I slide myself up on top of the table and watch the sexy Camden in the Kitchen Show.

Cheerier now, he flips a bottle of dressing and tosses a bag of arugula behind his back, making a proper spectacle of his work. Rolling my eyes, I say, "Of course you have a flair for the dramatics. You're a footballer through and through."

He quirks a brow. "Are you saying footballers put on a show?"

"Well, not all, but some definitely do. It's so funny how you guys flail wildly and make a big scene whenever you get tackled."

He tsks and leans back against the counter, crossing his arms over his chest. "Indie, I know you're incredibly smart, but please allow me to educate you about my sport."

His dress shirt pulls at the biceps and I suddenly picture him shirtless—ink on display, abs rippled just how I know they do. His slacks are bulging, revealing what I know to be plenty of—

"Up here, Specs." My eyes shoot up to find him watching me with an amused expression on his face.

"I'm listening," I state defensively.

His eyes crinkle, clearly pleased by my objectification. "Our pitch is huge. Over one hundred yards. And there is only one ref and two linesmen to keep up with twenty-two players over all of that space. You absolutely have to call attention to something that happens. Not dramatising a tackle could cost you the foul call you deserve. And drawing a foul is a vital part of strategy."

"But some get penalised for over-dramatising," I state, revealing

I may know more about football than I care to admit.

He slants his eyes and approaches me, tucking himself between my legs. My wine glass presses between us again, just like that other time in my kitchen.

"In my world..." He brushes his lips along my jaw, pushing my loose strands of hair with his nose before whispering in my ear, "... that's called passion."

I turn my face to kiss him, but he pulls back before our lips can connect. "Come now, Specs. I'm here to pamper you tonight. Not tell you all the reasons why football is the best game in the world."

By the time he plates our salads and refills my wine, I feel warm and fuzzy all over. Having him here makes me that way.

We're sitting across from each other at my table when I blurt out, "So do you want to talk about what happened to you earlier today?"

He shakes me off. "I'd rather talk about you. I feel like we do a lot of talking about me." I half smile and he continues, "The Penis List. We didn't really discuss it in full detail. It's very...peculiar."

I give him a rueful smile. "Yeah, I am a bit of a head case. I thought you'd have sussed that out by now."

"I'm aware. But lucky for you, the crazy ones are usually the most fun." He winks and then adds, "So tell me how it came about. Why would you think you need a list? You're smart, gorgeous, fun. You could have hundreds of blokes if you wanted. Why the need for a guideline?"

I try to conceal my grin. "Well," I begin, "I told you how I skipped a few years of school, right?"

"Yes," he replies.

"Being three years younger than all my classmates at an all-girl boarding school was pretty awful. All the girls were getting their periods and wearing C-cup bras. I didn't even need a training bra until I was fourteen."

"Your tits came in just fine." He shoots me a creepy smirk that has me shaking my head. "I would have liked to have been your classmate in school, though. All that hair, those glasses, and boobs… You would have had trouble getting rid of me."

"Anyway, perv, remember how you wanted me to tell you dirty stories about things that went on at my school?"

His mouth falls open. "God, yes. There are stories, aren't there? You were holding back on me."

I wince. "I don't think they're very interesting myself. But having been all girls with limited supervision in the dorms created some interesting use of free time. The older girls were so hyper-sexualised and curious, they experimented with each other—"

"Stop," Camden says, silencing my words. "How old were you at this time?"

I shrug. "They were probably fifteen, so I would have been twelve."

"God, this would be so much better if it happened in University."

"Sorry to pummel your fantasy. Anyway, I wasn't in the same place they were in…both in maturity and in puberty. I think they kind of targeted me for that."

He frowns. "What happened?"

"Well, a few of the older girls convinced me to sneak out of the dorms one night. They said there was an abandoned school bus in the woods that other girls were star-gazing from at night through the busted roof. I was going through an astrology phase and I guess it felt nice that they noticed. So I went with them.

"I crawled up the bus steps all excited for stars, but walked in on a bunch of kids all having sex instead. Like, right next to each other and everything."

"Good grief." Cam's disgusted face is comforting. It took me a long time to realise what those kids were doing wasn't the normal way to go about having intercourse. I thought I was alone in my repulsion at the time. "So what did you do?"

"I was only twelve and still so underdeveloped and naïve that I just started bawling. I ran out of there and never spoke to those girls the rest of my years at that school."

"Kids can be the worst kinds of sods."

"I remember thinking that if that was how normal people behaved, I didn't want to be normal. I couldn't imagine losing my virginity that way. After all of that, it was so difficult for me to open up to girls. I didn't have a single true friend until I met Belle in med school. It even took some time for me to share all this nonsense with her. But once I did, she helped me see that it would be better to have a game plan to empower me instead of me being scared of the unknown."

"It's not a horrid idea when you put it like that," he says with a thoughtful look. "What did your parents say about that bus incident?"

I shake my head. "I never told them. Their work is their priority, so I've never really had a relationship with them like that where I shared school stories. And my grandmother was so old, I couldn't stomach the idea of telling her that sort of thing. She would have lost complete faith in humanity."

He gets a desolate sort of look in his eyes. "I can't imagine what that kind of family would be like. Bloody hell, mine knows everything about me at all times. We are in each other's business, in each other's homes, eating weekly meals together, traveling together, and going over match footage. Vi gives the best gifts, and Tanner is constantly pranking everybody. Gareth has such a large heart, but it's silent and that makes me scared for him. And Booker is still so impressionable. Ensuring he's on the right path is so important. My family, Indie…I cannot escape them even if I tried. Your upbringing is like another world to me."

His rant is unexpected; my reaction to it even more so. His long string of words feels like a knife repeatedly jabbing my heart with every bullet point he ticks off. They sting, even though I know he doesn't mean for them to. He's obviously releasing something that weighs heavily on him; but, out of nowhere, the twelve-year-old girl inside of me begins to weep, which is odd because I've never allowed myself to feel upset over something I've never known. My family is my family. I don't know any different. I've created a life of near solitude for myself, so why are his words cutting me so deeply?

My face heats as the presence of tears swell in my eyes.

"Fuck, Indie." Camden's face falls as he drops his fork. The chair scrapes loudly against the floor, and he rushes over to me. He squats down beside me and cups my face in his hands. "I don't know what I said. Christ, I'm so pent-up about my family lately, I think I blacked out. I didn't think."

I stiffen and turn away from him. "Please don't look at me," my voice cracks. "I'm fine."

"God, no, Indie. I have to look at you. I caused this. I am such an idiot. Please. Look at me so I can make this better."

"There's nothing you can do to make it better." I laugh-cry an awkward, mortifying sound. "This is so stupid."

"No, it's not. If it involves anything about you, it can't possibly be stupid."

"Please, Cam. Just go. I need some space." This is worse than the time I told him I was a virgin. I want to die. I want to crawl into a hole and die.

"No," his voice is earnest. "You don't need space right now, Indie. Let me show you."

"Show me what?" I huff in frustration and snap my eyes to meet his.

My embarrassment is almost snuffed out entirely by his expression. I don't see sorrow or pity or judgement. I see…more. Unexpected…more. I gaze into the sapphire depths of his irises and I feel…lost.

Camden's eyes follow the movement of my teeth chewing on my lip. His dark lashes fan his cheeks in that utterly beautiful way he has about him. Swallowing once, he strokes his thumb down my cheek over and over, watching me as if he's trying to count every freckle on my face. Finally, he pulls my mouth to his and brushes his tongue along the opening of my lips, requesting entry. I comply because I'm desperate to feel like anything other than that lost, lonely girl I reverted into thirty seconds ago.

His hands move down to my thighs, and he deftly turns the chair so he's now centered between my legs. When I grip the back of his head, he suddenly lifts me up and we're moving, my legs tightening around his waist as we go. His hands slide up the bottom of my shirt, stroking the small of my back and dipping down into my underwear as he stops beside the wall.

Holding me with one hand, he pulls my bed from the wall and lays me back on the lowered mattress, keeping himself on top of me. His lips persistently kiss away at all my heartache. My thighs clench him to me, relishing the feel of his weight. His pressure. His closeness. It's comforting. It's soothing. It's all-encompassing. I yearn for him to fill a space in me that I didn't even realise existed until this moment.

What happens next is like nothing I ever imagined. Expected. Or asked for.

Camden Harris makes love to me.

Slow, tender, passionate love.

He gently peels off every article of my clothing and then his own. His eyes hold me so captive that I can't even bring myself to glance at his body on display before me. His muscles were something that I admired before. They distracted my thoughts on more than one occasion. But right now, all I can look at are his eyes on mine as he lowers himself onto me.

The firmness of him against the softness of me.

His blue eyes swim back and forth, sparkling with something. Something profound. Something I want to feel with my bare hands. Something I want to reach out and pull inside of me—to hold and to cherish, even if it is just for a short time.

He inhales sharply when his naked tip brushes between my legs.

His voice is rough and pained when he says, "Indie, you don't even know what you are. You don't even know what you do to me."

My breath comes in harsh and goes out shaky.

"I've never, in my life, cared like this," he murmurs against my lips. "I feel different with you."

My abs tighten against his body when his thumb trails over my nipple.

"You're different," he whispers into my ear. "You're special," he says against my cheek. "You're challenging." He closes the space between us and kisses me deeply.

My eyes flutter closed and, with every stroke of his tongue, I inhale his words of affirmation. I accept them with each burst of oxygen.

Tears slide down my temples and into my hair over the realisation that I've never felt this level of devotion before, both for him and from him. It's more than I've ever felt about anything in my entire life.

He moves his mouth down and kisses every inch of my body, whispering reverent words against my flesh. Slowly, they begin to chip away and break down the dark, secret place in my heart.

"I can't believe I get to see you like this." He moves back up to my face. "You're raw. Open. But only to me."

I swallow hard and give him the slightest nod. It's so subtle that no one else in the entire world would notice it. Only him.

In this moment, we're beyond the words of everyday life. We're communicating more than vocal abilities allow.

And when he pushes into me, hard and bare, with zero barriers left between us, the entire act is not mind-blowing.

It's life-ruining.

It's as if I'm on a merry-go-round that is moving so fast, the world is a blur all around me. The only thing in focus is the man sitting on the ride beside me.

When I finally allow myself to come apart from his words and his touch, I throb everywhere. My body trembles from head to toe. The ache in my chest is so strong it feels as if it could arrest at any second.

Then, just when I think things can't get any worse—when I'm certain I can't possibly feel anything more—he lies down beside me, pulls me into his arms, and softly whispers into my ear, "Thou art mine."

24 The Cut

Camden

INDIE LETS ME HOLD HER UNTIL SHE FALLS ASLEEP. SHE DOESN'T pull away. She doesn't ask for space. She doesn't even go to the bathroom to clean up. She just curls up inside my arms, silently asking me to hold her. To be close to her. *To not give her space.*

No words are exchanged over what I revealed while we made love. I think that's what we did at least. I'm not even sure I fully know what I admitted. I just did what my body demanded that I do. It wasn't a premediated act. It wasn't me trying to be Penis Number Two. It was spontaneous and extraordinary.

The last thing I feel before sleep takes me is the sting of tears behind my closed eyes as a painful realisation overcomes me.

I wake to a noise and crack my eyes open just in time to see the bathroom door shut. The sound of rain pattering outside fills the quietness of her flat. The grey, hazy morning light casts a foreboding sensation over me. Glancing at the clock, I see it's only six-thirty in the morning. I roll on my back to assess my injuries.

Knee feels fine.

Head feels groggy.

Heart feels fucked.

With a heavy sigh, I drop my feet to the floor and slide into my black boxers, wincing at the memory of the fact that I didn't use a condom last night. I've never not used a condom with anyone. Ever. How stupid can I be? We hadn't even talked about birth control and I just pushed into her, completely bareback, like the biggest arsehole on the planet. I sit back down and drop my head in my hands, wishing someone would punch me in the face.

Despite all of that, a more poignant thought pushes itself to the surface—the thought that had me overwhelmed and moved me into a place I never thought I'd be with a woman. It's what enabled me to breathe in the scent of her all night long and fantasise about how life could maybe be different. And that maybe different is okay.

I want her.

In the early morning light of day, with no tears in her eyes, and no roaring desire to comfort her and make her feel special, I still want her. I want her for more than what our arrangement originally stated.

I want her for many, many days.

Maybe an infinite amount of days? Hell, I don't know. Wanting someone like this is new to me. The passionate footballer inside of me is screaming, *long term*, which is insane. And utterly mental.

But I've been awakened by Indie and I have to tell her.

The door opens and my head snaps up to see her pause in the doorway. I stand up from the Murphy bed positioned right in the middle of her small studio. She's so close but feels so far away. She runs a bare foot up the back of her calf, her legs naked beneath a long grey tank top. Her red, curly hair is knotted on top of her head and thick black-framed glasses line her pensive brown eyes.

"Can we talk?" I ask and make a move toward her.

"Yes, but just…don't touch me." Her words sting and she rushes out her next sentence. "I can't think straight when you touch me, Camden."

I can respect that I guess, but I'd be lying if I said it doesn't still sting. She drops down on a wooden kitchen chair and pulls her legs up to her chest, yanking her tank over her knees. I'm standing six feet from her but can see the regretful look in her eyes, plain as day… and it guts me.

Swallowing slowly, I say, "Indie, I need to know. Are we…safe? I didn't use a condom and, fuck, that was so wrong of me. I can't tell you how sorry I am. I know I'm clean, but are you on anything?"

Her head tremors with an awkward nod. "Yes, we're fine. I'm on the pill."

I sag with relief but still register her clipped tone. Knowing that was the easy question would be comical if I was in a laughing mood. But the tightness of her posture gives me an uneasy feeling.

I sit on the edge of the bed and watch her carefully. "What are you thinking?"

As if her words have been on the tip of her tongue, she asks, "Was all of that an act last night? A performance? Were you trying to draw a foul?"

Wounded, I reply, "No."

She stares back at me accusingly. "It wasn't?"

"No, Specs. I'm not that good of an actor. Did it feel like an act?" She remains silent. "Did you want it to be an act?"

Her face sparks with anger. "Yes! This was supposed to be casual, Camden. We just met. I've never even been with another man. This isn't how this was supposed to go."

"Well, sorry for mucking up your plans," I snap. "I didn't exactly plan for this."

"But you can stop it!"

"No, I bloody can't, Indie! It's not a fucking valve I can shut off."

I stand up, no longer giving a shit how much space she needs. I yank the other dining chair from its place and slam it down in front of her. When I sit, my knees graze her toes. In response, she squeezes her legs to her chest like a shield of armour.

Ready to lay all my shit bare, I pierce her with my eyes and say, "I want you, Indie. For more than five days. I want what I feel when I'm with you."

"Camden—"

"Bloody hell, I'm falling for you!" I yell. My breath sputters out fast and ragged as the words tumble out and suspend in the air, floating…and then drifting…and then sinking as her eyes blaze fire against them.

"You hardly know me." Her tone is contrite and it enrages me.

Through clenched teeth, I rebuff, "I know enough to know that I've never cared about anything like this in my life. Nothing, Indie. Nothing has felt like this. Do you hear what I'm saying? Because it takes a lot for me to admit that right now. I feel like…I feel like…" I rake my hand through my hair, trying to find the right words.

"Like what?" she snaps, losing a chink of her armour.

"Like I've been playing pretend my whole life!" I throw my hands out and slide closer to her. My hands shake from the ache I feel to hold her. To embrace her. To make her understand. To break down this unapologetic wall she has built around her. I reach out to touch her but stop myself. My voice is low and urgent. "When I compare my feelings for you to my feelings for *everything else*, they're so different."

As if completely oblivious to the insanity coursing through my veins, she groans, "No, Cam."

"Yes, Indie."

"No."

"YES!" I shout and make a move to kiss her. The heels of her hands slam against my chest, stopping my momentum. Cupping her face, I look at her pleadingly. "I've given you the tools to juggle, Specs. Just juggle already."

Her eyes are wide and accusing as they flick back and forth between mine. "That is *not* what my pun meant. And stop calling me that!"

"Puns can have all sorts of meanings. That's the beauty of them." Her defensive hands soften when I lean in. "Why can't you consider, even for a second, that you might like me, too?"

"Because I don't, Camden. Not like that."

"Indie," I exhale, pulling my hands from her face and clutching hers to my heart. "I'm wide open on the table, bleeding all over the bloody place. Stop holding back and feel this." My heart pounds beneath her touch, drumming away with anxiety.

With desperation.

With hope.

"*Feel me*," I croak, my shaky voice revealing how anguished I am.

Her brown eyes are wide and watery. Her cheeks are warm and flush. Every part of her face screams indecision, giving me a tiny ray of hope that perhaps I'm getting through to her after all.

When I move to kiss her again, she shoves me back. Then, without warning, her body climbs on top of me. Her legs wrap around my waist as she straddles me in the chair. With a throaty sigh, she slams her mouth to mine. Her hands greedily slice through every strand of hair on my head, tugging at the length on top. It's unrestrained and ravishing, and I'm completely overcome. She thrusts her tongue so deep into my mouth that I close my eyes and wince in shock but also in victory.

Her hand reaches between us and frees me from my boxers. I'm rock-hard in her grip as she positions me between her slits and falls down on top of me all in one motion. Squeezing me inside of her, she breaks our kiss and screams out.

My head falls to her chest as I utter her name over and over and over. She clutches me to her and rides me like I didn't even know she could. Bobbing and bucking, squeezing and releasing. Frenzied, I free one of her breasts and suck so hard on the nipple I'm sure it'll leave a mark. With every plunge, she takes me deeper inside of her. So deep I can't hold on much longer. The desperation in her body is alarming. I hold her as tight as I can because, even though I'm inside of her, I still feel like she's pulling away.

With only a few more thrusts, she screams out my name with her climax and I roar with her, emptying every part of myself inside her. Bare and wet, pulsing and kneading. She cradles me to her like I'm the only thing keeping her upright.

Our breaths are hot and ragged as the rest of the world slowly comes back into focus and we both realise what just happened. She finally pulls away from me, and what I see before me is a statue version of Indie Porter. Gone is the soft, beautiful girl whom I made love to last night, or even the one who climbed on top of me just a few minutes ago. Now she's hard and cold, without a trace of emotion on her cherubic face.

She stands up, pulling her shirt down and crossing her legs while she looks away from me. "See? That's what we are."

My mouth falls open as I tuck my limping dick back inside my boxers. "What?"

She looks at me with a flat expression on her face. "Sex. Fucking. That's all we are, Camden. That's all we can ever be." A spark of determination now invigorates her eyes. "I'm sorry, but you knew what I wanted from you. And you were using me just as much as I was using you."

"How did I use you?" I croak.

"To get you through this recovery," she states, her jaw taut with determination. "I've turned into a codependency for you. I'm like a painkiller you're hooked on. I see it all the time with athletes recovering from injuries. You're using me to make yourself feel better, and you're turning this into more than it is."

"Bollocks!" I stand up and move toward her. "You think you're nothing more than sex to me?"

"No, I think I'm more." She raises her chin. "I'm your doctor…

your surgeon. You are my patient. You said you didn't want a girlfriend and this was all temporary."

"I don't want a girlfriend," I snap. "I just want you. I want you in ways that supersede labels." I pause, waiting for my breathing to slow but then growl out, "Stop holding back."

"I'm not holding back." Her tone is verging on manic.

"You are! Bloody hell, Indie." I turn and kick back the chair that mocks me with memories of passion. Ramming my hands through my hair, I grip my neck so hard I can feel the vertebrae. "I've done things with you that shows another side of me to you. Let this happen."

"There isn't another side to me. Our original arrangement is all I'm capable of, and we've already gone way too far."

"We haven't gone far enough, Specs." I move to reach for her face but she pulls away, forcing me to clutch my hands into fists of frustration. She's like a bloody football I can't touch.

She's going to ruin me.

"I thought you could handle this," she states coolly, and I hear a deafening finality in her voice.

"So did I," I whisper and huff out a pathetic laugh. How could I have gotten this so wrong? The one time I open myself up and allow myself to care about something more, it all implodes in my face.

"You can't change the rules on me," she adds stiffly, barely making eye contact with me despite my close proximity. "I have a plan and I'm sticking to that plan."

"Oh, your precious fucking cock list," I huff, leaning in, my voice visceral. "It's ridiculous, Indie. Your plan is a child's idea to solve the problem of being a virgin. You don't fuck like a virgin, so stop acting like one."

I don't even feel the impact of what just happened until seconds later when the heat of her strike spreads across my cheek.

"Get out!" she growls, clutching her hand like she hurt herself more than she hurt me. Her face and voice are riddled with so much emotion that I can't bear to look at her.

My jaw muscle ticks as I walk around the room and grab my clothes up off the floor. Steeling myself to look at her one more time, I pause at the door and say, "The irony of all of this is that you are still the one doing the cutting."

Penis Mission

Indie

The door slams and I wait for the tears to come. I wait to feel bad about what I said or did. I expect regret and remorse to consume me. I wonder when what he said will begin to bother me.

Instead…I get nothing.

The fire in my palm turns to ice.

I'm numb.

I'm a rock.

I stare at myself in the bathroom mirror and looking back at me is a blank canvas. Nothing to connect to. Nothing to interpret. Absolutely zero symbolism in the curves of my face. If I was to say a pun about myself, I'd say, "'Much ado about nothing.'"

This…is me.

As the days pass by back at work, the same four words continue on repeat in my mind.

I'm charting.

"I'm falling for you."

I'm setting a bone.

"I'm falling for you."

I'm eating lunch.

"I'm falling for you."

I'm having a conversation with Prichard.

"I'm falling for you."

Speak of the devil. I feel my mobile vibrate in my pocket while walking out of the post-op room where I was checking on a patient, whom I did a shoulder replacement on earlier this morning.

I answer my mobile and adjust the iPad chart in my hand. "Hello, this is Dr. Porter."

"Indie…Prichard here. I just realised that I'm going to be in the OR for the next four hours with a double knee replacement."

"Okay," I reply, hearing the buzz of the OR behind him and realising he's probably operating as we speak.

"That Harris footballer is coming in today for another MRI. I want to make sure his graft is looking perfect, so I'd like you to be the one to take him to radiology. Not an intern. Got it?"

My chest feels tight. "The radiologist will be doing the scan, so I don't know why it matters who takes Mr. Harris to the room."

"Indie," he warns. "Harris is a VIP and I want you on it. We're representing the hospital here. I shouldn't have to explain myself."

His tone is final, and I know I've already argued more than I ever would have regarding any other patient. "No problem, Dr. Prichard."

"Cheers."

He hangs up and leaves my stomach swirling. I knew Camden was coming in today because I can read a schedule. But my hope of avoiding him until his surgery was just thwarted by the man who's supposed to be my mentor.

It's been ten days since I screwed Camden Harris on that chair in my flat. That stupid, stupid chair. My stupid, stupid brain.

I thought I could fuck away the feeling. I only had intercourse a handful of times and I suddenly thought I could use it as a dagger through the heart? What's wrong with me?

I'm not ready to see him. I can't even cope with everything that was said between us that morning in my flat or the night before in my bed. Now I'm being forced to pull my big girl knickers on and face the man who touched me in a way no one ever has.

Bloody hell.

I hate sex!

And of course we had every kind of sex imaginable. Oral, slow, kinky, hard, tender. Earth-shattering. Then he had to add personal sentiments on top of that. Why? The words he spewed at me were so intense, my chest could hardly stand it.

What did he expect to happen? Did he think I'd drop everything and start up a relationship with him? My patient? Relationships for me are difficult enough when sex isn't involved. I can barely keep up with Belle's mood swings. Plus he's so clearly on another level. It would be an utter disaster.

I'm not a footballer's girlfriend. I'm a planner with goals. I make a course for myself and focus on the steps I need to get me there. I checked the Penis Number One box! This is why I never should have tolerated him pretending to be a number two.

The more I stew on it, the angrier I get. Camden veered completely off my course. He went rogue and didn't give a damn what I wanted.

The worst part of all is that…I let him.

Just for a moment…*I let go.*

Guilt consumes me as I recall how I let him hold me—how I let the warmth of his body comfort me instead of terrify me. I allowed myself to feel him, skin against skin, inside of me, and it didn't send me into a panic like I thought it should have. It felt…right. He whispered those words in my ears, and I closed my eyes and let myself believe them. I let myself be a different person. I thought, just for the night, I could play the part. I could feel cared for. Protected. Treasured.

Just for the night.

Then reality crept in with the morning sun.

It was as if I turned back into a pumpkin.

I *lost* it.

Like, completely lost it. I turned back into the self that craves space because she doesn't know any different. The self that didn't grow up cuddling with a mum in a rocking chair, or even holding her gran's hand when she crossed the street.

I had to put a stop to what Camden and I were doing and give us both a strong dose of reality. He knew I had a plan, yet he tried to bulldoze himself right past it without a thought about what I needed. I wouldn't be taken advantage of like that.

So now, here I sit, at the hospital—the place where it all began—trying to convince myself that what happened with Camden in my flat was nothing.

Maybe it was all a scheme. He's a player after all. He probably just wanted more sex. He hasn't called or texted. That has to mean something. Not to mention, there's no way a man like Camden Harris—a football-playing, lady-chasing, vagina-ruining bloke—could fall for the awkward, introvert with intimacy issues.

End of.

This MRI today will be a piece of cake.

"Hiya there, Doc," Tanner says brightly as I round the corner to the waiting room where the nurse told me Camden Harris is currently waiting.

I thought my stomach was going to drop when the nurse paged to tell me he arrived. But seeing him in the flesh, sitting right next to his grizzly bear of a brother, is a thousand times worse.

His blonde undercut is longer than the last time I saw him, but he has it lazily swept off to the side and it looks perfect in that unkempt sort of way. He's dressed in jersey shorts that reveal an ample amount of his muscular legs, black trainers, and a fitted blue T-shirt that makes his dark, smouldering blue eyes look positively dirty. But there's a hardness around the edges as he looks at me.

I swallow and adjust my canary-yellow glasses. "Hello, Tanner, nice to see you again. Camden," I add, looking back at him and trying not to let my insides turn into pudding.

"Dr. Porter." His voice is low and flat. Emotionless. And extremely formal.

Tanner leaps up out of his chair. "You'd be proud of our boy, Doc. He's been doing two-a-day workouts all week."

My brows lift as I watch Camden stand up slowly from his own chair, clearly much less enthusiastic than his brother.

Seeing the look of surprise in my eyes, Tanner adds quickly, "They're all physical therapist approved exercises, don't worry. He's just a machine ready to get back out on the pitch. He's probably worried I'll steal his spot with the Gunners if he's not careful."

My jaw drops and I turn my wide eyes to Camden. "You got an offer from Arsenal?" I want to reach out and grab his arm, but I resist…barely.

His eyes narrow and he grinds through clenched teeth. "No."

Tanner laughs. "I just meant his spot that's coming to him. It's only a matter of time." He pats Camden's stiff shoulder, frowning inquisitively at him.

"Just shut it, Tanner, will you?" Camden mutters.

Tanner looks even more confused.

"Well, I'm glad to hear you're doing well," I add, trying to break the tension and gain control of the emotional torment I feel inside of me. *Time to be a doctor, Indie.* "Erm…if you'll follow me, I can take you to radiology. Tanner, you can wait here if you'd like."

"Sounds great. I'm sure I'll find something to occupy myself with." He winks at me playfully and flops back down in his chair.

I turn on my heel and grip the stethoscope around my neck so hard I think I'll leave bruises. I hate that I reacted the way I did at the mention of the Gunners wanting Camden. If he did get an offer, it has nothing to do with me. I shouldn't have to remind myself of that.

I can feel the heat of him behind me as I weave us down the corridors of the hospital toward the older part of the building that radiology occupies. His mere presence brings back so many unwanted memories. Hot memories. Sexual memories. Memories of passion… Like the way he took me from behind in the Cry Room, the dirty words he said, the firm grip he had on my arse. He carnally fucked me as if he was a slave to his passion and I was the desired craving. Just thinking about it causes a stirring between my legs.

Feeling the deafening silence thickening, I slow down so he can walk beside me and ask in clipped tones, "So your physical therapy has been going well?"

I chance a glance at him, and his eyes narrow as he watches the air in front of us. "Very well. My knee feels fine."

"Good. That's good."

More awkward silence.

"Be sure you don't overdo it, though, all right?" I add as we turn another corner.

He cuts me a look. "What happens if I overdo it?"

My brows lift, extremely comfortable answering this type of question. "Well, the graft only allows for the natural movements of everyday life. Things like running, walking, jogging, moving around in your home and work." My cheeks heat as I think about the movements we did together in both of our homes and elsewhere. "It can be pushed some, but not with the brute force involved in athletics. Twisting, pivoting, things that use the eccentricities of your knee's full range of motion. All those movements can injure the tendon the graft is attached to. Just be careful you're not pushing the boundaries."

He huffs out a laugh.

"What?"

He shakes his head.

"What?" I ask again, adjusting my glasses.

He stops so fast I have to turn and walk back to him. Glaring at me, he says, "I'm aware you don't like boundaries pushed. I don't need a reminder."

My face drops. My mouth falls open. My heart feels heavy. "Camden, I'm so sorry. I didn't mean—"

"What exactly are you sorry for, Indie?" His tone is acidic as he says my name through clenched teeth. The muscle in his jaw ticks angrily.

I glance down the hallway as someone walks by. Otherwise, we're completely alone in this very bare, very dank hallway. "Well… for a lot. But mostly for flipping the script on you so much. I could have handled everything better."

"How so?" he asks quickly. "Would handling it differently have changed the end results?"

My eyes soften. "No."

"Then you handled it fine." His eyes are slits.

"Camden—"

"Indie, I have loads of girls I can ring any time. I've already had a couple call this week, so don't trouble your mind with any more thoughts of whatever brief thing we were."

It's not a physical slap, but it hurts so badly my eyes sting. "Fine then." I turn back on my heel and don't slow my pace until we reach radiology.

I glance in through the thick window and the tech indicates he needs five minutes. I bite my lip. I don't know how I'll make it five full minutes. I want to leave now. I want to run away from this horrible, awkward, unpleasant sensation that's consuming my body.

"Find yourself a number two yet?" Cam asks, leaning against the hallway wall as if we're having the most casual conversation ever.

I nearly growl, "No. And it's none of your business."

He laughs. "Hey, I'm just curious. You seemed pretty determined and it's been a while since I last saw you. I figured you've been busy."

"Not as busy as you apparently," I snipe.

He huffs out another exasperating laugh. He's laughing! He's laughing as if this is any normal day and what happened between us was nothing. Then that voice in the back of my mind pipes up and reminds me that it was nothing. It reminds me I all but yelled that at him. What we had was just sex. I was just his doctor. He was just my patient.

"I have a right to be curious. I was a part of the list after all," he drawls and pats me on the shoulder like a guy. "Plus, we're mates, right?"

My eyes turn to saucers at his platonic touch that feels like hot coals against my skin. "Mates? You think we're mates?"

Shrugging his shoulders, he replies, "We're a bit more than doctor/patient." He winks and the look in his eyes is pure evil. "What was it you called us…Oh yes, 'just sex.'"

"Someone could hear you!" My eyes scan the hallway for anybody within listening distance. He's being so careless, I can't take another minute. "They'll come get you when they're ready." I turn to leave, but his hand flies out and grabs my arm.

"Indie," his voice is pleading. It's a tone I recognise better than the one he's been giving me. I want to lean into it and let it comfort me. It's the tone that brings back so many memories of fun and lust that it physically hurts my ears.

I turn back to him and look right up into his eyes. "No, Cam. I'm done. You're making me feel small and silly and stupid and childish just like *they* did."

"Who's they?" he snaps.

"Those girls! Those girls from school I told you about in confidence because I thought you cared. Because I thought we were friends who could trust each other. Because you came to my home and we shared a meal, and I thought that meant something. I didn't tell you so you could use it as ammunition to hurt me."

"It did mean something. And I'm sorry." He slices his free hand through his hair and looks down the hallway. His jawline is taut with emotion, but he's never looked more beautiful. He looks back at me and his ice blue eyes are now warm and soft again, just as they were the night I last saw him in my flat. "Indie, I hurt you because I was angry. But you hurt me because you don't care enough. One is certainly worse than the other."

His words are so true I want to wish them away the moment he puts them out into the universe. For some strange reason, they make me think of my parents and the fact that I don't even have a framed picture of them anymore. The one I had when I was six was at my gran's house and got boxed away in storage with the rest of her things. They care about me, but never enough.

I want to ask him, "what's enough," because I genuinely don't know. But the one thing I do know is that I probably can't feel it. I feel my lower lip wobble, so I pull it into my mouth to chew on in a vain attempt to hide how this encounter is affecting me.

His grip on my arm softens as he moves his thumb to stroke the inside of my elbow. His blue eyes are soft and sympathetic when he says, "Look, we had a fun time while it was good. Let's just leave it at that."

I nod woodenly, knowing that this peace offering is probably more than I deserve, yet, for some mysterious reason, I don't want to accept it.

Suddenly, the radiologist swings the door open and we spread apart instantly, both looking anywhere but at each other. He doesn't seem to take notice and ushers Camden in for his scan.

I can't bring myself to wait. The radiologist will have to see him out. He's given me a peace offering and I need the space to accept it. What Camden and I had was fun while it lasted, but now it's over and I need to move on.

"We're going out," I proclaim, pausing in front of the on-call room door where I find Belle standing at her locker. This sense of urgency has been coming on ever since Cam left a few hours ago. "We're going to get dressed up. I'm going to let you do my makeup, and we're going on a mission."

"Well, yeah," Belle replies. "I already told you a few days ago that Old George has Irish Way playing in the beer garden. I got us tickets for tonight, our first Tequila Sunrise night. Don't you remember?"

I bite my lip at the realisation of how utterly vacant I've been all week because this doesn't ring any bells. Well, no more. I'm done feeling the sting of that slap on my hand. Cam's completely over me and probably off screwing a new girl as we speak.

"That's right." My eyes narrow with strategy. "Old George is perfect."

Belle frowns. "Indie, you've been weird all week. What is going on with you? I saw Camden Harris' brother Tanner today at the hospital, so I know he was here. Did something happen between you two? Your eyes look a bit more Tarsier Primate today than usual."

A tiny part of me wants to tell Belle everything—to blurt out every nasty word that was said between Camden and me. But then I would have to tell her I let him push into me without a condom. That I knew he was doing it and I wanted him to do it. That I craved the feeling, but then, like a lunatic, I wigged out on him afterwards. I accepted him, rejected him, and then slapped him. She'll think I have schizophrenia. Sharing will only shine a bigger light on how truly detached I can be, and I don't want Belle to see that side of me. She's the one person who embraces my quirks. I don't want to wreck it. Plus, I need her to keep me going on this Penis List mission.

I defiantly raise my shoulders and reply, "Nothing bad happened with Camden. I accomplished my goal, so it's time to move down the list. Tonight we're on a Penis Number Two mission."

She eyes me skeptically. "Shag 'em and bag 'em is more my gig... But hey, you are officially deflowered, so who the hell am I to judge? Just call me your wing-woman, darling."

"Two more, please!" I shout down to the cute bartender and blink slowly, appreciating the cut of his jeans. "You know, those jeans would look even hotter on a footballer," I slur over my shoulder to Belle. "God, they can wear jeans!"

"Too right," Belle growls, raising her glass in a toast to hot thighs. "I'm craving a footballer for myself right about now."

My brows raise. "I'm not craving a footballer. Come on, we're here for Penis Number Two. Stay focused."

"Well, Stanley is right there. Primed and ready." She points toward the end of the bar where Stanley quickly looks away.

I shake my head. "Why does he always end up everywhere I am?"

"Because you invite him," she sings.

I sigh. "I know. He asks and I don't want to be mean. Stanley is a nice bloke."

"So why don't you put him out of his misery and shag him?"

"His eyes are too brown," I grumble.

She begins to argue with me as the bartender sets down our tequila. We grip the glasses in our hands, do a quick cheers, and gulp down the spicy liquid.

"Tequila Sunrise!" Belle shouts, giggling happily. "Well, just straight tequila I guess, but the sentiment is there."

"Tequila Sunrise," I murmur, propping my head on my hands.

Belle whacks me on the arm. "All right, we're good and buzzed now. It's time to get serious about Penis Number Two before we get so pissed we can't pick a good pecker."

Turning away from the bar, we lean our backs against the dark lacquered wood and admire the scene for a moment. Old George's beer garden is a gorgeous outdoor sight at night. It's located in the alley behind the pub and is completely ensconced in high lattice fencing covered in crawling ivy. Rustic picnic tables fill the left side, but they've removed several for a small dance floor and the band on the right. The ground is all original cobblestone—there's probably horse manure stamped into the divots from the Medieval era. Because of this, you can always spot the regulars from the tourists. The regulars are in sensible flats while the tourists wobble around awkwardly in heels. It's not a proper night at Old George if you don't see at least three girls take a tumble. Top the entire scene off with string after string of Edison bulbs and you have the most gorgeous, glowing, backyard party you've ever seen.

"I love Old George," I coo.

"I know, love. You look fab tonight, too. Have I told you that?"

"You look better," I murmur.

Belle is kitted out in black leather leggings and a studded, black tank top that makes her look as badass as the combat boots she's rocking. I'm a bit more colourful in floral print leggings and a fitted white T-shirt that Belle says makes my tits look great. Wearing my hair down is usually the only accessory I need to spruce up an outfit. That and my black vintage eyewear.

"Okay, so let's do this." Her gaze narrows on the crowd. "Are you sure you don't want to give Stanley a shot."

"I'm sure."

"So what's the type you're looking for?"

My face turns serious. "Penis Number Two type. Sweet, sensitive, and a nurturing lover. Must cry when he comes." I giggle as I remember that little tidbit from our list.

"I meant physically," Belle says around the straw of her drink.

My brows rise. "I don't know…I guess I like light hair."

“What else?”

“Maybe tall and broad.”

“Yes…”

“With eyes that smoulder.”

“Got it.”

“And I wouldn’t say no to some abs.”

“What about another crack at Penis Number One?” she asks, her eyes locked on something behind me.

“That’s not what—”

She grabs my chin and turns my head toward the far back corner of the beer garden. Despite the darkness, I can make out the outlines of two huge, strapping men sitting on top of a picnic table. It looks like a hairy and non-hairy set of twins.

“Oh no,” I say.

“Surprise!” she giggles and clutches my arm, yanking me in that direction.

26
Things That Make Me Go Hmmm

Camden

I AM A MAN WHO GETS WHAT I WANT.

I am not a man who's used to losing.

I've lost a handful of football matches, tickets to Coldplay once, and a bet with Vi over how much food her dog, Bruce, could consume in thirty seconds.

This isn't a proud list.

Now I can add Indie Porter to it, file it away, and move the hell on. She's a different calibre of the birds I shag, so that's why I'm still smarting over the whole ordeal. I guess rejection wounds even the most confident of footballers. So in the interest of moving on and gaining back some of my "Camden Harris, knicker-dropping smirk" mojo back, I let my brother drag me out tonight.

"I still can't believe you bagged your doctor!" Tanner takes a long drink of his beer, then puts it back up to his eye socket. With the other eye open and on me, he adds, "I did not take her for the monopoly squirt and split type. Do not pass Go, do not collect two hundred pounds."

"If you don't knock it off, I'll give you a matching set," I growl through clenched teeth, balling my fist up beside me. "I'm not kidding, Tan. Leave it."

"That info was well worth the shiner," he states, happily rolling the condensation-soaked beer bottle on his eye.

I take a drink of my own beer, mentally junk-punching myself for the eighteenth time tonight for telling him about Indie and me. Or at least telling him a tiny version of it. I'm not about to tell him she was a fucking virgin. I'd never hear the end of it.

I'm not proud of spilling the beans. But I am a bloke, and ever since he got back from their match last week, he hasn't stopped bragging about the threesome he had on the road. It's not uncommon for him to brag about his conquests, but for the past ten days I'd been slowly dying on the inside over this Indie thing. I was holding on by a thread.

Then today, after my MRI, he started talking about having a threesome with Indie and her coworker, Belle, who apparently chatted with him in the waiting room while I was suffering through a little piece of redheaded hell. My possessiveness got the better of me. I blurted out that I'd screwed Dr. Porter because I knew he'd shut up then.

You see, my brothers and I have an understanding about women. We call it the Bacon Sandwich Rule. If I lick a bacon sandwich, that means it's mine and they can't touch it. Ever.

We apply this same well-thought-out and highly-sensitive philosophy to women, and it's worked well for us…until today.

The punch went a little something like this:

Tanner starts, "You fucked the redhead?"

"Stop."

"What was it like?"

"Stop."

"Were her tits big? They look big."

"Stop."

"Was she wild? She looks like a screamer."

"Stop."

"Did she suck you off? God, I bet she gives good head."

"Stop."

"How were her nipples? Pink or pale pink?"

"Stop."

"Did she call out my name when she came?"

PUNCH.

I know it was probably a bit dramatic, but bloody hell, Tanner can be a sod. This isn't the first time we've rowed over a girl; however, it is the first time I've punched him over one. It evidently still didn't teach him because he won't stop running his mouth.

Regardless, I didn't punch him because I'm still pining over Indie. After our talk today, I know that ship has sailed. Whatever fucked-up thoughts my mind was having over her are well and dead now. I truly think she is incapable of feeling. She's got her head in the sand so far, she wouldn't see a connection with someone if her glasses were binoculars.

She set me up so perfectly, though, like a master heartbreaker. When we fucked on that chair…I had hope. But after it was over and I realised she was just saying goodbye, I knew I was doomed.

After that, all sorts of self-doubt began creeping into my mind. Hell, if I can get it in my head that I care more about her than I do about football, my mind is fucked. Maybe tonight is just what I need to get my shit straight again because it's time for Camden Harris to stop acting like he's on his man-period.

"Hello, boys. Fancy seeing you here!" a voice says from behind me, and I snap my head around to see who it is.

Nothing could have prepared me for who stands before me.

"Dr. Ryan," Tanner leers. "Nice to see you again."

"Call me Belle," she says with a giggle.

"I prefer Dr. Ryan if it's all the same to you. And hello to you, too, Dr. Porter."

Indie's eyes haven't left mine the entire time. She's staring at me with a sort of shocked, embarrassed half smile—one that makes me wish I could read her mind. I know I just saw her today, but seeing her now, under the moonlight, dressed in street clothes with her hair down…well, she looks like the woman I used to know. Not the one I forced myself to make peace with earlier today.

Belle jabs Indie in the ribs with her elbow.

"Ouch," Indie says through clenched teeth. "Hi, Tanner." She looks at me. "Hi, Cam."

"Hello," I reply. "Is seeing you here really just a coincidence?" If so, the fates are cruel, cruel bastards.

Her brows lift. "I have a feeling this isn't a coincidence."

She looks at Belle and Tanner, who both smile knowingly.

"I'm a huge fan of Irish Way," Tanner says, breaking the tension with a comment about the band. "And I just happened to run into Belle today, and she had the inside scoop on where I could score some tickets."

"We love Old George," Belle adds, walking over and sitting down on the bench beside Tanner's feet. "This is our hangout spot, and it's fun when bands play here."

Tanner begins small talk with Belle while Indie remains standing here, staring at me awkwardly. She shifts from one foot to the other as she plays with the frame of her glasses.

I could tell Tanner we need to leave. I could leave by myself. I could go to the bar and get a drink, go to the loo, go to another pub, go hit on a different girl, go crazy!

But I don't.

"Can we go talk for a minute?" I ask, sliding off of the table, not waiting for her response.

Tanner watches me like he thinks I'm going to go take her to the toilet and fuck her.

Indie looks at Belle and gets a silent nod of approval. When she turns to walk away, my hand instantly goes to the small of her back. I hear her sharp intake of breath, so I pull my hand back and clench my fist, wishing Tanner's face was nearby again. Indie Porter likes space…and, fuck, I wish I didn't want to be inside of her right now.

She stops by a thick cluster of ivy, away from the crowd of people, and turns around to face me. She crosses her arms over her chest. The warm bulbs cast a halo around her head and it all seems ironic.

"Do we have a problem that I don't know about?" I ask, stuffing my hands into the pockets of my jeans. They're one of my tightest pair, but today I noticed that my stitches are completely dissolved, so this is the first time I've been able to wear them in two weeks.

Her gaze slides down my abs and lingers somewhere around my legs. "What makes you think we have a problem?"

"Because you look like someone kicked your puppy."

"I've never had a puppy." She glowers before my meaning finally dawns on her. "I'm fine."

I nod. "Good. We can be around each other, can't we?" I ask out loud, wondering the same thing myself.

"I guess so. Does your brother know about us?" She looks down and I can see the shame blanket her. As much as I don't want to, I take it personal.

"He knows, but don't worry about him. He's a sod but he's a decent sod." I watch her face and register the tension knitted between her brows. I can't help myself as my hand reaches out and lifts her chin. I pin her with a serious look. "He won't judge you, Indie."

She exhales when she sees the sincerity in my expression. "Good. So are you really just out for a fun night with your brother, or is this where your book club meets?"

My brows lift at her little attempt at a joke. It feels like the Indie I grew to like. "Book Club meets on Sundays," I wink. "What about you? Tequila Sunrise night I take it?"

Her eyes flash with a tiny level of anguish over how well we know each other. Our late-night pillow talk saw to that. "I'm off for four days this time," she replies.

I want to ask her what her plans were for tonight—if she really was going to try to find her number two—but I bite my tongue.

"Let's go try and have some fun." I toss an arm around her shoulders and exhale when she doesn't tense this time. She actually tucks into me a bit, and the familiar scent of lemons and freshly washed hair makes my heart pound.

The four of us commandeer the corner picnic table that is now littered with empty beer bottles and a pizza we all shared. The band is loud, but not so loud that you can't hear each other talk. It's also not so soft that you feel like you have to fill the awkward silences with chatter.

It's the perfect spot because there's less lighting back here and, so far, my brother and I have gone relatively unnoticed, aside from a couple blokes who wanted to talk football in the loo.

It's always the loo where they get ya. Dick in hand, minding your own business, and bam. "*You're a Harris, aren't you?*"

The ones that get me in the loo never know which Harris I am. They just generalise and try to play it off that I'm a twin so that's why they couldn't tell. Tanner and I haven't looked alike all season, but whatever. People are in love with the idea of us all on one team, playing for the hearts of East London. If I become a Gunner and break up our trio, the Bethnal fans will be devastated. But I can't think about that right now.

The night carries on and it's a bit odd having a normal outing with Indie after everything we shared. Tanner and I are on one side of the table, and Indie and Belle are on the other. It's so ordinary but it feels right. It makes me wonder what life might be like if I was in a relationship. Perhaps it wouldn't be as bad as I'd always thought.

At one point, I get the sense that Tanner and Belle know each other more than they're letting on. Something about the way he says her name, "Dr. Ryan." I'd make a mental note to pester him about it later, but that means he'd pester me about Indie and I don't want that hot, hairy mess coming at me.

"Oh my God, are you two the Harris twins?" a blonde croons as she wobbles up to our table in four-inch heels. She's standing closest to me.

"That we are," Tanner answers with his familiar prowling leer.

"I'm a huge Bethnal Green fan…You guys are like, the best." The girl steps in closer and touches my shoulder as she stumbles. "You had a great season."

I smile politely as her hand squeezes repeatedly. My eyes move to Indie when I hear a heavy sigh from across the table. Her mouth is hanging open a bit and she's watching the girl with a definite curl to her lip.

"Would you want to dance?" the blonde asks, looking back and forth between Tanner and me.

"Which one are you asking?" I ask, unable to stop watching Indie out of the corner of my eye.

The blonde smiles knowingly. "Both of you." Then she giggles in a way that makes my balls crawl up inside of me.

"Fuck. Off," Belle growls, and all of our eyes fly to her. "Seriously. Are you blind? We're sitting right here."

The girl crosses her arms over her chest and cuts a determined look right at Belle. Then she glances at Indie and rolls her eyes. Looking back at Tanner, she says, "You're not seriously staying here with these two frumps, are you?"

Belle slams her fists down on the table and shoots up while Tanner's hands fly out to grab hold of her wrists. I remain silent and watch Indie as she frowns down at the table. She's not moving to calm Belle down. She's not glaring back at the girl. She's just retreated completely inside of herself and blocked it all out.

Tanner's voice is garbled from restraining Belle when he says, "Thanks for saying hello. Have a nice night."

The girl cocks out her hip with an obvious look of disgust. Then she turns and totters away, trying not to fall on the jagged cobblestone and looking like a complete prat in the process.

"Relax, Tony the Tiger. She's not worth messing up your surgically magical hands." Tanner releases his grip on Belle.

She sits down in a huff. "Well, the cheek of her! Talking shit about us when she's the one who looks like a prostitute."

"You could have gone with her if you wanted," Indie blurts out and her eyes are pinned right on me. "Nothing here to stop you."

My gaze narrows at her obvious meaning. "She's not exactly my type."

"What's your type?" She tips her beer and takes three long swigs in a row lowers it and wipes her hand across her mouth.

"I don't know. I'll let you know when I see her," I answer through clenched teeth.

The tension is heavy as Indie's toffee eyes stay locked on mine. Is she picking a fight? Is she trying to bait me? I shouldn't have to remind her that she's the one who told me to fuck off before.

I should be angry, but my strongest emotion right now is turned on. I'm turned the fuck on by Specs and the possibility of her being jealous.

"Camden gave me this black eye," Tanner blurts out of nowhere.

Indie's mascara-lashed eyes are drooping when she looks over to him. "That's what looks different," she replies as she quickly chugs down the remainder of her beer like she's on a mission. She grabs another one out of the ice bucket beside me. "I could hardly see it around all your hair and all this…nighttime. Gosh, that beard!"

"Don't mock the beard!" Tanner crows.

"What did he punch you for?" Belle asks, and I reach out to take the beer from Indie's hand.

She hands it to me without hesitation as she waits for Tanner's answer. I tip it to my lips and drink down most of the contents. She doesn't look like she needs more to drink. I hand the bottle back to

Indie, who scowls when she realises it's mostly empty.

"A girl," Tanner responds. Before I can stop myself, I punch him hard in the shoulder. "Ooof, bloody hell, mate. What was that for?"

I roll my eyes and rest my arms back on the table. "Because you're an arse."

Indie's brows raise. Then they narrow. "Another girl. No surprise there. We all know Camden's quite experienced." She takes a drink of the empty bottle and then sets it down on the table with a huff. "You've got the next round, Belle."

"All right, I'm going." Belle unfolds herself from the table, a look of discomfort marring her features.

"I'll help you." Tanner stands like he too wants to get away from this awkward situation. "Those drinks are very heavy. You'll need a muscled figure with my sort of stamina to help you carry them."

"You're a gentleman and a scholar, good sir." Belle mock bows to Tanner before they shuffle off toward the packed bar area.

I envy their light-hearted banter. Indie and I used to have that. Not all this tension and these narrowed eyes and passive aggressive comments. I watch her pick at the label of her bottle, away with her own thoughts. I'm craving the old Indie—the one with a fiery temper and a knee-jerk reaction that makes me smile.

"If I didn't know any better, I'd say you were jealous."

Her brows lift as she looks at me. "Good thing you know better." She's not letting any cards show tonight. "So tell me, is it normal for two brothers to punch each other over a girl?"

I purse my lips. "It's normal for us to fight. It's how we communicate I guess."

She nods like this is a completely foreign concept to her. "And then you guys make up, just like that?"

I lean forward and reply, "I think even Tanner knows when he deserves a punch."

Her eyes rove around my face. We are so close I can smell the beer on her breath. I prefer the lemon scent, but it doesn't mean I wouldn't kiss her if I had the chance.

She tucks her hair behind her ears and says, "I suppose it's nice you guys are related, and that you have family around who cares about you enough to punch you in the face over some girl."

She's fixating on this girl. I'm torn between being honest with her and telling her that *she* was the girl, or letting her stew with curiosity.

Before I can decide, she continues, "I never had that." She frowns down at the table. "I never even had a pet. I wanted a gerbil once, but my gran said no because I wouldn't be around long enough to take care of it."

"That's no good," I reply, the corner of my mouth turning up at her memory.

"Yeah, you know, my gran died two years ago and I realised at her funeral that I never hugged her. She raised me and I never hugged her my whole life." I watch Indie in eerie silence as she rubs her pointer finger over the rim of the glass bottle.

"My parents came home for the funeral and I spent three days straight with them, which was so weird because it was awkward, as if I didn't know them and they felt like strangers. When it was time for them to go, I drove them to the airport because they had to get back to work…I remember getting out of the car and wanting to make sure I hugged them. I had this desperate need to hug them…because, you know, they were getting on a plane, and you never know when a plane could crash and the only people genetically wired to love you unconditionally are going to go down in flames.

"So I went to hug my mum and she stopped me in my tracks like this." She reaches across the table and grips my biceps. She looks at the physical representation like she still can't believe it. I can't much either. "Then she said, 'Indie, I think I'm getting a cold. Better keep your distance.'"

The weight of the words suspends in the air as she releases my arms with a sad smile. I'm frozen, unmoving, and still feeling the harshness of her grip on my arms.

Shaking her head, she tips the empty beer bottle onto its side and rolls it along the bumpy ridges of the wooden picnic table. "Who keeps their daughter at arm's-length like that? At the time, I tried to believe that she cared enough to not want me to get sick. But when I was driving home, all I kept thinking was, 'What kind of mother doesn't hug their child at the airport?' Hugging at the airport is such an epic moment. There are YouTube montages of awesome hugs at airports. There are homeless men who hold up signs that say 'free hugs,' and they aren't worried about getting sick."

She nods a few times before her eyes snap to mine. "I bet you a million pounds I bury my parents before I hug them."

I feel like I was just shot in the face. Like a million times. Or kicked in the ribs after they're all broken and I've been bleeding internally for hours.

She frowns and looks over her shoulder. "Where's Belle with those drinks?" She moves to get up from the table and I reach out for her hand.

"No more drinks," I beg, my eyes stinging.

She grimaces and then looks at my hand on hers. I don't know if she doesn't feel the tears falling down her face, or if she just doesn't want to acknowledge them. "It's Tequila Sunrise time. You know how important that is to me, Cam."

"I do, but let's go dance instead."

She contemplates the idea. "Dancing is part of the approved list of items for a Tequila Sunrise worthy activity," she says, bobbing her head thoughtfully.

I don't wait for her answer. I stand up and make my way around the table toward her. She won't make eye contact with me, but when I reach out, she puts her hand in mine and stares at our fingers linked together. Tears continue to slide out over and over, but I still don't say anything. Words aren't what she needs right now.

The music isn't slow. Not at all. People are dancing wildly around us, but I tune it all out. I wrap her in my arms and clasp her head to my chest. I begin slowly rocking her to the music, alternating between holding her, squeezing her, and running my fingers through her hair the entire time. Her shoulders shake every once in a while and I know she's crying. All I want to do is take away the pain. I don't want anything more in this world than to take away this pain she has in her.

My desperation to do this for her trumps football. It trumps my family. It trumps my desire to kiss her. What I want for her to feel in this second supersedes any sexual desire I've ever had for her.

I need her to feel *this*.

"Let me take you home," I whisper into her hair, loud enough she can hear me.

Her eyes shoot up to mine and the pain in them guts me. "No," she exclaims. "I couldn't stand it."

My face falls. "Why, Indie?"

She shakes her head side-to-side like the answer should be clear as day. "Because I'm not right for this. I'm not right for you."

I cup her face in my hands, my jawbone ticking with ferocious need to make her see. "Indie, *please*. Let me take you home."

She jerks her head out of my hands. "No, Cam. This was a mistake. I don't want you."

Her words feel final as her watery eyes dry up, piercing through me once again.

"Just go find one of your hundreds of girls at your beck and call. Or that girl you punched Tanner over. If she's worth fighting your brother for, she's who you should be with."

"She was you," I growl, stepping back into her space.

Her face crumples in pain, and she walks backwards away from me. "If she was me, I feel bad for you because I'm not worth that."

"Indie—"

"I'll see you at your surgery, Camden."

I want to chase after her. I want to say more. I want to show her my heart again, but I don't…because I've already said too much. None of it will matter anyway.

She stumbles back over to the picnic table, grabs a confused Belle's hand, and drags her toward the door and out of my heart.

For good this time.

27
Hard Pass

Camden

THE NEXT THREE DAYS AFTER OLD GEORGE ARE PRETTY GRIM. My body swirls in doubt and desperate thoughts of self-preservation. This is worse than the first time Indie blew me off because now I've seen more of her heart. I know more of her darkness. She showed me why she's so damn attached to that stupid list, and it's not something I can fix because she doesn't want me.

So instead, I'm trying to figure out what the hell happened to me. I went from being on top of my game, pulling birds from my brother like it was nothing, to an emotional and physical cripple.

If I knew this was how feelings felt, I'd have avoided them like the horrid STD they are.

I head to Tower Park, hoping that standing on the pitch and looking up into the empty stands might give me some much needed perspective. It's the place where it all began for me, so surely I can find some clarity there.

I drape myself out on the grass, deep in thought, but even this grass feels different. This pitch that I look at like hallowed ground feels pokey and all wrong against my back.

Where have my balls gone? I can't control Indie. I can't control my dad. I can't control the surgery. I can't control my recovery. But above all, I can't get away from this deeply rooted fear of what my life could be like without football. It's all making me crazy.

Feeling out of control is not an emotion I appreciate. I can't gain power over a damn thing in my life and it's eating me alive. I'm due to get the surgery on my knee in a week, and my entire body is roaring with anger over so many things that I think I might explode on the table.

Before I know it, I'm pressing the buzzer to Vi's flat in Brick Lane. I need to talk to her more than I need to talk to anybody.

She lets me up, so I step inside the private alley lift that takes me to the eleventh floor of an old period building. Her flat occupies the entire floor. It's a symbol of how different our dad treats her over us. Don't get me wrong. Vi deserves every penny. She's been the voice of reason for our family since the day she could speak. This is a small price to pay for how much she's helped all of us.

But she's a camera bag designer and not exactly making the kind of money it would take to be able to afford a London penthouse like this. She moved out of our dad's Chigwell house a few years ago and bought this flat with a trust that he'd set aside for her. So it's her money and she invested it wisely. Regardless, he's never set up trusts for the rest of us. Gareth says it's because we make more than he did back then. I think it's because he doesn't want us to be able to quit football.

When I walk in, Hayden meets me at the lift with Vi's dog, Bruce, on a lead. "Hey, Cam."

"Hey, Hayden, how are you?"

"Good. You okay?" he asks, frowning at me. It's the first time I realise there may be some physical representation of the lack of sleep I've been getting the last few nights.

"I'm good. Just need to talk to your baby mama if that's all right."

"Hey, I'm making an honest woman of her eventually." His grey eyes flick to the balcony where she must be sitting. He smiles fondly. "We just mixed up the order a bit."

I offer a polite smile. "As long as you keep her happy, that's all that matters. We won't give you the Harris Shakedown if you keep that smile on her face."

Hayden chuckles. "I'm highly familiar with the Harris Shakedown. I think it was five days straight you guys stalked outside my home last time Vi and I disagreed."

"It was more than a disagreement," I grumble defensively. The bastard nearly broke her heart.

He sighs and pins me with an intense stare. "Cam, I was an idiot. Without question. But sometimes a bit of perspective changes things. That time was a vital part of our story." He reaches down and grips the thick leather cuff wrapped around his wrist. "And you know what? I wouldn't change that now."

"You wouldn't?"

Shaking his head, he replies, "Nope. I'll win your sister back as many times as I have to."

"I'm out here!" Vi yells from outside, interrupting our impromptu heart-to-heart.

Hayden tilts his head with a smile and moves aside for me to walk by. "I'll let you get to it."

"Cheers, Hayden." I move through the living room and step onto their huge terrace. The shrinking London sun casts a grey haze over the incredible view. "Bloody hell, I want to move."

"Well, you should," Vi says and I glance over to find her stretched out on a lounger, book in hand, looking like the epitome of happy and healthy. "It's not like you don't have the money."

I shrug. "I've never cared much because we're never home."

She shoots me a puzzled look. "But you care now?"

I exhale heavily and sit down across from her. "That's what I'm here to talk to you about. I need you to stay calm, Vi. And I need you to know that I've thought about this long and hard, and nothing is going to change my mind."

She sits up to face me so we're knee-to-knee. Clasped fists to clasped fists. Pensive expression to pensive expression.

"I'm not going to have the surgery next week."

"What?" she nearly screams.

"Hear me out," I remind her. "Because you're the only one I'm going to say it to this way, and I want you to know the truth."

"Okay," she grinds through clenched teeth.

"I don't want the surgery next week because I'd rather live with this graft in my knee and never know if I can play as good, rather than get the graft out and find out that I can't get back all that I lost."

She exhales heavily three times like she's doing Lamaze breathing. "Vi, calm down."

"Camden, no."

"Vi…it's my decision. This is what I want."

"So you're scared? Why? What changed? You weren't scared to have the first surgery," she says, her blue eyes wide and watery.

"I didn't have time to think about it," I reply. *Plus, I had Indie by my side.*

"Did something happen between you and Indie?"

Her question doesn't surprise me. I knew she'd go there. She's been calling or texting almost every day, asking how things are with her. "No. This has nothing to do with her. It has to do with me making a decision for myself and not for anyone else."

"Cam, I can see it in your eyes. You're lying. Tell me the truth. What did she do to you?"

I sneer, "Why do you think she did something to me? Isn't it far more likely that I kicked her to the curb?"

Her chin drops. "Drop the shield, I'm not shooting at you."

"Vi, this isn't about Indie. But I'm grateful for my time with her. I learned a lot. People can survive with torn ACLs and live perfectly normal lives."

She clenches her jaw. "How could she say such a thing?"

"She's a doctor and it's the truth. But it doesn't matter. I can't take this pressure. This weight. This…everything. It's too much. I'm telling you because I love you and I don't want you to be disappointed in me. You're the one person I can't take that from."

"But football is everything to you. It's everything to all of us." Her voice is panicky.

I want to growl, but I'm staying calm because she has a baby inside of her and I need to be gentle. "I just need some time to decide what *I* want to do for a change."

"You're so talented, Camden," her voice sounds defeated.

"That's not the point."

She sighs dejectedly. "This is not going to go over well."

28

I Need Space for My Space

Indie

"INDIE," PRICHARD SAYS, STOPPING ME IN THE HALLWAY ON MY way to Patch Alley.

I do my best to suppress a heavy sigh. "Hi, Dr. Prichard." I enunciate his name more forcefully than necessary, attempting to put extra focus on the *doctor* part of my address.

He grasps my elbow and guides me away from the hustle and bustle, into the darkened hallway where stretchers are stored. His touch feels like needles. "I have excellent news."

"I was just paged for an ortho consult on a little boy," I say, pointing to where I was heading.

"This won't take long." His eyes crinkle on me in that way that makes me feel squirrely. I've done my best to avoid him since that odd moment in the scrub room, but with Camden's surgery coming up, there's only so much space I can create.

"*The British Medical Journal* will be here on Monday for the Harris surgery. They want to interview me…and you." He seems to bite out the last part. "They are interested in talking to you about the research you did in med school."

My mouth drops open. *The British Medical Journal* is even bigger than the one that published my research before. "What do they want to know?"

"Nothing too technical. They want to do a human interest piece on how you are one of the youngest published practicing doctors operating on a top-level athlete. They want to talk about your upbringing, your research, the procedure we're doing on the Harris patient. Everything. The hospital is very keen about this idea."

"Wow," I reply still feeling a bit stunned. To have a medical journal interested in me at all is a tremendous honour. But a human interest piece? About my background and Camden? Nerves erupt inside my belly over how awkward this could be for me in more ways than I can even admit.

"I thought you might be pleased." Prichard's brows rise and he gets a smug look in his eyes. "I have a bottle of vintage Dom we can share after the surgery to celebrate."

Realising that his hand is still on my elbow, I force out a smile. His advances are becoming more and more obvious. It's not against hospital policy to date a member of the staff; however, when I'm already fighting against other residents' perception of me, attention like this will not help me get ahead.

"We'll see." I step away from him, but he steps back into my space—so close that I can smell his cologne.

"Indie, I hope you can see what a good team we make. Together, I can really see big things happening all around."

I stare back at him in wonder. It's such a jarring juxtaposition for someone so handsome to say things so obviously creepy. When he has the entire hospital flocking at his feet, I wonder why he puts so much focus on me.

"Well, Dr. Prichard, I have a patient waiting, so…"

"Of course." He smiles and winks. I turn and haul arse out of his space, away from his scent, and retreat into my own thoughts.

"What was it you did, little man?" I ask, sitting down next to a wide-eyed little boy whose tiny form takes up only ten percent of the stretcher we're sitting on.

His lower lip protrudes as he's doing his very best not to cry again. "Well, I was chasing my sister…and she went downstairs real fast and I wanted to get her…and so…I didn't."

"The steps are wooden. There's no carpet, or padding, or anything. He screamed so loud. I just know something is broken."

I look over at his mother's face and see matching wide eyes tear up as she watches her four-year-old son clutch his arm protectively to his chest. It took a solid ten minutes for me to get him to stop crying and finally talk to me.

"It hurts," he mumbles again.

An idea comes to mind. "Hey, Limerick, do you like football?"

"Yeah, my dad says, 'Go Gunners.'" His voice wobbles as he sniffles.

I smile. "So you're an Arsenal fan? That's a great team. Do you want to know something really cool?"

"What?"

"I treated a professional footballer here in this hospital not very long ago."

"Who was it?"

"He's a striker. He's very big and very strong and has scored lots of goals this season. But do you know what else?"

He looks at me with wide, puppy-dog eyes.

"He was scared, too."

"He was?" A light turns on in his eyes.

"He was. And do you know how I got him to not be scared?"

"How?"

"I had him sing a song," I lie. I can't very well tell him that I snogged his face off. "Do you like singing?"

"Depends on the song."

"Humpty Dumpty seems to make sense here."

He grins and says, "I know that one."

"Come on then, let's hear it!"

I get him going on the nursery song before he lets me touch his arm. Eventually, around some giggles and some pitchy notes on my part, I'm able to do a full manual exam.

"Limerick," I whisper and he stops singing. "You're a better singer than that footballer."

He beams and then drops his face to serious. "But he's probably a better footballer."

"Only until you get bigger." I ruffle his hair and tell his mother that someone will be by to take him to X-ray. I suspect he does have a hairline fracture but, depending on the location, he could get by with a brace and not a full cast. She seems grateful, and I make a mental note to relay the singing bit to the radiologist.

"You know, that's the third time you've brought him up in random conversation since we came back to work yesterday." Belle pushes herself off the nurse's station counter and jogs to catch up to me as I make my way to the on-call room.

"It is not," I defend. "And don't you have better things to do than watch me with a patient?"

Ignoring my last remark, she continues, "Yesterday you yelled at Stanley when he said footballers are all poofs who like to put on a show. And last night you ripped my head off when I asked you why you were reading a sports medicine textbook."

"I just had to look something up," I argue, still annoyed by my newly found interest. Ever since I saw Tower Park and felt the grandness of it all, my brain won't shut up.

Thinking about Tower Park evokes a most unwelcome memory of how Camden held me on the dance floor as I cried the other night. How embarrassing and humiliating. For some odd reason, it's always been easy to open up to him. I reveal things to him that I've never even told Belle.

The rest of my time off was very un-Tequila Sunrisey. Belle kept pestering me about why I was emotional when we left Old George that night. I lied and told her I was allergic to the ivy on the walls and had accidently touched some. She made me take medicine and spent the night with me to make sure I didn't go into anaphylactic shock.

I'm grateful to be back at the hospital now, letting work consume my mind instead of thoughts of Camden.

His surgery is in just a few days and I have to stop thinking about him. I can't think about how he felt when he held me at Old George, or how incredible my first time with him was, or how funny and charming he is when he puns. I don't give a toss if he meant what he said that morning I threw him out of my flat. It was a mistake when I cried in his arms at Old George—a lapse in judgment. I'd had too much to drink and didn't know what I was doing.

So I detached. I pushed him away not once, but twice. In my experience, that's how most relationships are. Distant. Here one minute, gone the next. No goodbye hug. No thoughtful words. No grand gestures. Just a departure. That is what Camden Harris would have turned into if I gave too much of myself. If I allowed myself to depend on him for my sole happiness, he'd become like all the other absentee figures in my life.

I just wish I knew why this is all still bothering me so much.

"And those two instances don't necessarily have to do with *him*," I say to Belle as we reach the on-call room door. I turn, pressing my back against the door, and add, "I'm just applying the knowledge I gained from that experience to the real world."

Her eyes narrow. "Please." Reaching behind me, she quickly shoves open the door and sends me flying backwards.

Thankfully, a pair of able hands catch me. "Indie, are you okay?" Stanley's big brown eyes look down on me all soft and worried and still a bit wounded. He hasn't lost that look since that night at the club over a month ago.

"I'm fine, Stanley. Cheers." I right myself and pull out of his arms, staring down at the floor. I feel his eyes on me as he shuffles his way out. I exhale as the door closes behind him. "Gosh, this place can feel so stifling sometimes." I drop down onto the bed and Belle flops down next to me.

"I don't know what you're moaning about. You have Penis Number Two right there, ready and waiting for you. That's called easy-peasy convenience if you ask me."

The idea of having sex with Stanley churns my stomach. "I'm not having sex with Stanley."

"Why not? You've completed number one…You were so keen on number two just a few days ago."

"I can't do it."

"You said you were ready. I think experiencing a guy like Stanley could be good—"

"Maybe we can wait until I get the feel of the first cock out of me, all right? Not all of us are like you and can hop from one dick to the next without a care in the world." My breaths come out fast and heavy as my words slice into Belle's unsuspecting guts. I wince at her crestfallen face.

She rears back from my attempted embrace. "Fuck. Off. Indie." Then she stands up and storms out of the room, leaving me completely shattered in her wake.

I could laugh…if I didn't think it might make me cry. If space is what I wanted, then I've certainly achieved it now. First Camden, now Belle. My eyes sting with unshed tears. Tears that I refuse to release. Tears that I won't permit to drop. Tears that have no business coming from me. This is all ridiculous.

Pushing Camden away was the right thing to do. The presence of *The British Medical Journal* cements that fact. I couldn't operate on him if we were still together. Plus, what we're doing with sports medicine is so much bigger than some crush. Walking away from Camden was necessary. He is my patient. Nothing more. I'm making history here, and all of this will work out just fine.

"Erm…Indie?" Stanley interrupts my thoughts, peeking his

head around the door. "There's someone here to see you. I put her in the consult room down Hallway D."

"Who is it?" I ask.

"She didn't want to say."

She? I think to myself, standing up and smoothing my scrubs into place. Who on earth?

I make my way to the room where we take patient's families to tell them bad news. It's not a good room. It's a very bad room with mauve cushioned chairs and dusty silk flowers. I hate the room.

When I open the door, my eyes fall on the back of a slender blonde who's looking out the window on the far wall. When she turns around, my heart sinks.

"Vi," I say, my eyes wide with frozen shock. "What are you doing here?"

Her lips are curled, nostrils flared, and eyes razor sharp, focused on me. "What did you do?" she asks, her voice low and controlled.

I frown as she advances toward me. She looks as if she wants to hit me. "Is everything okay?"

"No, *Dr. Porter*, it's not. Tell me what you did. What else did you say to him?"

My face is the picture of horrified. Did Camden really tell her everything about us? I begin stammering, "I don't…I just…We couldn't—"

"Why would you convince him not to have the surgery? You're his doctor! This is what's best for him. This is what's best for the hospital. If he leaves that stupid graft in, he won't be able to play football or anything ever again. Tell me what you said to him."

My head spins. This is nowhere near what I thought she was accusing me of. "I never told him not to get the graft removed, Vi."

She looks me up and down as if she doesn't believe a word I'm saying. "Did you tell him people can get by without repairing their ACL? Did you tell him not everyone has the surgery?"

My mind flashes back to our first two nights together in the hospital, and she's completely right. I did say all of that to him. But I didn't say it because I thought he shouldn't do it. I said it because… because…

I care about him.

"Vi, I said some derivative of that, but I didn't mean for him…Of course I didn't…He's a career athlete." I'm tripping over my words. "He has to have the second surgery. There's no question."

"We've been trying to convince him for two days. He's not budging!" Her clear blue eyes are wide and wild and a bit scary, if I'm being honest. "What the hell happened between you two? I never would have given you coffee had I known you would do this to him."

"What does coffee have to do with anything?"

She shakes her head and rolls her eyes, clearly not giving up that nugget of information to me…the chosen enemy. "You have no right to judge our family or how we operate. None."

"I never said I did!"

"Yet you passed judgement on our dad. He said you questioned him the day before Cam's surgery. God only knows what you said to Cam. And then you hooked up with him outside of the hospital just to further insert yourself into his life and mess things up. I let it go because I could see how happy he was around you. And I know he's a charming sod. But you! I never expected you to mess things up like this. This has to be grounds for malpractice! Who do you think you are?" Her voice is so loud it rattles the light fixture.

Her anger doesn't scare me, though. It doesn't intimidate me. It enrages me on behalf of myself and what Camden and I are…were. I won't let her twist what we had together into some sick sadistic game I was playing with a patient. I won't.

"Look. I'm no one, all right," I begin, ready to unleash everything inside of me right now. "I'm no one except the one person who maybe looks at your brother a bit more objectively. I don't see him as a footballer athlete. I see him as a man. A patient at first…but then, a man. A lovely, kind man who has more going on for him than football."

"Football is his whole life—"

"I'm not finished!" I nearly growl.

She closes her mouth.

"Everything I said to him was because he was alone and hurting. You guys are around him all the time, yet you don't *see* him. You don't see the fear he has. You don't see the look in his eyes when I talk about inserting a scope into his leg. You don't see that maybe the fact that your mum had two surgeries and still died in the end could be causing him some turmoil. You don't see that a meeting with Arsenal at the hospital puts pressure on him when he's already crumbling inside, because in his mind, he is *broken*! Vi, he's been a footballer most of his life. He identifies himself with it. He thinks that's all that he is. This kind of injury messes with more than just his knee."

Silence stretches out and tears well in Vi's eyes as she shakes her head back and forth. She attempts to speak but stops herself, covering her mouth to hide her emotions.

"But you're not completely wrong here," I say with a tender touch to her shoulder. "I have been completely unprofessional and could probably lose my job after all of this. I wouldn't blame you if you wanted to turn me in. I deserve it. I deserve worse."

She looks down and swipes haphazardly at her wet cheeks.

"But please don't turn me in because you think I was trying to manipulate your brother. I wasn't. I cared about Camden. I still… care." The words ache in my throat like a tight knot that refuses to turn into a full-blown cry. "But he got confused about what we were. It's probably my fault. I should have put a stop to it before it was too late."

Vi moves toward me with a pleading look in her eyes. "Maybe you can get through to him? Make him see sense? I don't know what happened between the two of you. He won't say a thing and it's killing me to not know."

My chin wobbles at his loyalty. Despite me hitting him, despite me rejecting him twice, despite me having sex with him and then kicking him out, he's protecting me. He could be bad-mouthing me all over London or cost me my job and I would deserve it. But he's not. "I can't tell you what happened between us. Just that I wish I were wired differently. Maybe if I was more like your family, things wouldn't have gotten so complicated between us. I really do still care, though."

Vi's eyes are on mine and she gives me a small, imperceptible nod. "I didn't see Cam." Her voice cracks. "You're right. I didn't see." She sniffles and wipes her nose with a huff of disappointment. "He's my baby brother," her shoulders lift. "I just want what's best for him. Our family is unique, but you have to know it comes from a good place. Maybe we made some mistakes, but football isn't just a game to us. It's not our way of life. It's what brought us back to life."

"I actually know that," I say with a heavy exhale and nod encouragingly. "Despite everything I said, Vi, I know that Camden loves football. I think he's trying to convince himself that he doesn't, but I saw his face at Tower Park that day. I know what it means for him to play with his brothers. To have you in the stands...or holding his hand before surgery. I respect your family so much. I envy what you guys have. It's completely foreign to me, but to have that level of love and devotion in your everyday lives," I huff out incredulously. "Your baby is going to be so lucky."

A surprised smile spreads across her face as she touches her stomach. "It means a lot to hear that." Tears well in her eyes again. "We don't know any other way to be a family, you know?"

"Nor do I," I reply quietly, feeling the sting of realisation overwhelm me.

She swallows and nods definitively. "I should be going. I'm sorry I came here and melted down like this. My Momma-Bear Ninja is strong."

I smile, but her words don't bring me comfort. They bring me jealousy. Acute, heavy, surprising jealousy.

She makes her way to the door and calls back, “Take care, Indie.”

“You, too, Vi,” I croak and turn my back to her so she can’t see my face crumple over the realisation that overcomes me in that moment.

29 Space is Just a Sequence of Letters

Camden

"CAMDEN, WHAT IS ALL THIS NONSENSE ABOUT YOU NOT wanting to have the surgery?" my dad growls into the line. "I can't even believe I have to have this conversation with you."

Sighing heavily, I turn the volume down on my earbuds and hit STOP on the treadmill. I could kick myself for answering, but if I didn't, he would have stopped by. "Dad, this isn't your decision."

"You're my son. I'm your father. How can you possibly think that I won't have a say regarding this?"

"You're my father? That's a laugh." I grab a hand towel and wipe my forehead.

"What on earth—"

"You're my manager. That's why you're talking to me. Not because of fatherly concern."

He harrumphs. "I seem to remember raising you. That doesn't entitle me to being labeled your father?"

"I think you can thank Vi for some of that."

"Damnit, Camden, I'll drag you to that hospital myself if I have to."

"Great, I look forward to it," I bark.

"Did that meeting with Arsenal really mean nothing to you? Good God, it's what we've all dreamed of for ages."

"No, it's what you've dreamed of for us. I don't know what the hell I want anymore."

"Camden, you're just scared. An injury can mess with your mind. Stay focused, Son."

"I'm tired of everyone telling me what to do!" I roar into the mobile, tipping over the edge completely. "I'm not letting you all back me into a corner. I have my own bloody mind and no one is pushing me around anymore. It's over. I'm not having the surgery on Monday. End of."

His heavy sigh is trembling with barely contained anger. I can picture him pinching the bridge of his nose in disappointment. In a flat voice, he says, "You're making a mistake."

"At least it's mine." I push END on the screen and yank my earbuds out before I chuck my mobile to the corner of the room.

I bend over to snatch up the whiteboard marker off the floor and scrawl out yet another pun on the mirrored wall of our gym. It fits well with the other puns I've been writing as they continue to slither into my brain unwelcomed:

Those who get too big for their britches will be exposed in the end.

Every calendar's days are numbered.

Marathon runners with bad footwear suffer the agony of defeat.

I can't seem to stop punning, no matter how hard I try. Or how embarrassing it might be. Tanner and I usually write inspirational quotes on the mirror to help us stay focused during our home workouts. Writing depressing puns doesn't seem to have the same effect. I read my latest one another time:

To write with a broken pencil is pointless.

I can thank my dad for the inspiration behind that one. What I'm seeing in the mirror these days doesn't impress me. I glare at myself, poking the six-pack on my stomach. I used to take pride in looking this way. I used to marvel at the results years of hard work and training afforded my body and my lifestyle.

But right now, I just don't give a shit.

I grab a large exercise ball and sit on it, bouncing to get my bearings. It's been three days since I decided not to have the surgery. I'm surprised my dad waited this long. He probably hoped someone else would talk me out of my decision. Vi is convinced this is all happening because of a broken heart, which is ridiculous because the only thing Indie Porter gave me was a much needed wake-up call.

For someone so inexperienced with men, she knows how to blow a guy off rather triumphantly. After dancing with her the other night, everything felt different. If I could get it in my head that I wanted Indie more than I wanted football, my priorities were obviously fucked. So I'm done letting everybody take what they want from me. I'm done being a bloody show pony for football, for the hospital, and for Indie. I'm so fucking done.

Plus, if I don't have the surgery, I don't have to deal with any of it.

Especially Indie.

Shaking my head, I lean back to do some crunches and attempt to drown out my thoughts. Just as I get started, I hear a voice down the hallway that makes me freeze mid-crunch.

"Look, I can text him and tell him I'm here and then this conversation will be over, or you can make this easier by letting me in to talk to him. You buzzed me up here, so I don't know why you're wasting my time."

"How do I know you're not going to inject some Jedi mind tricks in him like the other night?" Tanner's voice sounds defiant like a child.

"I didn't mess with his mind!"

I stand up to look out the door. I see Tanner at the end of the hallway, but I can't see *her*.

"Prove it," he jeers.

"Tanner," I bark.

He jumps, momentarily surprised by my voice. Then he holds his hand out to stop me. "Cam, don't sweat it. I've got this."

"I appreciate the bro barrier, but I can handle it."

He narrows his eyes and pauses for a beat. Finally taking a step back, he indicates with his hand for her to come through. I try to prepare myself for the sight of her, but it's useless.

Actually laying eyes on her is like a bolt of lightning. In an instant, I remember how she feels. How she tastes. How she adjusts her glasses when she's nervous. I remember the snappy look she gets in her eyes when I'm being a smartarse. I remember the heated colouring of her cheeks when she gets turned on. I remember all of that with a thunderous punch against my chest like I'm being resuscitated.

She's dressed in her blue work scrubs. Her hair is a wild mess on top of her head. Her name badge is still connected to her breast pocket and standard black frames rest on her nose.

She looks gorgeous.

Her eyes drink me in, too, probably because I'm shirtless and only wearing a pair of athletic shorts and trainers. I feel mildly grateful when it seems hard for her to look at me.

"Can we go to your room and talk?" she asks, adjusting her glasses.

I can't stomach the idea of being in my room with her again… so close to the bed where I first touched her. I tear my eyes away and reply, "No, but you can come in here."

I turn and walk back into our small gym, grabbing the exercise ball and flopping down onto it. I immediately regret the decision to bring her in here when I see her reading the puns on the mirror. Her mouth opens like she wants to say something. Just as quickly, her jaw shuts when she stops at:

Show me someone in denial and I'll show you a person in Egypt up to their ankles.

Jaw taut, she twirls on her heel to face me, crossing her arms over her chest. "Nice to know you've been talking about me to your family."

My face remains flat. "I haven't said any more to Tanner than what he knew before."

Her brows lift. "So he's that friendly to all the girls you bring home?"

I huff, "I've never brought any other girl here." I bite my tongue as soon as the words spill out. She doesn't need to know that. She doesn't deserve to know that everything I did with her was unique.

She fades away for a second, clearly lost in her thoughts.

"Did you come here for a reason, or just to get in a row with my brother?"

"I had a nice chat with your sister yesterday." My head juts forward like I couldn't possibly have heard her right. "She came by the hospital and told me you're not going to have the second surgery."

My family's constant need to meddle has reached new heights. "Sorry to mess up your plans," I grind out through clenched teeth.

She scoffs, "My plans aren't important here."

"Oh please," I hiss. "This surgery was going to be huge for your career. I'm not a dumb jock, Indie."

"I've never said you were. I've never even thought you were. Not once." She tightens the hold on her arms and glances down at my abs. "Do you have a bloody shirt you can put on?"

I roll my eyes, unsure if she's trying to make a joke or if I'm distracting her thoughts too much. Either option doesn't involve me putting a shirt on.

"Did you just come here to try and convince me to have the surgery? If so, you can save your breath. Everyone in my family has already tried. If they can't do it, neither can you."

She props her hands on her hips. "Why aren't you having it?"

"I need some time off," I answer like it's the easiest question in the world.

"So take time off *after* the surgery."

I shake my head. "That won't work."

"Yes, it will. Cam, the surgery wasn't meant for this. If you take any sort of impact with that graft in, you risk worse damage to it. Get the graft removed and then decide not to play."

"If I get it removed, I'll be convinced to play. I know my family, and I'm tired of doing what everyone else wants me to do all the time. It's time I do what *I* want. It's my knee."

"Your family loves you. They're just trying to do what's best for you. You're so lucky to have that. If it's me you're angry at, I'll take myself off of your surgery. I'll be as far away from that OR as humanly possible, okay?"

"Don't flatter yourself," I scoff. "You are not the reason for this. I couldn't give a toss who saws into me."

"There's no sawing," she groans defensively.

"The drilling."

"No drilling either."

"The burning of bone."

"Stop."

"The—"

"Camden, don't joke right now!" Her voice borders on shrill and she cups her face in sheer exhaustion. "This all got so messed up. I thought if I gave you space it might make things better. But now your family hates me, you're not having the surgery, and all distance did was make things worse!"

My eyes narrow on her. "I think you forgot that you're the one who craves space, Indie. Not me. I'm a Harris. Space is a made-up word to us." My voice is flat and emotionless even though she stares back at me with brown, watery eyes.

"I'm so sorry, Camden. For everything. I'm not built for any of this." She sniffs and turns her back on me to swipe at her face. Her hunched posture guts my insides. My instinct is to go to her like I did the other night. To touch her. To hold her and comfort her until those tears disappear or turn into laughter. But I refrain, because I know it's not me she wants.

Despite all of that, I offer, "It's not you, Indie. I've just lost the passion for it."

She scoffs and shakes her head. "You bleed passion. It's your best feature."

Her words slice through me. The personal comment sinks into my soul, reminding me of all that we've shared with each other. But she's still over there. I'm still over here. I have to stay strong because what I crave from her is more than this moment right now. Through clenched teeth, I utter, "Please don't speak like you know me." *I'm not sure my heart can take it.*

She nods and her eyes move back to the puns on the mirror. Without speaking, she bends over to pick up the marker from the floor. Finding an open spot, she scrawls something and then turns to look at me one more time. Her face is filled with emotions. Sorrow. Anger. Frustration. But mostly, she looks lost.

She hands the marker to me. "I hope you make the right decision for you, Camden. And no one else."

I watch her leave. Once she is gone, my mind screams at me to not read her words, but my heart overrules.

I move closer to the mirror: *What you seize is what you get.*

"What the hell does that mean?" Tanner's voice interrupts my thoughts. I turn and see him standing behind me, biting down on a banana.

I squint at it again. "The beauty of puns is that they can mean any number of things."

He shakes his head and watches me. "Serves you right for hooking up with a smart bird. Did she get through to you?"

I roll my eyes. "No, Tanner. Just leave it."

He pulls his hands back like he's not trying to pick a fight, his banana still clutched in one. "Slam your fist in the door as many times as you'd like, Brother, but it's not going to hurt anyone but you."

My jaw falls open. Then he walks out on me, too. It's not a pun, but I hear him loud and clear.

36
My First Pet

Indie

"So is that it then?" I ask, rushing into the on-call room and finding Belle flipping through a magazine as if she doesn't have a care in the world. "Is that the end of our friendship? Is that how these things usually go?"

"What the hell happened to you?" she asks, eyeing me from the cot she's draped over.

She must be commenting on the fact that I walked back from Camden's flat in the rain. Or maybe she's talking about the fact that I'm losing my bloody mind and can feel myself imploding. Stanley takes one look at my crazy eyes and scurries out the door with his tail tucked between his legs.

"Let's talk about what *hasn't* happened to me in the last week, shall we?" I begin pacing in front of her, the squishy sound of my wet trainers sending chills up my spine. "I haven't managed to get Stanley to stop looking at me as if I'm a dessert buffet and he's on a diet. I haven't managed to get Prichard to stop making creepy comments to me. I haven't managed to lose my virginity and just move the hell on. I haven't managed to avoid hooking up with a patient. And now I haven't managed to keep a best friend! As far as relationships go, I'd say I'm doing a proper job of cocking everything up."

Her face twists into an unattractive sneer and she throws her feet down on the floor to sit up. "What the bloody hell are you going on about?"

"Well, I got in a fight with you and you don't even care."

"What makes you think I don't care?" she asks, her voice high and shocked.

"You didn't fight with me. Just like that, you walked out on me yesterday and I haven't seen you since. I thought caring about people usually means they…care! I thought that, even when you mess up, they fight with you. I don't know how to process these emotions that are crushing my insides right now."

"Indie—"

"You know how kids always remember their first pet the most?" I ask her, feeling as if I still can't quite catch my breath.

"I guess so?"

"They do. It's science. Their first pet reduces anxiety. Teaches them how to be social. Shows them unconditional love. Then the pet dies because animals have shorter lifespans than humans. But it's okay because the pet served its purpose. It taught the kid how to connect by choice instead of familial obligation. I never had that. I've never had a pet. You were my pet!"

"I was your pet?" Her face is completely disbelieving.

"This is a euphemism. Keep up."

"I'm trying!" she exclaims. "But your brand of crazy is of a special variety tonight."

"Look," I exhale and sit down next to her on the bed. Reaching out, I grab her hands and pierce her eyes with mine. "I've been used to solitude and living my life with my own thoughts. It's been easy for me because I never grew up in the same place or around the same people, so I never really formed relationships. It was me and school. Detaching kept things simple.

"You're the first thing I haven't wanted to detach from, and I'm dying on the inside because I hate what I said to you. You're not a slut. I would never think that about you. I was just mad about something else and I used you as a punching bag I guess. I don't know why. I'll revisit that at a later date with a therapist."

"Your therapist list is getting longer and longer," she murmurs.

"I know," I half sob.

"So is that an apology?" she asks.

"Yeah, I guess so," I shrug.

"Fine."

"Fine?"

"Yeah sure, fine. That declaration was pretty dramatic, but you're going to have to do a lot worse to get rid of me. Using me as a punching bag is called love, darling."

I freeze for a tiny moment before throwing my arms around her neck and hugging her to me. A real, genuine hug. I know I'm getting her wet but I don't care. I thought I was okay being alone. I thought space is what I craved, but it's not. Things have changed for me. My brain hadn't had time to catch up to that fact. In my arms is my unconditional best friend. My family. I care about her.

"We've never fought before," I croak.

She pats my wet back gingerly. "No, we haven't. I would have remembered if this is how you behave after a fight. I wish I would have recorded it."

I smile and then release her to hunch over and hold my head in my hands. "God, what a mess I've made these last few weeks."

"What's going on? Because I know that rant wasn't all about you apologising for a snarky comment."

I swallow hard. "Camden Harris said he was falling for me."

"He what?" she screams. "When? At Old George?"

"Before," I reply.

"Before?" she screams again.

I shush her. Then I spill every last sordid, awful detail. Even down to the goodbye sex I gave him on the chair in my flat, the crying on the dance floor at the pub, and the conversation I just had with him in his gym.

"Christ, Indie, you skipped to the finish line," Belle says, shaking her head back and forth in wonder.

"Stop," I groan. "Help me figure out what to do. I mean, if I did dive into more with him, a relationship or whatever, I don't know if I could survive losing him. I melted down over the thought of losing you and we've never had sex!"

"This is true. We'll save the *Vagina List* for our thirties." She waggles her brows, and I huff out a pathetic laugh at her joke.

"What if I don't know what love even feels like? I think I love you, but what the hell do I know? You're just a girl I make Penis Lists with and tell all my secrets to. Whatever you and I have isn't normal, is it?"

"What's normal? Who cares about normal?" she shrugs. "You do what feels right."

"But how can I date a Penis Number One? He's a player. Won't I get my heart broken?"

"Indie," she says with wide, shocked eyes. "You're like the dumbest smart person I know."

"What the hell does that mean?" I baulk.

"Camden isn't Penis Number One." She reaches out and grabs my shoulders so I'm facing her more clearly. "He's Penis Number Three."

My hands cover my cheeks and they feel as if they might melt off my face. "No."

"Yes."

"No."

"Yes! Indie, he is the perfect mix of One and Two. He said 'Thou Art Mine' right after he made love to you. That's the stuff love stories are made of."

I shake my head in disbelief. "I don't know if I'm capable of more yet. I always thought I'd live a little before I found a Penis Number Three."

"Well, he's certainly shown himself to you already, darling. You just have to decide if he's worth it."

31 Close Enough

Camden

Me: I'm coming for the surgery tomorrow. Don't make a thing of it. Don't pull out from doing the procedure. Let's just pretend we don't know each other and get through the day.

...

...

...

Indie: I'm glad.

She's glad, I think to myself as I ride in the car with my brothers to the hospital. It's six a.m. and the London sunlight hasn't even touched the surface yet, further darkening my mood. But it's okay, because Indie Porter is "glad." I'm glad she's glad. I'm glad that I tormented myself over the decision for hours and she gets to type back two fucking words in a text.

I'll be glad when this is over and I can get back to my life, whatever it may be.

"Camden," Tanner says from the back seat, shaking my shoulder to get my attention. "What do you call cheese that is not yours?"

"I don't know, what?" I ask, turning my head to look at him.

"Nacho cheese!" His eyes crinkle as he bursts out laughing. I can actually see his mouth smile now that the season is over and he's trimmed his beard at last. Booker chuckles quietly beside him, and I glance over at Gareth in the driver's seat whose shoulders shake with silent laughter.

The corner of my mouth tilts up.

"That's a pun, right? Did you like it?" Tanner asks, his voice bright and innocent.

I shrug. "It's all right," I say while trying to stop my smile from growing. "Are we not picking Vi up?" I ask Gareth as he misses the turn for her flat.

"No, she's meeting us there." His jaw seems more tense than usual, which makes me frown.

A few minutes later, we pull up to the hospital. I get out of the car and stare up at the building like it's the single solitary cause of all my stress. Not Tower Park or the match where I injured myself…but this building.

Unwelcome memories of Indie flood my mind. I never had a problem sleeping alone in my entire life. In fact, it was rare I ever slept over at a woman's flat. But one injury and a sideways glance from a pretty doctor and Camden Harris turned into an emotional pansy.

She was so nervous and unsure in those early days with me—terrified of getting caught—but there was a spark in her eyes that cannot be denied. Was it just the adventure she sought? Not actually me? Perhaps that's where I got everything so twisted.

After we check in, a nurse ushers me up into a small, private pre-op room. It's got one window, one chair, and one small bed—quite opposite of the lush suite I stayed in before.

She hands me a white hospital gown and bootie socks. "I'll be back to start your IV once you've changed."

"Do you want some space?" Gareth's deep voice asks, piercing me with a million silent questions. "I can get these obnoxious sods out of here."

I glance over at Tanner, who's currently shoving Booker into the wall over and over like a bouncing pinball. A small smile lifts my face and I shake my head. "You guys can stay."

"Cosy," Gareth murmurs and smirks at me.

I change and get situated on the bed. Shortly thereafter, the nurse returns. The three of my mammoth brothers in here along with the nurse makes for some tight quarters, but I like the distraction. Also, I feel touched that none of my brothers have brought up football all morning.

Just when I begin to wonder where Vi is, I hear a voice clear in the doorway.

My dad, Vaughn Harris himself, is standing at the threshold with a tight smile on his face. "Hello, Camden," he drawls, nervously unzipping his Bethnal Green jacket.

"Hiya, Dad," I say, my face the picture of shock.

Vi steps out from behind him, a meek smile on her face. "Hey, Cam. You look good. You all ready for the day?"

I can't stop staring at my dad as I say, "I guess so."

"Good. That's good." She clears her throat rather obnoxiously. "Gareth, Booker, Tan…why don't we go get some coffee for everyone. No coffee for you, Cam. Sorry. You can have some after."

I nod woodenly as everyone makes their way out of the room. The nurse is working away on my arm, oblivious to everything.

After exhaling a heavy breath, my father nods his head once and steps into the room like it was the hardest decision of his life. He swallows hard as he eyes the nurse fiddling with my IV.

"There you go. All set now," she says brightly. "I've pushed some meds in there to relax you. It will be another thirty minutes. Then we'll come wheel you to the OR, so just try to relax." Then she looks from me to my dad before making a hasty retreat.

"Are you…all set?" Dad asks, standing awkwardly beside my bed and squinting at the machines like they might tell him something. His hands shift along the open zipper of his jacket.

"Ready as I'll ever be," I sigh.

He nods and purses his lips together before saying, "I'm glad you decided to go through with the surgery." The words get stuck in his throat on their way out but I get the idea.

My brows lift. "It doesn't mean I know what I want to do after all of this is over." He closes his eyes like that comment is painful for him, so I add, "I mean it, Dad. I hope you're not here to convince me to do something, because it won't work."

His blue eyes find mine and he shakes his head adamantly. "I'm not here to do that, Cam. I swear. I'm trying to respect your wishes and understand all of this. But I have to be honest. I can't wrap my mind around the fact that you don't like football anymore. I thought being a Gunner was what you always wanted. I don't know how I got so off the mark."

I recoil. "I do like football, but not like this. Not when I feel like half a man right now."

He gets a pained look in his eyes and grabs the chair, bringing it to the side of my bed. Resting his elbows on the mattress, he presses his hands together and says, "Son, you are not half a man. You're not even three quarters of a man. Even as you are now, Arsenal still wants you. They even sent me a letter of intent saying they want you to sign."

"They what?" I ask, my jaw dropping in disbelief.

"I wasn't going to say anything because that's not why I'm here, but I can't help it. I'm so bloody proud of you! I've kept you with Bethnal longer than I should have because it was our home and I love seeing you play with your brothers. But now you have the opportunity to fly, and I'm so chuffed that I want to shout it at the top of my lungs."

I can't believe the words he's just said. A letter of intent? While I'm still injured? How is that even possible? "I don't even know what to say, Dad."

"Don't say anything. I just want to be proud of you. But I need you to know that if you don't play football again, I will *still* be proud of you."

I swallow hard and reply, "It's not that I never want to play again. I guess I just need to feel good enough to fly on my own first, Dad." I stare down at my knee that looks perfectly normal, and I still can't figure out how one appendage can muck everything up like this. "After my injury, when I thought I might never play again, I realised that I don't know who I am without football. For so long, I let it be the only thing that mattered."

He releases a shaky sigh and pinches the bridge of his nose. "Son, I understand that more than you could possibly know."

"How?" I ask. "Your life's passion is football. Our whole lives, that's what we've always known about you."

"That was only after I lost your mother, Cam." His voice cracks and the deep creases around his eyes stack on top of each other as he attempts to hide his emotions. "Christ, I don't know if I can talk about this."

My eyes sting as I see painful tears form in his. He never speaks of Mum. Ever. Last year, Vi gave us all a book of poems that she found of Mum's, and I thought he was going to lose it. The poems were all penned by her and were so incredibly personal. They exuded who she was and what she loved out of life. I swear I could remember how she smelled just by touching the papers.

A grave look washes over his face and he shakes his head. "Camden, I loved your mother with everything inside of me. My heart, my brain, my guts, my everything. Football was just a game I played. I never loved it because there wasn't room in my heart to love anything else. She filled me with so much passion. Then we had you kids, and when I saw her as a mother, my insides grew. Football still didn't compete.

"Then she started to die on me," his voice wobbles and he covers his mouth. My jaw clenches at the intense pain he still feels after all these years. After a few seconds, he continues, "I put her through painful surgeries to try to give us more time with her. But when every bloody doctor came out with those masks on their faces and that look in their eyes, I knew it was all for nothing."

"Dad, I'm sorry...I didn't—"

"I don't talk about it because I'm ashamed. I couldn't cope with the idea of losing her. With every passing day, she got worse, and my insides deteriorated more and more. My passion died. I was awful to her in the end. Gareth even had to step in a couple of times. When I think about how I treated her and all that he had to shoulder at such a young age, the guilt consumes me. Before I knew it, she died and I was drowning in so much regret that I thought if I could just focus on you kids, things could get back to how they used to be. I could find my passion again. But I was a crap father. If it wasn't for Vi, who knows how bad things would have gotten."

I reach out and cover his clasped hands on the mattress. "You did the best you could, Dad."

He shakes his head, apparently not believing me. "When football came back into my life, things magically got better. Watching you boys practise with Bethnal Green made me happy because it made you happy. I let football become my new passion.

"Then you went down at that match. After your brothers carried you off the field and we came into this hospital, I couldn't just sit around and do nothing like I did with your mum. I couldn't wait for everything to come tumbling down around me again."

"So you started talking to Arsenal," I say, seeing the picture come into focus so much more clearly now.

"I'm not proud of the way I handled things. I wanted to look past the present and focus on the future, which was wrong. So I'm here now and I'm not going to talk to you about Arsenal, or Bethnal Green, or football anymore. If you don't want to have this surgery today, let's postpone it. We have loads of time."

I look closely at my dad, who's gazing at me with wide, open, accepting eyes—eyes that are telling me he'll drive the getaway car.

This is a man who knows love. Not the love of football like I always thought. He loved my mum. He loved her so deeply that he lost himself when he lost her. I can relate to that. Maybe I can find my passion again someday, whatever it might be.

I swallow around the knot in my throat and say, "I want to have the surgery, Dad. And if you're okay with sticking by my side, I'd really like that, too."

His blue eyes pierce through my soul. "I'm not going anywhere, Cam."

A while later, the nurse returns and her mouth drops open at the sight of my completely packed room. Dad is in a chair that he pulled up next to my bed. Vi is sitting at the foot with Hayden now tucked up next to her. Gareth and Booker are sandwiched shoulder-to-shoulder on the window ledge, and Tanner slides himself up off the floor at her entry. Everyone has coffee in hand except me.

"It's time." She smiles awkwardly and stands back from the door.

"I'll walk down with him," Dad says right away.

"No, Dad, I'm good. You can go to the waiting room with everyone else. I'll be fine."

"Are you sure? I can walk down with you," he says again.

"Or I could," Vi adds, her clear blue eyes touching me with motherly softness.

I shake my head with a laugh. "No. I'm good you guys. I promise. Go get more coffee. I'll see you all afterwards."

After a handful of awkward hugs, Tanner comes in last and whispers, "You've never looked uglier."

I punch him in the ribs before he pulls away, smiling as the wind gets knocked out of him. "You're pretty much insulting yourself there, Twin Genius."

He waggles his eyebrows at the nurse and makes his way out of the room.

"I apologise for him," I state in a nonplussed tone.

"Oh, it's fine," she giggles. "You have a lovely family."

That I do, I think to myself as she pushes me out the door.

"Ah, Mr. Harris." Dr. Prichard's voice bellows from around the corner, causing the nurse to stop us in the doorway. "I was just coming to see you." He's out of breath as he grabs hold of the side rail of my bed. "Are you excited to get back on your feet?"

"I've been on my feet quite well for the past month now thanks to you," I murmur. "But yes, I'm ready for all of this to be over."

"I'm sure you are. I have a paper here I am hoping we can get you to sign before we wheel you in. It's a basic release form to use your name in a medical article. *The British Medical Journal* is here to do a human interest story on Indie and me, and they'd like permission to reference you by name in the article."

My cheery mood plummets as he hands me the piece of paper. "Does Dr. Porter know about this?"

His eyes squint a bit. "Yes, as a matter of fact, I told her several days ago. She's quite keen. Her med school research project on the graft we placed in your knee is the talk of the hospital."

"Right," I grind out through clenched teeth. Shaking my head, I sign my name with the pen he hands me and feel something sharp digging into my back.

"Thanks, Son. We'll see you in there…or after." He winks and scampers away with an infuriatingly patronising waggle to his walk. He hasn't a care in the world, oblivious to the fact that he's completely crushed mine.

Here I thought Indie came to my flat to talk me into having the surgery because there was an ounce of her that actually cared—a tiny shred that might want what's best for my well-being.

Well, Camden. This isn't the first time she's made you look like a fucking wanker.

If I could be any more done, I would be on fire.

As we begin moving down the hallway, I lean forward in the bed and ask, "Nurse, can you check my back and tell me if there's a knife sticking in it?"

32 Draw A Foul

Indie

I PRESS DOWN ON THE METAL BAR WITH MY FOOT TO KICK ON THE water in the wash basin and begin the exhaustive process of scrubbing in for surgery. I don't wear rings, watches, or bracelets because it's one less step I have to deal with. I start with rubbing the antimicrobial soap scrub on my hands and arms, then move to cleaning out the subungual areas with a nail file. After that, it's the two-minute timed scrubs on each side of my fingers, between my fingers, and the back and front of both hands. Finally, I move on to my arms. The whole process lasts ages.

Ages that I can do nothing but think about Camden and what he's doing. Who's with him? How he's feeling? Is he nervous? Did he have a blowout with his dad, and is that why he's having the surgery? I want to know all of these things and could have figured a lot of them out if I'd stopped by his room before the procedure. But I was a coward.

My heart is over-flowing with new feelings. Feelings that don't do well bottled up. Saying any of this to Camden right now would be selfish, though. This procedure is difficult enough on him without adding our personal drama into the mix. I just have to hold my tongue, get through this, and hope that we can figure things out afterwards.

"Ah, Indie! There you are," Prichard's voice says from behind me as I go to do my final hand rinse. "You're scrubbed in early."

I want to tell him it's because he tried to kiss me the last time we were in this room together, but I bite my tongue. "Just wanting to make sure everything is setup right."

He cuts me a look as he ties his mask around his face and says, "I just came from Mr. Harris' room."

"Oh?" I ask, trying to remain calm but wanting to know everything in an instant. "How did he seem?"

"He seemed fine. Just fine. I got him to sign a release form so you can reference him in your interview with *The British Medical Journal* after surgery. It was something the hospital PR gal said we needed. I reserved the consult room in Hallway D for you to sit and talk with them when we wrap up here."

"You told Cam—I mean, Mr. Harris about the article?" I ask, my voice tight and pinched.

Prichard moves over next to me at the basin and eyes me from behind his mask. "I did. Is that a problem?" he asks, revealing nothing with his eyes.

"No, no problem at all," I grind, grateful that Prichard can't see me chewing on my lip nervously behind my mask.

He begins scrubbing in, still watching me instead of his hands. "He seemed a bit put-off by it, but he signed anyway."

My mind goes haywire.

What must Camden be thinking? Does he think I only came to him because of the article? Damnit, I should have told him! Why do I suck so bad at relationships? I can't seem to stop screwing things up with him. Maybe I can catch him before the surgery.

Movement through the window to the OR catches my eye, and I see a nurse pushing Camden in on a stretcher. The pained look on his face makes me feel a sudden and overwhelming urge to draw a foul.

33 It's Dr. Porter, Bitch

Camden

An overwhelming sense of Déjà Vu casts over me when the nurse positions me in the OR. Once again, Dr. Prichard says something that leaves me reeling minutes before I'm going to be put under. God, what an arrogant arsehole.

And, once again, Indie is in the forefront of my mind. After everything my father said about my mum and how she was all he loved, I wanted it. I wanted a chance to care for someone that much. To put it above football. Above everything.

And, bloody hell, I hate the fact that after all he said, it was Indie's face that crept into my mind. My heart. My soul.

But if what Dr. Prichard said is true, then I've been reading her all wrong since day one. When I held her in my arms that night at Old George and felt her pain, I wanted to move mountains to take it away. I would've given anything. Been anything. Done anything. I wanted to be whatever she needed in that moment.

I think some deep, dark part of my mind thought that when this surgery was all over, there would be hope for Indie and me. That maybe by getting me out of the hospital and away from the stress of her job, we'd have a fighting chance. Her coming to me a couple days ago to convince me to have the surgery filled me with the hope that perhaps she cared more about me than she did about all this hospital bullshit.

Now it's all for naught.

Now it feels like all of this was truly just so she could get ahead. They say the apple doesn't fall far from the tree. Well, maybe she's just like her family and is incapable of truly hugging someone and accepting all that entails.

She used me like a puppet, and lying here on this table while they literally stick cords to my body means I'm still letting her pull the strings.

It has to stop.

I shove away a hand that's sticking a pad to my chest.

"Mr. Harris, we're just getting these in place. Then we'll have you move to this table."

"I'm not doing this." My voice sounds distant and mumbly.

"What's that?" a mask-covered face asks, moving to stand over me.

"I said I'm not doing this. I don't want the surgery." I swallow against the meds coursing through my veins and will myself to think clearly.

"Mr. Harris," a new nurse states, joining the other person standing above me. Her brows knit together as she adds, "We can give you something stronger for the nerves."

"You already gave me a bunch of shit and I hate it. I said I'm not having this surgery. I meant it. Get me out of here." I move to sit up but my head spins.

Several hands reach out and grab my shoulders, attempting to lay me back down. But I'm stronger than all of them, even doped up on painkillers. I swing my legs off the stretcher, wincing at the rubbing sensation in my knee that I feel whenever I twist it a certain way. It's probably the magical graft that Indie put in—the one that needs to come out. Well, fuck it. It can wait. I begin ripping off the sticky pads on my chest and sides.

"Mr. Harris, please! We can help you with whatever you need."

"I need to leave," I growl, but my dramatic scene comes to a screeching halt when familiar toffee eyes find mine.

Indie is standing four feet in front of me, gowned completely in blue from her head to her toes. Red, curly hair peeks out the bottom of her scrub cap as her eyes squint sympathetically through cheetah-print glasses. She's holding her freshly washed hands up in front of herself, and her mouth is covered by a mask as she asks, "Cam, what's the matter?"

I laugh incredulously and glance over at Dr. Prichard. He's currently scrubbing his hands in the sink and watching the scene through the window like the creepy voyeur he is.

"Like you even care," I answer.

Pulling her brows together, she takes a step forward. "Of course I care. What is it?"

"You could have told me about the medical journal. You could have mentioned it and I would have listened. But this was all an act, wasn't it? All you care about is this bloody surgery and getting your name on paper."

Her face turns pink as she looks around the OR. "Can you all please clear out?" she asks firmly.

The staff stare in wonder, unmoving.

"Clear out!" she shouts, and everyone scampers with a jolt out the door, leaving us behind with only the hum of machines and the beeping of monitors to keep us company.

Despite their departure, I can feel their eyes on us through the windows. Indie notices the same thing and sighs heavily at the ridiculous fishbowl we find ourselves in. She turns to face me again, pulling down her mask and revealing those large red lips that are now pursed into a frown. "I wanted to tell you about the feature, but not until you made up your mind about the surgery."

"Why the hell not?" I bark.

"Because I was afraid that if you knew about it, you'd go through with the surgery just for me and not for yourself."

This gives me pause. "Thinking pretty highly of yourself again I see."

She rolls her eyes. "No, I think highly of *you*, Camden. And I think you're the type to put the well-being of others above your own." She swallows nervously. "What's really wrong? It's more than the article."

I squint harshly at her, frustrated that she really doesn't see it. All the possibility. "It's everything. And it's nothing."

I move to stand up, but Indie moves closer to me and reaches out. Her hands are cool and damp on my arms. I pause, watching her chew her lip with worry.

"You need this surgery, Cam. That's not me speaking as your doctor but as your friend. Regardless of whether or not you ever kick a ball again in your entire life, you're going to want a properly operating knee."

I shake my head angrily. "You think we're mates? I can't even trust you right now."

"Of course you can," she says urgently, looking up at me with wide, hurt eyes.

"Well, what am I supposed to think, Indie? I get here and find out about this publication right before I get wheeled into the place where you're going to dice me up. My dad shows up and tells me all this stuff about my mum that makes me think of *you*, and I feel like the biggest jerk on the planet because I'm in this alone. I'm fucking lost and the only thing I know I want, I can't have!"

"What is that?" she asks with a gasp.

"You! Bloody hell, I want you, Specs. After all this bullshit and stress and low after low, all I want is you. But you don't want me."

She makes a move to reply but I cut her off.

"Everybody is pulling strings and, no matter what I do, I can't seem to get away from them."

"I'm not pulling strings, Cam. I care about you." Her voice trembles.

"You care about the surgery."

I move to slide off the table, but she holds me still again as she snaps, "Stop saying that!"

"Fine, let's just get on with the surgery," I mutter, feeling completely mind-fucked to my limit. "Maybe when I wake up I won't remember any of this."

"Camden—"

"Leave it. I mean it. This injury has fucked with so much more than my knee."

"Damnit, Cam," she growls and grabs my face so hard I feel every one of her fingertips pressed against my skin.

But the next thing I feel is not hard and biting.

It's soft and supple.

It's her lips on mine.

They stroke my mouth over and over, and the sensation is so perfect that I'm certain I am dreaming.

"What are you doing?" my voice quakes as our mouths break apart. Her face is centimetres from mine, yet I squeeze her arms in my hands, fearful they might disappear beneath my touch.

But the warmth of her laboured breath feels so real.

Staring at my lips, she whispers, "I'm finally juggling."

Once again, I swear I am dreaming. Brown eyes crawl up my face and lock on mine. I tilt my head and pull away from her for better perspective. There's no way she just kissed me in her OR. There's no way she just repeated that pun she wrote inside my novel so long ago. My brain has to be messing with me, and this is all an illusion from the IV drug cocktail that nurse gave me.

She moves toward me again, and my eyes swim with desperation as I cup her face in my hands. "Don't kiss me again, Indie." My voice is thick and heavy. "Because I'm trembling from how badly I want you. And if I kiss you, I will lose my fucking mind."

"So lose it with me," she says simply, with all the confidence in the world. Then she whispers three words against my lips that make me come completely undone. "I am thine."

Just before she touches her lips to mine, my eyes begin to sting, so I hold her away from me to stare at her one last time. The warmth of her cheeks against my palms confirms that she is real and this is happening.

Swallowing hard, I whisper back, "Thou art mine."

No more words are needed. No more questions are asked. No more strings are pulled. Simply put, we create the most soul-crushing kiss of all time. We are two hearts connecting on another worldly plane manifesting in this physical act right here. All the anger and frustration between our communication issues comes to a head with the pure, undiluted honesty of lips, tongues, hands, and bodies.

I wrap my arms around her ribs and hug her tightly, pulling her as close to me as I can so I can feel every beat of her heart. But realisation of what we're doing and where we're doing it dawns on me much too quickly. I regrettably pull back. "What did you just do, Specs? You're going to lose your job."

"I don't care." She smiles with hooded eyes and moves to kiss me again.

"That was a stupid thing to do, Indie Porter. This was a great opportunity for you," I murmur, staring down at her swollen lips and aching to touch them again.

She huffs out a soft laugh. "I think it's the smartest thing I've done all week."

I groan and hug her to me. Her selflessness is utterly mind-blowing. Shocking, unexpected, and fascinating on so many levels. Then, in a flash, my arrogance drops. "If you walk out there and tell my brothers I needed a kiss before surgery, I'll make you pay."

"Never," she smirks and kisses me sweetly for good measure. "I think I was the one who needed the kiss. But I will say, if I'm going to lose my job over a kiss, that one was definitely worth it."

She pulls away when we hear giggles waft through the door that

Dr. Prichard is now waltzing through.

With a heavy sigh, he says, "I thought you were smarter than this, Indie."

She begrudgingly releases me, takes a step back, and straightens her posture. Shooting Dr. Prichard a hard look, she replies, "It's Dr. Porter. Please refer to me as such from now on."

With that, she walks out with her shoulders held high and I do nothing to conceal the Camden Harris proud-as-fuck-smirk on my face.

34
All In A Day's Work

Indie

"TELL ME WHAT I'M HEARING ISN'T TRUE," BELLE SAYS, RUSHING up to me in the on-call room.

"It's probably true," I reply while stuffing my locker belongings into a garbage bag. "What'd you hear?"

"Indie Crazy Girl Porter! Did you seriously snog Camden Harris in your OR?" Belle knocks the bag out of my hand and turns me to face her head-on, practically slamming me up against the locker. My face evidently tells her everything she needs to know. "What the fuckity fuck?"

Shaking my head, I say, "I didn't plan to do it, but I had to do something."

"Why are you emptying your locker?"

Swallowing, I reply, "Because I just left the chief of surgery's office. I'm suspended for a year and I have to redo my internship when I come back."

"What?" she screams.

"Belle, it's fine. It's probably better than I deserve."

"So is Camden in surgery then?"

"No." I roll my eyes. "Prichard threw a huge fit about the OR not being sterile anymore and postponed everything."

"Bloody hell. What about *The British Medical Journal* article?"

I shrug. "I'm sure there's nothing they want to talk to me about now. I threw it all away."

"For a footballer."

I smile. "For a footballer."

"Look how you just said footballer with a sleazy smile! God, you're completely smitten. What are you going to do about your suspension, though? You'll fall so far behind. This is terrible."

I shrug. "I'll figure it out. I mean, I'm still young. I have plenty of time to catch up. I just can't believe I have a job to come back to." I flinch as I recall the chief's face as he ripped into me about my immature and unprofessional behaviour, which he's totally right about.

"So what are you doing now?" Belle asks.

"The chief said I have to be out of the hospital immediately."

"God, Indie, I'm so sorry."

I purse my lips. I suppose I should be more devastated than I am. If I'm being honest, though, the only thing I want to do is talk to Camden. There's still so much explaining I have to do. I want him to understand me. I want him to know why I behaved the way I did and pushed him away. One public display of affection doesn't make up for all the heartache I caused.

I throw my bag over my shoulder. When I open the door to leave, I find Tanner looking up and down the hallway.

"Tanner?"

"Oh, Indie...Dr. Porter...Bugger, I don't know what to call you."

"Indie, please. Where's Camden?"

He swallows once and replies, "Some prat tipped-off the paparazzi. It's a freaking nightmare outside the hospital. It had to be someone from the OR. There's a photo and everything."

My heart drops. "No."

"'Fraid so, love. You snogged him globally now."

Everything feels tight, claustrophobic, and royally screwed up. This is even worse than my suspension. This is the hospital's reputation on the line. A photo being leaked from the OR is a huge *Patient Data Protection Act* violation.

As my mind reels with this new information, I hear Tanner say to Belle, "Nice to see you again, Dr. Ryan."

"What did you do to your face?" she snaps.

He strokes his chin, looking defensive. "What do you mean? I trimmed it up."

"But it's not all long and nappy anymore." Belle's face looks angry.

His brows lift. "No, apparently the birds don't like your face to look like their grandmother's vagina."

"Not all birds," she grumbles.

"Tanner," I bark, breaking up the weird energy crackling between these two. "Where is Camden?"

"He's waiting for you in a black cab out back. We tried to get him to leave to get the mania away from here, but he refused to go without you. Right now Gareth is out front doing an impromptu press conference to distract them so you guys can get out of here."

"Oh my God," I groan as the insanity continues to build, but I don't have time to freak out any longer.

Tanner grabs my bag out of my hands and clutches my arm. "We need to go." He begins running me down the hallway toward the same area Camden left the hospital last time. Belle follows, her eyes wide and disbelieving at this whole ridiculous scene laid out before us.

When we reach the door, I squint through the pouring rain and eye the black cab parked along the sidewalk. Tanner attempts to tuck me under his arm, but the brake lights flip on and the car shoots into reverse right toward us. He opens the door and chucks my bag in, stepping back so I can slide in next. I look up at him in confusion when he doesn't hop in behind me.

"I'll catch a ride with Gareth and give you guys some…space." He winks and slams the door shut, backing up to stand beside Belle under the overhang. The two glance at each other for a moment and then watch us pull away.

"Hey, Specs," a familiar voice utters. I turn to see Camden sitting across from me in the cab. Facing me, his legs are stretched out wide in black jogging pants. His white T-shirt is splotched with rain on his shoulders. He looks perfect. "Tough day at work?"

I laugh in a way that verges on crying and launch myself onto him. I straddle him and hug his neck so hard, I think I might break him. When I finally feel as if he's not going to slip out from under my hands, I loosen my grip and pull back. "I'm so sorry for all of this, Camden. It's all my fault."

His blue eyes widen. "Your fault? I'm the reason this is turning into a circus."

"I know, but none of this would have happened if I wouldn't have kissed you like that." I cover my face with my hands. "I'm such a freak."

He pulls my hands down and cups my face, stroking small lines on my cheekbone as his eyes pin me with a million questions. "Indie, just tell me what that kiss meant. I have to know if it means what I think it means because you give me so many mixed signals. Just be honest with me now. No more walls. No more space."

"Okay," I reply, wincing as I slide off of his lap. I tuck my legs up under me and turn so I can face him. He rests his hand on my shoulder and rubs it encouragingly. "I guess you could say I was trying to draw a foul."

His face drops. All happiness and good humour instantly gone. "I think that's the sexiest fucking thing I've ever heard."

He moves in and presses his lips to mine, kissing me desperately and snaking a hand up my scrub top. I want more, so much more, but I have to hold back so I can get this all out.

I push him away. "There's more I need to say."

He half smiles and pulls his hand out from under my shirt. "I'm listening. I promise."

I pull his hand up between us and twine my fingers with his, staring at the vast disparity. His hand is large and tan and rough. Mine is small and pale and soft. So different, but together, so beautiful.

"I've never had any real relationships in my life, aside from Belle. No family meddling. No screaming, protective sisters. No ridiculous, hairy brothers. But since I've met you, I want that. I want sarcasm, I want drama. Hell, I want cheeky squeezes over coffee in the kitchen. I want to go to dinner with your dad, even if it means I get into a fight with him about you."

He pulls me into his chest and sighs heavily. "I want that, too."

"And I want this," I say, squeezing around his waist. "I want affection. Lots and lots of affection. It might take me some time to get used to, and I might hate it at times when I'm feeling stressed. But I want you to keep helping me accept it."

"I can do that," he murmurs and drops a soft kiss on my head.

I pull back so I can look into his eyes for the next part. "Camden, I want you. I want more. I want lots more. I know my words are horribly delayed, but I'm falling for you, too."

His eyes crinkle with a smile as he cups my face in his hands and brushes his lips against mine. The kiss is honest and pure, not overtly sexual like all of the others. It's perfect.

When he pulls away, he says, "When you walked out on a surgery like that for me…Well, I don't know if there will ever be a moment in my life that tops that. I bleed passion for you, Specs. I'm not sure how much longer I can keep my hands off of you."

"Does that mean you want to score right now?" I ask and shoot him a lascivious smirk.

"Let's shoot for a turkey." He winks and tips me onto my back, moving over top of me on the cab seat. The feel of his mouth on me is heavenly as he kisses and licks my neck in the most delicious ways possible.

When he comes up to claim my lips, I stop him mid-action and whisper, "I have no idea what a turkey is."

He laughs. Really laughs. And it's my favourite Tequila Sunrise moment, ever.

After having the cab circle around Camden's flat to ensure there are no paparazzi, we leap out of the car, both vibrating with a need to touch each other. It's been only a couple of weeks since we were last intimate, but I already feel the build between my legs for what I know he can give me.

By the time we tumble into his lift, he's already slipped his hand inside my knickers. "God, Cam!" I brace myself on the side of the lift wall. He's standing behind me, and the reflection of his hand buried in the front of my scrubs as he nibbles my ear and does that thing to my clit again has me nearly tipping over the edge. "You have to stop. I'm going to fall."

"I'll catch you," his warm breath chuckles in my ear. "God, I missed you, Specs. It's been too long since I've touched you like this," he says, continuing to defile my vagina with his expert fingers.

"I missed you, too," I moan and tip my head back on his shoulder.

"I've never missed anyone like I missed you. When we were apart, I smelled lemons everywhere I went."

I close my eyes and drink in his sweet words like the best cup of hot tea.

"I'm going to make you happy, Indie. I'm going to show you there's more to me. I can do the boyfriend bit if that's what you want. I'll show you what we can be together."

My hand reaches down and stills his movement. I turn my head and look into his eyes. The vulnerable gleam staring back at me has me turning in his arms. He removes his hands from my trousers and holds me around the waist. I can feel his strained erection, but I ignore it because he needs to hear what I'm about to say. "I just want you. I already know there's more to you. I saw more the day you came rolling into my hospital."

The corner of his mouth tilts up. "You're really mine?" he asks, a sad flicker on his face as he awaits my answer.

I cup his face in my hands and press my forehead against his. "As long as you are mine. Now please, make love to me so I can say those words back to you this time."

He inhales my words with a deep, swirling, simmering kiss that leaves me breathless. When the lift chimes open, he walks me backwards, never detaching his lips from mine. He manages to unlock the door and then pulls me up so my legs wrap around his waist as he carries me to his bedroom.

Everything feels different. Now that I've embraced this closeness that I feel for him, it's as if my heart can finally accept what he's been showing me all along. Those moments of vulnerability in the hospital; how tender he was with me when we had sex for the first time; how he looked at me when I walked barefoot on the Tower Park pitch.

Before I know it, I'm naked in his bed and he's on top of me, dropping searing hot kisses on all of my naughty parts. When he comes back up, I wrap my legs around him and grip him between us, stroking the smooth skin of his head against me and staring deeply into his eyes. I have a moment of realisation over how beautiful our first time together really was. He was there for me, just like this. Tuned in to me, tender and caring. *Loving*, even though neither of us even knew it yet.

He slides into me, and I stare at him despite the overwhelming fullness and wonderful pressure we're creating between our bodies. His eyes are locked on mine, too. The passion displayed there for me makes my heart expand.

More than I've ever felt before.

35 Gunning for Me

Camden

THE NEXT MORNING, I'M NOT SURPRISED WHEN I COME OUT OF my room to find my dad, Booker, Tanner, and Gareth sitting in my kitchen. Booker is propped on a stool at the counter. Tanner is perched on the counter, and Gareth and Dad are occupying two seats at the table. Everybody has coffee in hand.

"It's not even the day after a match," I say, striding over to the coffee pot and pouring myself a cup. I empty the last bit and immediately begin making a new pot. "To what do *we* owe this pleasure?"

Tanner's brows lift knowingly. "Is Indie still here?"

I hit the coffee to brew and turn, leaning back against the counter. "She is. Out cold still."

"We wanted to talk to you," Tanner says, shifting nervously on the counter. "I'll start. We still want you to have the surgery, Cam. Not to play football, but to have the choice to play if you ever want to. I think you're going to get to a point in your mind when things all click into place, and you're going to realise this is all just a mental healing that's happening. Then you're going to wish you had the graft out so there's no delay in chasing your dreams. I know what you went through sucked, Cam. I could feel it myself…in ways only a twin brother can. But I think you're wrong to take football off the table entirely."

He exhales heavily and looks around at everyone else like he forgot people were here.

"That how you feel, too, Gareth? Booker?"

Gareth replies first. "You're too good of an athlete to be walking around with something foreign in your body, Camden."

"I'd just hate to see something bad happen if you leave it in," Booker adds.

"What do you think, Dad?" I ask, looking over at him and taking a sip from my mug.

"I'm not here to push you into having the surgery. This is something your brothers wanted to do. I thought we should give you space, but since they are all too thick-headed to listen to their old man, I'm just here to referee."

"You don't want me to sign that letter of intent?" I ask, quirking a brow at him.

He shifts in his seat, clearly fighting the inner manager inside of him. "Only if you want to."

"Is that letter of intent even still valid? After that photo got leaked yesterday?"

He purses his lips. "It is…but with some conditions," he clips out, clearly uncomfortable with this line of questioning.

My brows lift. "So you've spoken to them."

"They rang me," he replies, and his eyes cast down like he's ashamed for taking the call.

"What are the conditions?"

He sighs. "Camden, we don't have to discuss this now."

"What are the conditions?"

He clears his throat. "They want you and Dr. Porter to do an interview with a high-level tabloid. Nothing sleazy. *Vanity Fair* or *Hello!* magazine to explain your relationship. Take the seediness out of it and put some good PR out there for the team and the hospital. That's when you'd announce your new position as a Gunner."

"Is that it?" I ask and all of my brothers' heads snap to me in shock.

Dad shrugs. "Pretty much. There are some monetary negotiations I have to discuss with you, but…Camden, I'm sorry…What are you saying right now?"

I take a drink and set my mug down. "I'm saying that I'm already having the surgery as soon as they call me back with the new scheduled time. I'm even letting that prat, Dr. Prichard, do it just so they don't look at Indie any more negatively than they already are." I exhale a deep breath as what I'm about to say becomes a huge declaration in my mind and my heart. "And even though I'll probably bleed green and white my whole life…red is a great colour on me."

"Fuck yes!" Tanner exclaims, leaping off the counter and hugging me ferociously. "You're going to be a Gunner? Bloody hell, Booker, Bethnal better move up next season because I'm ready for a chance to kick Cam's arse on the pitch. Dad, I don't want to be a striker anymore. I want to be a defender. Gareth, you lucky sod. You better crush him when they play Man U."

Gareth does that whole shoulder-shaking laugh thing and Booker's eyes light up like a Christmas tree. Dad watches me from the table as my brothers all hug me with congratulations. When they're done being the dramatic footballers they are, he stands up and walks over to me.

Putting his hand on my shoulder, he eyes me hard and says, "Did you find your passion again, Son?"

I smile back and a softness creeps into my chest. "I think I found a couple."

36
Girlfriend, M.D.

Indie

I WAKE COMPLETELY WRAPPED UP IN CAMDEN. HIS BRACED LEG IS tucked between my bare legs, and his arms hold me from behind. Every piece of my exposed skin is nearly encompassed by his.

I think I've got the hang of this spooning bit, I think to myself.

I separate from his grasp and slip out of bed with a big naked stretch. I toss on the red Gunners jersey he gave me last week and make my way over to the hotel window. I pull back the curtains and admire the early morning view of Baltimore, knowing full well I could drive a truck through this room and it wouldn't wake Camden.

It's been two weeks since I kissed him in my OR, and now we're on our honeymoon.

Of sorts.

Except for the whole surgery part.

And the fact that we didn't actually get married.

So it's not so much of a honeymoon as it is a getaway that involved an operation with a high-level surgeon at John Hopkins Hospital.

Two days after my suspension, the chief called the Harrises and me back into the hospital for a meeting. Apparently they discovered the photo from the OR that was leaked to the media came from

Prichard's mobile. The whole ordeal was a huge violation of the *Patient Data Protection Act* and they were desperate to make it right.

Part of the agreement was to send Camden to the States for the second half of The Wilson Repair. Then they offered me my job back.

I declined instantly.

There's no way I want to go back to a place that let Prichard get away with what he did. Plus, that would put me right back under his tutelage and I can't stomach the thought.

So now, here Cam and I reside, in a lush hotel in Baltimore, waiting for our flight home later tonight. His surgeon yesterday was so confident in Cam's recovery that he said he should be able to train with Arsenal immediately after we get back.

I was beside Cam through the whole process, but not in an official medical capacity. Strictly as his girlfriend...waiting room and all.

My mobile begins vibrating on the nightstand. I tip toe over to it and see Belle's name on the screen.

"Hello?" I whisper and head back over to the window.

"Hey, how's he feeling?" Belle's voice coos into the line.

"Good. He's still sleeping, but the surgery went great yesterday, and he said he had no pain last night."

"That's fab. Did the surgeon say if he can start training straight away?"

I nod even though she can't see me. "Yes, we fly back home tonight, and the surgeon said he can start tomorrow if he'd like."

"That's incredible."

"Yeah, Cam was pleased." I smile at his large, sleeping body lying so peacefully on the bed.

"So do you want to hear some dirt?" Belle's voice sounds conspiratorial.

My brows lift. "Sure."

"There's a group of six nurses that have come together and are all filing sexual harassment claims against Prichard."

"What?" I gasp.

"Yep. The prat poked his last hole at work, I'd say."

"I'd say, too. Wow." A chill runs up my spine.

"So if he gets sacked, do you think you might reconsider the offer to come back to work?"

I pull my lip into my mouth and begin chewing away at it. "I'm not sure."

"What do you mean? If he's gone, you can get back on track. What's stopping you?"

I exhale heavily, not entirely sure I am ready to get into all of this quite yet since I haven't even talked it over with Cam. "You know, Belle, since the moment I was suspended, I've felt a huge weight lifted off my shoulders. Things feel different now, as if I have more options. Honestly, I've been reading a lot about sports medicine."

"Is that a euphemism for sex with a footballer?"

"No! Don't be daft." I can't help but smirk.

"Well, I'm guessing he's lying naked in your hotel bed right now, even though he's only one day post-op." I cringe and she laughs knowingly into the line. "So what will you do, darling? Because I know you have a plan stewing in that big brain of yours."

She knows me so well. "I think I'm going to talk to Camden's dad about job-shadowing Bethnal Green F.C. team doctor. It'd be great experience, and I think I could have something to offer the world of sports medicine beyond surgical."

"Of course you could. You're my wunderkid!"

Rolling my eyes, I ask, "Do you think it's crazy? I'm sure it wouldn't be a paying job. I have some money saved, but things might get tight."

"So you move in with me. Or get some guilt money out of your parentals. Plus, I bet that that Harris brother you've got wouldn't mind sparing a zero from that big fat contract he just signed."

Her last suggestion makes me frown. "I'm not taking money from Cam."

She tsks. "I know you won't. I'm just saying you have options. I've been trying to get you to move in with me since med school. This sounds like an exciting prospect."

Her encouragement touches me. "But it's sad I won't be working with you anymore."

"Oh, it's okay," she scoffs. "I won't be here much longer anyway."

"Why do you say that?"

"Well, I meant to tell you sooner, but we had that little fight and then you got Harris'd. I got a fellowship position offer with Dr. Elizabeth Miller. She's a high-risk neonatal surgeon at the Chelsea and Westminster Hospital."

"I've heard of her!" I screech, quickly pressing my hand over my mouth. "She's like the American badass in the world of high-risk pregnancy surgery. Belle, this is huge."

"I know. I can't believe I was selected. You'd think they hadn't met me or something," she giggles.

"Shut up, you're brilliant. So I guess you've picked your specialty then?"

"I guess I have."

A moment of heavy silence stretches out between us.

"You're going to save babies, Belle." My smile couldn't be wider, and I'm shocked when my chin begins to wobble.

"Tequila Sunrise, Indie." Her voice catches a bit, and I'm transported back in time to the moment we saw that baby die of SIDs. That moment we started living our life to the fullest.

"Tequila Sunrise, Belle."

We discuss the particulars a bit more. By the time I hang up, I feel a renewed sense of determination to get back to London and put my plan into action. Belle and I have grown up so much in a matter of weeks and our futures look very bright indeed.

We say our goodbyes. Then I walk over to the bed to try to rouse Camden. "Mmmm, stroke lower, Specs. You know what I like."

I giggle and slip back into bed with him. "You like everything."

I kiss his shoulder.

His sleepy blue eyes pop open. “I like you,” he growls and pulls me on top of him, rolling us over to the other side of the bed where he proceeds to remind me just how much he likes me.

37 Bodily Harm

Camden

2 Months Later

"I'M NOT KIDDING, TANNER. YOU NEED TO PUT THE FEAR OF GOD into the team. If anyone even makes a backhanded comment that could be remotely toward Indie, Camden Harris Fists of Fury will fly," I bark, while standing in our kitchen and using wild hand gesticulations to demonstrate my point.

Then I add, "First they'll get your fists. Then Booker's fists. Then my fists once you guys get back to London and I get a hold of whoever had the nerve to look at her funny. You think we can cart them to Manchester so Gareth can have a crack, too?"

"He's full on psychotic now." Gareth's deep voice cuts into my tirade as he murmurs to Indie. They are sitting across from each other at the kitchen table, both apparently judging the show.

"I think you're overreacting just a titch, Cam," Vi states as she waddles over to the stove, stroking her now protruding belly.

"You think?" Hayden laughs, pulling Vi away from the oven and bending over to grab the large pan she was about to take out.

I look at them with wide, horrified eyes. "There's more where this is coming from, Hayden and Vi. Just you two wait 'til my niece is born. She's not going to have a bloke get within a mile of her without the Harrises bringing the pain!"

They burst out laughing and Tanner pipes up next. "I'm with ya all the way, Cam. The best defence is a good offence." He sets his fists up in front of his face and takes a couple jabs at Booker's shoulder.

"Lay off," Booker bellows. "Vi, you might want to keep that wee babe in there as long as possible. It's not safe out here. And, Camden, you do need to relax. We're going to take care of Indie. She's shadowing the team doctor, not giving sponge baths to the players."

I groan at the thought of all those players in the changing room. I've been in that changing room, I know what it looks like after a match.

I exhale heavily and mope my way over to Indie. Flopping down in the seat next to her, she cradles my head as I rest it on the table in a proper pout.

Last week was my first match, and this week she begins her job with Bethnal. We've only officially been together two months now, but I'm still dreading the idea of being away from her.

She nailed a meet and greet with the team doc, just like I knew she would. Apparently she had over-prepared for the meeting and created some injury prevention technique plan for footballers. She blew the staff away.

She is a bloody genius after all.

Even though I'm pouting because this will give me less time with her, I couldn't be more proud.

Indie's voice is determined as she interjects, "I think it's good we're going to have some time apart during your season, Cam."

My head pops up to look at her in horror. "What on earth does that mean?"

Her cheeks redden. "You completely embarrassed the lot of us when you flew up into the stands and kissed me after your first goal as a Gunner last week. We really don't need extra media coverage."

"That stadium kiss was well worth the ten thousand pound fine,"

I state confidently, staring back at Indie and marveling at how it's still fun to just look at her. Sometimes I can adjust my gaze the slightest bit and make her blush.

She grins and blushes.

I smile.

"I didn't completely hate it, I guess" she murmurs with a smirk and leans into my embrace.

I press a tender kiss to her temple and move my hand between her legs under the table. "That's called passion, babe. I thought you were a quick study." I whisper the next bit into her ear. "Let me take you to bed and educate you again."

She bites her lip with a giggle. "I think I'm going to like sports medicine."

"Enough," Vi chimes in. "I've seen enough of you two snogging to last me a lifetime."

Gareth and Booker both chuckle while Tanner says with a playful smile, "We can pull it up and watch it on *Match of the Day* highlights if you'd like."

"Not again!" Indie bellows, her face dropping to serious in two seconds flat.

I smile lasciviously and recall the similarly horrified expression on her face last week. My brothers and Dad were all at their own prospective matches so she was seated with Vi and Hayden.

It was a great day.

It was the moment that I realised I love her.

The roar of the crowd was deafening as I moved the ball down the Arsenal pitch. It was like there was an invisible string between my toes and the leather as I skirted past defenders left and right. I closed in on the goal and my pace halted as I pulled my boot back and shot. I

clutched my hands into fists as I watched the keeper's glove grapple desperately to get a single hair on the ball. When it slipped past him and touched the nylon netting, I no longer saw football.

I saw red.

A beautiful, vivacious, red-framed glasses-wearing redhead seated on the goal side just behind the place I sunk my ball.

Before I could register what was happening, I was sprinting away from my teammates who were all trying to tackle me in celebration. I leapt over the security barricades, past the guards, and climbed up a long row of concrete steps.

I could feel several fans giving me matey pats on my back as I passed them, but I had tunnel vision for my ultimate goal, who was wearing a red jersey with the Harris name on the back.

As I approached, I registered that Vi was bawling huge, fat tears that I could see from a mile away as she clutched her shaking stomach. Hayden was laughing and holding her under his arm. Indie just looked mystified. Shocked. Disbelieving. My large presence in my kit with my boots clacking against the pavement stupefied my genius of a girlfriend.

"What are you doing?" she asked, staring up at me as I closed the space between us and cupped her face in my hands.

"Kissing my best goal on the lips."

"I think you mean best girl, you show-boating footballer—"

I pressed my lips to hers.

Scoring my first goal as a Gunner felt like a million pounds.

Realising I love Indie Porter…felt like a billion.

38
Lot More Than Coffee

Indie

THE DELICIOUS SCENT OF COFFEE INVADES MY SLEEP, ROUSING me in the way only a fresh cup can. I crack my eyes open and see a very sexy hand holding a very cute mug in my face. I smile and sit up.

"What's this?" I ask, taking the pink mug from Camden and eyeing the thick black text on the side that says: *These Glasses Make Me Look Sexy.*

He sits down beside my legs as I lean back against the headboard. Waking up with Camden still gives me butterflies. Seeing him almost every day still makes me smile. Snuggling him in bed doesn't make me uncomfortable anymore. It makes me happy.

The more time I spend with him, the more comfortable I become with this whole lack-of-space business. Any time I feel myself pulling away, Camden has an uncanny way of turning things dirty and making me forget all about that separation I thought I needed.

Cuddling isn't so bad when you just let yourself enjoy it instead of mentally freaking out over the after effects. And since I no longer care about my Penis List plan, I've realised that Cam gives me all the Tequila Sunrise life experiences I could ever want.

We've even got his little *ritual* down for the mornings he has to go to practise or matches. Apparently it was a solo job before I came along, but Cam says making me a part of his visualisation technique is sure to make him the best striker Arsenal has ever seen. I don't mind, even if he does like to shout "Goal!" after he comes.

God, he really is a pig.

I smirk around a sip of the coffee he brought me and eye him appreciatively propped on the edge of the bed. He's dressed in a soft white cotton T-shirt that he seems to have an endless supply of and a pair of jersey shorts that reveal his muscular thighs.

"Didn't like me using the standard black coffee mug anymore?" I ask.

"I thought it was time you had your own," he exhales heavily. "We've been together for three months now, you know."

"Three months? When did you start counting?"

"You were mine the day of my injury, Specs. You just didn't know it yet." He leans over and kisses my forehead, sliding his fingers through my hair as he drops more kisses all the way down to my neck. "You look good with my coffee in your hand."

I frown. "You're so weird about coffee. The first time I came here and your sister gave me some, I thought your head was going to explode."

He squints at me thoughtfully for a moment before standing up and striding over to his dresser. When he returns, he's holding an intricately carved keepsake box. He opens it up and sifts through several sheets of loose leaf paper until he finds the one he wants.

Holding it out to me with a nervous twinge in his eyes, he murmurs, "It's a poem my mum wrote." My eyes fall to the paper scribed with carefully written words by a woman he knew very little before she died. "Read it," he instructs.

<u>**Your Favourite Girl's Cuppa**</u>
When you handed me that cup,
you handed me your heart.

When you inhaled that roast,
you inhaled our first start.
When you laughed around a sip,
you soared into my mind.
When you poured me some more,
I gave you all the love I could find.

Coffee is more than a cup of caffeine.
Coffee is the drink you sip from for dreams.
Coffee makes moments more than a scene.
Coffee makes love become everything.

When you have true love in your heart,
coffee in bed is the best place to start.

When I look up, I can't hide the tears in my eyes. "Camden," I croak and he half smiles.

"I love you a latte, Indie," he rushes out anxiously. The dopey look on his face makes my heart swoon. "I just wanted you to know that."

The words fall down on me in the most delicious way possible. The scent of coffee all around us makes an instant memory fold in my mind. He watches me, nervously awaiting my reply.

Because I promised never to hold back from him, I inhale deeply and answer, "Well, I love you from my head tomatoes."

His gaze narrows, having to think it through for a bit and then he laughs. Really laughs. It's a great laugh. It's a laugh that zings you right in the knickers and makes you laugh along with him.

His mock impressed face nods before he replies, "You've been sitting on that one for a while now, haven't you?"

I giggle. "Maybe."

His face grows serious, but that smile stays in his eyes. "I love you," he says, cupping my face and pressing a soft kiss to my lips.

"I love you," I repeat. "And there's nothing punny about that."

THE END

There's more Harris Brothers Love coming!

Be sure to email me or post a review of *Challenge* and cast your vote for which brother's story you want next! And sign up for my newsletter to be notified of the next Harris Brothers release date.

www.AmyDawsAuthor.com

***Challenge* is a spin-off from the London Lovers Series.**

MORE BOOKS BY AMY DAWS

The London Lovers:

Becoming Us: Finley's Story Part 1

A Broken Us: Finley's Story Part 2

London Bound: Leslie's Story

Not the One: Reyna's Story

A London Lovers/Harris Brothers Crossover Novel:

Strength: Vi Harris & Hayden's Story

The Harris Brothers Series:

A spin-off series featuring the football-playing Harris Brothers!

Challenge: Camden's Story

Endurance: Tanner's Story

Keeper: Booker's Story

Surrender & Dominate: Gareth's Duet

Wait With Me: A Tire Shop Rom Com

Pointe of Breaking: A College Dance Standalone by Amy Daws & Sarah J. Pepper

Chasing Hope: A Mother's True Story of Loss, Heartbreak, and the Miracle of Hope

For all retailer purchase links, visit:
www.amydawsauthor.com

ACKNOWLEDGEMENTS

Now that I've written my eighth book, I'm confident enough to realize that no book process for me is the same. If I could sum up what writing *Challenge* was like using one word besides "challenging" ...it would be tumultuous. From moving into a new house to traveling to three different countries, I have learned that I am not Super Woman, and to try to write a book amongst all of that madness was simply that...madness!

But I made it and I'm happy...I think. Ask me over drinks to be sure.

Regardless of everything, I do truly love this story and these characters. They have the best banter I've ever written between a couple, and I loved dipping my toes into full-blown rom com.

And now I'm grateful to thank the people who helped get me here. Because there were a lot for this one.

First of all, my beta readers and proofers. I tortured them with this book. This is the first story that I have had to tell my beta readers they need to re-read before reviewing because the changes were so extensive. I sent them multiple updated files, I hounded them for feedback, I asked them to talk out characters with me, and I messaged them constantly. It was painful. But we made it. And it truly was something I couldn't have done without them. So, thank you all for being there for me and for Cam and Indie!

Belinda! My footballer/British muse. You are the one who inspired these wacky Harris Brothers of mine back when I wrote *That One Moment*. Thank you for being my voice of fun for these boys and the wonderful sport of football.

My editor, Stephanie. Thank you for editing my book in the middle of Hurricane Hermine. Your roof was leaking, your power was going out, your lawn was flooded, and your potted plants were flying, but by George…you stuck with me. One of these days, I won't have a painful deadline! That's a lie, I probably always will.

I have to give a personal shout out to one of the most incredible authors I know, Staci Hart. Staci, I've never met anyone like you. I've never seen anyone find the people they want to surround themselves with in life, and then spend countless hours trying to raise them up as high as they can go. You work tirelessly to help others and ask for nothing in return. From beta reading, to helping me with my cover, to introducing me to your incredible author family, I'm overwhelmed. I can't fathom how you see so much in me, but I am grateful. Thank you for being my biggest cheerleader with this book. I'm keeping you and your tribe forever. I want to be you when I grow up.

My hubby. The dude who doesn't watch soccer (football). You may not have helped me with the technicalities of this sports romance book, but it's you that holds the family together when I disappear into another story. Thank you for making meals, getting school supplies, buying the groceries, and not yelling at me too much for letting Lolo eat Lucky Charms in bed every morning.

Lolo. My daughter. My best friend. I've read articles about how you shouldn't be best friends with your daughter because you need to be a mother and enforce discipline. Screw it. You're mine and I don't care what people say. Thank you for the hugs that you don't even know how bad I needed and the snuggles that make all this hard work worth it. Thank you for asking the most thoughtful questions at bedtime every night. It's probably my favorite thing about you.

My angels in the sky, my special six. I still haven't forgotten you. I may think of you a little less, but it's only because you are all so innately a part of me that I carry you with me every day…with every breath…with every heartbeat. If I'm overly emotional, it's because you six taught me what it's like to feel. And I still wish you were here instead of there. But then that would be a very different story.

MORE ABOUT THE AUTHOR

Amy Daws lives in South Dakota with her husband and miracle daughter, Lorelei. The long-awaited birth of Lorelei is what inspired Amy's first book, *Chasing Hope*, and her passion for writing. Amy's contemporary romance novels are mostly London-based so she can fuel her passion for all things British.

For more of Amy's work, visit: www.amydawsauthor.com or check out the links below.

www.facebook.com/amydawsauthor
www.twitter.com/amydawsauthor
instagram.com/amy_daws_author

Made in the USA
Monee, IL
09 September 2024

65309759R10185